The War, The Bones and Dr. Cowie

by

Lexie Conyngham

First published in 2016 by The Kellas Cat Press, Aberdeen.

Copyright Alexandra Conyngham, 2016

ISBN: 978-1-910926-14-7

Lexie Conyngham

With thanks to Eleanor, who gave me her skeleton!

Chapter One

There was no siren that first night, but when the aeroplane came over she woke immediately. She knew at once by the droning blare of the engines that it was too low, too fast. Without further analysis she rolled out of bed, shoved her feet into her shoes and her arms into her coat sleeves, pulled a beret on to her head, then snatched up her bag and a torch, all without needing to turn on a light. In less than two minutes she was outside in the lane, pausing at last to listen to the sound, finding her direction.

The aeroplane must have flown almost directly over the cottage. The engines howled, stuttered: for a brief second there was silence. Then a great flare of flame flashed out of the darkness, with a hollow whoomph. The machine had crashed.

She began to hurry up the lane towards the flare, trying to remember the shape of the place in daylight. She had only been here a day, and had spent that in the cottage and the village, registering with the Food Officer, stocking up, cleaning, airing. If she had cast a glance this way she had seen only farmland and trees, stone dykes and the muddy lane, and the land rising away from her. She stumbled and switched on the blackout torch, though it was almost useless for anything but showing her the general direction of the lane. Her eyes down on the dark path still held the image of the flames ahead.

She could hear shouting, in the distance. Could there have been survivors? She wondered what kind of aeroplane it was. The engines had not sounded British, at any rate. How many in the crew?

In a few minutes the familiar smell of smoke filled her nostrils, and as she glanced up from the lane she could see, through gaps in the hedge, figures against the flames. There had to be four or five of them. Then suddenly she heard the clank of a bicycle behind her and a voice called 'Hi, watch out!' She jumped aside, and automatically flicked her torch towards the face of the cyclist. It was a policeman.

'Who the hell are you?' he demanded, catching his balance. 'Get that torch out my eyes!'

'I'm a doctor - Marian Cowie. I saw the crash. A German plane, I'd say.'

'Aye, well, time for all that later. If you're a doctor you'd better come on with me.' He slid off the bicycle and wheeled it rapidly up the lane, Marian following, trying to keep focussed on the man's lean back. Young and full of himself, she thought. Then she grinned in the darkness – he probably thought the same about her.

In a minute they came to a gate that she would probably have missed. The policeman hauled it open, leaving the bicycle propped against the dyke, and strode off up a sloping field, leaving Marian to close the gate after them.

The aeroplane had crashed, as far as she could see in the light from the fire, where the field met a sharp rise in the ground. It had gouged furrows in the earth, which was otherwise pasture: peering around she could glimpse shadowy cattle huddled away from this unpastoral intrusion. The policeman, ignoring them, stamped forward confidently. Now that Marian could see the figures by the fire more clearly, she realised that four of them wore Home Guard uniform and carried rifles. The fifth had his hands above his head.

'Yous were here quickly,' she heard the policeman call. There was more than a hint of suspicion in his voice.

'We were over at the station,' said the Home Guard sergeant. 'We saw her going over. There's one that's dead, and one that's injured.'

The policeman contemplated the wreckage, his head on one side.

'That there's a Heinkel. There should be two more, do you think?'

'Aye, I think so.'

'Hi,' said the policeman, who seemed to think this a suitable greeting. 'You there, Miss Doctor. Could you take a shuftie at this mannie here? Sergeant says he's injured.'

Marian came forward hesitantly, not quite sure how to

approach a potential patient with four rifles pointed at him. He had his back to the glare of the fire, which was already beginning to die down, but the Home Guard sergeant produced a torch that was more effective than her own, and flashed it first at the airman, then at her.

'You'll be Mrs. Cowie's granddaughter, will you, Doctor?' he asked.

'That's right.'

'Aye. My name's John Leslie – I do the chippie work round the place.'

'Marian Cowie. How do you do.' They shook hands formally, and oddly she felt better. 'Can we ... could you move your men around so that I can get at him?'

Leslie saw her problem at once.

'Right, you two, there. Pat, you get behind him. Sandy, are you all right, son? Grand.'

The soldiers adjusted their positions, and Marian moved closer. The airman was watching her with curiosity, she thought, more than anything else. He was not much taller than she, his eyes bloodshot in the torchlight. Beyond that it was hard to determine anything distinguishing: his uniform was grubby, and his face was blackened.

'Do you speak English?' she asked.

'Little,' he replied.

'I'm a doctor. Are you hurt? Injured?'

He began to move a hand, then paused, eyed the soldiers, and started again more slowly. He pointed to the small of his back.

'Hurt,' he said firmly. 'Very hurt.'

'Anywhere else?' she asked, with an inclusive wave of her hand. She still held her medical bag. He shook his head, and winced a little. The change of angle showed her that he had marks down the side of his face. She put out a gentle hand and tilted his head towards the light to scrutinise him more closely. Burned skin had flowed down from his temple to his jawbone. 'Hurt?' she asked. He nodded this time, more cautiously. 'Can you walk?' She found herself making walking movements with her fingers, and stopped, feeling silly. He understood, though, and took a couple of steps forward, but they were weak and anxious. She nodded.

'He has facial burns, at least, and I think he has really injured the base of his spine,' she told Sergeant Leslie. 'I have some morphine in my bag – I could give him a shot, and I'll dress the face. Do you have a stretcher?'

'Not on me,' said the sergeant, with solemn humour.

'Then you'll have to help him to the lane, and let him take his time. It'll be hard going for him. Could I have some torchlight, please?' She already had her bag open on the grass, and was sorting through her bottles. It was the matter of a practised moment to inject the airman, slowed only by showing him what she was doing, saying the word 'Morphine' a couple of times carefully. Then she set to with a dressing for his face, working as well as she could in the torchlight. 'Where can he be taken?'

'There's the War Memorial Hospital at Insch,' said the policeman, suddenly reappearing. 'But he'd need to be under guard, till we could get him away to Peterhead or Aberdeen Prison. Or I could put him in the cell at the police house.'

'Ach, Argo, you'd not put an injured man in that hole,' said Sergeant Leslie, with fatherly reproach. 'You've been storing coals in it.'

'That's none of your business!' snapped P.C. Argo. 'And how would you know, anyway?'

'We could take him up to the farm,' said an older, heavy soldier. 'Mr. Blaikie would lock him up good and solid.'

'Aye, Rab, but Mr. Blaikie's buildings are better for keeping in beasts than keeping in airmen,' said Sergeant Leslie.

'Hem,' interrupted one of the other soldiers, the one called Pat, politely, 'what about the cellars at the castle? They're clean, and they lock: they're a bit chilly, but we could keep him there till morning.'

P.C. Argo was not too keen on that solution, either.

'I couldn't ask Mrs. Forbes to take in an enemy alien, now, could I?'

'Ah, but Major Forbes is home. It'd be up to him.'

This seemed to be the answer to the problem: Major Forbes could evidently be safely approached and trusted to comply and to cope with the situation.

'Then you can get him away to the prison hospital in the morning, presumably,' said Marian, trying to bring the matter to a resolution.

'That'll be fine,' agreed the sergeant. 'Geddie, Sandy, will you take him over there, then? Tell Major Forbes I'll be over later if he wants to ask me any questions.'

'Are you no coming with us now, Sergeant?' said the younger man, Sandy. He had a face that appeared, without being deformed exactly, as if it had been pushed sideways. Without his uniform Marian would have put him at around twelve.

'P.C. Argo and I will need to see round the rest of this guddle,' Leslie nodded at the wreckage. 'And maybe Dr. Cowie here will help? Dr. Hanson was at the station when we left,' he added to P.C. Argo, 'there was a mannie had caught his hand under the wheel of the luggage trolley. Sailor going to Fraserburgh – sleeping on the platform.'

'Aye, who'd travel these days?' Argo agreed. He and Sergeant Leslie turned and began to walk over to the wreckage. The fourth Home Guard and Marian watched the airman being led away, his legs distinctly wobbly, then followed the other two. Sergeant Leslie had paused for them to catch up.

'I'm sorry, Miss – I should have asked. Are you up to this?'

'I haven't seen a 'plane crash before,' said Marian honestly, 'but I've been working in London.'

The sergeant drew in breath in a reverse whistle.

'Aye, I thought I'd heard that. You'll likely have seen worse than this, then.'

'Come on,' interrupted P.C. Argo. 'I want these other fellows accounted for as quick as we can.'

It had taken Marian thirty-eight hours to travel from London to Aberdeen, a cold, half-blacked out, confusing journey, interleaved with unfathomable delays and diversions. An invading German with a railway timetable would not, she thought, have been at a particular advantage. She was used enough to sleeping in her clothes, but sleeping with other people made her uneasy, particularly as those people came and went in the course of the journey: a middle-aged woman dressed in black; a middle-aged man like a solicitor escorting two bewildered schoolboys; a young woman slumped with her baby in the corner seat; and endless officers, young, old, in khaki, navy, air force blue, one in Lovat green, eventually all blurring into each other. She identified

Londoners on the train by contrast with the unBlitzed – the second winter of the war had been a hard one. Like herself, they were marked out by red eyes, a propensity to catnap, and overscrubbed white faces like worn-out bandages.

She left Aberdeen just when the eggy yellow dawn was already making flat black cutouts of the trees. Long pink and grey clouds lay like fish above the horizon. Some were underlit with burning red, as though they were still cooking over a fire. She was, as usual, hungry, and a cup of grey railway tea barely helped. There were of course no taxis, and she found she was not quite sure of the way, after all these years, but as she strode up the hill with her carpet bag and doctor's case she found that it had changed little after all: she crested the hill, left the cover of the trees and found the village hiding in the hill's shadow, matching her sharpening memory so closely she felt tempted to shout 'Snap!' The cottage was this side of it, the key under the curling stone by the door, and she found to her delight that someone had left a jug of milk and a loaf of bread on the kitchen table. Who had been expecting her? But news always travelled fast in places like this – you could hardly move without comment.

Sergeant Leslie, for example, had already known who she was. She followed his silhouette now, against the still-bright flames of the aeroplane carcase. The heat was no longer frightening, more soothing, like a cosy hearth. She knew the feeling from the end of a busy night in London, when the street still burned but there was nothing more she could do, and it was time to go home.

'Here's the dead one,' called the Sergeant, and she caught up and stooped to where a body lay neatly, safely distant from the fire. She used her torch again to examine it. There was a gashed black hole artistically placed just off centre on his forehead. She heard P.C. Argo come up behind her, and then squat down beside her.

'He's been shot,' she said, pointing to the hole.

'Hi!' exclaimed Argo again, and rose quickly.

'It wasnae us,' Sergeant Leslie responded wearily.

'Oh, aye?'

'I think he's right,' Marian intervened. 'This isn't a rifle shot. He was probably caught by ack ack fire coming over Aberdeen.'

'Dead before he got here, then, eh?' demanded Argo.

'He's coldish, despite the fire. I think he's been dead an hour or so.'

'Right, well, he's no going to belt off, then. Where's the other two?'

'That's the question,' agreed Sergeant Leslie. 'Let's take a wee lookie in the plane first, eh? Now that the fire's gone down.'

They approached with extreme caution, the Home Guardsmen with their rifles at the ready.

'Ow!' said Marian suddenly, and all three men snapped round at her. 'Sorry – caught my coat on something.' She peered down the faint beam of her torch. 'It's just a bit of metal sticking out. Sorry – didn't mean to alarm you.'

'You're all right?' asked the sergeant.

'Yes, yes, thanks.'

'Just as well – we're no carrying you down the hill,' said P.C. Argo flatly.

'There's no one in here, that I can see,' said Pat, the other soldier, who was using his own torch to examine the inside of the Heinkel. 'And if there was, he'd be dead. It's burned right round.'

'They must have got out, then,' decided Sergeant Leslie. 'The plane came in from that direction, just over your grandma's cottage, eh?' he asked Marian.

'It certainly sounded like it,' she agreed.

'So if they fell out before, they'll be back that way. And if they scrambled out after, they'll probably go the opposite direction. Dr. Cowie, if you come with me we'll head downhill, and if P.C. Argo will go with Pat ...' He waved at the other soldier, who nodded and turned on his own torch, starting to sweep the beam low over the rising ground. P.C. Argo, who clearly preferred giving orders to taking them, shrugged with bad grace, gave a sharp 'Right, with me, Farquhar!' and followed Pat. Marian and the sergeant turned down towards the village again.

Even in the darkness it did not take long to find their third crewman. The pilot had evidently bailed out, but something must have gone wrong, for he lay in the next field, his parachute stretched out beyond him pale against the dark soil. His head was bare, his hair faint blond, and his arms and the unbleached ropes and silk of the parachute was an extension of his own colourless hair, as if he were some kind of water spirit lying in his own stream. Marian checked for life signs, but there had been no doubt in her mind from the moment she had seen him that he was dead.

'He's broken his neck,' she told Leslie.

'Another for the mortuary,' remarked the sergeant, without satisfaction. 'I'd better go and sort out people to fetch the two bodies. And you'd best go home, Dr. Cowie – if the fourth man is about and fit you're not safe.'

'I could help search for him,' she tried.

'In the dark, with that wee bitty torch?'

'But what if he's injured?'

'I doubt they'll bring him to you, or to Dr. Hanson, if he's back. Away home to your bed – in fact, as I'm going that way myself I'll walk you to your door.'

He was as good as his word, marching Marian back to the cottage and seeing her safely inside, a guardian shadow by the gate. She went to switch on the light, then remembered that there was no electricity in the cottage. In any case, there were no blackout curtains yet – something else to be done. She took off her coat with a heavy sigh, laying it on the table with the torn part upwards. Then she felt her way to the bedroom, laid her shoes neatly in place, lay down on the bed, and pulled the eiderdown back over herself, listening – always listening.

She must have dozed in the end, for it was a surprise when she woke in the unfamiliar bed. She lay for a little, still listening to the silence, reacquainting herself with the cottage in early morning. Finally, she opened the curtains, ordinary but thick, and was shocked to see sunshine, liquid and glittering. She slid the window up but her skin jarred at the cold air, and she seized a woolly shawl from the back of a chair. Then she realised that the cottage was no longer silent – it was blanketed with birdsong.

For a long moment she had let it sweep over her, dazzled, deafened. Then, deliberately, she tried to unpick the tangled threads of sound. The wood pigeons were the easiest, their purring, repetitive coo a low note in the song. A blackbird came next, for she could see it perched on a rosebush, bright beak wide. Wrens she was sure she heard, for there had always been wrens, and the unbelievably loud pipe of a great tit whose family, generations back, had nested in the wild service tree by the lane. Then, to her delight, she caught the plump rivulet of the willow warbler's song, and gazing up she found it at the highest tip of a silver birch, green-yellow and confident, determined to be heard. An inventive song thrush tried to drown out all the rest.

Satisfied with this mental exercise, she turned away from the window and found she had been there for half an hour already. The loss of time unsettled her, making her feel a little dizzy, and she hurried to make up for it, washing in cold water and dressing quickly in fresh clothes. Tea and dry toast made breakfast – the milk was much thicker than she was used to in London, and the tea was nearly a meal in itself.

Today she would turn out the cottage and clean it thoroughly. At least she knew she could do that job: mending her coat was beyond her. For a doctor with a delicate touch, she had always been handless with a needle: when she had briefly toyed with the idea of becoming a surgeon, she had seen her mother shudder. She would have to find a seamstress in the village. But the cleaning was within her capabilities, and needed to be done. Her grandmother had made her usual winter pilgrimage to Aberdeen before Christmas, 1939, and had decided she was too frail to return to rural life the following spring: she had taken up residence near Marian's parents and was now ensconced, and no one had lived in the cottage since. Marian investigated under the sink and in the pantry, tied a scarf over her hair and an apron over her clothes, and set to.

No one came to disturb her, but it was not a lonely day. She was used, for one thing, to spending time on her own, but when she flung all the windows wide she found that not only were birds crowding the garden, but the road outside was quite busy enough to remind her that the village was not far away. Farm carts rattled back and forth, cyclists busied themselves presumably heading for the station – though so many? – including one gaggle of girls in overalls and a man with them, cycling with a curious clanking sound that drew her to the upstairs front window to stare out, whacking her head on the corner of the sloping roof. The cottage was typical, with two small downstairs rooms divided by a hallway with a central front door, a staircase leading to an upper hall, and two bedrooms sneaking glances from high-pointed dormer windows to both front and back, across the valley. The scullery and pantry were formed in an extension at the back, added just before the last war – her grandmother always called it 'the new bittie'. On investigation, Marian concluded that her grandmother had stocked the pantry around the time that it was built: it was full of jars and tins of museum vintage, along with boxes of soap and candles as cold and dry as stone. Grandmother had always maintained that soap well dried went further and candles well chilled burned longer – she had been fighting on the home front for years before the war started.

In the attic she found some heavy black petticoats, remnants of Victorian mourning fortifications, and spent half an hour suspending them from nails over the windows, rather proud of her improvised blackout. The waist tapes she used to loop up the curtains for daylight. If an ARP warden made it this far, he would have no excuse to fine her.

Somewhere in the middle of the day she made tea and toast again as a quick lunch, but by evening she was dusty, tired and hungry. She brushed herself off and washed her face and hands, put away the mop and dusters, and, wrapping a shawl around her shoulders in place of the torn coat, she headed off to see if the inn still provided an evening meal.

She was surprised at how dark it was already. In London she had loved the blackout, loved the way she could feel her senses stretching out as she made her footsteps softer and softer, padding the loud pavements in her cork soles. Here it was different and somehow more frightening, for the spaces were wider, there were no echoes off familiar buildings, no railings to brush along with her fingertips, no helpful white stripes painted on the kerb to catch her torchlight. She had not brought her pathetic torch, either – she had left it in the pocket of her torn coat - and stumbled down the hill trying to follow a spiky hedge with, she now realised, nettles in it. She was considering whether or not to turn back – but would she find her way back? – when she heard that odd clanking sound again, and bicycle tyres on the road.

'Someone there? Are you all right?' came a man's voice.

'Yes – just a bit lost,' she said, feeling much more vulnerable than she liked.

'Where are you heading?' He did not seem to be dismounting from the bicycle, and came no closer.

'The inn, if it's still there.'

'Oh, aye. I'll guide you down, if you'll follow my voice. I'll just ride slowly.'

A bit odd, she thought, but she followed his directions. The voice she was following, all she could detect of him beyond the clanking bicycle, was local but, she would have said, educated. She was rather unimpressed that he could not be bothered to dismount and guide her properly.

'There should be a little kerb to your left now,' he said, 'and if you step up and reach out, you should find the wall of the inn. Got it?'

She nodded, stupidly, then said 'Yes, thanks.' She was just about to stride out more confidently when he snapped,

'Stop!'

'What?' Her heart pounded.

'The village siren. You wouldn't know, I suppose, but you nearly walked into it.'

She reached out and found a wooden handle and a great round metal thing on a frame – painful on impact, she thought.

'Remember the kerb as you come out round it – nearly there,' the voice advised, and in a moment she found herself at the darkened doorway she vaguely remembered.

'All right now?' he called.

'Yes, thanks, but –'

''Night, then,' came the voice, and off he went, clanking faster now as even his shadow disappeared. 'Where does poor Pa go in the blackout?' came unbidden to her mind. There was nothing but darkness out here, so she fumbled her way through the blackout curtains and entered the inn.

The inn was cosy, old and a little bedraggled: it had been a minor coaching inn off the turnpike road north from Aberdeen. The landlady took temporary possession of Marian's ration book and disappeared, directing her to one of the old private dining rooms away from the public bar. Here there was no fire laid, but the warmth had spread from the rest of the building and the thick velvet curtains over the blackout blinds kept it in. Marian sat at the little table and stretched, rubbing her eyes.

The landlady returned.

'There's your tea,' she announced, setting down a tray. 'Your dinner'll no be long. Did you get the milk and the loaf?' she asked.

Marian blinked.

'Oh, it was you? Thank you so much – it was more than welcome. What do I owe you?'

'Och, never worry,' said the landlady. 'Times gone by there would have been a bitty of butter and some eggs, but you ken what things are like. I'm Netta Binnie, by the way: I'm sure you'll have forgotten. You would only have been a wee lassie when you were up here last. But I hate to think of anyone arriving in a strange place these days and having to sort out all the papers before they can so much as buy a pint of milk. I'll be back with your dinner.'

It took fifteen minutes: Marian had to remind herself sternly that this was not a Lyons teahouse. Mrs. Binnie had taken and reloaded the tray, this time with a napkin and cutlery and a large and elderly china plate.

'It's a potato and rabbit pie,' she explained. 'To be brutally honest, it's mair tattie than rabbit, but it's the best we have.' Marian welcomed it with open arms: the scent of the gravy alone was enough to tell her straightaway that it was the best thing she had eaten for a while. London's potato bars sold nothing like this. 'There's onion in it and everything,' Mrs. Binnie added. 'We have our own onions, thank the Lord.' She settled against the side of an armchair by the empty fireplace, folding her long red hands under her ample arms. 'I'd say that the one good meal in the day is necessary if you're working. You've had a busy day by the look of you: what have you been up to?'

It was said with a smile, and Marian did not find the question intrusive.

'Redding out,' she said, using her grandmother's word. 'The cottage just needed a bit of a dust and scrub.'

'And you'll have had a late night the night before, with that plane crash up by the fairy hill.'

'That's right. But I'm used to that.'

'Bad business, eh, though? Nae fine at all. John Leslie says there was blood everywhere.'

'Does he?' This puzzled Marian, but she put it down to

18

escalating gossip.

'And a prisoner and all. Did you meet him?'

'I did.'

'What was he like, then?' Mrs. Binnie's eyes grew sharp.

'Medium height, thin, about forty, I think. It was dark. He was polite enough.'

'He would be, with four rifles pointing at him.'

'He didn't give the impression of being very – warlike. I mean, there was no 'Heil Hitler' or anything.'

They both fell silent, thinking about the prisoner. Then Mrs. Binnie seemed to feel a change of subject was in order.

'And what like of plans do you have for while you're here? What are you up to?'

'I'm just taking a break from London,' Marian said smoothly. 'But I hope I can make myself useful while I'm here, though it's only going to be a couple of weeks or so.'

'A couple of weeks? My! It's hardly worth the journey – wasn't it a long one?'

'It certainly was – but there's so much to do in London I couldn't afford to be away any longer. Do you know if there's something I could help with just for a little while?'

'Well, the S.W.R.I.'s always keen to have us knitting comforts –'

'I can't knit!' Marian stopped her there.

'We could teach you! Or more up your street, maybe, we make up and roll bandages. But you're a doctor, aren't you? The best thing you could do is offer to help poor Dr. Hanson.'

'Is he the local man?'

'That's right. He's coming up to an age he'd like to retire, and he's no so well himself. Before the war started he told me he was starting the hunt for a partner who might succeed him, but of course that all went west and now he has no help and more work than ever, for he covers the factory by the station as well as the neighbouring practice – the young doctor there's joined the Medical Corps.'

'What about the district nurse?'

'About the same age, with a bad back. She's more ready to lie in her ain bed these days than visit someone else's. This place fair wore her out.'

'Then he certainly sounds in need of help,' Marian agreed. 'I'll try there. Even if I could help with his dispensing or something – '

'Oh, we have a pharmacist!' said Mrs. Binnie with mock grandeur, as if she was claiming to have a coach and four. 'For why I don't know. What kind of a thing were you up to in London, then? If you can say, that is.'

Marian swallowed a mouthful of pie.

'I work at a practice in the east end. And I volunteer with an ambulance unit.'

'Oh, aye,' said Mrs. Binnie, with a frown of concern. 'That'd be no easy work, I'd say.'

'No harder than anything others are going through. I think everyone has two jobs at present,' Marian said, but she noted Mrs. Binnie's unconvinced expression. Her gaze lay heavily on Marian but Marian felt up to it: she was pretty fit, she thought, for someone who had been working on about two hours' sleep a night for months.

'Aye, well, I suppose,' said Mrs. Binnie, shifting her broad hips reluctantly. 'There'll be men at the bar in need of ale.'

'I'll bring the tray back to the bar when I've finished, then,' Marian offered, and Mrs. Binnie nodded and left.

Marian finished every last scrap of the pie, examining the heavy pattern of the plate to make sure she had missed nothing. Maybe living in the countryside in wartime was not such a bad idea. She squeezed another cup of tea out of the pot, then stacked everything on the tray and went to carry it through to the bar. The passage outside was narrow and a little dim, and as she advanced down it she met a large figure coming quickly in the opposite direction, taking up almost all the space. He moved too fast for her to back, still bearing the tray, into her dining room, and in a second he was in front of her.

'Who do you think I am?' he demanded, without preface.

'Um ...' By the light of the nearest dim bulb she took in his outdoor face, spoon-shaped, with deepset blue eyes not used to close focus. 'A farmer?'

'Aye, I work the land. And it's hard work – harder than they loons ken how to do. But I'm no a coward, ye ken!' Veins bulged in the man's hands, rough hands that could harrow twenty acres without benefit of machinery. She squinted up quickly again at his face. She had feared anger, but all she could see in his far-seeing eyes was a kind of hurt desperation.

'I'm sure you're not,' she agreed, trying not to sound too patronising, too English.

'The sojer laddies there, they're crying me a coward because I'm no in uniform like them. I'm in a reserved occupation, ken? I'm the farm labourer out at North Meiklefold. It's a big ferm – it takes the farmer and his wife and myself and the orra loun to keep the place going.'

'I don't doubt it,' she said in answer to his sudden focussed gaze. She wished he would get out of her way – she was dead tired, the tray was heavy, and she simply wanted to go home and go to her bed. The big hands, one on each wall of the narrow passage and seemingly forgotten by the farm labourer, barred her exit still like knots on a rope, and no one else appeared behind her or behind him to remind him to move.

'An' I'm skilled, ken – they all said so. I can plough a furrow as straight as a town street – I'm no easily replaced by some wee lassie fae the Land Army.'

'No, indeed.'

'An' I'm no coward,' he added, coming back to his first point. 'I'd go out to France like the next man, or fly in one of them wee aeroplanes – I fancy that –' She struggled to imagine the bulk of him squeezed into the fragile cockpit of a Hurricane, and the way its balsa and linen would strain under him. 'I'm not saying I'd go in a boat,' he conceded. 'The sea's an uncanny place, no the territory for a farming loon. But the Gordons or the Air Force could have me any day, if Mr. Blaikie didna need me more. I'm no coward, I never have been. I'm no feart of anything. Except only the once,' he said suddenly, and his blue gaze clouded so dramatically that she caught her breath.

'The once?' she repeated, unable to stop herself. He hardly seemed to have heard her, but his corduroy face dropped its creases all at once, his gaze still far away, and he said nothing for a long moment. She found herself counting his long, damp breaths as if she were taking his pulse. Then, softly, but audibly, he began to speak again.

'It would have been twenty year ago,' he said. 'Twenty year

ago, for it was the year young Dod Blaikie died. In fact, it was that very week, for I was sent out with my dog Moss and Mr. Blaikie's gun, to shoot rabbits for a stew for the day of the funeral. He was a grand lad, Dod Blaikie, but Moss was a grander dog. I'd had him from a pup, and I tell you that dog could read my mind. There wasn't a place he wouldn't have followed me – or run on ahead, as it turned out.

'Well, I'd started late with the rabbitting and we hadna had much luck, and it was dark when we turned for home. That wouldna bother us – Moss could see a black sheep in the dark and I wasna far behind when I was young. There was a thin, underfed wee moon now and then, and between times it was grey black. We were over in Copse Field – you'll no ken it, but there's a fringe of woodland and scrub, or there was then. The scrub's all back and ploughed up now. The quickest way back fae there is along by Loch Essie, where the ground drops away sharp-like and there's a wee pathie by the loch shore. They say that in times lang syne folks quarried there, and that's why the cliff's so steep and the loch's so deep. I'm not so sure, myself – or at least I'm not so sure it was *folks* that did the quarrying. You'll see why I might have my doubts.

'The night was cool enough, but it seemed to get colder still as Moss and I skittered down the pathie to the loch. It's dicey enough in daylight, that wee bit: I lost my footing a couple of times, and Moss went down it on his hunkers with his front legs braced. We must have skited a few loose chuckies into the water, I suppose, between us, and there were a few splashes – maybe that's why it happened. Maybe it would have happened anyways. We stopped a minute at the water's edge, just to catch our breath and our balance, but the chill was on me at once like nothing I'd felt there before – I thought I was coming down with something. Then I heard Moss shiver, too, and I kenned it wasna just myself. I bent down to pat his head, though I couldna see more than a shadow of his white markings in the dark, and I wasna that surprised to feel his hackles right up and his ears twitching like crazy. It was as if he couldna tell whether to prick them or lay them flat.

'I straightened up. The bag of rabbits wasna heavy, but it was awkward like, and I tied it more securely round my chest. Then, as quiet as I could, I reloaded both barrels of the gun and took the safety off. I suppose I thought it might be poachers, which would explain why we'd found so few rabbits – it didna explain the terrible cold, mind you.

'"Come on, boy," I said quietlike – as much to myself as to Moss, and we stepped out along the pathie. Ye ken how narrow it is there. The cliff goes sheer up on one side, not less than twenty feet, and the loch is at your feet and already twenty feet deep at the other, and in between there's about four feet of rocky grass that the sheep keep low. As we stepped out, the wee slithery bit of a moon slipped back out of the clouds and showed us the way, for which I was thankful enough. That's that last thing that I remember thinking – and then it happened.

'There was an almighty rush of water, like a dam burst. I whipped fast around me, thinking I'd see the cliff come down round us, or the pathie give way. I didna. Instead I saw something you'd never believe.

'Bursting out of the loch came a figure. Not just any figure: a monster, a giant. His head and shoulders broke the surface, and the waves it made seized my legs, soaked me to the thighs. I staggered, backing up to the cliff. Moss was already by me on a ledge, barking as if he had no choice. When I looked back, the monster was clear of the water to his waist, tossing back his head, shaking the loch water off in a silver spray of drops. He cleared his nose with a terrific snort, then sniffed hard. He flung something away out of his huge hand and I caught just the sight of a couple of human skulls fleeing off like broken nutshells. The next second he was staring straight at us.

'Two michty strides and he was out. The water ballooned in front of him, each great leg kicking another wave against us. Then there he was on the path, a wall between us and home, dripping as the water ran back round his feet into the loch.

'Now I wished the moon had stayed behind the clouds. Maybe I wouldna be here the now, but at least I wouldna have that sight haunting my dreams for the rest of my days on earth. Lord, he was enormous. He stood mair than twenty feet tall, but slouched over, his arms hanging in front of him like one of they apes in the books. Weeds dripped and slithered off his bald head, and in the moonlight at least his skin was rough and greenlike – he was like a damp corner in a harled wall. And the reek of him was unbelievable. I've pulled a dead Scotch mule out of a bog two weeks after she went missing, and it was something on to that – only a thousand times worse. I choked in my throat and Moss stopped barking, and all the while the thing just stood and eyed us, with a scance that said that it wasna sure whether or no we was worth the bother.

'Then just as I was beginning to wonder if we could make it back the way we came, the thing opened its mouth wide and let out a roar like nothing on earth, like the cliff cracking above us, like the ground wrenched open at our feet. The sick moonlight glinted on sharp, unnatural teeth and a tongue like fresh leather. And Moss, my poor Moss, clapped eyes on him, and ran.

'Brave dog, he didna run away. He ran at the thing, full pelt. With one great swinging hand, the monster plucked him up, and tossed him casual-like into his gaping mouth. There was one last heroic bark, cut off, and then a terrible crunch, like stones falling, and Moss was gone. Then the thing turned back at me.

'I had the shotgun in my hands, but my heart was thumping so hard that it looked like I was beating time with the barrel. Then the gun went off in my hands, both barrels, though I wouldna go so far as to say I fired it. I was kinda surprised to see that I had hit it: the monster batted his slimy chest where the pellets had gone in, but just as if it was midgies. Then the thing took a step towards me, and I saw, as if it mattered, that it had long, webbed toes on its bare feet. I swallowed hard. This was it, I thought: one more step, a crunch, and that'd be me away with Moss.

'When another wave hit my legs, I was too bothered with keeping my feet and being terrified to look away. But when another roar came, and it wasna from the monster, I risked a peek at the loch.

'Believe it or not, there stood another big yin – the very twin of my fella. There he stood, up to his oxters in the loch, roaring his shiny green head off. For a minute I thought I'd gone wud altogether. Then the first monster hauled himself round, and let out another skraich, and though it was hard to gather the specifics, it was pretty clear that neither was too pleased to see the other.

'The first one stepped back, away from me, and turned towards the second. The second started towards the bank, weeds slipping off his arms and chest, while the first was making faces at him like he'd eaten something that disagreed with him – I hoped it was my poor Moss, taking his revenge. Then the first one stepped back into the loch and there they both were, thigh deep in the icy water, and the next second they were laying into one another like their lives depended on it.

'Blow after blow they landed, one monster agin the other, battering heads and chests, huge fists flailing and grabbing, the waters of the loch seething around them. Though the waves tugged my legs, I was frozen to the spot, half terrified, half fascinated, wanting to run and too scared to move. Still they fought, but it came to me bit by bit that the second monster, the one without the shotgun scars on him, was getting the upper hand. The first one was starting to slump around each blow, his shoulders sagging lower and lower, striving just to keep his balance in the water. At last the second monster got his michty hands round his brother's neck, the first monster could do nothing, and he began to slip under the water.

'Suddenly I saw that the minute he'd finished him off, the second beast would be after me. He was bent over the body, pressing it down, one foot now I'd say on his enemy as well as the big hands, and he had his back to me. My legs, shoogly as they were, suddenly remembered how to run as if someone had struck a match under my feet, and with a scrabble over the stones, I was off. And I never stopped till I was back at the farmhouse and the big door locked behind me.'

Marian found she was gripping the tray so hard her knuckles were white, and holding her breath. She breathed out slowly.

'Well, I'd say that anyone would have been scared then,' she agreed, bewildered. 'Don't let the lads at the bar bother you at all. You're a brave man, doing good work.'

'Aye, aye,' said the farmhand vaguely, as if he had run out of steam. 'Well, I'll let you go, now, lassie – I see you've a heavy tray there.'

He dropped his hands and pressed his great bulk against the passage wall, and she scrambled past. Nothing more was said.

Chapter Two

The reason she had gone back up to the crash site was seven-eighths base curiosity.

Mrs. Binnie's claim that John Leslie, the Home Guard sergeant, had said there was blood everywhere, had niggled at her mind during the night. John Leslie had seemed like a sensible man, not given to gossip. It had been dark, of course, when the plane crashed, and Leslie would have been back at the site next day, yesterday, while she was redding out the cottage. What had he found?

There had been no rain, fortunately, so the scene was very much as she had left it. The plane lay almost flat, a great bird that had folded and died of exhaustion, but with the smell of burned metal still strong. The two corpses had of course been removed: there was no trace of the one who had lain beside the plane, shot in the head, but the ploughed earth was roughed and gouged where the other airman, the one with the strung-out parachute, had been strewn. Hard as she examined them, she could see no blood in either place, and the man she had seen to, the one with the burned face and the injured back, he had had no gushing wound. She moved closer to the aircraft, warily, and was glad of her care for she found straightaway the spike of twisted metal that had ripped her coat that night. It was coated in a brown fluid that had dried and hardened in drips around the ripped metal – blood.

Well, there was a thing.

Either one of the Home Guard had cut themselves on it, or the policeman had, or she herself had. She knew that she was uninjured. There was, of course, a fourth possibility – and a fourth airman. Was their fugitive bleeding?

She began to examine the area around the metal spike: she

thought it must be a part of the landing carriage. She imagined it touching the ground, catching violently, being ripped off as the plane staggered down. There was more blood on the grass, and for a fanciful moment she thought that the plane itself had bled from its wounds. The blood on the grass formed a thinnish trail, almost invisible, leading alongside the plane, then round the wreckage of the broken wing, and towards the Fairy Hill, as she had heard Mrs. Binnie call it. The sharp incline of the hill had finally done for the plane, which had caught it between cockpit and wing. The broken cockpit had breached the side of the hill, but not by much: granite and gorse bushes were equal to anything the Luftwaffe could hurl at them.

She lost the trail quickly on the rough ground, and wondered what to do next. The last visible drop had fallen on a sparkling white pebble, about the size to sit comfortably in her hand, and she was torn between the need to leave the blood where it was and the desire to hold the smooth stone. She squatted down and quartered the ground with her eyes. On closer inspection, there were a number of the glistening white pebbles scattered on the earth and poking out of it. None of them was bloody. She plucked one out of its earthy bed, and stood up, dusting and stroking the smooth, cold stone in her hands. She turned slowly, scanning the field below her, as if she might catch sight of a wandering Luftwaffe crewman, but almost jumped when she saw another man strolling across the field, watching her unashamedly.

She shoved the pebble into her pocket, feeling strangely intruded upon. The man was tall and well-built, in the uniform of an officer of the Gordon Highlanders, with his long coat swinging into place as he stepped towards her, hands out apologetically.

'Hello, there,' he said, in a cultivated voice. 'I'm sorry, did I startle you?'

'Well, yes, you did, rather,' she answered, a little crossly. 'I was thinking.'

'Oh, dear! Then I'm *very* sorry.'

Feeling she was being laughed at, she met his eyes. For some unaccountable reason, her heart skipped a little beat and she found herself suddenly brushing the mud off her own skirts, suddenly aware of how filthy she must be after a morning's scrambling around about the wreckage, suddenly unaccustomedly anxious about her hair.

'I'm Neil Forbes – my mother lives over at the castle,' he explained quickly.

'Marian Cowie. I'm staying in the village.' She put her hand out and he took it briefly in his. 'Oh, sorry,' she said hastily. 'I've been – ah ...' Digging around for corpses and stray blood, she thought, but thought better of saying.

'I know,' he smiled. 'I've been watching. What have you found?'

'Oh, just a pebble,' she said, one hand going guiltily to her pocket as if she might be accused of stealing. 'But really I came up here because I heard that there was an awful lot of blood at the crash site, and I knew that the three airmen I saw probably hadn't lost very much, so I came to see what I could find out. I treated the injured man, you see, the other night, and I saw the two corpses that were here, but there's a missing man, and I wondered if the blood might be a clue.' 'Shut up, shut up, shut up!' she thought to herself, drawing to a halt at last. 'He'll think you're some stupid girl who can't keep her mouth shut. And aren't you?'

But Major Forbes was smiling broadly.

'Of course – you're a doctor, aren't you? A clever girl. You'll make a nice change from old Dr. Hanson if you stick around here.'

'Oh, I'm not sticking around – I'm going back to London very soon.'

'To London? What fun! I'm afraid I'm off back to France shortly.'

'Not so much fun,' agreed Marian.

'So what about some lunch while we still have time?' Forbes asked, still smiling. 'Unless you're planning to stay up here all day?'

He walked her amicably down the hill to the lane, very quickly discovering a mutual interest in popular music, sociable dancing, and birds. He pointed out a place by the lane where he had gone as a boy to listen to sedge warblers. 'I couldn't believe that anything not metal could make a noise like that.' They compared memories of the statuesque pelicans in St. James' Park, and reached the inn as she told him of the willow warbler she had heard again that morning. They were just about to go inside when she remembered something: and she had her medical bag with her.

'Do you mind?' she asked. 'I need to find the chemist – to replace something I used the other night.'

'Of course.'

The chemist's shop was in the village square, in a respectable old establishment on the far side. It was quite cramped inside, making Major Forbes vast by contrast. He stood patiently as she asked the man behind the counter for morphine. As he turned to fetch it, she recognised the chemist as one of the Home Guard soldiers from the night of the crash.

'You're Mr. – um – Farquhar, aren't you?' she asked.

'That's right,' said the chemist. 'The name's above the door.' He was a young man, with a face full of tension, as stiff and angular as a retort stand. He instantly made her feel nervous, but she was eager to know something.

'I don't know if you remember me – I was at the plane crash the other night.' She nodded apologetically to Forbes, not wanting to hold him back.

'Of course. The lady doctor.'

'I was wondering ... did any of you injure yourselves on the wreckage?'

Patrick Farquhar gave a little nasal laugh, quite humourless.

'Oh, the blood! No, none of us did. I'd say it's almost certainly the missing crewman, don't you think? When we went up yesterday we found a trail of blood leading on to the hill, but we lost it there. I assume you found the same thing?'

'That's right,' said Marian, feeling slightly deflated.

'Well, it wasn't from the man you fellows brought to us,' Forbes came into the conversation suddenly. 'There was no blood in the cellar after he left. Now, before you ruin my appetite altogether ...' He smiled at Marian and held out an arm. 'Come and have that lunch.'

The inn was the only place in the village to buy a meal. It had a grander appearance in the daylight, its whitewashed walls still bright and the archway into the stable yard well swept. Forbes stationed her in the same little dining room she had used the previous night, and went to order food. The lunch was the same delicious pie that she had had before, but aside from that the meal was very different: even at my advanced age, she thought to herself, reckoning up her twenty-seven years, it's still a little more exciting to be attended to by a handsome – extremely handsome! – officer than to exchange gossip with a plump landlady. She was just reviewing her plans for the afternoon in her head, wondering if he would propose anything that they might do together, when he laid down his cutlery and glanced at his watch.

'Oh, no – is that really the time?' He sighed. 'I'm afraid I have to catch the Aberdeen train – I have an appointment this afternoon. Will you come through to the bar with me while I pay? There's someone there I'd like you to meet, and he can walk you home – if you feel in need of an escort.' His smile was still magical: like a magnet, it drew a smile from her, too.

'What a shame. But of course, I'd like to meet your friend.'

The friend turned out to be a fellow Gordons officer, Allardyce by name. Forbes discreetly paid Mrs. Binnie for their lunch, and said goodbye to Marian in a way that unmistakeably meant 'And I'll see you again very soon.' She let out an involuntary sigh as he left the inn: Captain Allardyce stole an uncertain glance at her, and she immediately regretted the sigh. The young officer perched again on the bar stool, an elbow on the bar in an effort to look at ease, though Marian was fairly sure he was too young for his drinking career to have been much longer than his army one. He was small and would have been colourless, but his skin told of unaccustomed outdoor living, rough and red on cheeks, forehead and chin. His eyes were eager to please.

'So, are you a local man? From the village, too?' she asked kindly.

'No, not really – well, Aberdeenshire, yes. But I'm staying up at the castle tonight,' he explained. 'My people are missionaries and they're stuck in Singapore, so when we both had leave together Forbes asked me here.'

'That's decent of him,' Marian agreed. 'Do you like it here?'

'Oh, indeed! Lovely place. Very friendly, very traditional. Reminds me what we're fighting for.'

'Do you – ah – work with the Major, then?'

'Oh, yes! Well, you know they're giving him a gong, don't you?'

'Are they?' Marian felt a little flicker of pleasure, and something of her interest must have shown in her face.

'The whole Dunkirk business,' the young officer said, as if that should be sufficient introduction, the scene set, though his next words threw it away again. 'Not that we actually ever made it to Dunkirk, you understand!'

'Can you tell me about it?' Marian was curious as to how medals could be won in a retreat.

'I don't see why not: Jerry probably knows most of it, and very little redounds to our credit – except Major Forbes' part. You see, we were supposed to come home by the Dunkirk route, but first we had to hold a little harbour town in Normandy – sweet place, name of St. Valéry-en-Caux. Some day I might go back – wonder what language I'll need to speak? Anyway, there we were, holding St. Valéry so that our lot could march back through and we'd hold off Jerry until we were relieved. The fighting was nasty stuff: I hate scrapping through a town, in and out of people's houses, wrecking their precious things, hiding round a wall with some poster on it for something like ciggies or Cinzano, something in the real world, slithering on a newspaper that someone's been reading for the sports news. I don't like it. You don't know where you are, and it's as if the people don't either, as if they're all still there, living their lives, leaning over your shoulder as you pull the trigger, lounging against the wall you're crouching behind, watching you like a film, or just getting on with eating their dinner. Fanciful, you'll say! But I can't seem to shake it.

'Anyway, the fight was pretty bitter – there were rumours that the Frenchies had actually sent cavalry against the German tanks, would you believe? - and there was no sign of the relief, wherever the hell they were. And I was indeed crouched behind a wall with a ciggie poster on it, with four of my men, when there was an unholy crack above us and there's a bit I don't remember then. When I came to, the wall was all over us, bits of stone and plaster and poster on us and round us. I listened for a bit – well, just stayed still till I had accounted for all my limbs, actually – but I couldn't hear anything but the trickle of plaster and dust, and a blackbird singing in a tree just beside us. That made me wonder for a minute! Dead or alive? I thought. Then I felt the pain starting in my head, and I was pretty sure Heaven wouldn't contain blackbird's song and a headache like a knife in my skull, so I started very gently to wriggle out from the rubble.

'As it happened I was soon free, and I had a hunt for the men. Two of them had bought it, I'm afraid: a carpenter from Skene, who was as brave as a bull, and a lad named Hadden from Aberdeen, who had a job as a clerk but wanted to be a lawyer. Both good men: it's hard to get used to losses like that, when you've nattered with them at night and fought beside them in the day. Hadden's mother had already lost another son: that was a hard letter to write. Anyway, I knew we had to leave them, for Jerry was still moving about in the streets. My sergeant, Frith, was just working himself free, and another man, Scott, had to be dug out quietly, and brought round with water and a bit of a shake. We did a bit of a scout, from our heap of rubble, and realised that there was no shooting or shelling, and Jerry was definitely in possession of the territory.

'We heard the sound of trucks coming along the street, and three appeared, those grim grey things that the Reich use to lug their men around. To our horror, we saw that they were all filled with khaki uniforms! We could even recognise some of our colleagues, and almost all were wearing the Gordon badge – about fifty PoWs. I'm afraid we all swore most horrible at that – I never felt so sick in my life. But we kept under our rubble and kept our voices down, for we didn't want to be added to Jerry's guests. Instead we waited, sipping our water occasionally, for dusk.

'The twilight gave us our chance – that and the fact that Jerry was off having his dinner. Or at least we thought he was. We crept along as quietly as we could – we went by the street, for although we'd thought about crossing the back gardens, it would have taken much more effort and almost certainly one of us would have put a foot through a coldframe or something – probably me! The street was deserted, the shadows were growing darker by the minute, and we kept low. We were just passing one of the more prosperous houses near the edge of the town – there's a big sort of chalk lump north of the town, with woods on the top, and the main road west goes round it by the sea, and this fine house was by the road with, I suppose, its gardens going back up the hill. And we were eyeing up a Jerry guard post a few hundred yards ahead and wondering what to do about it, when suddenly a big staff car turned up on the other side of it. We hardly stopped to think: we scuttled into the big house as if we owned it, slid into the front room and hid below the windowsill, not a breath between us, watching the road and listening to the rest of the house.

'The staff car swept through the barrier and passed our new billet, but we didn't move. For one thing Scott and I were both still a bit bloody from our head injuries, and for another, we couldn't work out yet how to pass the guard post. We could climb over the chalk cliff, but we didn't know if the Jerries were in the woods or not. So we lay low, and speculated in whispers about the possibility of liberating some food from the kitchen – we were all pretty hungry, though if we'd known what real hunger was like then, we'd have managed a bit better! Anyway, we debated for a bit, and then we decided that the best thing might be if we all went together, covering each other's backs, to see if there was anything in the kitchen.

'There wasn't a squeak from the rest of the house, so with one eye on the front door, one up the stairs, and one ahead, we made our way to the back of the house where we found, as expected, a large kitchen with a pantry off it. In there there were sausages hanging up and plenty of apples from last autumn still in good state: with a quick grace to the absent (we hoped) owner, we took a few of each and started eating. No bread, unfortunately: too late in the day, but further investigation found a pot of broth on the stove and we took a ladle each of that. Scott and Frith were just taking their second and I was waiting my turn when there was a sound behind us and we all leapt for our weapons.

'The figure faintly silhouetted in the doorway was not wearing a round Jerry helmet, and letting my revolver drop a little I tried my school French.

'"Bonsoir, monsieur. Pardonnez notre – er – intrusion, mais –'

'"It's me, Allardyce!" said the figure, with the breath of a laugh, and there was Major Forbes. And heartily pleased we all were to see him! "Is it just the three of you?"

'I explained quickly about our two casualties.

'"What about you? Are you alone?"

'"No: I've a medic with me, but he's injured," Forbes said quickly. "Seen the guardpost outside?" We nodded. "I've found a way round it. Grab what food you can, and let's go."

'We did as bid, filled our packs with sausage and apples and took a final draught of that excellent broth. Then we followed

Forbes back into the hall and to a doorway under the stairs. The door lay open, and he led us quickly down into the darkness. As soon as I had closed the door behind us, he switched on an electric torch and we saw chalky stone walls, quite dry, and stone steps which took us up to a fine cellar. We realised quickly we were somewhere inside the chalk bluff behind the house. There was straw on the floor and some half empty wine racks lined one wall. In a corner, on a pile of sacks, sat a man in RAMC uniform, white as a fish and clutching a brandy bottle. One sleeve was ragged and bloody, roughly bandaged.

'"You fit, Doctor?" Forbes asked, hardly pausing. The medic tried to rise but we had to haul him up, and we corked the brandy bottle and stuck it in his pack. Forbes was already through another door in the far end of the cellar, and we were off, trailing quickly behind him down another passage, following another torch beam, but this time in rather more damp conditions. The passageway meandered up and down, sometimes about ankle-deep in water, pitch-dark and walled with the sticky, powdery chalk, and I must admit I was beginning to wonder if we wouldn't have been safer with the Jerry guard post. We stumbled over bits of rotten barrels and squashed through stuff I'd rather not think about, thank you, and still the Major led us on, as if he had all the energy in the world. It was a bit dizzy-making watching the bouncing torchbeam up ahead, with the men all outlined against it, and I was beginning to feel a bit at the end of my rope when the torchlight ahead suddenly turned upwards, and the Major called back in a sort of whisper,

'"Nearly there! Watch your step!"

'Next thing I knew we were once again heading up damp stone steps, then drier ones, then the Major switched off the torch and there was a faint creaking noise and then we pushed our way up through an ancient trap door. To my absolute amazement, we were in a small wood, and when I peeked about, dark though it was, I could see the chalk cliff north of St. Valéry behind us, looming against the night sky.

'"But why on earth –" I began, wondering who would have cut such a passage.

'"No idea, old man," replied Forbes, knowing at once what I'd been going to say. "Now, we'd better all take a slug of the

Doctor's brandy, and be on our way: I'd like to put a few miles between us and St. Valéry's dubious charms before first light."

'Of course there was nothing else to do – German patrols would no doubt be rooting round the place before breakfast. Frith was absolutely marvellous: Scott was still very wobbly, and Frith very nearly carried him that night. The medico and I propped each other up, and the Major led the way, scouting ahead and darting back to us – he must have walked three times the distance any of us did, but he never seemed to tire. Just before dawn he found a rough barn, a touch neglected, and we bedded down in that and ate some sausage and apple, and slept the sleep of the just.

'It must have been about four o'clock in the afternoon when I woke. My head was thick – brandy has never agreed with me, and the knock on the head hadn't done me much good, either. It took me a moment to open my eyes, and when I did, I realised that the Major had moved. The medico and Scott were still asleep, but Frith was on the ball as usual and nodded to where the Major was, at the same time putting a finger to his lips. Forbes was right behind one of the wooden partition things in the barn, part of a stall or something – not very well up in these country matters – but he was clearly trying to see, without being seen, something outside the barn. I concentrated, too. I heard voices. And I'm not the world's greatest linguist, but they were shouting in German.

'My heart fairly leapt, I can tell you. I think I'd sort of thought that with the Major leading us, we would have some kind of charmed life and never see a Jerry again! But it wasn't to be, of course: even from where I was, I could see a couple of grey figures in the yard outside. Forbes drew back behind the partition thing, and crept back to us.

'"Bloody Jerry is billeted in the farmhouse," he said with a delighted face. "We've been next door neighbours all day." My face must have shown my complete panic, for he grinned even more, and said, "Better wake the others – quietly."

'Scott and the medico were mercilessly roused, poor chaps, and we made the sitrep. We all rather looked to the Major for a plan, and fortunately we didn't look in vain.

'"This place is such a wreck," he said. "If you take a slant back there, behind those ladders, there's actually a big gap in the wall where the wood's simply fallen away. There are woods about fifty yards that way. Making a run for it has to be the best option."

'I glanced at Scott and the medico. I doubted that they could even make a brisk walk for it for as much as fifty yards, and I was still a bit woolly myself.

'"Maybe," I said, "if I were to go to the door there, with my revolver ..." I had some idea that I would be holding them back if I included myself in the walking wounded of the party.

'"And steal my idea?" snapped Forbes, with a wicked smile. "No, you're in charge of the retreat, Allardyce, my man. I'm off to bag a few Huns. Get ready to run."

'There was no denying the man – you simply couldn't. He crept back to his partition thing, with his revolver drawn. We staggered to our feet and huddled over to the gap in the boards. I glanced back to see the same wicked delight on Forbes' face as he ever so gently cocked the revolver, and nodded to me. Then we left. I never expected to see him again.

'I couldn't count the shots as we lurched across the rough field behind the barn. They were tangled up with bursts of machine gun fire, and with the beating of the blood in my head. Frith carried Scott and the medico and I bounced along together, and by a minor miracle we reached the trees without anyone seeing us. We fell into a ditch and took a moment to catch our breath and scout back to see if we could see anything. The little farm gave the impression of being quiet, but in the distance we could still hear gunfire – though it seemed to be further away than the farm.

'Well, I got my compass out and my map, and we sort of worked out roughly where we were, and roughly which direction to head in. We decided that Dunkirk was by now out of the question: if the Germans were as far as St. Valéry and holding, the road round the coast would not be a happy place to be. What were our options? We weren't remotely sure, but somehow or other we settled on heading for Marseilles, in the hope of a ship. We ate some food, drank some brandy and water from a pretty stream, and set off. I missed Forbes like a right arm – or perhaps like a right arm would miss a body, for I knew I was definitely only an appendage by comparison.

'We walked till after dark, and after some more rations we kept on walking. The roads we found were pretty quiet, but at one point I was sure I heard footsteps behind us. I motioned the others to pull into the ditch where there were scrubby bushes, and we froze as a figure came into sight round the bend. Then, to our amazement, we realised it was Major Forbes.

'He gave new life to us: we would never have walked all that way without him. It took us days, but despite running out of food, and having to borrow three bicycles to give Scott and the doctor a rest, and ducking out of the way all day, and flying like owls through the night, we finally reached the river – no idea what it's called – that marked the border of Vichy France.

'Now, this was a great achievement, but it was a big problem, too, for to cross it, we needed to pass patrols, and though we were no longer in anything recognisable as British uniforms (Forbes had retrieved some peasant-like garb off a couple of washing lines along the way, and we had sunk a bundle of our uniforms in a lake rather than attract attention by burning them), we needed papers, or to be able to swim well. Forbes of course can swim like the proverbial, and Scott said he was capable, but the doctor still had one arm out of commission and Frith, showing the first sign of anything like fear, said he'd rather shoot his way across the bridge than risk the water. It was pretty wide at that point. I think Forbes had the notion that we could swim ahead, as it were, and find something to bring back to get them across: at any rate, when he and Scott and I reached the other side, I was a bit knocked off course by the current and found myself blundering about in some reeds, and that's how I came upon the boat.

'It was a big old thing, fine for the five of us, and the oars were shipped in it. I showed it to Forbes like a puppy bringing back its first stick. Forbes gave me a quick pat on the shoulder and we all hopped in: Scott could have stayed where he was, I suppose, but good chap that he is he wasn't going to stay in safety while we fetched Frith and the doctor, who had seen what we had and were now up and waving on the far bank. We were a fair way from any bridge or road: who knows what the boat was doing there, probably for the convenience of a local farmer, but we felt pretty safe, and waved back. Then we saw, to our horror, two grey uniforms appear out of the scrubby woodland behind them.

'The Jerries were along the bank a bit, and because of some tall rushes in between, they couldn't see our lot and our lot couldn't see them. We couldn't signal to them to take cover, or the

Jerries would have seen us – they were already squinting across at us. Then Forbes came up with the best, the bravest idea we had ever seen. He waved at both our friends and at the Germans, and began to row towards them all across the river.

'I think I was sitting there with my mouth open. Scott, shaking like a leaf (and who could blame him?) rowed alongside the Major, clearly assuming we were rowing across to be shot. I sat at the little tiller, pretending I knew what I was doing with the current.

'It didn't seem a minute till we reached the other side. We reached the bank as near the Germans as we could get, so that Frith and the doctor had to spin round to see what we were up to. Then they saw the Germans for the first time, and froze.

'Forbes was ahead of the game, though.

'"Vous voudrez traverser?" he asked in very simple French, as if expecting the Germans not to understand.

'Jerry, an officer and an ordinary soldier, thought for a tick – translating in their heads, I thought. Then the officer nodded.

'"Oui, oui. Combien?"

'"Six francs tous les deux," said Forbes boldly – extortionate pricing, but the Germans clearly recognised that it was war time. The officer fished in his pockets and found the money, and tried to give it to Forbes as they stepped, uncertainly, into the boat.

'"Non, non, à l'autre côté," said Forbes. 'Et vous, mes braves?' he added to the doctor and Frith. They nodded, and scrambled down into the boat. I wish I had a photograph of their faces! They didn't know where to look, but kept their heads down. The Germans, neither of them boating men, held tight to anything they could reach as Scott and Forbes turned the boat and I helped them push off, jumping in after.

'This time, the crossing felt hours long. At first, no one spoke. Then the German officer said, as if he had been planning the words for a while,

'"Vous êtes tous très silents."

'"Ach," said Forbes, and spat over the side. "Mon ami ici," he said, jerking his head towards Scott, rowing silently beside him, "il a bu trop trop du vin hier soir. Il s'agît d'une jeune fille," he added, pretending to whisper. It took a second for the German officer to translate again, then he laughed heartily. Scott, sensing perhaps the meaning rather than understanding, contrived to appear more and more sullen, and the Germans giggled for the rest of the journey – easily amused, eh?

'Well, on the other bank they hopped out, paid their money and went off. The doctor and Frith got out too, and made a show of digging in their pockets until the Germans were well out of sight, when we returned the boat to the reed bed where we'd found it, and slid back into the woods. And there, in a clearing, I must confess that we danced a little jig, the five of us, and took a sip of the doctor's brandy, and toasted the valour of Major Forbes.

'After that incident, nothing could daunt us. We made it to Marseilles, where we were directed to a seamen's mission run by a diminutive padre of the Scottish church: he sent us off over the Pyrenees and we eventually took ship from Santander. By the time we came here, the Scottish church had told Mrs. Forbes that the Major was fine, and apparently they've even sent word to my parents in Singapore. But I'd be languishing in some German PoW camp if it hadn't been for Major Forbes.'

'Good gracious!' said Marian. 'That's quite a story.'

'Oh, yes,' agreed Allardyce. 'I've probably not done him justice. But I suspect that when this game is all over, there'll be quite a few stories about Major Forbes.'

'Well, thank you very much for telling me that one.' The second story she had been told in two days, she thought, remembering the lumbering farmhand the night before and his fantastical story of the monsters in the loch. 'Now I must be going, I'm afraid.'

Allardyce tried to down the rest of his beer.

'I'll walk you back – the Major said –'

'Not at all! I don't want to drag you away!' said Marian firmly, and the Captain subsided. She wanted to be on her own for a little, to think.

She left the inn with a wave to Mrs. Binnie, and turned right to walk back up through the village and up to the crash site again. The place was drawing her back, though she had other things on her mind – or more precisely, she wanted to review, with considerable pleasure, the couple of hours she had just spent with Neil Forbes.

She was determined not to care too much, this time. She had been caught like that too many times before. Yet she had a feeling, an instinct, which she would have liked very much to ignore but that it was borne out by Captain Allardyce's enthusiastic tale – this man, she was convinced, was lucky in war.

Happy reflections sped her back to the crash site, but as soon as she was near the Heinkel again, in the net of its burned metallic odour, even Major Forbes dwindled to the back of her mind and she began another careful examination of the wreckage, circumnavigating the broken plane until she arrived, once again, at the mess where the cockpit should have been. She stopped, crouched down, and surveyed again.

A few feet away, some lump of metal had gouged a furrow into the side of the hill, turning up toffee brown soil laced with roots and rocks. She stood up and ran a muddy hand through her hair, contemplating it. Could a body be hidden underneath? The Home Guard and she had assumed that the fourth crew member had escaped, but for some reason she felt sure there was something more here. Almost without making the decision, she found herself following the furrow towards the lump of wreckage, stepping slowly, examining the ground, imagining the course of the hot metal as it was ripped from the rest of the Heinkel, wondering if someone could have been torn out with it.

When she saw the curved whitish shape at first, she thought it was one of the odd quartz pebbles she had seen earlier, scattered by the crash. Granted, it was a large one: most of them were a couple of inches across at most, whereas the curve of this one suggested a diameter closer to eight or ten inches. Then with almost an audible click in her brain she recognised the little dip and lift of the top of an eye socket, and she was on her knees beside it.

A moment's work with her fingers and the top of the skull was revealed, the earth-filled eye sockets watching her indifferently. She sat on her heels and stared back. What on earth was this? Could an aeroplane crash do this? Was this her missing airman?

'Hey, there!' The voice behind her made her jump, as if the skull itself had spoken. 'Are you digging on my patch?'

She craned about her, trying to find the source of the voice – a man. She was kneeling at the edge of the fairy hill, just where it started to rise from the farmland to her right. Further round its base, behind her, hidden before by the gorse bushes, was a man, kneeling and leaning back on his heels much as she was. She pushed herself up and readied herself to apologise and explain to an angry farmer.

The man was on his feet by the time she reached him, and grinning, which she took as a reassurance.

'Hello,' he said, starting again. 'I'm Davie Fraser. Who are you?'

'Marian Cowie,' she replied, shaking hands. 'I'm helping investigate the plane crash. Is this your land?' She thought perhaps he was a tenant of the Forbes family.

'Oh, no,' Davie said. He was a bit older than her, she reckoned, with a crooked face, sharp-nosed. His voice was educated, but with a local undertone. 'This is Forbes land. I just meant that I'm doing a dig here.'

'You're an archaeologist?'

'That's the plan. This is probably a Bronze Age burial mound, and I'm hunting for the entrance.'

'You mean it's not a fairy hill?' she asked, with a serious face.

'Well, if you never see me again you can draw your own conclusions,' he said. 'Though perhaps the fairies wouldn't fancy me. What have you found? If it's Bronze Age, I'm bagging it.'

'Fair enough,' said Marian, 'but I'm pretty sure it isn't. Come and see.'

She turned to go back to her skull, and when he followed her she noticed he had a stick to lean on. He wore wide trousers, almost like Oxford bags. She wondered if the crooked face was related to the bad legs, automatically searching for a diagnosis, while he stopped and stared at the skull.

'I doubt that's not your missing airman,' he said. 'The rate of decomposition would be remarkable, don't you think?'

'I know. But it's not Bronze Age either, is it?'

'I wish it was.' He used his stick to push back gorse branches from the skull. 'They didn't tend to lay their dead on their backs – they preferred to curl them up on their sides. You've just found it?'

'Yes. I'll have to tell the police. Do you know where the nearest telephone box is?'

'It's down near the inn. You'd be as quick going to the police house. Do you want me to keep an eye on your friend while you go?'

'Oh, yes please. Do you mind?'

'Not if you're quick,' he said, settling himself into a comfortable standing position with his stick. 'You know where you're going?'

'Of course. I'll be as quick as I can.'

Marian stumbled over the tufty pasture to the lane and hurried back down to the village. She had seen the police house at the upper end of the square, just where the little village street of shops led off the road her own cottage lay on. It did not take long to reach it: the tiny front garden was already dug and sown in vegetable rows, and some hens pecked in a run safely away from the beds, but there was no answer to her knocking. She stood for a moment, wondering what to do, then saw a familiar figure in the garden next door. She was not absolutely sure, but tried:

'Sergeant Leslie?' and the man next door glanced up.

'Oh, aye, Dr. Cowie, isn't it?'

'That's right. Do you know where P.C. Argo is?'

'Is there some kind of a problem?' John Leslie frowned, concerned, propping his hoe against the stone dyke.

'Um ... Could you tell him that I've found another body – up at the crash site? But I think there's something odd about it.'

'Oh, aye?' Leslie's frown deepened. 'Is it not the missing crewman, then?'

'I don't think so.'

There was a moment of silence while Leslie took out a rag from his pocket and slowly wiped his big, hard hands, staring at some point beyond Marian's head. She began to wonder if he was as competent as she had thought him the night of the crash. At last he spoke.

'Is young Davie Fraser up there? The lad with the stick.'

'Yes, yes, he is.'

'That's fine. I'll tell P.C. Argo as soon as I see him.'

'Thanks. I'll go back up and wait for him.'

She began the climb back up the road and the lane to the crash site, wondering why John Leslie had asked about Davie, and found herself compensating with an over-loud 'Hello!' when she saw Davie in the distance standing like an illfed crow over the grave. He waved back. She waited till she had reached him, then explained, 'I've left a message for him. I'll stay till he comes.'

'He won't be long, I daresay,' said Davie. 'Life round here isn't as exciting as P.C. Argo hoped, so a body is likely to brighten his day.'

'Each to their own,' she remarked absently. 'Were you expecting bodies in your dig?'

'In a burial mound? Well, it would be the place for them, wouldn't it? A cist burial would be my dream. Just something bijou, a few bones, ashes on the floor, a nice clay beaker – that would be fine.' He made a wry face.

'Is that likely?'

'There's what we archaeologists are pleased to call a recumbent stone circle about a mile over that way, pointing this way,' Davie explained, waving a hand generally west. 'Lots of these quartz pebbles round it, too. And this is the first distinct feature in this direction, and here on the side of a hill, between the Don and the Essie – well, it's ideal. Then they say that someone found a lump of gold and a silver amulet here about thirty years ago – and all that together is a good reason to be here. But to be honest, I'd settle for a few nails, or a bit of sword hilt, or maybe on a good day a ring. There's not much in the way of metalwork round here, and progress is slow.'

'Are you with one of the universities?'

'No, hence the lack of a team of eager students digging away with me. I'm hoping to get one of them interested – after the war. Until then, I just burrow away in my spare time. Which is not something any of us has much of at the moment, eh?'

'So what else do you do?'

'I work at the paper factory. It's been on the busy side recently: we had a bit of a disaster, and so we have bings of things that need to be made all over again.'

'Very traditional, Aberdeen paper factories.'

'Oh, aye. We're all doing important war work,' he added solemnly.

'What, all that stationery, I suppose? We could paper every house in the country with the posters the Government churns out.'

He laughed.

'No, no, hush, don't tell anyone but we're building huge paper aeroplanes to drop folded paper water bombs on Germany. Much lighter than conventional bombers, cheaper of course, and cause almost as much confusion.'

'You're joking!'

'Of course I'm joking!' He frowned. 'Well, I think I'm joking. Well, I am this week – you never know what the boffins will come up with next.'

'Aye, that's very true.' She turned her back to the hill, aware of the proximity of her feet and the skull. A figure was coming up the lane, in a dark uniform. 'Oh, now – there's the policeman.'

'I told you he'd not leave it long,' said Davie. 'Well, I'll leave you to it. I'd better get home for my tea or I'll be nibbling the paper tonight.' He set off. She watched him swinging across the field towards the lane – left leg, then, she thought, not the right. A war injury? If so, he must have had it early in the war – his face had that habitual drawn expression of someone for whom every step is wearing.

Davie nodded at the policeman as they passed: the policeman did not. P.C. Argo carried on up the field to where Marian was standing.

'I hear you've found a body,' he announced, 'and it's no one of our airmen.'

'That's right – here.' She drew him over to where the bare skull gazed peacefully out of the earth. 'What do you think?' she asked after a minute.

'I suppose the crash couldn't have driven him into the ground,' Argo remarked, grudgingly.

'No. And anyway, the flesh wouldn't have decomposed in two days.'

'It could have burned off in the fire.'

'There's no evidence of burning on the skull, anyway.'

'Maybe the Nazis have some chemical thing now that disposes of the bodies – in case we learn anything from them.'

A myriad of objections to this rose in Marian's mind, but instead she said,

'I doubt that.'

Argo glared sharply at her, as though suspecting her of Nazi sympathies.

'Well, if it's not the airman, we'll have to sort out who it is.'

'That's why I called you.'

'It's not recent, then.' Argo judged. 'It could be something

Davie Fraser's been digging up.'

'No, it's not that old, and it's lying on its back – Bronze Age burials were on their side.'

Argo gave a snort: he did not approve, it appeared, of Bronze Age burial practices. She had the impression he would have issued them with some kind of caution if he could have.

'So we need to know how old it is,' he established at last. Marian wished he would ask a direct question, though of course, she herself had no idea yet how old the burial was. 'You could do that. Dr. Hanson's pretty busy at the moment.'

She lost patience with him.

'But do you know of anyone missing? Anyone around here? It wouldn't be recent – maybe an old case?'

P.C. Argo applied his mighty brain to a review of crime in the Burgessie parish. Then a sly smile spread across his face.

'When I came up here fae Aberdeen – they wanted new blood and modern ideas, for P.C. Robertson had been here about a century – old man Robertson sat me down in the police house and handed over all the cases that were still open. Not many, nor anything very momentous, you can imagine, but I had to take him seriously, of course. Then, like his winning card, he pulled out a file of papers, not too thick, but a bit faded, like.

'"This is the Barclay case," he announced, all solemn. He seemed to think I would know what he was talking about, so I acted a bit excited like and said could he refresh me with the details. He settled in his chair, all pleased, and set to.

'"You wouldna have been more than a lad," he began, "when the dreadful disappearance happened. It was just after the Great War – 1921, in fact. She was a maid at the big house, you ken, not more than a girl herself, and gey bonny.' He went a bit wistful when he said this, and it crossed my mind he'd fancied her himself. 'There had been an army of servants at the big house before the War, but no so many after, and there were few enough to ask what might have happened to the lass. There was a cook, of course, a steward, some gardeners – not as many as had been – and twa-three maids. The housekeeping staff had little to do with the gardeners, they told me, but there was gossip that she had been seeing some man, certainly. No one could put a name to him, so he wasn't from the village. Some thought he might have been a friend visiting the family, but I had my own theory."

'I said the right things to push him on a bit –'

'Wait,' said Marian, 'what age was this girl?'

'Nineteen, I found out from the papers,' said P.C. Argo.

'Well, that might fit. There'll be signs on the skeleton, if we're lucky – age, and possibly sex.'

'Wait,' said P.C. Argo with a sly smile. 'I gave the old fellow all the encouragement he needed, and on he went.

"'The family was definitely hiding something. But the problem was that the whole thing happened just about the time that the laird went off to Africa with his daughter. I never had the chance to question them. Mrs. Forbes was always very protective of young Master Forbes, and he was only a lad at the time himself. Mr. Forbes – well, it tore my heart to think he might have had something to do with it, for he was a good man, but the conclusion was obvious. Mr. Forbes had taken advantage of the lass, and she'd fallen into the family way, and they had had to do away with her."

"'That seems a bit ... hard on the lass," says I. "Would it not have been easier just to send her away?"

"'Oh, she must have tried to put some pressure on Mr. Forbes," says P.C. Robertson. "And the way I see it, the girl, Miss Forbes, she must have seen something, and they took her away to stop her telling. They gave it out that her father was taking her out to Tanganyika to marry her off to some rich colonial. Mr. Forbes was in East Africa at the end of the War, and it got under his skin somehow – and Miss Forbes was a fine lassie and never afraid of anything. But they never took the maid with her. She was never seen again."

"'And what about the boyfriend? The man who was seen with the maid?"

"'Ach, I dinna think there was anything in that. Everyone gossips about maids. She was a bonny lass, as I've said, with – what do they call it? Strawberry blonde hair, and green eyes. The other maids were most likely jealous of her. And however good the laird was, she had the kind of looks it would be very hard to resist."

'Then something went click inside my head. Strawberry blonde hair and green eyes? Disappearing in 1921? with a strange man? I tried very hard not to smile, for I realised I had solved the poor old fellow's old case.

'"What was the maid's name again?" I asked as if it had just slipped my mind.

'"Jessie Barclay," said P.C. Robertson, and I swear there was a tear in his eye.

'I couldn't help smiling then, and P.C. Robertson frowned at me, more puzzled than anything.

'"P.C. Robertson," says I, "when I was twelve, a young couple came to live in our stair in George Street. She was expecting a child, and she had a healthy boy a few months later – my own mother attended her. They had both been in service, so I learned over the years, him to a man from the West Coast, her to a family in the country, and they'd met when his man visited her family. She had the most beautiful strawberry blonde hair, and she was the first person I'd ever met with green eyes. And to her own name she was Jessie Barclay."

'Well, you should have seen his face – it was a picture. He didn't know whether to believe me or not – and you could see he was torn for if she was alive his theory was wrong, but if I was right, then she was alive! And I think he had never wanted to believe the old laird had anything to do with it – he was traditional like that.'

'So did you make sure you were right?' asked Marian, 'for otherwise the date of Jessie Barclay's disappearance would make her a prime candidate for that skeleton.'

'Of course I was right,' said P.C. Argo, without hesitation. 'P.C. Robertson took down all the details, and I heard from my mother he was round asking questions, and he shook Jessie Barclay's hand as if he would pull her arm off. She's in Aberdeen, with two sons in the Air Force and a daughter riding a bicycle for the A.R.P. She's no in that hole over there.'

'Oh, well. Good for Jessie,' said Marian, reluctantly.

Chapter Three

P.C. Argo had not, contrary to Davie Fraser's expectations, lingered long on the hillside. He was less than bothered by Marian's find.

'If it's no the missing airman – and you seem fairly sure about that –' Argo added, regarding her sharply, 'then it's no going to be top priority for a whilie. There's a war on, do you ken.'

'It's still a dead body, though. What do you want me to do?' Marian asked, intending a rhetorical question, but Argo did like to be turned to for instruction.

'I want you to dig up the rest of it and get some definite facts about it. You said yourself there's no much to go on at the moment. Then you can write me a report on it, and I'll see what I can do,' he finished with an attempt at benevolence. She drew breath to snap back, then let it out again. Why not? It might be something useful to do in her spare time while she was here. Someone had to find out what the body was, and she found she liked very much to be out in that field by the fairy hill, in peace.

A small flock of pigeons – ten or twelve of them, rose suddenly from the copse beyond the lane with a sound like falling playing cards. Suddenly she saw them wheel and turn against a bright-burning building, confused, thinking it was daylight. The roar of the blaze filled her ears, and she could feel the heat on her face and hands ...

'... clothes missing from her washing line, which could well be that missing crewman. So you see, there are much more important things to be done than to investigate some skeleton that's been in the ground for twenty years or more.'

'What?' Marian's world spun like the wheeling pigeons.

'You said yourself,' said P.C. Argo again, with heavy patience, 'that the bones must have been there for a whilie. It's just no urgent.'

'I understand. I'll do what I can,' she agreed. Satisfied that his authority had been recognised, Argo strode off, back towards the village. The light was dimming, and there was little else she could do in the evening dusk. She gathered her medical bag and the bits and pieces she had brought with her, and wondered if it was too late in the day to call on the local doctor.

She walked down the hill, dreaming of tall officers with deep blue eyes. She was nearly at her cottage door when she heard a clanking, and happy voices coming up the hill from the village. She glanced back as she closed the garden gate. It was Davie Fraser, pedalling slowly up the lane, accompanied by a couple of laughing young women in overalls and headscarves. He waved cheerfully at her, and she waved back, trying to work out what was wrong with his bicycle. Then she realised: it had only one pedal. Davie's left leg hung on one side of the frame, and on the other, his right leg slammed the pedal down and twisted to draw it up again, doing all the work. The clanking this caused reminded her of her first evening in the cottage and the man who had guided her to the door of the inn, without dismounting from his bicycle. It must have been Davie: there was a minor mystery cleared up.

She smartened herself up, abandoning her muddy clothes for brushing down later, and set off further down the hill to visit the doctor.

Dr. Hanson lived in a fine granite villa which sat up in a supervisory position the village square, to the south west of the village. While the lane to the main Aberdeen road ran downhill, the doctor's property rose above it with assurance. The broad front overlooked a sloping garden bordered by rhododendrons in bud, but the centre of the smooth lawn had been gouged out, defiantly, to form a vegetable bed in which the remains of last year's brassicas huddled alongside a couple of wavy rows of leeks. The steep driveway probably eliminated the frailest of his patients, Marian thought, seeing that an extension to the near side of the house was signposted 'Waiting Room', and the nearest broad bay window was heavily netted, presumably as a consulting room. A shaded desk lamp glowed through the net – the blackout would not come into effect for a few hours yet, and it would take a Nazi with good eyesight to pick this dim light out of the dusk.

The front door was answered by an elderly maid, who,

explaining that the last patient had gone, announced her straightaway to the doctor. Dr. Hanson stood in mild surprise as Marian entered, and came round his formidable desk to shake her hand.

'I heard you were in the neighbourhood,' he said, 'and I intended to pay you a visit, but my time is rarely my own these days. I'm delighted you pre-empted me.'

He was a small, precise man, with delicate, yellowish hands and an open expression that Marian was sure his patients trusted. His moist blue eyes were shrewd, though. He was a good deal older than Marian had expected, and she wondered how he was coping with his extra workload.

'Someone suggested that while I'm here – I don't know for how long, a couple of weeks, perhaps – you might appreciate some help. But I don't want to interfere, of course.'

'Not at all, not at all! I'd be glad of any assistance. My neighbouring colleague has flung himself into the thrills of the R.A.M.C., along with my own two sons, leaving the old, ah, dinosaurs like me to deal with the boring work of general practice. Aye well, I suppose I did the same myself in my day. We seemed to have been much more serious about it back then – all King and country. Nowadays it's how the pay compares with agricultural work, and whether basic training is tougher than howking tatties.'

They talked for a little of the practice, its extent, the general run of patients and the interesting ones, the district nurse's bad back that laid her in her bed half the month, the differences made by absent husbands and fathers and the influx of paper factory workers. Dr. Hanson made a few gentle enquiries as to Marian's own background, her training, and what she had been doing in London for the last few months. It was agreed that Marian would cover a day that week and two days the following week of visits and afternoon surgery, 'just purely,' Dr. Hanson said with a smile, 'to allow me to catch up with everything else. I find I'm forgetting the normal standards of decent living - like offering you tea! Would you care for a cup? We could retreat to a more sociable part of the house, too – though I'm not sure where the fire's been laid.' He frowned, but rang the bell for the maid.

'I'm perfectly happy here, but I'd love some tea,' said Marian. An idea had just struck her. She waited until he had spoken to the maid, then told him about the skull she had found at the fairy hill. 'I was wondering,' she added, 'seeing you've been here for long enough to know, if you can remember any mysterious disappearances in the last, say, thirty years? Anyone unaccounted for?'

'Disappearances ...' Dr. Hanson's face folded into a hundred wrinkles. 'I'm not sure that I can think of anything like that. I suppose you're regarding it as a suspicious death. I can only think of one of those around here in my time, and I don't think it'll solve your problem at all.'

'I wouldn't mind hearing about it, though,' she prompted, 'if there's the least chance ...'

'Well ...' Dr. Hanson considered. The tea arrived, with two plain biscuits and an apologetic shake of the head from the maid, who clearly did not consider them sufficient for a guest. She departed with an arthritic curtsey, and Dr. Hanson, who had been staring out somewhere beyond Marian, gave a little shrug and said,

'Well, I suppose.' He made himself more comfortable in the big leather chair, and nodded at her. 'You're an Aberdeen man, aren't you? You'll have done your carvery at Marischal College.'

'Well, yes,' she agreed. A vision of the clay-cold dissection rooms blinked in her mind, simple and clean, something from another life.

'My predecessor here was an Aberdeen man too – didn't move too far! Now, Dr. Striven, he was a bit of a character in his way. The life of a country practitioner didn't altogether suit him, for he enjoyed a degree of high living: the brandy and cigars could be indulged in at home, though they tasted better if someone else paid for them, but there were other things ...

'Now, he had a junior partner in the practice, a family man, and he encouraged him in the brandy and cigar line, too, but he found in the end that he grudged two quotas of luxury coming out of the practice income and not both going his way. So he acquired a practice accountant, a man by the name of Laing, in Aberdeen, and once a month he would post to him the practice income, in cheques made out to Laing, so that, he explained to his junior partner, Laing could take his commission before banking the rest. He pointed out to his partner that this removed the burden of accounting from both their shoulders, and his partner, who was not what you would call a canny man, was duly grateful, and the pair of them had another brandy. The thing was, Laing, clever accountant as he was, did not exist – he was a figment of Dr. Striven's extremely active imagination, and the cheques made out to Mr. Robert Laing were gradually deposited in an account of the same name at the Aberdeen County Bank in Union Street, by post. Thus the innocent junior partner had no idea of the practice's financial state, and took gratefully his allowance at the end of each quarter.

'Now, Dr. Striven had city tastes, and city – shall we say proclivities? The kind of thing you're warned about at medical school, that if you find evidence of it you're to give the – er – gentlemen concerned time and encouragement to quit the country. Well, Dr. Striven had never been caught, and he had no intention of anyone finding any evidence. But he knew that even a rumour of such a thing would destroy his career as a family doctor, so having invented a chartered accountant, it was no strain on Dr. Striven's imagination to invent a lady friend. This mysterious siren arrived at the surgery when no one else was there, her visits brief and infrequent, her car, driven by a swarthy chauffeur, smart and neat, her dress variable but always including a black feather boa. Of course no one ever saw the lady, but as cleverly as Dr. Striven dropped the hints, more and more of the villagers heard of her and one or two even believed they had indeed seen her, zipping about in her car or walking with the doctor, or they had seen the swarthy chauffeur catching a swift cigarette as he waited for his mistress. The power of suggestion can be tremendously strong: perhaps Dr. Striven should have followed the field of brain medicine, and kept himself out of trouble.

'Now, Dr. Striven was a man very much like the rest of us in many ways. Sometimes he thought things through and prepared them carefully, and sometimes he acted on impulse. And in general, very much like the rest of us, what he thought through and prepared carefully went rather better than what he did on impulse. But when something in what he had prepared went wrong, Dr. Striven acted on a very bad impulse indeed, and that was the undoing of him.

'His partner, a fine doctor and a slightly too simple man, hailed from Liverpool and had gone to medical school there, so who knew what fancy took him one day to Aberdeen where he found himself by chance in the neighbourhood of the address of the egregious accountant, Mr. Laing. As it happened he had a few minutes to spare, and went to call on the man, a matter of courtesy only.

'But for a professional man, Mr. Laing was surprisingly hard to track down. If the address the good doctor remembered was correct, then the accountant lived in a very sorry little stair above a humble dairy in Union Grove, but no one in the dairy had heard of him and his name was beside none of the bells at the door. With no time left to investigate further, the doctor returned to the village the next day, and during a dinner break in their busy day he joined Dr. Striven for a cup of tea in Dr. Striven's consulting room – this very room - and mentioned his fruitless search for Mr. Laing.

'"Perhaps you were at the wrong address, old fellow," suggested Dr. Striven, hiding his beating heart well. "The number, I believe, is 138."

'But just too late, he saw an envelope in his own handwriting in front of him on the desk, addressed to Mr. R. Laing, C.A., 183, Union Grove. But it was not that which gave him away, but the involuntary jerk of his hand leaping to cover the envelope. He looked up at his partner, and his partner, innocent that he was, saw the guilt in Dr. Striven's eyes.

'"Is there something you would like to tell me, Striven?" he asked. "Is it possible that you have been deceiving me? Tell me straight, man – does Laing exist?"

'Dr. Striven let out a heavy sigh.

'"No, no, he does not." He slumped forward in his chair, elbows on the desk, a most unphysicianly posture. "I should have told you long ago, old fellow: I wish I had."

'"Then what are you hiding?" asked his partner. "You may speak freely to me – that which must remain confidential will not go beyond this room." He spoke in a manner that could hardly be mistaken, and for a moment Dr. Striven had a wild hope that he could pass this off as some scheme to cover an unsuitable – and indeed illegal – dalliance. But then, just as the hope flashed in his mind, his partner smacked his forehead and cried,

'"Of course! It's the money!"

'"I'll give it all back, I promise," Striven gabbled, but even as he thought how dim his partner really was, he knew it was too late.

'"I need that to get my lad through the University," said his partner. "Damn' sure you'll give it back."

'"Of course, of course I will," said Striven, trying to sound calmer and more calming. "See here, I've some guineas in a bag in my coat. Let me give you those – as a promise of the rest."

'He rose carefully from his chair, sliding up his sleeve as he did so the sharp brass letter opener from his desk. He made for the coat stand by the door, but in an instant the letter opener was through his partner's coat and deep, deep into his back. There was a little choking sound, and his partner was dead.

'Well, there was the act of impulse, and now Dr. Striven knew he had to think things through carefully again. First he drew the blind, which he often did for patients, anyway, so that would arouse no suspicion. Then he went into the passage, and locked the front door, after checking to see that no importunate patient had intruded into the barren waiting room, which used to be the other front room. Then he called the maid, not the brightest of girls, and sent her on an errand. Confident that he was now alone in the house, he went back to his room and with considerable effort he carried his partner's body slowly across the passage to the other consulting room, and closed the door.

'Where was he to put the body? He wanted to keep it on its front for there was still some blood oozing from the wound. He thought of laying it under the window, where no one glancing in would see it, but if anyone came through the door it would be in plain view. The rug over the consulting room couch was not long enough to hide anything on the floor below it, but if he rolled the body under the couch and arranged the rug artfully, it might give the impression that a patient had slid off the couch to stand up and had partially pulled the rug with them.

'He did it quickly, and then studied the effect from several angles, with and without his spectacles - he was very short-sighted - before he was satisfied. Then he left the consulting room and locked the door. A glance at his pocket watch told him he had only a few minutes left. He hurried back to his own room, took one of the cloths and dipped it into a bucket of soapy water he always kept there during the working day. Wringing it out, he swabbed down the plain wooden chair his partner had been sitting in, and scrubbed at the floor beneath it – fortunately he had always planned his room to take account of patients who emitted any quantity of bodily fluids or partially digested foodstuffs. In a moment or two, nothing about the floor would arouse suspicion. Then he examined his own appearance in the mirror on the back of the door: there was a spatter of blood drops up his face and neck, as he had thought, but only a few drops on his lapel, which he quickly scrubbed, and a dribble on his collar. He always kept a spare collar in his desk drawer, so this was soon remedied. He doubted that anything had caused a moment's concern in the limited mind of his maid, who was used to the milder disadvantages of being servant to a general practitioner.

Then he went to unlock the front door, just as the afternoon's first patient chapped it. The patient was his own, and Dr. Striven took him straight in to his consulting room. Thus he settled down to give his attention to the ailments of the villagers for the rest of the afternoon.

Of course, after a while his maid, who acted as receptionist, began to remark that each time she went to collect his next patient from the waiting room, there were even more of his partner's patients not so patiently waiting. At last, he raised his eyebrows, and went through to see. He said to them,

"I hope my partner's not keeping you too long today. Mrs. Geddie, when is your appointment?"

"It was at two o'clock, Doctor, and here I am still two hours later and neither hide nor hair of anyone to take care of my poor toe."

"Oh, dearie me!" exclaimed Dr. Striven. "What on earth has become of him?" And he went and knocked on the door of the other consulting room, which mercifully his partner did not answer. He tried the door, aware that the patients nearest the door of the waiting room were watching him, then with a worried frown he unlocked the door with his own keys, and stuck his head in. "No sign of him! Well, that's very strange." He paused for a moment, doing his best to act indecisively while praying that none of the patients would think to stand up and come and inspect the room more closely. Then he thoughtfully closed and relocked the door, and said,

"Perhaps he was unwell and went home. Is there anyone here

for anything urgent?"

A few, including old Mrs. Geddie, waved their hands.

"Then if I can hurry my own list a little,' he said, smiling at them encouragingly, "and if you don't mind waiting a wee bittie longer, I'll see you."

'The patients were pleased with this arrangement for the most part, as much as patients ever are, and Dr. Striven worked hard to see them all and let them away before his evening meal time.

'Now, Dr. Striven lived in this house, of course, on his own apart from the daily maid. The maid cooked and served Dr. Striven's dinner and evening meal, then left, and the doctor would put his own dishes in the sink for her to do next morning. That night, though, he left his dishes in the dining room and hurried to the kitchen to stoke the fire in the stove, and got out all the pots and pans he could find. He took them two by two to his partner's consulting room, and as he brought them back, filled with neatly butchered joints of middle-aged physician, he topped them up with water and set them to boil. He had to make three more trips to the well, and there was much swabbing to be done in the consulting room, but in the end nothing was left there but a suit of clothes, a bunch of keys, a watch and chain and a pocket book. Through the house was a fine smell of cooking meat, and they say that that night an unusual number of stray dogs and even the occasional tramp lingered in the village, sniffing the fragrant air.

'With everything well stoked and covered, Dr. Striven decided to take a few moments to cover a little more of his tracks. His partner's house was not far away, and to pre-empt any ventures on her part, Striven went to call on the wife.

'She opened the door herself and it was clear by her face when she saw him that she had been expecting her husband. Her expression swam from disappointment to anxiety.

'"What's the matter, Dr. Striven?" she asked.

'"Matter? Nothing at all," he replied. "I came to ask after your husband."

'"George has not come home," she said, clearly trying to keep herself under control. "I thought you might know ... was he all right at work?"

'"He seemed perfectly well this morning," said Dr. Striven in all honesty. "I have not seen him this afternoon – in fact, I believed he had come home, perhaps feeling unwell. I had to deal with his afternoon patients." He was quite proud of the slightly heroic tone in which he produced this.

"'Oh, I am sorry," she said automatically. She was a well-mannered sort. "But where could he be? He did not mention any emergency? A call to one of the farms, perhaps?"

"'No, not at all. I am very sorry not to be able to help you, madam, but as I said I came here seeking information myself. Perhaps you would send me a message when he does return safely?"

'And taking his leave, he returned to his cooking.

'When he had a moment again, he collected the appointment book from his consulting room and took it to the kitchen. There he carefully sliced out the page with the afternoon's appointments and recopied it, but including, at 1.45p.m., an entry for 'Mrs. ...' and then an illegible squiggle, as close as he could approximate to his partner's hand. Then he replaced the book, and attended again to culinary affairs.

'It took longer than he had expected to boil down the various parts of his partner. However, in the early hours of the morning he finally scraped the last of the bones clean and placed it in a box, and took the remaining meat in a bucket in several trips to his neighbour's pigs. The pigs were unnervingly grateful: Dr. Striven made a mental note not to buy any pork for some time. Then he cleaned the kitchen, washing the pots and pans in yet more water, tamped down the stove and as a final touch, fetched his dinner dishes from the dining room and placed them as usual in the sink. He checked his watch: the maid was due to arrive in two hours. Well, she would just have to wonder about the still-warm stove: it would have to be one of life's little mysteries, if she even noticed. She was not, he was glad to say, the sharpest of girls. He retired to bed, taking the box of bones with him and setting it carefully inside his wardrobe.

'The next couple of days were uneventful. During the day he assumed an anxious frown as he dealt with both sets of patients and his partner's increasingly fretful wife, whom he tried very hard not to think of as the widow. At the same time, he worked hard to convey to the woman, without actually saying so, that the practice was on a very poor footing financially. He led her, as a man innocent of leaping to the conclusion himself, to believe that his partner had taken as he disappeared a sizeable proportion of the practice funds. He used his previous methods of sowing the seeds of rumour to hint at the mysterious 1.45p.m. appointment, and had the satisfaction by the end of the week of hearing from his maid that in the opinion of the village gossips, his partner had absconded with the lady in the feather boa, and that Dr. Striven was regarded with considerable sympathy locally. And in the evenings, after the maid had left, Dr. Striven carefully went over the boiled bones, examining them for any distinguishing marks, and cautiously yellowing them with tea leaves and brown boot polish, to age them to something of the colour of the fine skeleton he had in his own consulting room.

'The following week's evenings he spent articulating his partner's skeleton with brass wire, and on Friday night he finally took down his old skeleton and hung his new one in its place, and on Saturday morning he tucked the old one in a suitcase, placed it in his motorcar and drove to Aberdeen. The medical library would be the place to find a likely student, he thought: he parked some distance away from it, and manhandled the suitcase into the building. He trusted no one would remember him from his own student days. He found a bench and sat down, the suitcase at his feet, and surveyed the scene.

'It was quiet, for a Saturday, but he did not even at that approach the first student that he saw. Instead, he waited, peering short-sightedly at each new figure crossing the hall, seeking any that was a little more threadbare, more lean and hungry, than the others. At last he saw one whose gown, he could see, was tattered at the edges, and whose jacket, when he saw it more closely, was shiny of elbow and deficient in buttons. Moreover, there was something a little familiar about him, which Striven took sentimentally to be a reflection of himself at that age – young, poor, carefree, and not yet a murderer.

'"Young man," he said, waving him over, "do I take it that you are a medical student here?"

'"I am, sir," said the student.

'"Long ago, so was I," said Dr. Striven, and paused just long enough to let his air of wistfulness envelope them. "Ah! happy days! But not always easy ones, eh? Tell me, young man, have you a skeleton of your own?"

"'Well – no," said the student, toeing the ground. "Not to study, sir."

"'Aye, well, I ken well what it's like when the funds – but we'll say no more about it, shall we? As it happens, I have reached the happy stage of retiring from practice, and I was looking for a good man who might take care of my old skeleton for me."

'The student's eyes widened in alarm, and Dr. Striven laughed.

"'No, no!" he said quickly. "I've no intention of donating my body to medical science just yet! I meant the skeleton someone kindly gave me when I was a student like you. It's here, in this suitcase. Would you like it?"

"'Oh, yes please!" said the student eagerly. "Can I take a look?" He knelt on the floor and opened the heavy case. A grinning skull, resting on the usual assortment of bones, greeted him.

"'Of course, you'll need to do a little work on re-articulation," said Dr. Striven. "I had to fold the poor fellow up a bit to fit him in. But I think you'll find he's all there."

"'And it is a he, is it?" The student fished out the pelvis and fingered the notches. "Oh, yes, indeed. But I can't afford you pay you at all, sir," he said suddenly, laying the pelvis back in the case. "Is there anything I could do for you instead?"

"'Not at all, not at all," said Dr. Striven, your complete selfless benefactor. "You don't even need to know my name" - which he had carefully removed from the suitcase. "I shall simply vanish and retire, and allow you to become acquainted."

'At this the student appeared very puzzled indeed, but Dr. Striven, short sight and all, did not see, for he had taken himself at his word and vanished back to his motorcar.

'Thus relieved of a superfluity of skeletons, Dr. Striven returned to the village and to his practice. Gossip died down over his partner's disappearance, though Dr. Striven kept up a slight contact with the wife in the hopes, so he said, that the man might have the decency to send the abandoned lady some indication of his whereabouts, or even some of the practice funds. Then, one day, the lady herself presented herself to him as a patient.

"'I am half ashamed to appear here," she admitted, "for you

know I have not the means to pay you and you can scarcely afford to treat me for nothing."

"'Dear lady," said Dr. Striven, his face all sympathetic concern, "you know that any service I can perform ... to a fellow sufferer ...""

"'You are very kind," she said. He put the slight sharpness of her voice down to her emotional state.

"'And what is the nature of the problem, dear lady?" asked Dr. Striven, slipping seamlessly into practitioner style.

"'Well, I suppose it's only natural, but ever since George - disappeared - I have had such trouble in sleeping."

"'That is indeed a natural reaction to all the worry you have had, but that is not to say that science cannot provide a way for us to re-establish your normal sleeping. The body can lapse into bad habits at a time of stress. Tell me, are you eating all right?"

"'Not very well, no ...""

"'Well," said the doctor, "one thing at a time. Let us find a gentle remedy for the sleeplessness first, and I often find that an improvement in appetite follows without any further intervention."

'He stood up to reach for his bottle of standard sleeping pills, then noticed that the lady's gaze had wandered, as the gaze of the fatigued often does, but it had settled, unnervingly, on the new skeleton.

"'Do you know," the lady said, slightly dreamily, "it's very strange, but I can't help feeling ... that skeleton really reminds me of George."

"'Oh, my dear lady," said Dr. Striven, in his deepest tones of sympathy, "You see the tricks the mind plays when deprived of sleep? It is a dreadful thing, though we take it so much for granted."

'But she still stared at the skeleton.

"'Tell me, Dr. Striven," she said, "does that skeleton show any breaks? I mean, when it was – alive, did it ever break a bone?"

"'Not at all," said the doctor with confidence – he had been over every bone at least four times. "I got it from the best of sources. It's always a thing of pride for the medical student, his first skeleton." And he was rather proud of himself, despite his frantic heartbeat, for not having told an actual lie. Nevertheless, he poured a few more sleeping pills into the brown bottle, and decided to play it safe.

'"These are quite mild, so I'd suggest you take three of them at first to start the attack strongly, as it were. Take your system by surprise, bowl it over, then we can ease off gradually later."

'"Thank you so much, Dr. Striven." The lady roused herself with a little shake. "And about payment –"

'"Don't even think about it, dear lady," said the doctor, pressing the bottle into her hands. "It's the least I can do." The lady left, and he breathed a heartfelt sigh of relief. If she took three of those pills, she would have no more doubts about skeletons, and the chances were that the village would simply reflect on the tragic story of an abandoned wife. If she didn't, no matter: she would put the whole thing down to fatigue when she felt more like herself.

'Well, the lady took the pills home with her, but she did not take three, or two, or even one. Instead, she handed the bottle to her son, who had obtained leave from the university to visit his mother in her distress. The son, whose name was James, took the bottle and examined them.

'"Father dispensed these, too," he said. "Dr. Striven makes them up himself. They are quite strong – how many did he tell you to take, again?"

'"Three," said his mother, with a faint smile.

'"Then," said James, "I fear we must be on the right track."

'"But how shall we follow it to its end?" his mother asked. "Let's sit down with a cup of tea and have a think. But there's no sugar."

'"No matter," said James. "If we're clever, there'll soon be sugar again."

'A few days passed. Dr. Striven noted that his late partner's widow was still in the land of the living, and in fact seemed much improved.

'"Aye, well, never mind," he thought to himself: as long as she didn't go speculating about his skeleton to all her afternoon tea circle, it would be fine.

'Then one morning, as he sat at his desk, speaking authoritatively to old Mrs. Geddie, she interrupted him suddenly.

'"Doctor, I hardly think that's respectful. Or appropriate."

Stopped in mid-stride, Dr. Striven stared at her with his mouth open, trying to think what he had just said. Then he turned to where she was pointing, and despite all his anatomical expertise, he knew his blood was running cold.

'The skeleton had one long hand up to its chest, and between the carefully articulated fingers, like a sweet posy, was a little bunch of black feathers, the kind you might find on a lady's boa.

'He stuttered some apology to Mrs. Geddie, got rid of her, then quickly rearranged the skeleton and flung the feathers in the fire. He glanced about the room, but nothing else gave the impression of being out of place. That evening he questioned the maid, but the girl was as thick as mince and he had no satisfaction. He locked up with particular care after she left, and went to bed. He did not sleep well that night.

'Next morning there was nothing amiss, nor the next. But the following morning, the skeleton had moved again. This time its hand was at its face, and when he went to move it he found a cigar between its excellent teeth. Closer examination showed it to be his late partner's favoured brand.

'This time he went about the room minutely. Again, there was no sign of a break-in, but when he opened his desk drawer, where he had secreted his victim's keys, pocket book and watch and chain, he found that they had all vanished. He swallowed hard, and for a long moment he eyed the skeleton as though it was likely to tell him something. Then he shook himself hard, and swore he would sack the maid.

'That evening he did so, despite her protestations of baffled innocence. He had no wish to prosecute the case, for it might be thought somewhat suspicious that he was pursuing the theft of his partner's belongings, when his partner had, presumably, taken them with him when he absconded. Indeed, he was pleased, he told himself, to be rid of the things, and quite pleased to be rid of the maid, of whom he had never thought highly.

'The next morning dawned fair, and though there was no hot water ready for his shave, he felt contented. The place was locked up like a bank, the evidence had all gone, and his partner's widow had not pursued the strange notion she had had of the skeleton. He stoked the kitchen stove, boiled water, shaved at the sink, and returned to dress upstairs. Once down, he decided to reassure himself about the skeleton before he made himself breakfast, and so he went to his consulting room.

'What he saw nearly caused a fit. The skeleton, draped in his watch and chain, was sitting at the desk with, in front of him, his pocket book, his keys, and a glass of brandy. With a cry, Dr. Striven slammed the door, grabbed his coat and ran from the house – but he was not alone.

'His motorcar was not a good morning starter, and he flung himself at the handle like a madman, jerking it round till the car choked into life. He threw his coat on to the back seat, leapt in and set off. The one thought in his mind was to drive to Aberdeen, clear out the bank account in the name of the invisible Mr. Laing, and go – where, he could not think, but Aberdeen was a harbour: he would see where the first boat was going, and take his chances on that.

'Once in the town he tried to concentrate: he knew he had been driving erratically. Dodging around the trams in the Castlegate, he pulled the car in beside the bank, and spent a few long moments controlling his breathing, smoothing his hair, reining in his galloping thoughts. Then he stepped out, reached for his coat and felt in the pocket for the bank book he had kept there these last few weeks, ready for an emergency.

'It was gone.

'He tried to remember when he had last seen it, and could not. Never mind, he thought: they might still – if he brazened it out – if he went to Laing's accommodation address and brought back a letter from the bank – maybe they would let him – the thought of driving back to the village to search for the book appalled him. He drew a breath, and went into the bank.

'"Mr. Laing?" the clerk said, misunderstanding him. "You've just missed him, I'm afraid. And I don't think he'll be back – he's just closed his account." And he picked up a familiar bank book from the counter in front of him, and let Striven see the name on the front – Robert Laing.

'With a cry of despair, Dr. Striven turned from the counter and blundered out of the bank, then sank down on the curved granite steps, his head in his hands. He needed that money to make good his escape: there was little enough in his own account, and closing it might draw further attention to himself. What in the name of heaven was he to do?

'Slowly he became aware of someone sitting on the steps beside him. He was almost afraid to look, for in a second his mind had conjured a picture of the skeleton, following him here, companionable with its brandy and cigar. Then he heard a slight chuckle, and forced himself to turn slowly round.

'There sat, to his surprise, the medical student to whom he had given his old skeleton. He was close enough to be sure, despite his eyesight. The young man was smiling at him, sympathetically, it seemed.

'"You've had a bit of a shock, haven't you?"

'Striven could do nothing but nod. Perhaps the student had some medication about him, something that would ease the pain ...

'"All that money – clearly, Laing was not a man to be trusted, was he?" Striven blinked. "In fact," the student went on, "Laing was not a man at all."

'"Are you Laing?" asked Striven, quietly. He felt he could believe anything.

'"Laing? No!" The student grinned. "But I do appear familiar, don't I? That's why you chose me to give me your old skeleton, isn't it? I rang bells."

'Striven nodded. He had the curious feeling of receding, backing out of the world. He could have sworn that he was sliding back down his life, as well, turning into a child again. Kindly Mr. Laing, the accountant – that was a big word – was standing over him, explaining something very complicated, but it wasn't anything that mattered much. If he was polite, perhaps Mr. Laing would give him sixpence.

'James Hanson – for it was I – saw that my father's murderer had slipped away somewhere I could not follow. I pulled him up gently to his feet, and took him to the police station. What followed was perhaps routine: the skeleton in his consulting room was examined and found to match my father's physical details absolutely – of course he had never broken a bone. These were the days before our infamous colleague Buck Ruxton, of course, but nevertheless the presence of my father's watch and pocket book, traces of human flesh in the nearby pig trough, and traces of blood on the chair and floor, were enough to convict Striven. Old Matthew Hay found him insane, and he ended his days in a secure hospital, as innocent as a child. And when I qualified, I took over the practice here.'

'And your mother?' Marian asked. 'Could she really stay here?'

'She could – she did. She's buried in the kirkyard, beside my father. Oh, she was a strong woman, my mother, and a clever one – she loved my father very deeply, I believe. Striven never took much account of women, which was a mistake. His maid was the first to come to us and tell us that she thought there was something wrong. When he gave me the skeleton in the suitcase, I thought at first it must be my father's, but it didn't match – far too tall. That made us look elsewhere, and the maid let me in the first night until I found my father's own keys in Striven's desk. Aye, well, colourful days – but no spare victim, as far as I know, to fit your skeleton. Unless there really was a lady with a black feather boa.'

Marian reflected a moment, horrified at the story.

'But weren't you scared to confront Dr. Striven? When you knew he had already killed your father?'

Hanson gave a little dry laugh.

'He was indeed much bigger than me. But we were at a busy street corner in Aberdeen, for one; for another, it was quite clear to me that Striven was a broken man. He wasn't basically at heart an evil man, I'd say. He hadn't spent years eaten up with jealousy, or hatred, he'd simply tried to protect himself, financially and socially. But here – if you want stories of the village, you should go to the schoolmistress. She knows a hundred local stories, if she'll tell you them. She's a shy lass, but that doesn't mean she doesn't have a brain.'

'The schoolmistress – right, I'll try her,' Marian agreed.

'Like me, she enjoys learning for learning's sake: she doesn't just collect facts like some schoolboy with an aircraft spotting book. And once you get her going – but there, we're all story tellers, aren't we?'

Marian laughed.

'I don't think I am!'

Chapter Four

'I have nothing against women studying medicine, nothing at all. Some of them make very fine doctors, just as some men do. What I object to is the female medical student who marries straight from university and never practises. What a waste!'

'But I won't do that, Dad.'

'How do you know? Some young medic as earnest as yourself brushes against your scalpel hand at the dissection table, or some handsome brute catches your eye on the rugby field, and the next thing you know it's marriage and children and sweet domesticity, and all that hard work gone to waste.'

'It won't happen to me, Dad! I'm going to be a doctor, a proper, practising doctor.'

'Well, we'll see,' he had said, with a knowing smile. Marian had been determined from that moment to prove him wrong, to make him proud of her. Sometimes Marian wondered if what he had actually known was that the very suggestion that she would not practise would be enough to drive her to it: if so, he had been absolutely right. There had been earnest young medics, and handsome brutes, and Marian had laughed and danced and picnicked and always, always, came back to her work, leaving them, who knows, heartbroken? But leaving them, at any rate. Now the image of Neil Forbes' face, deep blue eyes glowing, swam before her eyes, and if she concentrated she could hear his carelessly clipped, warm voice, laughing easily with her as they walked down the hill to the village. With a little imagination, she could see the whole adventure that Captain Allardyce had told her about, from St. Valéry to Marseilles. Yes, a man lucky in war. Was war like cards? Lucky at cards, unlucky in love, her grandmother would say. Would Major Forbes be worth giving it all up for?

She turned over in the dark bedroom of her grandmother's cottage, flexing her toes in the thin socks she had taken to wearing with slacks – they were more comfortable to sleep in than stockings, and tougher. Her shoes and medical bag, beret, torn coat and torch lay neatly arranged on and by a chair by the door. It was remarkable, she thought, how little sleep one really needed to function normally. She wondered how the night was going in London, and where her colleagues were working. Were they all safe, this time?

It was Thursday morning, and she had promised Dr. Hanson that she would cover his surgery and visits on Friday, so determined to waste no time she ate breakfast as dawn was breaking and was back on the fairy hill as soon as the light was good enough to dig by. She had found an old Brownie camera in her grandmother's cupboard, something she used in her artwork, no doubt, and there was some relatively fresh film to wind into it, which was lucky: such things were not easy to come by these days. The previous afternoon she had arranged some gorse twigs over the part of the skull she had already exposed, partly to protect it from careless feet, and partly to hide it from casual eyes, though it seemed unlikely that anyone but Davie Fraser went up there much. She had not seen the Home Guard around yesterday apart from meeting John Leslie when she went to fetch the police constable, and if the search for the missing airman was still going on with any enthusiasm it was not happening up here by the crash site.

Using the film sparingly and with great deliberation, she took a shot of the partially-exposed skull, then laid down the camera on her folded coat and began, with a trowel she had found in her grandmother's shed, to chip back the earth from the bare bones. She worked slowly and cautiously, her mind focussed on the emerging jawbone, the neat rows of teeth, the arching ribcage still filled with earth, the collar bones and shoulders and delicate upper arms. The skull was what her old lecturer would have called 'ladylike': the shape of the forehead was light, the jawbone neat, a balance of probability that the body was that of a woman. Or a girl: the cranial sutures across the top of the gritty skull were not all sealed up, so she had probably not reached full maturity. And now, already, on the ribcage, she was meeting finger bones: had someone tenderly laid her hands across her breast before turning the cold soil back in on her?

'Would you like a cup of tea?'

She jumped. Heart spinning, she turned on her heels to find Davie, with a cheery smile and a Thermos flask, and two enamel cups.

'I always bring an extra one in case someone is interested enough to visit,' he explained. 'I'm sorry I've no piece to go with it, though – if you really fancied it you could have a fishpaste sandwich from my lunch?'

'I wouldn't deprive you!' she laughed. He looked as if he needed feeding up, certainly, though perhaps it was just the strain of all that limping. 'Have you been up here long? I didn't hear you.'

'I saw you arrive,' he admitted, 'but you were very determined and I'd just got going myself, so I didn't disturb you. How's it going?'

They both scanned the pathetic shape of skull and ribcage and arms.

'All right, so far, I suppose,' she replied.

'Is it a girl, do you think? It's small.'

'Yes, I think so. I'll know better once I see the pelvis, of course. And young – early twenties at most.'

'Have you any idea who it is yet?' Davie asked, after a contemplative sip of tea. 'Did P.C. Argo solve the case?'

'He told me a story about a missing girl in the village, but then he also told me how he'd solved it so it wasn't her,' Marian said, with raised eyebrows. Davie gave an amused snort.

'Aye, they're good at telling stories round here,' he commented.

'So you're not from around here, then?'

'Me? No, I'm from Banchory. Thirty odd miles away, and a different world.'

'So you wouldn't have known of anyone disappearing twenty or thirty years ago, then?'

'Twenty or thirty years ago I doubt I'd even heard of the place,' Davie replied. 'Most people round here would have been here, though. Even with the war, there aren't that many incomers, really, apart from the factory workers like me. Oh, and old L.C.R., of course.'

'Who's he? or she?'

'He's an archivist, a curator from the Record Office in

Edinburgh. He's up at the big house, standing guard over registers that have been moved there for safety. Maybe we're not supposed to know that, but he's quite open about it. He's done some work on local history, by the way, so even though he might not have been here himself thirty years ago, he might well know something about stories from around then.'

'I must talk to him some time, then.'

'He'll like that ...' said Davie, absently. They fell silent for a moment, still gazing down at the exposed bones.

'May I take a look at your dig?' Marian asked. 'I'd like a break from this one.'

'Be my guest!' Davie waved her towards it. Round the steep curve of the fairy hill she found a small, deep square cut from the side of the hill, about a yard each way. Around it, she could see other places where Davie had evidently done the same thing, then backfilled the holes.

'They're test pits,' he explained, seeing her frown. 'I dig out a square yard down to see what might be there. Then I draw it –' he nodded to a thick pad of paper poking out of a satchel '- and record anything I find, and fill it back in. It saves me shifting round too much, of course – archaeology for the immobile!' He folded himself irresistibly down beside the pit, and picked up a narrow trowel.

'So what are you hoping for here? Is it like that Suffolk one – what was it, a couple of years ago: it was in all the papers ...'

'Sutton Hoo?'

'That's the one – most unlikely name. Wasn't it a Saxon king or something?'

'They don't know, but it was likely to be someone important. Raedwald is the prime candidate, or a bloke called Aethelhere. I've lost you already, haven't I?'

'Raedwald or Aethelhere, I'm with you.' He was easy to listen to, though he kept digging while he talked. He had long, elegant fingers, she noticed: surgeon's hands.

'There was no body, anyway,' he went on, 'but it was clearly a burial site. There were the remains of a boat about eighty feet long, and lots of bits of metal work – the rivets from the boat were the real key to the shape of the dig, but of course what people remember are the gold artefacts.'

'Of course – buried treasure!'

'I doubt I'll find anything like that here. Some of the villagers say I might find one of St. Angus' victims. But in some ways I'd rather get the rivets than the gold.'

'You're a strange man.'

He returned her smile.

'No, it's true.' He rolled over to rest on his hip, facing her. 'The gold is fine, and it must be dead exciting to find it – incorruptible in the earth. But what does it really tell you? There was a helmet at Sutton Hoo, just a plain, tough old helmet, a few animal patterns on it but nothing fancy. But that had been on a man's head in battle. He'd sweated into it, cursed its weight, thanked his gods for it when it saved his life, pulled it off with a grunt at the end of the day and surveyed the battlefield as he rubbed his bare head, taken it home and cleaned it off for next time. That's history. And I'll tell you another thing,' he went on, rolling back to dig on irresistibly, 'however big a man he was, I'd be prepared to bet that he was at least once damned scared in that helmet.'

She pictured it: the warrior with his precious helmet. It must have been made to fit him, or it would have been horribly uncomfortable. She began to think about skull shapes she had seen, and how awkward some of them would have been to fit. A helmet was a very personal thing.

'See this.' Davie had been scratching in the soil again, and now he had something rounded in his hands. 'Catch!'

She put out a hand and the object fell smoothly into it. It was a pebble.

'Quartz pebble,' Davie explained. 'When they're clean they gleam white, almost sparkling. People have noticed that they appear in large numbers at sites that the old Celts regarded as religious: shrines, holy wells, saints' graves, our own recumbent stone circles here in the North-East, that kind of thing. Someone brought that from the beach somewhere, stuck it in a little bag at their belt, or wrapped it in their pack, and carried it here to set it at this place. Why? What did they think they were honouring? Christian or pagan? Did they belong round here and travel to the sea specially, or were they passing through? What did they eat – did they bring some fish back, too? Were they asking some special favour from their god? What? A good harvest? A child? A cure? Success in battle? Inspiration for their party piece at that night's feast?'

'All right, all right,' she grinned ruefully. 'I shan't even consider gold in the British Museum again – if it ever comes back to the British Museum.'

'Oh, gold tells us things too. Just don't run for it and dismiss the rest. And I tell you, if someone promised me gold artefacts in a boat burial here, I'd row the boat here myself.' He had rolled on to his hip again, and leaned on his elbow to brush off his hands and check his watch. 'Time to go, unfortunately: got to get back to folding those paper aeroplanes. Better look the other way,' he added with a self-mocking grimace. 'I rise to my feet with all the grace of a paperclip unfolding.'

She laughed, and watched him anyway, with a doctor's eye. He was awkward, but with a kind of practised awkwardness that almost was grace. Definitely the left leg, completely useless – with callipers, she thought? A wound to the hip joint causing paralysis, perhaps, wasting of the muscles of the upper leg. He caught her eye again as he arranged his stick and his satchel, with amusement, as if he wondered how long it would take her to solve the puzzle or to ask him outright. Then he waved goodbye and swung off down the field, passing over the rough pasture with ease. She watched him, still analysing, and took a sip of her tea. It was stone cold.

She worked till after dinner time, then went back to the cottage to change for going into the village. She took a basket and her rationbook, and was pleased to be able to find bread, butter, plenty of winter vegetables, and wonderful unrationed fish. Her meat ration went on sausages: the excuse was that the ration went further, but she had always been secretly partial to sausages, even the watery wartime bangers. With her basket much fuller than she expected, she took the precious groceries home and made herself a sandwich, then returned to the village around the time she expected school to be out.

The school was a small, symmetrical granite building in the centre of the village, on a slight rise. It shared its grounds with a solid and ugly Victorian house, and what had been rough, unmade-up school yard was now partially given over to vegetable beds and a row of neat rabbit hutches. Even as Marian was examining this over the wall, the two end doors opened and within seconds the streams of boys and girls collided and the yard was full. She was bewildered by their instant activity: some were running in mad circles, some sharing some treasure in a huddled corner, some skipping, some tossing marbles. Several had already kicked off their hard boots for the walk home, and were rounding up younger siblings with world-weary solemnity.

She moved to the gate and watched, wary in an unfamiliar setting, waiting for anyone to appear likely to be a teacher. The children were multiplying like bacteria on a microscope slide, running and whirling and bouncing off each other. She was about to take her courage in her hands and edge through the crowd when a voice came from about her right elbow.

'Who are you, Miss?'

She jumped and glanced down to find a pale lad with black hair creeping over his forehead. He wore a jersey which was mostly navy, then branched into an astonishing spring green at the waist and cuffs.

'Ahm, I'm Marian Cowie,' she said, under the impression that perhaps the teacher had sent him out to enquire. 'Dr. Marian Cowie.'

'Oh, aye, a doctor, eh?' said the boy, and produced a kind of writing pad from his pocket. He licked a pencil and wrote down 'Dr. Marian Cowie.' The writing pad was made of scraps of used paper, tied with a loop of thin twine. The pencil was very short.

'Is the teacher in the school still?'

'Oh, aye.' He broke off to surrender himself to a hoarse, smoker's cough. 'And what,' he went on, after a mighty spit of phlegm, 'is your business round here?'

'What are you,' she demanded cheerfully, 'a policeman in the making?'

He gave her a lofty stare.

'Nah, nay a pollisman. I'm to be a journalist. Ken?' She nodded, but he was not convinced that she fully understood. 'See newspapers? Somebody writes all that stuff, ken? And that'll be me.'

'You're not from round here, though, are you?' she asked, suddenly realising.

'Nah, I'm in frae Glasgow.' His air of easy superiority, the tounser's sophistication amongst the teuchters, suffered an abrupt dent as he gave a yell and dived into a miniature brawl a few yards away. He emerged dragging, by the collar, a small girl with the same pale complexion and the same swag of black hair. 'I tellt ye before, Agnes,' he admonished her. 'I dinna care what they cry you, Miss Liddle says you're no to wallop them. Now, away and play nicely: this is nae the Gorbals.' He gave her a light shove between the shoulder blades, then turned apologetically back to Marian. 'I'm Cammie, by the way, and that's my wee sister. We've been evacuated, ken.'

'I thought most of the evacuees had gone back,' said Marian.

'Aye, well, Ma and Da were killed when the Singer Sewing Machine factory was hit last month,' he said philosphically. 'It was incendiaries setting fire to the woodyard, ken.' He observed her keenly. 'You'll be the lady that's been in London. I hear tell it's rough down there, too.'

'Well, we're coping,' she said quickly. Was this an appropriate conversation to have with a young lad? 'And do you like being up here?'

'It's all right,' Cammie decided, after some thought. 'Miss Liddle's grand: she's going to help me get on to a paper when I'm old enough. But I'll tell you: yon porridge makes me boke. I'd rather have a jccly piece and a pint, and none of that fish, either.'

Marian was distracted from this telling culinary criticism by the appearance of a woman at the nearer doorway of the school building. She was small and bespectacled, and wore a tweed suit and sturdy brown boots. She had an empty basket in each hand.

'Where are my boys and girls for the hill?' she called, in a high, cheerful voice that surprisingly carried over the whole school yard. Half a dozen of the children, including Cammie and Agnes, ran immediately to her. Marian made her way further into the school territory unnoticed, as the teacher handed the two baskets to the tallest boy and the tallest girl.

'Here are the damp cloths for over the top,' she went on, light and precise. 'Remember where we found some good plants before? Up by the loch on the mossland there. Be careful, and keep well away from the edge of the loch. Do you hear me, Agnes?'

'Yes, Miss Liddle,' said Agnes, an angel in a muddy skirt.

'Well done, children!' She gave them a smile that hugged

them all, and they ran off through the gate with a flutter of waving hands. Marian found herself smiling, too, then she approached across the yard.

'Miss Liddle?' she asked, still smiling. At once a veil seemed to drop over the teacher's face, and she was nervous and stiff.

'Yes?' she replied, almost inaudibly.

'My name's Marian Cowie – my grandmother has the cottage at the top of the village.'

'Oh, yes?' Miss Liddle did not meet her eye, but hunted for something minute and unspecified in the pockets of her coat. Absently, she watched the last few children leaving the yard. Marian took a deep breath. Miss Liddle was much less approachable up close.

'Dr. Hanson sent me, Miss Liddle. He said you might be able to tell me some of the history of the village. You see, I've found a body.' This may have been a mistake. Miss Liddle jumped like a hare at the very idea. 'Well,' Marian tried to soften the account, 'I've found – some bones, up on the Fairy Hill. I think they've been there for a little while, and I was wondering if you knew anything of the history of the site, something that could help me work out who – whose they might have been?'

Miss Liddle was silent for a moment, apparently making the effort to assess Marian discreetly. Marian stayed quite still, as if she were trying to win the trust of an injured bird. Miss Liddle's gaze flickered back and forth, taking in Marian's face, her handbag, her face again, her shoes, her face again, and her gloves. The gloves were the final arbiter.

'Will you come into the schoolroom?' she asked. 'It will be warmer in there.'

The schoolroom smelled of woodsmoke and chalk, but the children had left it neat and tidy. There were desks for two teachers: one was heaped with knitting, which on closer examination consisted of sweaters, balaclavas and socks, in the usual khaki, navy and airforce blue of comforts for the troops. The other held a pen tray and inkwell, a couple of small volumes which appeared to be the school logbook and register, a basket of knitting in progress, and a stone jam jar of daffodils and forsythia.

'I'm afraid I'm on my own these days,' Miss Liddle said with an obvious effort. 'Miss Laws has joined the WAAF. It was a little tricky for a while when we had the rush of evacuees: they brought their teacher with them, of course, and they had school in the morning and we had it in the afternoon, but things are never that simple, are they?' The little rush of information ran out. She added quietly, 'Then most of them went home.'

'Except for Cammie and Agnes, I suppose,' said Marian. Miss Liddle gave her an alarmed glance.

'You know them?'

'I met Cammie at the gate, that's all,' Marian realised she had stepped too far again into Miss Liddle's ground, and metaphorically backed off. 'He's a bright lad.'

'Oh, very much so, very much so.' Miss Liddle tailed off, then pulled herself back with 'And there are a few others, too, of course: ones who have lost their mothers or whose parents have had to go away to work, or who are still worried about them being in Glasgow ... I fear there are even some for whom the removal of their children has come as a relief.' She stared down at her desk for a long moment. Then as if she had found some inspiration there, she pulled over the chair from the other desk for Marian, and sat herself behind her own desk. It seemed to help.

'Now, Dr. Hanson sent you, you said, I think?'

'That's right. He said there was no one to equal you on the history of the village, and you would, ah, be able to tell me some stories.'

'I see. I wonder which ones he had in mind ...' Miss Liddle pondered, her fingers reaching out irresistibly towards the knitting basket. Her hands were small and white, but with signs, Marian saw, of recent wear: the knuckles were a little red and swollen. She fiddled with the knobbled end of a needle, digging her nail into the wood. Then in a decisive moment she pulled the knitting from the basket, arranged the wool to flow freely, and pushed the stitches up ready for a new row. She took a deep breath.

'Well, if it's stories about the village you're seeking, you'll need to hear the story of St. Angus.'

'Agnes? Wasn't she the one with the eyes?' Marian's Established Church upbringing struggled with her liberal education, to the benefit of neither.

'No,' said Miss Liddle. 'That was Lucy. I think Agnes was the one with the breasts – as it were,' she added, with unexpected humour. 'But no, this was Angus. The story is said to come from the Middle Ages, or earlier, when apparently they went through a spate of burning Christians around here. It is unlikely, certainly, but it is an old story.

'You see,' said Miss Liddle, the knitting already moving fluidly along the needles, 'in the olden days, this little village was a place of some consequence. The clue is in the name, I suppose – Burgessie, the burgh on the Essie river. We had our own market place, our own burgh court – now in abeyance – a provost and burgesses, believe it or not, and all the signs of grandeur and all the privileges of rank. And one of the most significant, grand and privileged persons in this fine burgh was Angus, a weaver burgess. Unfortunately he was also the most rank.

'His fine house was in the market square, with a grand garden full of flowers and herbs, workshops for the tradesmen, fine parlours and bedchambers for the family, where the rushes on the floor were mixed with lavender and lady's bedstraw, and were swept out every day. He had a grand chamber with a Flemish carpet on the floor and some of the merchants he entertained there were even permitted to tread on it, while they sipped thimbles full of Rhenish wines and nibbled oranges and raisins and other exotic sweetmeats. It had balconies overlooking the market square, all the better to keep a needle-sharp eye on all the activities of the town.

'His lady and his daughters knew well how to bear themselves in the finest silk gowns in the most expensive dyes, and how to hold the sweetest nosegays beneath their delicate nostrils the better to disdain their fellow townsfolk. Humble tutors taught them music and dancing; a grovelling foreigner taught his son French and fencing. No doubt it was to raise the town to the same level of elegance that he neatly carded out tenants who failed to pay their rent on time, particularly the elderly and infirm who were no great ornament about the place, and a poor investment. A merchant who sipped the Rhenish wine and nibbled the raisins but chose not to fulfil his side of the bargain soon found his business unravelling, his house burning, his wife ailing, and his daughter pining for some mysterious stranger who had left her a mother before ever she would be a wife. There were rumours, too, of an old woman – aye, and a young man, too – who had owned properties which lay in the way of Angus' business expansion plans, and who had found themselves pinned unexpectedly at the bottom of the loch. And it's a very deep loch.

'Now, these were those unregenerate and unhappy days when townsfolk hereabouts found the very idea of the Church a strange and terrifying thing, and believed that anyone associating with a Christian could be susceptible to contamination. One of the best disinfectants of course, is fire, and so any Christians that could be discovered soon found themselves at the centre of considerable conflagration, and though they might have come out of it cleaner, they also came out of it dead, which is discouraging – as it was intended to be.

'Around this time Angus was anticipating becoming Provost, as had been his dearest ambition for some years. There was one other man who might be considered more popular than Angus amongst the other burgesses, but for one thing he was not quite so rich (and inducements to voters can be expensive), and for another thing he had not enjoyed the best of health for some months, despite Angus' kindliest attentions with specially selected wines and sweetmeats, and talk had begun amongst the burgesses, source unknown, that he was really not up to the job and that it would, in fact, be doing him a kindness not to elect him.

'Of course, such matters were not discussed in an open meeting, and anyway, the business of the day was far too compelling. A journeyman baker had died recently, leaving two pretty daughters of around marriageable age, and it had just been discovered that the two girls professed to be Christians. Well, there's nothing like a good burning for rousing the townsfolk, but when the fuel is young and pretty the whole thing reaches a brand new height. They had to be convicted, of course: the law has to be allowed its authority, or you simply have a lynching, which lacks gravitas. But the authority of the law was a simple matter, for it could be considered in the nature of a byelaw, so the Council could do the convicting any time it suited them. And in any case the girls were all too ready to be convicted. It was almost indecent, the way they clamoured their silly faith, it was more like a schoolgirl crush than anything. And in fact, Angus' rival for provost tried to argue for a bit that the girls were quite young and that they would grow out of their folly, and that pleased Angus, for it meant a few more votes had definitely moved to him. The Council voted, the girls were convicted, John Leslie was told off to get firewood ready and a sum was fixed to pay for his apprentices to build the pyre, a date was arranged, fine weather was invoked, and Angus invited the Council members to view the festivities from his fine balcony, and for dinner afterwards. It was a Provostly thing to do, he felt, and would demonstrate for all the burgesses to see his complete suitability for the post.

'The day of the burning was to be a public holiday, and he was exceptionally busy the day before overseeing his apprentices who had to make up for their time off. The apprentices, of course, like apprentices the world over, did not see things the same way – a holiday was a holiday, and that was that – so they needed close watching or the profits would be down. His elegant wife was whipping the servants into a frenzy in the house to make everything perfect for the burgesses and their families – she knew well the value of promoting her husband's career. Angus was particularly irritable as the mother of the two Christian girls had turned up first thing to beg him for mercy for her daughters. She had been a dignified kind of woman, but of course Angus could do nothing for her, which rather took the shine off being thought so influential in the first place. Angus was feeling hot and bothered, and as he was on his way from the workshops to the attic to fetch something the apprentices were incapable of finding, he thought he might just take a wee rest on the back stair. He sat heavily on the narrow wooden tread, closed his eyes and took a few deep breaths, feeling the sweat prickling his back in the cooler air, away from the hot workshop.

'After a moment or two he felt better, and still with a sense of urgency he pawed and stretched up from the step and turned to go on up to the attic. He nearly tripped over the child who had evidently been sitting just at the back of him. The child was smiling at him, and as he stooped to shove the child aside he stopped, for it was not the cheeky grin he expected. Who was this? He thought it must be one of the servants' children, perhaps brought in to help this busy day. The professional woven into the back of his mind noted, absently, that the child's robe was of a rather fine linen – where was that from?

'"Go on about your work," he snapped, though he did not touch the child, but squeezed past.

'"Thank you for your goodness, St. Angus!" called the child. He stopped, not sure if he had heard aright.

'"What was that?"

'But the child was already scampering off, with a chuckle that just for a second touched what might have been his heart. Then he went on up to the attic, and forgot all about it.

'An hour or so later, Angus was in the workshop on his own, for he had sent the apprentices out to make deliveries – in two different directions, for to send them together would take twice as long, and he had had to put up a coin as a prize for the first back. He was sorting out materials, still on his tired feet, making sure that when the apprentices returned they could get straight back to work. His journeyman had stepped out for his dinner and apart from the distant scuffles of the servants, all was quiet.

'Angus became aware that he was being watched, a tingly feeling in his broad back. Behind him he found another golden-haired child, standing beaming at him, quite at home in his workshop.

'"What is it?" Angus snapped, thinking the child must have been sent with a message for him.

'"St. Angus, you will be eternally blessed!" cried the child.

'"Get away out of here, and less of your impidence!" he shouted, but somehow the child was already gone. Again, it left an impression in his mind of some very high-quality white woollen cloth, far too good for a servant's brat. Cross at these petty interruptions, Angus stamped off to find his wife.

'"Oh, grand," said she, pulling off her apron. "I was on the point of calling you for your dinner."

'"Well, I might as well have it while I'm up the stairs, I suppose," he said grudgingly. "But I came to say could you not get the servants to keep their brats in the kitchen? I've tripped over two of them already today."

'"Brats?" asked his wife, but her mind was more on the linen she was folding. "I don't think any of the servants has a child just now – not one young enough to be called a brat, anyway."

'Dinner was served and eaten with an air of urgency, the emptied dishes whisked off before Angus could wipe his bread round the last of the gravy. He decided that that was what made him feel a bit uneasy in the stomach after his meal, all that haste, that and all his running around in the morning in the heat. He heard the town clock strike the hour, and decided he would allow himself half an hour to lie down. There was no sense in doing so much today that he wouldn't be fit to enjoy tomorrow. He pushed his chair back, ignoring his wife's haste to tidy it away against the wall, and went upstairs to his bedroom.

'There, his bed was a particular source of pride: carved posts, dark red damask curtains, cool white linen sheets – and both of the two golden-haired bairnies sitting side by side on the edge, wide-eyed as if butter wouldn't melt in their smiling mouths!

'"What ...?" he began, but he was really not feeling fine. He wanted to cry out at the children to go away and leave him alone, but somehow the room was growing unsteady, and he was swallowing more often than he should, and it was awfully warm.

'"St. Angus, your sacrifice is your salvation!" One child seemed to be calling from far away.

'"Blessings upon you, St. Angus!" called the other, and their voices tangled together, and their faces faded, and he fell upon his bed, dribbling a bit into the precious dark red damask.

'With his eyes closed, he could see why he was so hot. It was the next day already, the girls were being burned, and the two golden-haired bairns were dancing around the fire, calling to him.

'"St. Angus! St. Angus!"

'"Don't call me Saint!" he cried at them. "I don't believe in this Christianity!" But the fire burned higher and the children danced faster and the light and the heat and their golden hair spun into a blur and he knew no more.

'When he woke, his mouth felt like unspun fleece. He staggered back downstairs and into the kitchen, where he took a great sup of water from the water barrel, and drank and drank until he felt like the barrel himself. It was still the day before, the girls were still to be burned, and there was still a wheen of work to do, so he wiped his forehead on his sleeve and pushed through the busy servants back into his work room.

'The apprentices jerked up like puppets when he appeared, making their best efforts to pretend they had been working hard all along, and began to argue over which of them had earned his penny for being first back. Angus set back to work again, growling at them half-heartedly, and for the rest of the day the workshop was undisturbed – or so he thought, though he often saw a movement from the corner of his eye, which melted to golden nothing when he turn his aching head to look properly.

'When the work was finally finished, he sent the apprentices to their beds, listened for five calculated minutes to his wife's satisfied summary of the day's work, and then pulled on his second best doublet and went out. At the local inn, he knew he would find the other burgesses in a similar state after today's hard work. He called for a pot from Mrs. Binnie's equivalent of the day, and sat himself down at the long table, drawing the other burgesses closer to him with a gesture.

'"I've been doing a bit of thinking, lads," he said, when he had them all close enough to hear his low voice. "You see this burning thing tomorrow –"

'"Oh, aye," said one, "the best thing this town's seen for a long whilie. Every spare bed is filled with visitors. They've come fae so far as Ellon!"

'"Aye, the market'll do passing well tomorrow," said another.

'"And the weather is set fair," said a third. "Oh, it'll be a bonny, bonny day!"

'"And of course," said the first, Jamie again, "we're all looking forward to your fine hospitality! My wife's been stitching and clipping all day, every last wee fold perfect – and that's just the underpinnings!"

'They all laughed, except Angus, who shifted in his seat. His back was still hot and prickly, though the inn had no fire lit yet this warm summer evening.

'"The thing is, lads," he began again after a lubrication of ale, "I wonder if we're been a bitty hasty here."

The other burgesses stared at him.

'"Hasty?" Jamie asked, puzzled.

'"Aye. I mean, these are only young lassies, scarce let go of their mother's apron. What are we doing burning them for something that's – well, when it comes down to it, who are they harming but themselves?"

Sandy frowned at him.

'"But isn't that just what Davie said at the last meeting? That they were too young to know their own minds? And you said – aye, I mind it," he added, "you said that what was but mild in the child would grow strong and sour in the woman, and it would be kinder to burn them now than to let them grow into a bitter and suspicious old age, shunned for the contamination they bore, lonely in their folly."

"'I'm sure I didna put it quite like that," Angus said uncomfortably, but the others nodded eagerly.

"'Aye, aye, you did!" said Jamie. "Well remembered, Sandy! 'Strong and sour', that was the very way you put it, right enough!"

"'Likely he's taken a fancy to one of the lassies," suggested Donald, nudging Jamie.

"'Or to the mother," added Jamie, 'for she's a bonny enough quine herself."

"'I have not," said Angus sharply. "I've barely seen the lassies and the widow is nothing to me. I just think we're rushing into things."

'Sandy scowled, but examined Angus more closely.

"'Is it not well you are? I mean it as a friend, Angus – you're no looking yourself, lad. Finish your drink and away home with you, and fetch yourself a good night's sleep, and the whole matter will have a much finer face in the morn."

'Angus did not take much persuading, for truth to tell, he did not feel like himself at all, and he was a man that was never ill. He contributed little more to the conversation, but supped his ale slowly, and when it was finished he slipped away from the table and went home to his bed.

'But all that night his dreams were the same. The girls were on the pyre, arms raised, singing. The children skipped and danced about the flames, calling to him.

"'St. Angus! St. Angus! Thank you!"

'Then the girls would see him, and would break off their singing to cry out,

"'Thank you, St. Angus! Thank you!"

"'Don't call me Saint!" he heard his own voice insisting. "Don't call me Saint! Your saints are good – I'm no good man. I'm cruel and violent and – and greedy and selfish. I am no Saint!"

'On and on the dreams ran, as Angus tossed and thrashed amongst the rich damask and the fine linen. Eventually a strange thumping and rustling penetrated into his nightmare, and he surfaced to the light of a fine new day. Staggering to the window, he saw outside that men were taking the faggots out from a cart to build the pyre, while John the carpenter put the finishing touches to a sturdy stake in the middle. Angus gasped and ran downstairs, dragging his boots and breeches with him.

'"Stop that!" he cried, pausing in his doorway to pull on breeches and boots. The workmen stopped, puzzled, automatically obeying such a figure of authority. But Sandy suddenly appeared from the other side of the cart.

'"Angus, my man, are you still sickening? Did you not go home to your bed as we told you?"

'But Angus was staring past him. The two golden children were already there, watching the pyre builders, watching Sandy, watching him, all with a kind of knowing concern. Angus saw they were holding hands.

'"Who are those two brats?" he asked, but not as if he expected an answer. Sandy glanced around vaguely, and shrugged. The workmen started again, dragging the scraping faggots off the cart and bouncing them on to the growing heap.

'"Go on, now," said Sandy. "Go and wash your face and dress in your finery. It's going to be a grand day – and another grand step on your way to being provost," he added in a lower voice, with a smile. And he burled Angus around, gently enough, and poked him back into his house, pulling the door closed behind him.

'Angus did as he was told, though the washing, the shaving, the brushing, the scenting, the dressing, none of them were as real in his mind as the dreams from the night before. His wife bustled around him, perfecting the girls, polishing the boy, testing the servants. She probably looked wonderful. The guests began to arrive, and he and the family awaited them in the grand room upstairs, encouraging them to eat the expensive sweetmeats, urging them to quaff the expensive wine. The doors to the balcony were open, the fine cloth of curtains and drapes heaving a little in a refreshing breeze. The sounds of the growing crowd swelled easily up to their ears, and the smells of warm unwashed bodies and cheap hot food fought with the delicate perfumes of their own assembly. When a cheer went up, and was sustained, they knew it was time to assemble on the balcony.

'Outside, a path had opened in the crowd, and down it, in bare feet and plain sarks, came the two girls. Their hair was loose but

their hands were bound, but when Angus saw their faces they were
full of light. He groaned to himself – time was running out. But
what was he supposed to do? Throw away all his ambition on this
pair of journeyman's lassies? He peeked around for the two
children, and quickly saw them, standing by the pyre, but they had
their backs to him, facing the girls. Though they were in the way,
the crowd seemed not to see them – only the girls fixed their eyes
on the golden heads, and smiled.

'The town jailer brought the girls forward and lifted them, one
by one, to the stake, tying them firmly in place. Then he appeared
to say a word of farewell, and laughed, and jumped clear. The
crowd fell silent, and suddenly Angus realised that the girls were
singing.

'Everything was very still. Then the jailer drew a torch from a
brazier at hand, and touched it to the dry faggots. The crowd
surged with a cheer, and the balcony party applauded decorously.

'But the two children turned, and stared straight up at Angus.

'"Quickly, St. Angus, quickly!" they called. "Now is the
time!"

'Angus saw it, too. He leaped over the draped balcony rail,
drawing his knife as he went. In seconds he was on the pyre,
slicing and slicing at the ropes binding the girls. The younger girl
was free, and then the elder. One by one he lifted them and swung
them, not noticing his fine sleeves rip, swung them high out of the
flames. He gasped with the effort, and his mouth filled with sparks.
He was to burn instead.

'"Oh, God!" he cried, an oath he swore often enough, but gold
and scarlet the flames roared in answer.

'And the people in the place that day saw a great light in
Heaven, and the flames of Heaven surged down to meet the flames
of earth, and twisted in them and tied by them they saw Angus
lifted up, higher and higher, and vanish into the sky. And some
said they heard still the girls singing, and Angus with them, but
those tending the poor girls said they were beyond singing just
then.

'When the earthly flames were doused, not a trace of Angus
was found except the knife he had used to cut the girls free. The
people of the town, knowing they had seen something far beyond
the ordinary, ensured that the girls were pardoned and returned to

their mother, though pardoned for what was no longer to be a crime, for the greater part of the town turned to the true faith that day. And Angus' widow and bairns left for who cared where, and his fine house was taken down and a church replaced it, and its first dedication was to St. Angus. And those who were there at the very first service swore afterwards that they saw two strange children there, with happy smiles and golden hair, and in remarkably fine white clothing, but at the end of the service, where the congregation produced such music as has never been heard since, the children were gone.'

There was a long silence in the schoolroom, only underlined by the slight scuffing of the wooden knitting needles.

'What an extraordinary story,' said Marian at last, finding she had tears in her eyes. She did not like to cry in public.

'If you read the oldest kirk session records in the church there,' Miss Liddle nodded towards the high schoolroom windows, 'you'll find mention of the church being dedicated to St. Angus. Other than that, it's just a story – I suppose.'

'Thank you,' said Marian.

'You're welcome,' Miss Liddle smiled shyly.

It was only when Marian was back out in the playground that she realised that the story had not, in any practical sense, helped her at all.

Chapter Five

At first it seemed fortuitous on Friday morning when Marian woke to rain. It was the kind of rain that simply fills the air with water, making it hard to tell one from another, and rendering any umbrella completely redundant. Digging on the Fairy Hill held little charm today, so she was glad to have something else to do instead, covering Dr. Hanson's rounds and surgery. By the time she had paid her first visit, and her shoes were twice their own weight with mud, she had changed her mind about her good fortune.

Dr. Hanson had waved her off very cheerily at his house – the house, she supposed suddenly, in which his father had been murdered. Adopting a sort of fisherman's hat and waterproofs he was going to set off for the paper factory to carry out some medical duties there, but he had very kindly lent her his motor car for her country visits. She had driven a few times before, on the relatively smooth cassies of Aberdeen, but she was sure she knew what she was doing once Dr. Hanson turned the engine over a few times. The car was smaller than her father's Daimler, and more suited for the terrain, she was convinced, though the blackout slits over the headlights gave it an air of calculation she was not entirely happy about. She had a large umbrella, a short list of patients with some highly confidential notes, her medical bag, a map and a basket of bottles wrapped in sacking, which Dr. Hanson explained were the various prescriptions the patients she was going to attend might be likely to need – easier to have them with her than to have the trouble of going back. She was painfully aware of her ripped coat, but she had compensated with a very professional, serious hat in charcoal grey. Lady doctors in particular, she had found, had to dress with authority.

The first case was a tenant farmhouse full of measles: five red-headed children all in the one room, all between five and twelve, all on the point of riotous recovery - a blur of red spots. The mother blinked at the daylight when she answered the door, and when Marian introduced herself she reached out a hand spontaneously and clutched Marian's wet sleeve. Marian felt it was more relief from her children she required, and a little adult conversation, for the children were going on well and as soon as the mother could let them outside the whole household would be much the better for it. Barring their convalescence the children were ridiculously healthy: her memory wandered into London lanes opened wide by a German bomb to reveal the rancid poverty within, the first time fresh air had penetrated since the places were built.

Here, the kitchen was clean and she accepted a cup of tea, but noting some fine mending in a basket by the stove, she tried her best to hide the botched job she had made of mending her own wet coat. There was knitting, too: Marian was starting to feel reproached by the capacity every other woman seemed to have to knit everything from balaclavas to battleships. The mother had a weathered face with a flat forehead running straight down into her nose without dipping, giving her a bruised look, though there was no other obvious sign of any injury – Marian made a mental note of it, all the same. She finished her tea, said goodbye to the herd of spotty bairns and the smiling mother, and left.

The farm track was steep and treacherous, the rough grass and gravel in the middle of it threatening at any moment to gouge off crucial parts of the car's underside. There might have been a good view from it, if she had not had her eyes firmly on the road and if the rain had not still been thick as fog. She bumped and lurched her way back to the road, shaking raindrops from her wet hair, and after consulting her map she headed west again, searching along the soaking way for a cairn of white-painted stones that would indicate the end of the lanie to North Meiklefold, where the Blaikies farmed.

This farm track was better-kept, though the white paint on the stones had not been redone for a few years. Someone had spread chuckies in the deeper muddy puddles and the car only skidded a couple of times as she chugged along in what she hoped was first gear. The wipers swiped the screen like mad pendulums, and she wondered if they would eventually fling themselves off. At North

Meiklefold she was able to stop in the concrete yard which was not quite as muddy as anywhere else, though there was plenty of evidence of the morning's milking. Switching off wipers, lights and engine with relief, she picked her way round the worst of the pats, and made her way to the farm kitchen.

Mrs. Blaikie was slim and efficient with grey in her hair and white on her nose from the flour she was turning into bannocks. A junior farmhand, Richie, the orra loun, sat in splendid luxury in an old bed recess, propped up on the kind of grey, patternless cushions that frequent farm kitchens, with a knitted blanket (more knitting) over his lower half. He had broken his leg tripping over a plough, which Mrs. Blaikie, talking without pause, clearly regarded as hilarious. Richie was more inclined to dramatise his condition, particularly as it was serious enough for him to have been brought in from the farmhands' bothy to sleep in this privileged position by the kitchen stove. Marian had a feeling his recovery might take a while. She adjusted his bandages and splint, and gave him the analgesic medicine that Dr. Hanson had made up for him. It was immediately snatched away by Mrs. Blaikie, who was omnipresent, and placed on a high shelf along with, Marian noted, a bottle of very cheap whisky. She suspected it had been brought by some other visitor to the invalid's couch.

To her immense relief, Mrs. Blaikie had finished griddling a bannock or two by the time she had finished attending to Richie, and made her another cup of tea. Marian was beginning to wonder if, in fact, general practice might have its appeal. The bannock was light and fluffy, with a scraping of jam on top – 'proper jam, none of that rubbish the W.I. makes down south, if you'll believe the papers,' remarked Mrs. Blaikie. She herself did not sit down with her piece but was constantly moving, stirring a stockpot, flipping bannocks, and then flicking wide a door that had been ajar on the stove to reveal something moving. Marian contained a squeal, then saw it was a lamb, impossibly small, wrapped in a sack. Mrs. Blaikie whipped it out and took a baby bottle of milk from yet another simmering pan on the stove, and managed somehow to hold gulping lamb and emptying bottle in one hand while she slid bannocks off the griddle with the other hand, wrapping them quickly in an old cloth. It was exhausting to watch her.

Back out in the yard, the motor car had decided with a sly

expression that it was to go no further. The engine ground over but would not catch. Marian wondered if water had got into it, which she seemed to remember might not be good. She had no doubt that Mrs. Blaikie could start it in an instant, but as she was hesitating, a man appeared from one of the farm buildings and she recognised the other farm hand, the one she had met at the inn – the one who had told her the story of the monsters in the loch. Was that the same loch where the schoolchildren were sent to pick some plants by Miss Liddle? She supposed it must be. Did Miss Liddle know this story?

'Hallo?' she started, and the man wandered towards her. 'I'm sorry, I don't know your name, but we met at the inn the other night.'

'Oh, aye?' The man eyed her dubiously, and she wondered if he had been too drunk to remember her. Then light dawned on his spoon-shaped face. 'You're the doctor lassie came to the airyplane crash with us.'

One of the Home Guard, of course.

'That's right. I'm Marian Cowie.'

'Rab Geddie,' Geddie nodded at her, then as an afterthought wiped one huge hand on his trousers and proffered it. Marian was pleased she had pulled her gloves back on. 'Are you up here about the crash?'

'No, I was here to see to Richie's leg,' Marian tipped her head towards the farmhouse door.

'Oh, aye,' he said again, with a sigh. 'He could have done it at a better time, mind you, with lambing just starting. Tell me, Doctor, you wouldn't be able to give me a wee tonic or something, would you? See, as I say lambing's already starting, and there's ploughing to be done, and all the time the Home Guard have our duties too, and I ken fine Mr. Churchill can move the sun and moon around to suit himself but damned if he can put any more hours in the day for me.'

He was not the only one, either, thought Marian, wishing for more hours in the day. If a woman's work was never done, what about a woman's war work? never mind the men.

'I have nothing with me, I'm afraid, Mr. Geddie, but the chemist in the village will have something, I should think. He'd be well able to advise you.'

'The chemist in the village? Oh, aye. I canna mind when I was last in there. But I ken Patrick Farquhar fine, for he's in the Home Guard too. I'll see what he says, right enough.'

He was about to wander off again when she remembered to ask him to help start her motor: a flick of the wrist at the starting handle and the engine turned with a satisfied purr, recognising authority. He waved her off, standing solidly in the yard, as she started back down the North Meiklefold track. She thought back to the night he had told her the story of the monsters – the first story she had heard in the village. 'They're great story tellers round here,' Davie had said. How many had she heard already? But thinking about Rab's story, she began to wonder. Had it been a warning? He talked of monsters, monsters which tossed human skulls around like nutshells. Crunching on bones ... had Rab known about the skeleton at the Fairy Hill? Did he know who the monsters were? An image of his great powerful hands flashed into her mind. Was he one of the monsters?

The third patient was, on the map, more accessible. The place was a cottage, neat as a surgical instrument tray, and so symmetrical that Marian was surprised to find that there was not a doorbell on each side of the door. She rang it cautiously, and straightened her hat.

The door was snatched open to reveal an elderly man in a dressing gown. His pyjama trousers, visible beneath it, were pressed into a perfect pleat as if he expected to wear them to the office. He was also wearing a collar and tie.

'Yes? Can I help you?' he demanded, standing to attention.

'Hello, Captain Brown? I'm Dr. Cowie – Dr. Hanson asked me to call on his behalf.'

'What?'

'I'm the doctor.'

'Rubbish,' stated Captain Brown, with certainty.

'I beg your pardon?'

'You tell Dr. Hanson I'll see him and no one else. I pay him good guineas for his attendance. I'll not pay for any jumped-up district nurse hardly out of finishing school.'

On this welcoming note, he slammed the door.

Her fourth call was up another track off the main road, but this time she knew she would never persuade the motor car to climb it.

She climbed out and reached back in for her medical bag and the basket of bottles, took a moment to pull her hat firmly down on her head, and began a steep ascent.

She had been fogged all morning by a sense of unreality. Now it intensified: how had she come to be here? Where were her flagged pavements, her corner tea shops, her busy buses? Where were the nightly raids, the blazing fires, the urgent sirens? Where was her war?

Stopping, she turned back and gazed about her, down the hill. She could see no one. There was no human sound, no motor, no voice beyond that of the birds muttering in the wet hedges. There had to be a better place to be, a more useful place. Her colleagues needed her. She would go back soon – she would go next week.

She stumbled on sharp stones and slid on mud, and the rain pasted her hat to her head and began to trickle down her collar. Once or twice she wondered if she was on the right track at all, for trees grew down over the path, which lay deep between unkempt, thorny dikes, and had to be scrambled round, and at one point the track disappeared altogether and could only distantly be distinguished starting again on the other side of a field. At last she saw a run-down cottage standing in a little garden, where the kale stalks lay pale on the earth as if the winter's snow had only just left them. A stream ran past the gate, such as it was, and she scrambled across with a half-step, half-jump to find the inhabitant of the cottage standing, arms folded, in the doorway, watching her with a smile that was less than kindly.

'Mrs. Geddie?' she called out, first to make sure and second to reassure. She was half-ready to jump back over the stream again if Mrs. Geddie was to be anything like Captain Brown.

'Fa're you?' The old woman took in Marian's soaked hat, roughly-mended coat and filthy shoes and stockings in a superior glance. She herself could have been costumed to portray a peasant from any era, from the Bronze Age forward. Her face was so wrinkled it could have been knitted. She must have been at least a hundred.

'I'm Dr. Cowie, Mrs. Geddie. I'm helping Dr. Hanson today.'

'Oh, aye?' It was remarkable just how much amused disbelief could be injected into these two sounds. 'Ye'd better come in, then. Just leave your shoes at the door, there, for I've not long swept the floor. It would have been better if you'd fallen into the burn and washed some of that clort off you first.' She turned her back on Marian and waddled back into the cottage, thick with shawls.

'So is himself coming later?' she asked, when Marian had pulled off her shoes. To her surprise she felt, as much as saw, that the floor was earthen. Her damp feet were simply collecting more mud as she stood there. If it had been swept recently it was the only thing that had seen any attention. Everything else was thick with dust. Davie Fraser would have a field day excavating this.

'No, he's not coming at all today. He's had to go to the paper factory by the river.'

'Oh, indeed? That's the story you're telling me, is it?' She gave a little chuckle. 'Playing hard to get, that's closer to the truth. He thinks if he abandons me to some nursie for a week or so I'll be pining for him. Well, you needn't tell him I was asking after him at all. We girls have to stick together in these things, don't we?'

'Oh, ah, yes. Now, Dr. Hanson says it's your chest that's giving you trouble. I'll just fetch out my stethoscope ...' Marian set down the basket of bottles and rummaged in her medical bag.

'But tell me, do you not think he's a braw man, the doctor?' Mrs. Geddie went on as though she had not heard. She swung a kettle over the fire, and went to an ancient dresser to retrieve, clinking unsteadily, two cups and two saucers. Marian was vaguely surprised to see that they were china, under the glour, and not pewter or even wood.

'Would you like to sit down and let me listen to your chest?'

'Oh, there's no need for that, on a wet day like this. Baring my poor chest would do more harm than good, do you not think? And forby, there's no good baring it for you, when it's the doctor I'm after. Has he not sent you with my medicine? That's all I need.'

'I think it's all here,' agreed Marian, and she handed the woman the last four bottles from the basket. Whatever was in them, she half-hoped some kind doctor would prescribe it for her when she was a hundred.

'That's grand, that's all I need.' Mrs. Geddie took them and set them on the dresser, and handed Marian four empty bottles 'for next time'. Then she picked up the largest of the four bottles, popped out the cork, and took a huge swig. 'Aye, indeed. That's grand. The mixture as before – fine, fine.' Her hands now suspiciously steady, she poured tea into the cups and handed one to Marian, who still stood in the middle of the little room, soaking up mud through her stockings. Mrs. Geddie perched on a plain bench, and gazed up at her in a calculating way.

'You've been seeing Neil Forbes, I hear.'

'What?' Marian was completely taken aback. Her heart fluttered at the sound of his name.

'Aye, well. He'll be away back soon.' Mrs. Geddie mouthed her cup in satisfaction. Marian paused, then decided to plunge in.

'I've found a skeleton on the Fairy Hill,' she said. 'Maybe you've heard about that, too. Would you have any idea whose it is?'

Mrs. Geddie laughed.

'Oh,' she said, 'you'll find plenty to tell you stories round these parts. You'll maybe even tell a few yourself one day. But my story-telling days are over – that is, till I tell the story of my fine doctor and me – the fairy tale romance! So if you're after him yourself,' she stood suddenly, making Marian wonder if she was really as old as she appeared, 'you'll just have to ca'canny! Now, away with you! And take your slabbery shoes with you: you'll need to scrape them off as you go back or Mr. Blaikie'll be after you for taking his good loam.'

In seconds Marian found herself standing on the path with her medical bag, a basket of empty bottles and her shoes only half on her feet, and the door closed in her face. She took a moment in the rain to fasten her shoes properly, and sighed as she set off back down the hill to the car. Maybe general practice was not for her, after all.

Muttering to herself as she drove, she returned to the village, her patients at least seen, and parked Dr. Hanson's motor car back on his drive, checking three times that she had the handbrake fully on against the severe incline. He had asked her to come to lunch so that they could discuss the morning's visits and the afternoon surgery, but it was early yet, so she squelched down to the inn and found Mrs. Binnie, source of all information, peeling potatoes for the dinner.

'A seamstress? Oh, aye, there's one in the village – you've no need to go far. Go on down the hill to the old tollhouse – ken? The one with the roundy window in it. Mrs. Angus down there does all kinds of needlework.'

The roundy window turned out to be a round bay with two windows in it, pointing in two directions so that the tollkeeper could see approaching traffic. The house stood at the junction of the main road from Aberdeen and the turn-off to the village, where two large granite rocks stood like guardians – perhaps further indication of the village's former high status, just as the schoolmistress had said. Mrs. Angus, too, she thought – any connexion with the putative local saint?

Her knock on the door was answered by a loud squawk, and she was taken aback until the door was snatched open and she found herself being handed a wailing baby, which she had evidently just woken.

'Come in, then, come in.' The woman who had left her with the bairn was already off, disappearing into another room. Marian stepped straight into a living room, the room with the bay window, the baby howling in her ear. The bay held a Singer sewing machine painted like a canal narrow boat, with fabric hanging from it. There were baskets of material – lovely material, some of it – and baskets of what else but wool?, and empty baskets, all around the room. The air was tickly with escaping fibres, and her head was starting to sing with the baby's screams. She tried to jiggle it, but that seemed to make things worse. Paediatrics had never appealed.

The fire was lit in a fireplace so large this must originally have been the kitchen, though the fire itself was tiny. Beside it stood an old-fashioned pine cot, black with age, with the blankets half pulled out, just as the crying baby had been picked up.

Just as Marian was about to go and search for her, the woman returned and snatched the baby from her as suddenly as she had passed it over in the first place. A bottle was inserted in the infant's open mouth, which closed on it like a trap. Silence fell.

'Right, then, shall we start again?' asked the woman. She was sharp as a needle. 'How can I help you?'

'I'm looking for Mrs. Angus, the seamstress,' Marian explained.

'I'd say you'd found her,' said Mrs. Angus with a quick, thin smile. 'What is it you need doing?'

'It's this coat,' Marian pulled up the hem to show her. 'I've ripped it, and it's my only coat here.'

'Had a go at mending it yourself, I see,' Mrs. Angus remarked, and her eyes were already picking out Marian's unpractised stitches.

'Ah, yes, sorry – I was never any good with a needle.'

'I'll remember that if I need to go to you for stitches,' said Mrs. Angus, still examining the gashed tweed. Then she glanced up and laughed at Marian's contrite expression. 'I cannot do it today, but if you can leave it with me ...' She glanced out at the unrelenting rain. 'I'll lend you one of my own, if you like.'

'That would be very kind!' A few months ago she would have said that the seamstress was a good deal too thin to go borrowing coats from, but she had lost a lot of weight in London – hadn't everyone?

'Here, take that wet one off but don't put it down on anything, all right? I'll fetch one for you and hang that one up.' She departed again, this time taking the sucking baby with her, reminding Marian of Mrs. Blaikie and the lamb. Mrs. Angus was middle-aged, though, so whose was the baby?

Mrs. Angus returned quickly, bringing a coat in a lovely brown tweed and wearing a blue one herself. The baby was now wrapped in a thick shawl. Marian tried on the brown coat, and wondered secretly if she could persuade Mrs. Angus to swap it for her own. It was beautiful.

'Brown goes well with that reddish sort of hair.' The seamstress stood back and assessed the impact. 'I'm not sure about that hat. It's the wrong colour and I'm guessing you've slept in it.'

'It's the rain,' said Marian.

'True.' Now Mrs. Angus' sharp eyes unpicked her words, seeing what lay behind them. Not a woman to miss much. She held up Marian's own coat on its hanger. 'This one's fine. Where did you get this?'

'Selfridges, in London.'

'Oh, aye. Very nice. A good cloth. Mines is from Watt & Grant.' The odd Doric grammar still twanged in Marian's ear. With a flick, Mrs. Angus turned the coat and examined the buttons, then hung it on a rail by the wall. 'I'm away out just now,' she explained, gesturing to her own coat, 'to see P.C. Argo. Someone's been in and taken food from my pantry and eggs from my hen house, and German or Scottish, I'm not having it.'

'You think it was the missing airman?' Marian was slow to understand.

'Who knows, these days? This is my grandson, by the way,' she explained, jiggling the baby who was almost asleep. 'My daughter's away sewing camouflage netting in Aberdeen – doing her bit, as she says. I'm sure she could do a bit better than that, but there you are.'

She packed the baby quickly into a large black pram which was standing outside the door under a shelter, and together they set off back up the hill, while Mrs. Angus discoursed on Aberdeen fashion houses and advised on places to find a new coat.

'Falconer's have a lovely range this season,' she was saying when she broke off. 'What in the name of glory is going on now?'

They had reached the lower end of the green, where P.C. Argo, angrily pale, was attempting to hold back a small crowd of onlookers.

'I tellt you to stay back!' he was saying.

'But what's the matter?' someone called out.

'Is it the missing Nazi?' shouted another one.

'It's not the missing airman,' snapped Argo. 'Just stay back and stay calm.'

'Calm?' said one woman. 'If you'd tell us what's going on we might be less likely to worry.'

Argo sighed sharply, and as Mrs. Angus ploughed her way through the crowd using the pram as a battering ram, he once again pulled on the rope he had strung across the street to encourage the crowd to stop pushing against it. Marian stood on tiptoe to try to see better. At their end of the square amongst the crowd, some of whom were wearing gas masks, she could see Mrs. Binnie, and Davie Fraser with his bicycle standing alongside a rather lovely blonde girl – lovely but perhaps dim? she thought, uncharitably. There was another rope just beyond the Post Office door further up the square, with what must have been the other half of the local population behind it, and as she surveyed the scene she noticed that at the schoolhouse opposite a row of little faces lined the windows. She thought she could make out Cameron, who was taking notes.

'So come on, then,' Mrs. Angus had reached her goal and pitched the pram across P.C. Argo's path. 'What's going on here?'

Argo glared at her, but Mrs. Angus' glare was sharper.

'Someone reported a powdery substance left on the pavement outside the butcher's. We have reason to believe it might be some form of chemical attack.'

'Chemical attack?' repeated Mrs. Angus. 'Oh, aye, because Burgessie's first on Hitler's list for targets.'

Several people laughed shortly, but someone, Mrs. Binnie, Marian thought, took it more seriously.

'Well, what about that plane that crashed the other night? What if there was more to it than just a bomber?'

'Aye,' someone else helped the story along. 'And what about the missing airman? What if he parachuted out with chemicals to lay traps for us?'

'Or what if he's someone Hitler wants dead before he's caught? Maybe someone else has orders to spread the powder to kill him!'

'Or maybe the missing airman *is* Hitler, fleeing his would-be assassins in Berlin,' suggested Davie Fraser, though Marian had the impression that one was a little tongue in cheek. The lovely blonde creased her brow charmingly in concern.

'Oh, for goodness' sake,' snapped Mrs. Angus. 'Let me see it. It's probably baby milk.'

'I can't let you near it,' said Argo. 'We're waiting on the army to come and look.'

'And how long will they take?' asked Mrs. Angus. Several people agreed. 'And how stupid would they think you were if you'd called them out and that was all it was? Have some sense, lad.'

It seemed to be the word 'lad' that stabbed deepest.

'Right, then,' said P.C. Argo, slightly pink. 'And let everyone be witness you did it of your own free will.'

'Never otherwise,' said Mrs. Angus, and leaving Marian with the pram she dipped neatly under the rope and led Argo across to where a galvanised bucket had been upended on the pavement. Marian noticed that despite herself, Mrs. Angus was holding her nose, though how that would help against a gas attack was debatable.

Mrs. Angus reached out her free hand and tilted the bucket to one side, revealing a small pile of whitish powder. She stared at it for a moment, then carefully replaced the bucket. She returned to the rope slightly faster than she had left.

'Well, it's no milk powder,' she announced. 'But on the other hand, I'm no dead.'

Several heads nodded wisely, though there was a small discussion just behind Marian on how long some chemicals took to take effect. Then there was a long silence. No one gave the impression of knowing quite what to do next.

'Someone's waving at you,' Mrs. Angus remarked, nodding up at the farther rope.

'Oh!' Marian's heart leapt. It was Forbes.

'I'd better go and say hello,' she said. Mrs. Angus nodded sharply.

'Aye, he'll be away back soon.'

Marian worked her way round to the side of the square and walked unchallenged up by the schoolyard wall to the other end of the roped-off area. The crowd on the north side was equally sprinkled with gas masks and equally focused on the upturned galvanised bucket outside the butcher's. Forbes came to meet her.

'Hallo!' he greeted her. 'What a splendid hat!'

'Don't tease,' she said, 'the rain has ruined it. You're not here to deal with this chemical attack, are you?'

'Not my field,' he admitted, smiling. 'But if we can persuade Mrs. Binnie to return to her kitchen, would you like to join me again for lunch and a dry-out by the fire?'

'I can't, I'm afraid,' said Marian, half-disappointed and half-glad that she had a good reason not to appear too eager. 'I'm lunching with Dr. Hanson.'

Major Forbes was crestfallen enough to please her.

'Then you're once more abandoning me to Captain Allardyce. How can he compare?' Then a thought occurred. 'I've been meaning to ask you – are you coming to the party?'

'What party?'

'It's just a village thing, in the community hall. They've been kind enough to organise it to celebrate my little medal – congratulating the local boy, you know.'

'Your medal?' Captain Allardyce had mentioned it, she remembered.

'My M.C. Luck, really, but there we are. Now, the party's

tomorrow at six – you'll be there, won't you? Captain Allardyce is bailing out, back off to the south, and I must have one friendly face there!'

'If I won't throw the numbers, or anything ...'

'Oh, it's not like that. Ask Mrs. Binnie – she knows all about it. Now, I must go and meet Allardyce, if you'll excuse me. I can't pick you up, but I'll see you there, shall I? Around six?'

'Lovely,' Marian nodded. What would she wear? She watched him go, delighting in the authority of his movement around the square, then turned back to scan the crowd for Dr. Hanson. Instead, she saw someone waving at her from just round the corner of the Post Office. The wave was a little frantic. Puzzled, she took a few steps away from the back of the crowd and went to see who it was.

It was the farmhand who had told her the story of the loch monster. She struggled to remember his name ... Geddie? Yes. He was hiding round the corner of the Post Office, clutching a brown paper bag and stuttering in agitation.

'Doctor! Doctor, you've got to help me!'

'What on earth's the matter?'

'See all that?' He waved his hand backwards to indicate the square. 'That's all my fault.'

'Your fault? How?'

He blew out hard and rolled his eyes, as if wondering where to begin.

'You ken you told me to get a wee tonic? For lambing?'

'Ah, yes. I did.' She reckoned he needed a stiff whisky, not a tonic.

'Well, I came down to see what Mr. Farquhar at the chemist's would recommend. There was this grand stuff, he said, called Allenbury's Diet, so I bought a nine shilling tin. Allenbury's Diet – you ken the advert, 'Steady Nerves!'. I took it outside and I wanted to take a wee shuftie at it, so I opened it up and damned if I didn't spill a wheen of it on the pathie! It was a damned shame, but I thought nothing more of it and I went into the Post Office to get a postal order for my mother – ken, I send her a wee bit of money each week on a Friday, she's up by Nairn with my sister. And when I came out, they was just roping off the square. And I wondered what was going on, and so I asked and then I realised it was me! What am I going to do? They've called out the sojers and everything. I can't tell them it's just a bit of tonic.'

'Are you sure that's what it is?' asked Marian, trying fairly successfully to keep a straight face. 'Are you sure that what they've found is what you spilled?'

'Well, it's in the same place,' said Geddie, reasonably. 'It sort of bubbled up a wee bit when the rain fell on it. I thought it would wash away – I never thought they'd call the army out. How could I show my face at the Home Guard again?' His face was stretched long with dismay. Marian thought hard.

'May I see the rest of the tin?'

Geddie opened the brown paper bag and showed her a large tin of Allenbury's Diet. She fished it out, and noted that the seal was broken. Inside, the whitish powder filled around three quarters of the tin. She sniffed it. It did not smell like milk powder, anyway, and it certainly looked like the powder she had seen from a distance when Mrs. Angus had lifted the bucket.

'All right, let me deal with it. Stay here in case I need you.'

She returned to the green, where the crowds had grown slightly. Who would have thought so many people lived in Burgessie? She hunted around the crowd for the chemist, but did not see him. Instead, she made her way through to the rope line, and found John Leslie.

'I've reason to believe,' she began, 'that the substance under the bucket might be Allenbury's Diet. You know, the tonic.'

'What makes you think that?' asked John Leslie, interested.

'I've heard – someone's told me that they spilled it. They're a bit embarrassed – maybe we could ask the chemist? It had just been bought there – he could confirm that.'

'The chemist's was closed for lunch when we cordoned off the square –' Leslie began, then broke off. 'There he is. Mr. Farquhar! Pat! Could you come here a minute, please?'

The chemist sliced slowly through the crowd like a rather bad-tempered cheese wire.

'What on earth is going on here?' he asked, peering around the square.

'Could we maybe have a wee word? Maybe in your shop?' asked Leslie. He nodded at Marian. 'Shall we go along? Here, Jackie, keep an eye on this rope for me a minute.' He lifted the rope and led the way over to the chemist's shop, and Farquhar, frowning, leaned past them to unlock the door. They stepped inside, and Marian immediately noticed the Allenbury's advert.

'Are your nerves feeling the stress and strain?' it read, under a drawing of a pretty and determined ambulance driver. 'If so, try a cup of Allenbury's Diet night and morning!' It hadn't had much effect yet on Geddie.

'Have you had many customers this morning?' Leslie asked, in a kind of blend of neighbourly interest and sergeantly enquiry. Farquhar shrugged.

'The usual, I suppose.'

'Anyone in just before you closed for your dinner?' Leslie was more specifically helpful. Farquhar looked mildly surprised.

'Only Geddie.'

'And what did he want?'

'He said he needed a tonic during lambing. He's always a bit anxious at this time of year, but of course with Richie's leg it's worse just now. I sold him some Allenbury's Diet.' He waved at the poster on the wall. 'I thought he was pleased enough with the idea – took the largest size, though I suggested he might want to try the small size first.'

John Leslie met Marian's eye and shrugged, with a grin that was half-amusement, half relief.

'I'd better go and break it to P.C. Argo that he'll have to ring the army again,' he said, and left.

'So is anyone going to tell me what's going on, then?' asked Farquhar stiffly. Marian quickly explained. Farquhar scowled. 'The usual hysteria. I can't quite see Hitler concentrating his resources on a little village in the Garioch, can you?'

'It did seem a bit unlikely,' Marian agreed. 'But poor Geddie is mortified.' Farquhar snorted, his narrow freckled nose white. 'I'd better go, myself,' she added, remembering Dr. Hanson. But Farquhar was suddenly inclined to conversation.

'Are you here for long, then?'

'Just a couple of weeks, at most. I've lots to do in London.'

'But you've been digging around up on the fairy mound, then?' he asked. He was not good at pretending to be casual.

'It's just the skeleton, really. That is, it's not just a skeleton, it's a bit of a mystery, but what I mean is it's not a large scale investigation at all ...'

'My father was interested in that place. He and the laird had a great plan to dig through the whole thing once.'

'Oh? When was that?'

'Oh, before the last war. I was only a boy at the time. You see,' he pulled on his white coat absently, twitching the buttons closed, 'there had always been a local legend, pretty vague, really, tales of a golden boy who haunted the mound. Maybe haunted is a strong word – people had seen him from time to time, for as long as anyone can remember.' He shoved his fists into his pockets.

'What do you mean, a golden boy? Painted gold?'

'As I say it was pretty vague. My father and the laird were intent on being amateur archaeologists – I'm sure Mr. Fraser would despise them,' he added with a curl of his lip. He glanced about, as if to judge whether or not another customer might be likely to come in. His eyebrows rose wearily, and he leaned back on the bench behind the counter, and stared up at the ceiling.

'They dug there for a few weeks one summer, and found nothing of any use to anyone. But they were sure there was something there, for no good reason that I could see. So on they went. And one night, just as they were about to finish for the night and go home for their dinners like sane individuals, they finally found something. It was at dusk, and the laird had lit a hurricane lamp. He was leaning over the hole my father was digging, just to see if the last scrapes of the day might produce something, when the light was suddenly reflected back with a warm gleam. Without a word they set the lamp to one side and worked with their fingers, easing back the earth from the metal, gently and gradually freeing it from where it had lain heaven knows how many years. And yes, it was gold: crushed and folded and flat, but gold unmistakeably. There was a piece of silver, too. They set them to one side and dug more, but nothing else appeared that night, so they carefully wrapped the precious finds in a piece of old sacking and took them back to the castle. They laid them out on the library table and brought lamps.

'There they found that the silver was an amulet of some kind, in the shape of, they thought, a running deer, with some kind of dark red stone set into its head between the antlers – probably a garnet. There was a loop for a chain but no chain was left. It had a certain charm to it, but they quickly turned their attention to the gold.

'They could see at once that it was exquisitely worked, ornate with a plaited pattern and abstract shapes. It had clearly been very fine: my father said it weighed slightly more than a golf ball, but it had been flattened and worked until it was thin and broad, and had been, they thought, some kind of breast plate. However, it was small: it could only have been worn by a youth – and at once they thought of the golden boy.

'My father stayed there for his dinner and they retired to the library to discuss their finds again, but at that point he found that he must have left his pipe out by the mound, so the pair of them took the laird's hurricane lamp and headed out again into the summer darkness. It's not that far from the castle to the mound, as you know, but as soon as they entered the field where the mound is, my father said he could feel something strange. Not a chill, as ghost hunters so often say they feel: he felt a kind of breeze, though he was sure no wind had got up, and the trees and hedges weren't rustling. He said afterwards that it was almost as if he was in a stream, and the air was water running gently over him and round him. It was odd, he said, but not in the least frightening.

'"What was that?" said the laird suddenly.

'"What – the breeze?"

'"No – well, yes, that too. I thought I saw something just there." He pointed into the dark to one side. My father peered, saw nothing, and turned back – just in time to see a movement on their other side.

'"There it was again!" said the laird.

'"Too fast for cattle," my father added.

'"Do you know," said the laird slowly, "it had a sort of golden look about it."

'"I thought that, too," said my father.

'They took another couple of steps, and then again saw a few flashes of gold, darting about them. They stopped, not far now from the mound, and then they saw him – a boy, not more than fifteen or sixteen, golden and bright – though when I asked my father what he meant by this, he said he was not sure. At any rate, the boy was fair-haired, and he was wearing the breastplate, back in its proper shape, and to go with it he had a spear banded with gold. And the boy watched them and laughed, and then cried out with a strange accent,

"'What would you know?"

"'Who are you?" replied the laird, though he had to clear his throat.

'The boy laughed again with delight, pointed his spear and spun around, light as feathers. Then they seemed to see him on a throne, and there was a crowd of people between him and them, misty, so that they could still see him glowing through them. He wore a ring of gold on his head, and the silver amulet about his neck, and he appeared to be talking, though not to them. Then the mist spread for a moment, and cleared again, and the boy was running, running hard but not moving, his spear in his hand, and then he threw it, and they could see it piercing the body of a boar, as misty as the people had been, and the boy leapt high in triumph. Then the mist surged again, and again cleared, and they saw the boy cloaked and sombre, bowing over some kind of altar, as flames rose. And then there was more mist, and out of it came a running battle, men with swords and round shields and leather helmets, and amongst them the boy, golden and bright, running with his spear and a golden sword. And as he ran, like fire on oil, a dark figure lurched from the mist, and plunged a dark sword through the firelit figure, and the boy fell, and my father said it felt as if his very heart had stopped in his chest. The golden body lay there, and the soldiers ran on and vanished into the night, and the dark figure too slunk away, and the boy lay there alone. And it was as if for a long time they were drowned in sorrow, and the whole world was dark.

'Then the body rose slowly into the air, until it seemed to be lying on an invisible altar. Then the boy pushed himself up on to his elbows, then on to his hands. Then with a fluid movement he was on his feet, and then he was dancing, dancing, molten spun gold, whirling, flinging his arms high, kicking out with his golden feet, faster and faster, higher and higher, until, with another delighted laugh, he vanished.

'And they knew then that because they had dug up the golden breastplate, no one would ever see the golden boy again. And they knew that the world would be the less for it, and they were sad.'

There was a long silence, and then Mr. Farquhar rubbed a long finger across a shelf beside him, and examined it morosely.

'What an extraordinary story,' Marian said at last. 'And what happened to the golden breastplate?'

'Well, of course the laird took it, even though it was my father who found it. My father never could see how the laird and his like took advantage of him. And the laird was the death of him in the end.'

'The death of him?' Marian was taken by surprise.

'Oh, yes. It was about twenty years ago. The laird was off to India again, and Mrs. Forbes was to accompany him in the car just as far as the tollhouse as she often did, then would walk back from there, so my father went to the tollhouse to wave him off. He caught his leg on a piece of rusty wire that night, somewhere near the tollhouse, and he died of blood poisoning the next day.'

Chapter Six

Marian spent the evening dithering in a pleasant fashion over which of her two smart dresses to wear to Major Forbes' party. Both were a few years old, dating from before the outbreak of the war, but were of good quality, and the dark blue one had been altered in London to update it only that winter. But it was perhaps a little too smart for a village party: she had only brought it with her in case she had to meet her parents for dinner in Aberdeen. Now she also allowed herself to toy with the idea that Major Forbes might just invite her to the castle for dinner with his mother, and she would like to keep it in reserve for such a momentous event. So in the end she opted for the pale green dress in a pretty glazed cotton, which was lovely to dance in, should dancing occur. She also remembered, as she hung it over the back of her bedroom door and eased out the folds of the skirt, that her colleague Richard had told her it brought out the red lights in her fair hair. She smiled: he had seen it by chance, as she headed out to a dance, and had paid her the compliment quite analytically, as if it had nothing to do with her. She found her best silk stockings and a pair of evening slippers, though she planned to carry them and change her shoes when she arrived at the hall. Never, she reminded herself, go out without shoes you can run in. Then she checked her medical bag, laid out her brogues, coat and torch, changed into slacks and went to bed.

Next morning was fine weather again, though the earth was damp. Good digging weather, she thought, gazing out at the shining wet garden as she ate blissful eggs for breakfast. She made herself a chunky sandwich and a flask of black tea and headed up the hill with her trowel, skirting the now familiar wreckage of the Heinkel to where what she thought of as her own body was concealed discreetly with gorse twigs. She brushed them carefully away, wondering as she did so how the hunt for the last Heinkel crewman was going. For a village that told stories all the time, it was remarkably reticent about progress on that matter.

The skull was as she had left it, pale moon-shaped in the dark earth. She knelt delicately beside it, touching the crown as if in greeting, and began to work her way along with tentative trowel scoops to where she expected collar bones and breast bone to start. The layer of grass was the toughest part, she found, and once it was peeled back like the skin of an orange the earth below it was yielding to her fingers and she worked quickly. Soon the arches of the ribs began to appear, all in place as neat as Dr. Hanson's skeleton.

Hunger pangs were the first thing to stop her, and she blinked in surprise at her watch to find it was already past one. She brushed the worst of the mud off her fingers, wiped them on the grass, and pulled over her basket with the sandwich and tea. Settling with her back against a stone, out of the wind, she munched quickly as she gazed down over the village, or what she could see of it through the trees coming determinedly into leaf. What were her ambulance crew up to today, she wondered? Young Crompton with his disastrous eyesight would be the medic: he was lazy, she thought, and over-anxious about going into tight spaces, not like Richard. She had been furious when her supervisor had told her he would be taking over her crew in her absence. She would need to get back soon, or morale would be in pieces. Next week, if she could get the papers, she would go back.

She drank down the tea, wincing at its black bitterness that made her blink hard. The drips were shaken over the grass and the flask packed back in her basket as she wondered how much longer she should spend up here. Mrs. Binnie was setting up the village hall for the party and she had offered to lend a hand. A couple more hours, she thought, to give her time to scrape all the mud off her hands and probably face, too, in cold water.

More aware of the time now, she set to to uncover more of the delicate ribs and the collar bones. She had uncovered most of the front of the ribcage by the time her watch showed two, and she was about to sit up when she leapt at a soft sound behind her. She turned quickly, half-expecting Davie Fraser, but instead found that Cammie, the Glasgow evacuee, was seated on a nearby rock with his notebook and pencil out, observing her with cool interest.

'Hello Cammie,' she said. 'Not in school?'

'Saturday,' said Cammie succinctly. 'What are you digging up there, then?'

She sat back on her heels and sighed.

'It's a skeleton,' she said reluctantly.

'Aye, I heard tell. Whose skeleton, though?'

'Well, we don't know yet,' she said. 'It's not the missing airman, though.'

'Of course no,' he said. 'How could he take his meat off and bury himself all in one night?'

'Nicely put,' she said ironically.

'Did you ken I was here?' he asked, almost allowing himself to sound eager.

'Not until just before I turned round,' she admitted. He was pleased.

'I crept up dead quiet. That's a lot harder in the country, I've found, unless you're a teuchter born and bred. A city lad like me, I need practice.'

'You did well this time, then. Why are you trying to creep anyway?'

'Well, journalists sometimes need to be where they're no wanted,' he explained. 'Did I tell you I'm to be a journalist? Miss Liddle's going to help me.'

'You like her, don't you?'

'Aye, she's grand. Never had a teacher like her. If I'd stayed in the Gorbals, see, I'd never even have thought of such a thing. I dinna think my teacher there had ever heard of a journalist.'

Someone who had benefitted from the war, then, thought Marian. It's an ill wind that blows nobody good.

'That teacher's long gone anyway,' said Cammie reflectively. 'I seen his close the day after it was bombed out. Just the yin wall all the way up, and there in his flat there was still the stove stuck to the wall, with the milk saucepan on it still with the yellow handle sticking out in the rain. They never found him.' He sucked his lips in, thinking about it, with professional detachment. After all, she thought, he had probably seen as bad things as she had. He was bleached out still, clearly a town boy, and she wondered if he would colour up like the country children at the school –

particularly with that cough, she thought to herself, as he rasped and spat again.

'Well, I'd better get down to the village,' said Marian, standing and dusting down her slacks. 'I've to go to Major Forbes' party tonight.'

'Oh, aye, we're going to that and all,' agreed Cammie. 'Can I give you a wee hand with that?'

He helped her tug the gorse bushes over the bones again.

'So was it Mr. Fraser had you digging bones up here?' he asked far too casually.

'Of course not – it was P.C. Argo.'

'Ach, the pollis,' said Cammie, spitting again. 'I doubt he's too busy to bother himself with an old pile of bones.'

'Not at all,' said Marian. 'He's asked me to report to him, so I shall, when it's all dug up.'

'Aye, well,' said Cammie, resigned, 'nae doubt you can tell me later. Whose bones do you *think* they are, even if you dinna ken?'

'I don't know,' said Marian honestly. 'Everyone tells me a story about it, and then it turns out to have nothing to do with these bones.'

'Oh, aye, them and their stories! Has Miss Liddle told you her story about the kelpie yet? The one that near ate her grandfather?'

'No, I missed that one,' said Marian with a wry smile.

'Aye, well, nae doubt it'll come to you. It's a gey good one,' he conceded, 'but mebbe no as a bedtime story,' he added with unexpected feeling, and they walked back down to the village together.

'It's just so good to find someone to help that's not got just the one leg, or that's holding three weans, or whatever, these days,' said Mrs. Binnie. Marian was holding instead one end of a trestle table, its splintered edge worn harmlessly smooth by decades of such handling, and Mrs. Binnie lifted the other end with a practised flip that locked the legs into position.

'Well, make use of me while you have me!' said Marian. 'I'll not be here long.'

Mrs. Binnie reminded Marian of the best of the ward sisters she had worked with, in Aberdeen and London: practical, skilled, sensible, good-humoured, with a lifetime of experience – a very present help in time of trouble to an inexperienced young doctor who was humble enough to ask.

'If we put these out and the cloths on them, then we can set out the cups and saucers ready. Some people have brought cakes and the like already – there are a few tins in the kitchen. We can set those out too with a clout over them and fill the urn, and then maybe we can have a fly cup ourselves. What do you say to that as a plan?'

'Sounds good to me!' She caught the end of the tablecloth that Mrs. Binnie tossed her, and between them they spread it over the trestle, shifting it with flat hands to even the ends. Though thin, it was bright white and crackling with starch. 'It's lovely of the village to put on something like this for Major Forbes.' She relished the feel of saying his name.

'Aye, well, a local hero and all that,' Mrs. Binnie responded with perhaps less enthusiasm than Marian had expected. 'And anyway,' she added after a moment, 'he'll be away again soon.'

Marian reluctantly felt that a change of subject was required. It was not difficult for her to find one.

'Are you local yourself?' she asked, 'or have you been long in the village?'

Mrs. Binnie's easy grin returned.

'You mean did I murder some poor body and bury them up by the Mound?'

Marian grinned back.

'I don't suppose you'd tell me if you had! And you'd probably have had a good reason for it.'

'Aye, well,' agreed Mrs. Binnie, 'there would have been a few over the years I'd have been glad enough to see the back of, one way and another. I doubt I'd have got away with it, though – or maybe it's just a good thing I think I'd be caught!' She surveyed the covered tables, hands on her hips, for a moment, then went across to a press and began to lift out cups and saucers. 'But aye, I'm a local quine, born and bred in the village. I don't know how far back it goes - maybe to Adam, for all I know – but my great grandparents lived here, I can tell you that.'

'That's probably far enough to do.'

'You'd think so, wouldn't you? Here, there are the cups that match that first pile of saucers.' Marian balanced three cups in each hand and took them over to the table. As she turned, there was a great crash behind her.

'Och, who put that up there?' sighed Mrs. Binnie, staring down at a carpet of china fragments at her feet. 'Well, they'll no put it up there again, onywise.'

'I'll fetch a dustpan and brush,' Marian headed for the kitchen.

'Under the sink!' Mrs. Binnie called after her. When Marian returned she had begun to pick up the bigger pieces and she flung them into the metal dustpan with a clatter. Then she took a long step to Marian's side of the mess, slipped on a stray piece of china, skidded, and in an effort to save herself swept three more cups off the shelf.

'Oh, blow!' she cried. 'Are you all right?' For Marian had already bent down to sweep up the first breakage, and the cups tumbled about her head.

A shower of broken china, sliding from a shelf as the wall gave way. The woman's body lay underneath, as though she had been trying to catch the plates as they spun and fell. A young woman, in a pretty flowered housecoat, wedding ring gleaming new on the dusty fingers, hair sparkling with shards of blue and white wedding present crockery.

'Yes, I'm fine,' said Marian, sweeping quickly and neatly. 'You? Did you hurt yourself?'

'No, I'm grand,' said Mrs. Binnie. 'Maybe I should be cutting back on these dangerous activities at my age! Oh, dear: I doubt the church will miss three old teacups, but I'd better replace the tureen. The minister's wife aye uses that for her soup lunches. Are you sure you're all right? You're a bitty peely wally there.'

'No, really,' said Marian, but Mrs. Binnie looked hard at her.

'No, I tell you what,' she said. 'Let's put the kettle on now. We can easy finish this later.'

While Marian made the tea, Mrs. Binnie sorted out the huge urn and set it to boil, which would take a while. Then they pulled out a couple of hard wooden chairs from the rank around the walls, and settled themselves with a large cup each. At the first sip, the hall seemed a cosier place, and Mrs. Binnie wriggled her shoulders as if easing out the stiffness. There was a comfortable silence for a few minutes.

'Aye, my great granny,' said Mrs. Binnie eventually. 'Aye, she was the one.'

'Mmhmm?'

'Oh, she was a canny one, my great granny. No bonny: that was her sister Constance.'

'Bonny Connie,' Marian remarked.

'Aye, I think she was cried that!' laughed Mrs. Binnie. 'But Gran wasna bonny. And guess what? She was Annie – Canny Annie!'

'Canny Granny Annie,' Marian corrected her, and they both giggled.

'You're as daft as I am,' Mrs. Binnie accused her, 'and no one would think it to look at you. But anyway, it was Canny Granny Annie that had to deal with the witches.'

'There were witches in the village?'

'Oh, aye, every village had its witch. There was Mrs. Geddie here for a long, long time, for instance.'

'Isn't there still a Mrs. Geddie? I think I met her yesterday,' said Marian, remembering the old woman who had her eye on Dr. Hanson.

'Oh, aye, there's always a Mrs. Geddie,' said Mrs. Binnie darkly. 'I have the impression that it was very much like the church: each parish had its witch and its minister, and then a few of each would get together for local meetings, coven or presbytery – very much the same, a lot of old wifies gossiping away about more than really concerns them.'

'Mrs. Binnie! And in the church hall, too!' They giggled again. 'But why did Canny Annie have to deal with the witches?'

'Well,' said Mrs. Binnie, 'tip that teapot into my cup again and I'll tell you.

'Now, as I've said, Annie was the plain sister, but she was clever and she was a hard worker, and she found herself a man, Hendry, and they married and they were very happy. He was a farm labourer, like to be overseer soon, and they had a bit cottage kept well, food on the table and a couple of healthy weans. Hendry was a very fine-looking man, strong and tall with sandy-red hair and bright blue eyes, and there were a fair few quines disappointed when Annie claimed him.

'So life was very fine, and there was a third child well on the way, though Hendry had to work long hours on the farm, often coming home long after dark.

'Then there came a time when a few strange things started happening to Annie. One morning, the milk had been sour, she could smell it even as it foamed from the cow and the cow herself gyped round at her with a face as much as to say, 'Whatever's happening back there has nothing to do with me!' Then the leeks all took some kind of blight, all in one night, and then another night all the skeins of wool she'd spun and dyed with nettles, and hung up to dry on a tree, were all snorled into everlasting knots by morning, though there hadn't been a breath of wind all night. And then there was the morning a slate fell from the roof as she opened the door, and just missed her, though she felt the breath of it on her cheek as she jumped back. Now, Annie thought about all these things, and noted that they'd been all around the house, but not in the house, and she wondered.

'Then one night, when the weans were away to bed but Hendry was late back from the farm, and she was sitting by the fire stitching at a new napkin for the next wean, she heard a sound at the door, a kind of futhering with the latch. Thinking Hendry maybe couldn't see the door properly in the dark, she upped and opened it, and there on the doorstep was a desperately ugly old woman.

'Though she was about Annie's own height, she was wizened and withered, her grey skin just louped over her old bones, hairy warts on her chin, her hair like dank straw, and her eyes all bloodshot and weepy. Beside her, Annie felt right bonny!

'"What is it you want, old mother?" she said, not rudely, for she was not an unkind woman, and forbye she thought she knew what she was dealing with here.

'"And you would be Hendry's lawful wife, then, would you?" says the old woman, looking Annie up and down. Again it wasn't an unkind look, but a wee shiver of fear ran up Annie's spine. But she knew better than to show it.

'"I am that," she said.

'"Then I'm here to warn you," said the old crone. "My sister has taken a fancy to your guidman, and she's a witch."

'"And what's that to you?" asked Annie.

'"My sister is a prideful old woman, and as ugsome as sin,"

said she, "and I cannot thole the old runk. I have no wish to see her happy in love."

"'Tell me, are you a witch yourself?" Annie folded her arms and examined her.

"'I am that," said the woman, as if it was neither here nor there.

"'But why then come to me?" asked Annie. "You're a witch and I'm just a woman. If you want her not to have him, you'd be far better to do something about it yourself." For her heart was beating twenty to the dozen and she was terrible feart for her husband, but Canny Annie would never let the witch see that.

"'Oh, but I cannot do it without you," says the old carline. "Can I come in by your fire and we can talk about what's to be done, you and I?"

"'It's a fine night," said Annie, though it wasn't. She snatched up her shawl. "Let's sit outside."

'So the pair of them settled themselves on the dyke, and Annie thought of her weans asleep, safe, she hoped, in the house, and she thought of the wean in her belly, and prayed that it was safe, too.

"'Now, what we'll have to do," said the witch, "is to find a time when my sister has lured your guidman off – it happens when he's walking home late from his work, after dark – and when we come up with them you'll have to distract her. For as you can imagine, she's none too fond of you, but being a witch she doesn't think you're that much competition."

'Now, Annie thought back over the soured milk and the blighted leeks and the snorled skeins and the falling slate and she wondered about that.

"'And what would you be doing while I'm distracting your sister?" she asked.

"'Oh," says the witch, "I'd be drawing the charm off your guidman. I can make a potion, you see, and have it ready, and when my sister is dealing with you, I'll fling it over him, and snatch him, and away."

"'You will, will you?" thinks Annie. But she says, "Aye, right, fine. When do you want to do it?"

"'I'll follow my sister and watch what she does," says the witch, "and it might be a couple of days or it might be a week, and if I see her with your Hendry, I'll come to fetch you on the back of the wind."

'"Whatever that might mean," thinks Annie, but she slips off the dyke and pulls her shawl around her and says, friendly enough, "So I'll see you when I see you, then. Good night." And back she goes into the house, and shuts the door.

'And Hendry came home an hour or so later and right enough, she could see he was in a kind of dwaum. But she said nothing: she considered in her mind, and she waited to hear from the witch.

'Well, for the next couple of nights, as it so happened, Hendry was home before dark, and a bit brighter than he had been that night. But on the third night he was late again, and when she heard a noise at the latch, she flung her shawl around her shoulders and hurried to the door, expecting it to be the old woman.

'Well, it was an old woman, right enough, but not the same one. This one was even worse-favoured than the first, with great cabbage ears that stuck through her thin hair, and one eye cloudy-blind, and teeth blacker than pitch. There was a bit of a whiff about her, too. But Annie folded her arms and propped herself against the doorpost, and said, friendly enough,

'"Well, mother, how can I help you?"

'"I'm told you're young Hendry's lawful wife, then?" said the crone, licking her lips horribly.

'"Dear, what comes of marrying a handsome man!" thought Annie to herself, but she said, "I am that."

'"Then I'm here to give you fair warning," said the old woman. "There's a witch has taken a fancy to your guidman, and I should know for she's my own sister."

'"Tell me," says Annie, "have you many sisters?"

'"Just the one, and isn't the one more than enough?"

'"And are you a witch yourself?" says Annie.

'"I am that," says the old carline, as if it was neither here nor there.

'"Then why come to me?" says Annie. "You're a witch and I'm just a woman. If you want her not to have him, you'd be better to do something about it yourself."

'"Who says I want her not to have him?" snapped the witch. "But supposing I didn't, then I'd be hard put to do it without his own guidwife. Can I come in by your fire and rest my bones, and we can talk about what needs to be done, you and I?"

"'It's a fine night," says Annie, though it wasn't, "and I had my shawl on to sit for a whiley under the stars."

'So the two settled themselves on the dyke, and Annie said another quick prayer for the weans in the house and the wean in her belly.

"'Now, what I had in mind," said the witch, "is to catch my fine sister in the act of tempting your guidman away. She takes her chances watching for him coming home after dark – she might even be with him just now, wheedling and wooing him. It's not fit at all, a living disgrace to the family. So if you distract her – and she'll want fine to know what you're doing there, for she doesna much care for you as you'd imagine."

"'And what will you be doing," says Annie, "while I'm distracting your sister?"

"'I have a kind of medicine," says the witch, "and all I have to do is fling it over him and the charm she has on him will be lifted. Then I can snatch him away."

"'You can, can you?" thought Annie to herself, but she said, "Aye, that sounds like a good plan. But when will you do it?"

"'Oh, I'll follow my sister and watch what she does," says the witch, "and as soon as I see them together I'll send a raven to tell you. Then you go fast to where the raven says and I'll wait for you there."

"'Well, I'll wait for your message, then," says Annie, slipping off the dyke, "and I'll see you when I see you." And back she goes into the house, and shuts the door. And in an hour or so, back comes Hendry, dandering along as if he's been hit on the head, but she says nothing.

'Now, Annie's own grandmother was a clever woman herself, and when she died she had left Annie her old receipt book. In it were the recipes for all kinds of things: failsafe meringues, soap, orange wine, cough medicine made with slaters, ink from oakgalls, all sorts. And Annie had read it through, and had tried some of the recipes, and others she had smiled at like a sensible quine, but still she remembered them. And so the next morning before dawn she took down the book from the shelf where it sat with the family Bible, and leafed carefully through the old pages till she had found what she needed.

"'Ane Receipt for to Remove ane Charme from One

Bewitched," it was called, and nothing could seem more appropriate. But she noted at the bottom, "This receipt is at its strongest when applied to the Bewitched Person in the very Presence of the Witch herself."

'So at dawn, which is a fine time for such things, and for the rest of the day, Annie carried out her household chores. But every now and then, she found five minutes to go about outside and find some of the ingredients for the recipe, and she blended them with dew, and stirred them well, and set the bowl aside on a high shelf to be ready when it was needed. And then she waited, and she wondered how the raven would give her a message, and how you rode on the back of the wind.

'It was a week of waiting, though it felt like more, before anything happened. She dreamed at night of ravens that came and preached sermons at her, and wild midnight rides on the back of the wind, but the details were hazy and when she woke she shook her head and they flew like dust from her hair.

'Then, one fine night, she had the children off to bed and was sitting by the fire, trying to seem the picture of the contented wife and mother, though her stitches were growing smaller and smaller as she dwelt more on her thoughts and less and less on what passed through her fingers. All of a sudden there came a sharp tap on the window, and she thought for a second that the glass had split. Then she knew it was the sound she was waiting for, and she rose and hurried to the door.

'There on the outside windowsill was a great braw black raven, as shiny as polished coal, with a canny eye in his head as he met hers, and jerked his head at her.

'"Good evening to you, Master Raven," said Annie, not feeling half as daft talking to a bird as she had thought she might. "Have you any message for me?"

'"I have that," said the raven quite clearly, so that she thought for a moment there might be a wee mannie hidden inside the bird, shouting through the open beak.

'"And what is it?" she asked.

'"The witch told me to say," and his voice was like a sharp tooth on bone, "that her sister is with your guidman at the crossroads by the tollhouse. You must hurry, for who know how long they will stay?"

'"Thank you, Master Raven," said Annie, and she offered him a piece of bread. The bird nodded, took the bread in its beak, and flapped away, quickly vanishing in the dusky dark. Annie turned and stepped back into the house, and lifted the bowl of potion from its shelf. As she reached the door again, she felt a lick of wind across her face, though none touched her skirts, and she stopped dead.

'"Master Wind," she whispered, "are you here with a message for me?"

'She felt the words breathed on her face, cold and damp.

'"The witch told me to say," huffed the wind, "that her sister is with your guidman by the tollhouse at the crossroads. We must hurry, for who know how long they will stay?"

'"But how do we go?"

'"Bind my tail about your waist," breathed the wind, "and I will carry you." And she felt a long tail of wind like a shawl flapping around her waist, and she drew it up with her free hand, and wrapped it around her and twisted it tight. It felt like a cold compress about her back and her stomach, and damp as an autumn dawn, but the wind held her tight and in a moment her feet were off the ground and they were off.

'It did not feel fast, for the wind did not rush through her hair and her clothes – how could it, when it was bearing her along? But it was only three or four breaths before she found stone beneath her feet, and took her own weight again, and felt the wind flick itself free of her and heard it sigh away. And she searched about her in the dusky light. There dimly was the darkened tollhouse, its rounded bay catching starlight in its little windows. There was the road, stretching out in four directions, and there, at the very crossroads, holding burning torches, stood the two witches. One stood each side of the road, and in the middle of the road, his shadowed eyes as blank as the tollhouse windows, was Hendry. She could have wept to see him, but she knew she had to do better than that. The bowl of potion was curled in her arm beneath her shawl, resting on her plump stomach, and she offered up another quick prayer, for her weans in the house, for the wean in her belly, and for her beloved Hendry. Then she drew herself up and stepped forward.

'"Well, mothers," she called out. "You've summoned me here.

What would you do now?"

'"She wants your guidman," cried the first sister.

'"So does she!" cried the second, her blind eye glinting fire from her torch.

'"But each of you told me you'd help me get him back, if I distracted your sister. I take it there's little chance of either of you keeping your word?"

'"Why would we have to do that?" asked the second sister, and she sounded truly puzzled.

'"We're witches," added the other.

'"Then it's time I took him for myself," said Annie, and with a sudden dive she flew forward. Suddenly the still air seemed full of stars: she flung her potion over Hendry, and at the same instant the two witches flung some potion at her and Hendry together. The liquors glittered and sparkled as they flew, and as if the wind had once more snatched her up she hurled herself at her husband and they fell to the ground together. He gave a surprised grunt. She glanced up, and saw the flying potion glide from one witch to the other. Then she heard two terrible cries, two terrible dragging gurgles, two terrible grating, creaking, groans, and then – silence.

'"What in the name of Heaven are we doing here?" came a voice from under her, and Annie quickly scrambled to her feet. Hendry sat up and stared about him, clutching his pow as if it might fall off. "And where did those come from?"

'She looked where he pointed. On either side of the road, just where the two witches had been, were two tall rocks, strange and mishachelt in the starlight. She shuddered, for she knew that the two witches with the potions they had tried to hurl at her had turned each other into stone. And there they are to this day.

'And Annie took Hendry and led him home, and he was fine from that day. But the wean, when it was born – well, my Great Uncle Andy was never the full shilling, if you ken what I mean, whether it was the worry or the wind or the flying leap she took to Hendry, or whether some of the potion splashed, we never knew.'

Mrs. Binnie let the silence rest in the hall for a moment, then raised her cold teacup and took a chilly sip. The chink of china signalled the end of the story – it was as good as the National Anthem in the cinema.

'That was a great story,' said Marian, stretching her stiff legs.

'Aye, well, it has the great virtue of being true,' said Mrs. Binnie.

'But you told it so well. I felt as if it was happening in front of me.'

Mrs. Binnie smiled.

'Well, we're all story tellers. We just need the right story. I could have told you the story of the ghost that haunts the inn. See, some evenings, when it's quiet, I notice a man sitting at the corner table, a pint of ale in front of him, though I never mind serving him. He's got this big beard and a gey thick jersey, and there's one of them leather rucksacks beside him. Now, there's not a body ever seems to notice him, ken, but no one sits at that table when he's there, however busy we might be. He just stares down into his beer, and he drinks it, and then he gets up to go, hoomphing himself into his rucksack straps. He walks past the bar to the door, and somewhere between the bar and the door he just fades away.' She glanced at Marian, as if expecting a challenge, but Marian kept her face straight. 'Aye, and every time he passes the bar, I feel like I want to reach out, to say Good evening, or Another one there, at all? but every time something stops me. And every time, for a whole night after, I'm that wracked with nightmares about what might happen if I did reach out, if I did speak.'

Marian shivered and frowned, but could think of nothing to say. She did not believe in ghosts, like a good scientist.

'Mrs. Forbes, now,' Mrs. Binnie was saying, as she stood to wash her cup. 'She has a grand story to tell. She was the daughter of the post mistress here, you ken, till she married the laird. You'll have to ask her to tell you.'

'Oh, I couldn't do that,' said Marian.

Mrs. Binnie eyed her thoughtfully.

'Aye, it must be hard enough for you coming here, like an extra ingredient in a stew that's already on the simmer. But you'll soon find your way. You'll have a story of your own to tell, no doubt. Now, better get on or this place'll never be ready! Ah, here's some more bodies to give us a hand.'

Marian smiled as other women of the village appeared at the door – Miss Liddle chivvied in Cammie and Agnes and a couple more pale city girls - but she was smiling more at the thought of herself as a story teller. What on earth would her story be?

Chapter Seven

Marian's heart gave a little jump of nervous excitement as she entered the village hall, looking forward to seeing Major Forbes but simply pleased to be out and sociable. She was beginning to feel more at home in the village than she had, than she had any right to be after only a few days and not much memory of the place from her childhood, and no intention of staying for more than a few days more. It was all very well helping Dr. Hanson and putting out cups and saucers for a party, but it was not exactly what she had been doing in London. She pushed through the blackout drapes, checked her lipstick in the little wall mirror by the cloakroom, quickly changed her shoes and followed the noise to the party room.

The room could hardly be the same one she had left, furnished with rows of crockery, this afternoon. Someone had cleverly arranged a few candles with a number of little mirrors, mismatched from all over the house, by the looks of it. The mirrors repeated the twinkling candles all around the room above head height, so that the very walls glittered. Just below the line of lights there was a string of bunting so faded and elderly it was likely to have celebrated some act of local heroism in the Crimean. Mrs. Binnie, coming up behind her, nodded to it apologetically.

'It would have been in the rag collection long ago, if anybody had kent it was in the back of the cupboard,' she explained. 'But nothing would do Cammie and Agnes but it was going up on the wall. I doubt it'll fall apart before the party's over! It's only held up by faith and cobwebs.'

'Well, it's the thought that counts, isn't it?' asked Marian. Mrs. Binnie always made her smile. 'The mirrors and candles are lovely, though! Was that your idea?'

'No, no,' said Mrs. Binnie quickly. 'That was Mrs. Forbes. She came down late afternoon just as I was leaving, with two baskets full of mirrors and a big cake in the back of the car. A grand use of her petrol coupons, no doubt! But there we are. It's gey bonny, isn't it?'

'Very much so.'

'Marian! You were able to come!' Major Forbes darted across the room to her, making her feel like a film star with six words. Mrs. Binnie faded away before she noticed. 'My, you're a sight for sore eyes! Come and dance.'

There was music playing, and a few couples had already made use of it, amiably pushing through the crowds in the middle of the room. The gramophone jumped occasionally if anyone shook the table it was perched on, but Cammie was seated next to it, changing the records when he remembered: he had his notebook, Marian saw as Major Forbes spun her beneath his khaki arm, and was no doubt writing an account of the event. He caught her eye and made a little note: something for the Court and Social column, she thought with a smile.

'I hope that smile's for me!' said Major Forbes. 'I could do with it: don't much fancy all this fuss on my account.'

'If it's any comfort to you,' she retorted, 'I should say the villagers are all very glad of an excuse for a party. I'm not sure anyone is even thinking about you.'

He pretended to be offended.

'Nonsense: they're just politely averting their gaze so as not to embarrass you! Before you came in they were queuing for my autograph, I promise.'

They both laughed at the thought. The music broke off, and there was a confused moment of applause and groans as the few couples muddled themselves again with the rest of the party goers. Then they fell silent as an authoritative throat clearing came from the shallow stage at the end of the hall. Marian peeked between the backs and elbows in front of her and saw a powerfully built man with a dog collar facing the audience with a mischievous glint in his eye.

'Ladies and gentlemen, could we have a bit of wheesht here for a minute? I'm sure you all remember why we are here this evening.'

There was applause, though beside her Major Forbes grumbled in her ear.

'Here we go!'

The minister waved the room to silence again with one hand. Marian noticed that his other sleeve was pinned up to his shoulder, empty. Not this war, though, she thought to herself: the close-cropped, receding hair was silver grey, though his eyebrows were arched high and dark.

'We're here this evening to mark our pride at the award of the Military Cross to Major Neil Forbes, son of this parish. Major Forbes, where are you?'

Everyone stared about and quickly found the Major, who made a show of reluctance as he allowed himself to be levered up to the little stage. He stood there eventually, beside the minister, clearly rather pleased with his reception. Everyone applauded again.

'Wait, wait!' said the minister. 'He hasn't had his presentation yet! I don't mean his M.C.: no doubt His Majesty will see to that without any help from Burgessie. But we have a little something for you, Major: who has it, now?' He hunted around, frowning over his spectacles. Miss Liddle, the schoolmistress, steered two small girls up to the stage and prodded them in the right direction. One was carrying a flat box, though only because she had won the fight: the other girl had a possessive hand over it, too. Their keenness each to be the only one presenting it caused some fumbling but eventually Major Forbes managed to take hold of the box and slide it open, producing something in a frame.

'Oh, how splendid!' he exclaimed. 'I can tell you, ladies,' he said, bending down to the height of the little girls. 'This is much prettier than a boring old medal, isn't it?' He stood straight again and held it out so that at least the people at the front could see it. There were appreciative oohs and aahs.

'Very gratifying,' said a voice to her right. She glanced round: it was a man's voice, but unfamiliar. A thinnish gentleman in pince-nez looked her up and down in a way that made her feel slightly uncomfortable. 'All my own work, of course – a presentation scroll, in case you couldn't see it. No doubt you will later: I'm sure the Major will make sure you get a good long chance to examine it thoroughly.' His voice was as nasally thin as he was, a verbal paper cut. 'I don't believe we've been introduced, have we? Lorimer Catto Rennie, of the Record Office in

Edinburgh.'

She reluctantly shook his hand: it felt like a fistful of old pencils.

'Marian Cowie.'

'Enchanted.' He did not sound it. 'You'll be wondering why I'm here in Burgessie, or one step beyond the middle of nowhere, as it might be?'

Marian found herself unwilling to admit any interest in him at all.

'We all end up in strange places in wartime, don't we?' she answered lightly.

'In my case, stranger than most,' he carried on, completely self-assured. 'I'm here on a terribly secret mission, to guard a part of the national records which are being held in apparently comparative safety at the Castle here, in case of bombing in Edinburgh. Of course, I'm delighted to be spared any kind of bombing myself, but I think I could bear a little of it just for a few decent concerts a month, or a little art exhibition of really good quality, you know?'

He smiled at her, the smile of an office guillotine.

'Oh! Lorimer Catto Rennie – you must be L.C.R.!' she said suddenly. 'David Fraser mentioned you the other day.'

His smile stiffened.

'How very charming of him,' he said, with his teeth forming a tight wall at the front of his mouth. Marian found it necessary to placate him a little.

'You must find it frightfully dull here,' she said quickly, not quite meeting his eye. 'How on earth do you pass your time? Apart from making presentation scrolls, of course.'

'I indulge in hours of cataloguing, undisturbed by public enquiries,' L.C.R. explained, managing to instil the words 'public enquiries' with a subtle mixture of horror and disdain that an actor would have been proud of. Marian glanced at him. He appeared tremendously pleased with himself, but he also seemed precisely aware of where each of his limbs was disposed, where every hair on his well-trimmed head lay – with just the least hint of a curl over his high forehead. She wondered if he practised being himself in front of the mirror each day. At that moment she was spared further speculation by the arrival of the beautiful blonde she had seen talking to Davie in the village the previous day.

'Lorrie, darling, here you are! Do introduce me.'

The accent was extraordinary, utterly Mayfair. The voice had been heard across hunts from Oxfordshire to Sussex for generations. Marian found herself blinking, but the smile on the beautiful face was warm and expectant.

'Joy of my life,' said L.C.R. grandly, 'this is Marian Gow.'

'Cowie,' corrected Marian, offering her hand.

'And this divine creature,' he added, 'is Joy Smith-Allenbigh.' He wrapped an arm about her in a way that left no questions as to their relationship. Marian managed to smile normally.

'How do you do?' said Joy, her handshake as warm as her smile. 'Are you something to do with the paper factory?'

'No, I'm a doctor,' said Marian.

'Gosh! How splendid!' said Joy. 'I'm afraid I should be far too stupid to do anything like that. You must be terribly bright.'

'Well …' said Marian. 'I'm not coming to work here or anything. I'm just taking a few days' break, and then I'm going back to London.'

'To London! How ghastly for you. Are you working in one of the hospitals?'

'No, I'm in practice and with an ambulance unit.'

Joy's expressive face widened in alarm.

'That's very brave! I wish I could be useful like that.'

'What are you up to, then?' Marian asked. She had met plenty of women like Joy in London, who felt that 'doing their bit' meant an endless round of parties to entertain off-duty officers. A few managed to squeeze themselves into well-tailored uniforms and drive a general or two around the Home Counties.

'Oh, I'm in the paper factory. That's why I asked. It's jolly hard work, but it's splendid!'

That was a surprise. Marian found herself warming to Joy in a way she could not foresee warming to L.C.R.

'David Fraser tells me you're doing very valuable work there,' she said, forgetting L.C.R.'s previous reaction to Davie's name. Joy smiled gratefully.

'Davie's lovely, isn't he? He's such a dear friend.'

Was he, indeed? She wanted to think that Davie wasn't the type to befriend someone like Joy, but she had seen them together more than once. And to be fair, Joy did seem nice.

Cammie slammed the needle down on the gramophone again, and *In the Mood* sprang out of the speaker.

'Come on, darling!' cried Joy, angling L.C.R. into a gap in the crowd and somehow making him fold himself in time with the music. Marian grinned, and turned away. Beside her she found a well-dressed lady who had paused to follow Joy with her eyes, a wistful little expression on her face. Marian almost walked into her, and apologised.

'Not at all, not at all,' said the lady vaguely. She pulled herself back into focus and examined Marian curiously. 'I don't believe we've met.'

'Marian Cowie,' said Marian again. 'I'm staying at my grandmother's old cottage up by the hill.'

'Oh, of course, of course. I'm Anna Forbes. Major Neil Forbes' mother.' She presented a gloved hand precisely.

'How do you do?' Marian took the hand with care: she felt the need to make a good impression.

'I noticed you talking with Mr. Rennie and Miss Smith-Allenbigh,' said Mrs. Forbes. Her words were arranged with care. 'She would be lovely for Neil,' she sighed.

'She seems very fond of Mr. Rennie,' Marian suggested gently, as much for her own benefit as for Mrs. Forbes'.

'Oh, that won't last. Mr. Rennie is simply entertaining himself, and she is very – she is a very generous girl.'

Marian wondered if that were some kind of euphemism, then decided that Mrs. Forbes would hardly wish that kind of wife on her son.

'I heard,' she said, 'that Major Forbes would be going back soon.'

'Will he? Who told you that?' Her powder-blue eyes widened. 'He can't be: he would have told me straightaway.'

'Perhaps I misunderstood. I have only been here a few days, and so many people have told me so many things … People have been telling me stories, you know?' she finished with an apologetic smile. Mrs. Forbes raised her thin eyebrows, and nodded.

'They do that, yes.'

'Someone told me that you tell a very good story, Mrs. Forbes,' she ventured.

'Really?' Mrs. Forbes frowned, but not angrily. Instead she appeared to be trying to remember something, as if Marian's words had triggered some thought in the back of her mind.

'Would you tell me, some day?' Marian asked, feeling very foolhardy. Mrs. Forbes gave a distant smile.

'I might, some day. Some day. Not today, though: not today.' Then she moved as if she had glimpsed something across the room, through the crowd. 'Excuse me, Miss Cowie.' She was gone, slipping through the dancers like a fish, surprisingly swift for her age. As she vanished, her son reappeared, taking Marian by the elbow.

'My mother been interrogating you?' he asked cheerfully.

'Not at all,' she replied. 'I was asking her if she would tell me a story. Everyone has been telling me stories!' she turned to face him properly, laughing. 'I never came across such a village! Will you tell me a story?'

Major Forbes turned away.

'A story? Oh, I have no stories to tell.'

The silence was briefly awkward.

'Shall we dance, then?' Marian asked quickly.

'Perfect.' He smiled then, and they took to the floor again.

They talked as they danced, as they had when they had met and had lunch. She felt clever with him and pretty, appreciated. It was very pleasant. They certainly attracted attention, and she wondered, as she caught some unsmiling eyes, if she was monopolising him to the detriment of some local girl who had hopes of a dance or two. At the end of the next record, then, she decided she could be magnanimous, and insisted on sitting one out.

'And if you want to dance with someone else, please don't feel you have to sit with me!'

'Am I being dismissed?' He grinned down at her.

'Not at all: you must do your duty, that is all!'

'Then I shall seek it out,' he said with a bow, and a moment later she saw him dancing with Joy Smith-Allenbigh. It would delight his mother's heart, she thought, watching them: perhaps rightly, she added to herself, as she saw he seemed to be treating Joy exactly as he had treated her. Well, they had only just met, she reminded herself firmly: what claims did she have on Major Neil Forbes? At that moment he spun Joy around in a neat little whirl, and as Joy laughed Forbes met Marian's eye, and winked. She jumped, and deliberately turned away, embarrassed in case someone else should see her delight.

She went to ask for another cup of tea, and queued obediently behind a great broad back that was somehow familiar. When the man turned, it was Geddie the farmhand again. His face was pink even before he recognised her, so she assumed it was beer rather than shame at his daft behaviour over the Allenbury's Diet powder. He gave her a funny little pat on the arm, as though he was concerned for her.

'I was thinking, Doctor, that I shouldna have alarmed you like that the other night.'

'The other night?'

'Aye,' he nodded vigorously, then regarded her with an anxious frown. 'It was you, was it no? In the pub?'

She remembered the passage blocked by his heavy frame, the huge fists loosening and tightening.

'When you told me the story – when you told me about the monster in the loch? Yes, that was me.' She did not want him to think she did not believe him – and truth to tell, now she was beginning to wonder which stories were true and which were not.

'Aye, aye, so I did tell it you. I began to wonder a bitty – the next day my memory wasna so clear … But that wasna the right story to tell a lady like you, not one with monsters in it. I should have mebbe told you the one about the dancing weasels instead.'

'The dancing weasels?' She tried very hard to keep her face straight.

'Aye, aye,' he agreed solemnly. 'Dancing in the middle of the road. I just caught sight of them round the corner and then they were off like lilties.'

She wondered how much he had had to drink that evening, and tried to give him a reassuring smile.

Cammie lifted the record off the turntable and replaced it with *It's a Lovely Day Tomorrow*. Denny Dennis had hardly drawn breath to sing when Forbes was back by her side, separating her from Geddie in a manoeuvre as slick as anything on the parade ground. It was not an easy song to dance to, but they managed something resembling a slow foxtrot, the exact steps mattering little as the dance floor rolling smoothly beneath their soft feet, the other couples hazy at the very edge of her vision as Forbes wrapped her against him and she allowed herself to be led, heedless of anything but him. Only a few gliding steps floated them far too soon to the end of the dance, like something being carried on the tail of the wind.

'Now, then,' the minister clapped his hands as the tune drew to an end. Forbes let go of Marian's gaze a moment after he released her hands, and made her a little mock bow, smiling in a way which made her shiver all over. Quickly she turned away. 'Miss Liddle has prepared some of the children to give us a little entertainment.'

Cammie, his face stoical, led Agnes and two other little girls up on to the shallow stage, and arranged them around a box which Miss Liddle slid along behind them. The two girls stood behind the box, and Cammie and Agnes to each side of it. He cleared his throat ominously: Dr. Hanson, who was standing nearby, caught Marian's eye in professional alarm.

'Ladies and gentlemen, we present the story of Major Forbes' escape to Marseilles!' he announced. He and Agnes pulled on pieces of wool, and a pair of sacking curtains, decorated with flowers cut from bits of old lace, opened to present a rural scene painted on the inside of the box. The story of Major Forbes crossing the river with the unsuspecting German soldiers was told using puppets on sticks with unconvincing German accents, the narration urged on by Cammie and Agnes in turns. The audience laughed and clapped and cheered as the curtains closed, and the box was slid back off the stage for the children to be joined by others from the school assembling in two neat rows to sing *Run, Rabbit, Run.*

The young, high voices spun around Marian, quick and eager, and she closed her eyes. *The school had been hit as the children were being led to the shelter: teachers and pupils were littered across the playground like toys left behind after breaktime. A blackboard, a thing every child thought was a permanent fixture, was broken over the top of some desks, flung off the wall by the explosion.*

She gasped and swayed, but a steady hand gripped her arm. She opened her eyes: Dr. Hanson was staring into them, concerned, kindly. She made herself smile at him to reassure him:

there was no sense in being another of his patients, instead of his helper. A few more blinks and the images of the bombed school faded from her memory again.

'Come with me and we'll get a cup of tea,' said Dr. Hanson firmly, managing to make it sound more like a social engagement than a medical treatment. She allowed herself to be guided away as the children filed off the platform to more applause. She glanced back to see where Major Forbes had gone, but he had been trapped in conversation by two elderly ladies, one on each side, more dangerous than Germans. Marian and Dr. Hanson passed Davie Fraser on the way to the tea table, two cups balanced one on top of the other in his free hand as he levered himself along with his stick. He grinned at her, his teeth like an over-filled toastrack.

'Not all for me!' he defended himself with a nod at the cups. 'Honestly!'

She watched him go, making his way efficiently, for all his limp, around the room to where Mrs. Binnie was taking a rest and a news with Miss Liddle. Miss Liddle was as closed and shy as ever, but brightened when Davie arrived with the tea. Marian had not seen Miss Liddle smile at an adult before. She watched him for a moment. He had been talking to almost everyone at the party at one time or another, taking people tea, making them laugh. For a moment she felt she had been left off his list: she wanted to claim some acquaintance with him, based on their brief meetings on the hillside, their shared diggings. There he was, off again with that disastrous limp. At least it kept him safe from warwork – she could not help feeling that it was older than a war wound, to have carved that face with its pain. He stopped for a word with L.C.R. and Joy, and Joy's lovely face lit up at his approach. Then he was away again, chatting to Patrick Farquhar, the chemist, and another man also in the uniform of the Home Guard: she remembered him slightly from the night of the plane crash. Andy, was it? or Sandy? The one who seemed a bit backward, she remembered. He looked far too young to be in any uniform above Boy Scout.

Dr. Hanson handed her a cup of tea and led her to a seat, then excused himself, explaining that he could see one of his patients approaching. He winked at her and quickly assumed a caring expression, and headed off smartly to her left. Just at that moment, from the right, appeared another familiar figure: the old woman she had been sent to visit, Mrs. Geddie. She was wearing a coat in a remarkable shade of violet, and a hat of independent means. Mrs. Geddie opened her mouth to speak, and her face soured.

'Fa's that handsome doctor off till, then, lassie?' she asked Marian.

'He said he'd seen a patient,' said Marian with a straight face. No doubt it was Mrs. Geddie he had seen, and made a run for it. Geddie ... 'Are you anything to the farmhand Geddie up at, er, Mrs. Blaikie's farm?'

'Oh, aye, lass, he's my third sister's eldest son's son. Fit d'ye want wi' him? He's no sick, is he?' She plonked herself down beside Marian.

'Not at all, he's over there.' The 'Mrs.' must be a courtesy title, then. 'I'm just fitting together the names in the village.'

'There's not so many to go round as you might think,' said Mrs. Geddie cryptically. 'Are they telling you stories, then?'

'Like there's no tomorrow,' agreed Marian.

'Aye, they do that an' all. Could you bear another one at all?'

'You have one as well?' Marian was scarcely surprised.

'Aye, if you've a minty.' Mrs. Geddie squirmed her way down into her chair like a nesting duck. 'Well, this would have happened a good wee whiley ago. I mean, I could maybe tell you about the wifie and the witches?' She eyed Marian sideways from under the brim of her individual hat.

'Canny Annie? Mrs. Binnie's told me that one.'

'Oh, aye, Netta Binnie? Of course, it was her granny, was it no? Aye, aye. Well, no that one, then. I'll tell you the other I had in mind, for it was longer ago and likely no one else will think of it. It was after the '45, ken? After Culloden. Aye, Culloden.' Another sideways look: Marian wondered if she was assessing whose side Marian might be on.

'A bad day for both sides,' Marian murmured diplomatically, and Mrs. Geddie nodded.

'Well, the laddie I'm speaking of, he was a fine upstanding loon. He was a devoted follower of the Bonnie Prince, and few more handsome on that battlefield. Tall and fair with blue een so bright you could blind yourself on them, and a fine pair of legs in his phillibeg, and all!' For a moment her gaze turned wistfully about the room, found Dr. Hanson, and lingered. Then she shook herself. 'Aye, well. His name was Ross, I believe, Donald Ross. And nae doubt he fought valiantly at Culloden, as all his side did – and doubtless there were one or two heroes amongst the Government troops an' all. And he was a lucky man, too, for he ended the day unscathed, and saw his Prince flee, and decided – as who's to say you or I might not, too, had we the misfortune to end in such a situation? – that fleeing was no a bad idea at that. So off he went south and east, away from that unchancy battlefield, squirrelling into the hedges and the woods and through the hills and the glens where only the kindly and the sympathetic lived and would help him – for these were the quick flying days between the battle and the terrible things that happened in those glens afterwards. And a'body with een in their heid would likely help him, the women in particular. When the ties of his white linen shirt were undone, as they were after the heat of that battle, you could have seen the muscles on his great broad chest, wi' the wee golden hairs shining – oh! He was bonny!'

'Mrs. Geddie!' Marian could feel herself turning pink, but the old woman chuckled with unashamed lasciviousness.

'Ye have to make the most of a thing of beauty, Miss Cowie, ken. Onywyes, off he flew from Culloden Moor on his braw, shapely legs, and hid his handsome face in the mud and the leaves, and it wasna long before he gained the house of his sister and her son.

'Now his sister had married a grand man, a laird, who had taken his own tenants and gone to fight for Cumberland at Culloden. His eldest son, though, he had left behind to mind his estates, for the lad was a bitty young to be dragged off to war even in those days. Peter, they cried the lad, and he loved his uncle Donald, did Peter, though he did not love his politics. Peter followed his father's Government line, and so did Jeannie Ross, Donald's sister, Peter's mother. They were aye sticklers for the Duke of Cumberland's gang, and thought the Prince was a feckless timewaster and a coward. Well, who's to say?

'But when Uncle Donald turned up at their door, Peter said no question but they would take him in and hide him, even though he knew from the village that the Government troops were flying after any rebel officers they could find, or anyone who had done any favour for the Bonnie Prince. Uncle Donald would be safe in a house that was so well-kent to be loyal. So they hid him easy enough, and thought they were far enough from the battlefield to be safe. His sister Jeannie was gey fond of him forbye, and she and her son did all they could to keep Donald safe and comfortable until he would sometime reckon he could get away to France or other parts.

'But the time came when Cumberland's men were nearing the village, all perjink in their red coats. Peter saw his uncle Donald was growing uneasy like, and he told him never to worry, there were all kinds of hidey holes in the castle and nae doubt they could persuade the troops to leave them alone while Donald hid himself. But there was a thing Peter never considered in the matter, and that was this: his uncle Donald was nothing more than a yellow-haired, yellow-livered, selfish coward.

'Now, Donald Ross had been trusted by Charles Edward Stuart, who was always a man who liked handsome people about him. He had given Ross some papers for safe keeping, papers he had no wish to fall into the hands of the Butcher Duke. Ross was with him on that, for if they were found on his person they would be the kind of thing that the Government would easy use to have him strung up on the scaffold. Ross did not think that hanging would be good for his bonnie face, and he had no wish for the romance of an early death. So he laid a wee plan to himself, and what he did was this.

'When he heard that the Government troops were well and truly on their way, and actually in very fact coming up the drive, he got his sister's workbox, a fancy thing with a lid, and he set it in the hall of the castle. In it he put the papers he was supposed to be keeping from the Government people, but he made sure there was a good big corner sticking out. Then he nipped out the back door of the castle, stole the clothes of a dairy maid – we'll no ask how he persuaded her, but nae doubt she did not go entirely unrewarded – and minced his way off down the lanies and out of the estate and off and away, and he was never seen again, in this part of the world, at any rate.

'But things went badly inside the castle. When the troops burst in Peter tried to persuade them by telling them where his father was, how loyal his family were, all the rest of it. The troops were having none of it, and then some promising young corporal spotted the papers in the workbox. They snatched them up, and saw what they were, and that was it: Jeannie Ross and her son were arrested. And in due course, they were hanged in Edinburgh, and Jeannie's husband always reckoned that he saw Donald Ross in the crowd that day, watching his sister and his nephew hang that had saved his life, and he never lifted a hand to save them in return.

'Jeannie and her husband had other sons and the family lived on, but dinna mention the '45 to them. A brother betraying his sister for his own skin is not the kind of thing to leave a nice taste in the mouth for a family.'

'True enough,' said Marian, seeing that the story was over. 'What a nasty man!'

'Aye, aye.' Mrs. Geddie sucked in her lips and contemplated the room. 'He was no very nice.'

'Thank you for telling me the story, though,' said Marian. Her head was feeling full. 'Does absolutely everyone in this village have a story to tell?'

Mrs. Geddie chuckled, still quartering the room with her quick eyes.

'Naw, naw, no a'body. But you'll soon be able to tell one of your own.'

'Oh, I don't think so,' said Marian. 'I don't have any stories to tell.' Just like Neil Forbes, she thought suddenly. Maybe they would have to make a story together. She smiled.

'He'll be away soon, anyway,' said Mrs. Geddie.

'What?'

'Major Forbes.' Mrs. Geddie nodded to the Major, who was making his way over to them. 'It'll no be long now.'

'I don't …' said Marian, between crossness and bewilderment, but as Forbes approached Mrs. Geddie favoured them both with a peculiar little smile, and headed for the tea table. She would be lucky, Marian thought: they were starting to clear up.

'Another dance?' asked Forbes, assured of her assent. She stood and joined him on the floor, easily finding space as some older couples had left. Others stayed in the chairs around the side of the room, gossiping. L.C.R. and Joy clutched each other and trotted about the floor, L.C.R.'s thin face rapturous. The minister was chatting with Dr. Hanson, pointing up at the candles and mirrors. Mrs. Forbes had gone home and left them to glitter. Mrs.

Binnie was chivvying clattering teacups towards the kitchen, while Miss Liddle was hovering over Cammie and involved in some negotiation probably regarding bed time. Agnes watched with interest. The room was wider, cooler now, and a little breeze tickled the ends of the blackout curtains: they would have to be careful or they would be fined. The Home Guard were presumably to be on patrol somewhere, so Sandy, Geddie and Patrick Farquhar had disappeared, along with the carpenter Sergeant Leslie. Marian found she did not much like the idea of Patrick Farquhar with a gun: there was something barely controlled in his eyes. She shook herself in surprise at this fancy, and concentrated on the pleasure of dancing with Forbes.

The music drew to a close, and Cammie lifted the arm off the record and slid the shiny black disc back into its paper wrapping, then slipped the parcel into the wooden box beside the gramophone, moving with the slow care of someone who knew he would be sent to bed the moment he had finished. Miss Liddle handed him his coat, and shepherded her four charges out into the night, calling a quiet goodbye to Mrs. Binnie as she went. Marian waved to Cammie.

'Walk you home?' asked Forbes, offering her his arm. She smiled, and took it.

'My shoes are in the porch,' she said suddenly, remembering.

'Oh, mine too! Shall we pop and hunt for them?' asked Joy, overhearing her. Marian slid easily away from Forbes and followed Joy to the front door, where they began a hunt through the pile of odd boots, sticks, umbrellas and other debris jumbled around the door.

'Major Forbes really is a dish, darling,' said Joy in a noisy whisper to Marian: Marian supposed she could not bring the volume of her voice down any further. She only smiled in reply, sure they could be heard from the hall.

'You were enjoying yourself, too!'

'Oh, I love a dance! Such fun. And back to work tomorrow: making hay while the sun shines, and all that!'

'How on earth did you end up working in the paper factory?' Marian asked, then regretted it. She was not sure she could face another story tonight: she was eager to be walking home with Forbes.

'Oh, darling, that's a story for another day! And frightfully dull besides. A doctor must have much more interesting things to do than listen to tales of silly old me tramping up and down the country trying to do her bit!' She cast an uncertain, sideways glance at Marian, who was taken aback: most of Joy's type whom she had met before were supremely confident. Perhaps Joy really was in awe of Marian's brains. Marian gave a little smile: where she had been brought up, brains were positively expected.

'Perhaps we could meet for a cup of tea some time before I go?' she suggested, surprising herself. Joy beamed.

'Oh, that would be lovely! What a super idea. Let's.' Joy put out a foot expertly to hold down the blackout curtain while she touched up her lipstick in the little cloakroom mirror.

'You girls ready yet?' came the Major's voice.

'All done?' Marian nodded. 'Then let's let our boys ferry us home. Absolutely!' she cried out, and the men joined them in the porch so they could blunder quickly through the blackout curtain together.

Outside it was the perfect night for a first walk home with a handsome man. The light breeze chased a few wisps of cloud across a sky sprinkled with stars. The air was mild, with all the promise of spring. L.C.R. and Joy were heading the other way, whether to the castle or to Joy's digs Marian preferred not to think. She liked Joy very much, but could not imagine her being well suited with cold, papery L.C.R. After Joy called goodnight it was still not silent: others were heading home too in different directions, calling good night, issuing reminders for the morning. When the voices died away they heard an owl sounding softly across a field, and a tiny whisper of leaves.

She and Forbes turned up the hill, towards the road out of the village. There was a faint aroma of whisky in the air: it seemed some of the men had been drinking, and she wondered if Forbes had indulged, too. She was about to draw breath to ask, just out of interest – whisky was not easy to come by - when there was a shout down behind them.

'Watch out!'

Then another.

'There he is, quick! Quick!'

They both spun round, eyes searching the dark road and what

they could see either side. A jumble of movement and sound barrelled up the road towards them. Confused, they both stepped forward, and running footsteps broke from the muddle down the hill and pounded towards them. A starlit figure bounded past, shoving them to each side with breathless strength. Marian gasped, staggered to catch her balance, and fell against the thorny hedge. She yelped, but the sound was lost in a bellow from Forbes as he righted himself and shot after the fleeing figure. As Marian hauled herself upright two more men ran up, people she recognised from the dance.

'What is it?' she called out to them.

'The missing airman!' they shouted back as they passed. 'Has Major Forbes gone after him?' one of them added, over his shoulder.

'Yes, yes,' she cried back, and began to jog after them. There was shouting up ahead, and her heart started to pound. Then a shot came. She staggered with the shock. They must be on the road to the bridge over the railway: there was probably a guard on it, and perhaps the airman had been trapped between the guard and Forbes, desperate and dangerous. She found a new turn of speed, caught up with the men from the dance who had run further, and saw the bridge ahead, caught in the starlight between banks of dark trees, as they turned the corner of the lane. There were figures on it, moving erratically.

'Halt, who goes there?' demanded one, and she could just see the wobble in his rifle as he tried to stop the other man.

'It's Major Forbes to you, you fool!' came Forbes' voice. 'Where did he go? Why didn't you stop him?'

The men from the dance ran up to the bridge, Marian just behind them.

'Where's the airman?' one of them asked. The other, more observant, gently eased aside the shaking rifle. 'Sandy, man, are you injured? There's blood on your head, lad.'

'Where's the doctor?' asked the other man.

'Och, he's away home.'

'No, the lassie. The one we passed: she's a doctor, too.'

'I'm here,' said Marian hurriedly, pushing her way forward. She pulled out her feeble blackout torch and tried to make some assessment of the situation. Sandy was propped against the parapet of the bridge, and the rifle slumped in his hands. 'Hello, Sandy, have you been hurt?'

Sandy, she remembered, the one who wasn't all there, or that was the impression she had. She touched him on the chin and angled his unresisting face towards her, seeing the swipe of blood on his forehead. His cap was missing.

'Did he shoot you? Did he hit you on the head?' she asked, vaguely aware of a clanking noise on the road behind them. Sandy shook his head slightly.

'He pushed me over.' His shoulders heaved suddenly, and a sob escaped him. 'I fell on the wall.'

'Never mind that fool: where is the airman?' demanded Forbes. He reached past Marian to take a handful of Sandy's rough wool uniform jacket. 'Where did he go? How in the name of hell could you just let him run past?'

'That's enough of that,' came a new voice. Marian spun round, surprised, but Forbes did not let go of Sandy's jacket – not until a long, pale hand reached round the other side of Marian and laid itself firmly on Forbes' own hand. Marian squeezed out backwards, trying to see what was going on. To her surprise she found Davie Fraser standing on her left, Forbes glaring at him from her right, his chin out, brow sunken. Marian backed a little further.

'Leave Sandy alone, Mr. Forbes,' said Davie politely. 'It's not going to help you find your missing airman any faster, picking Sandy up and shaking him.'

Sandy stared from one to the other man, dazed. Marian found she was holding her breath, her pulse loud in her ears. Davie's ghostly hand was steady over Forbes' fist, but the fist gradually loosened and fell, though Forbes' eyes never left Davie's face. Their hands fell apart slowly, like lovers saying goodbye, but otherwise neither man moved.

'I could knock you down with one blow,' Forbes snapped. Davie did not flinch.

'And would that make you a better person?' he asked.

'What?' Forbes was thrown off his stride.

'Look,' said Marian sharply, 'Sandy's near to passing out.'

Both men stepped back as if the spell had been broken. Marian seized Sandy and rubbed his hands hard, trying to see his eyes in the dim light to assess him for concussion.

'I'll take him away to the manse,' said Davie, 'if you'll give me a hand.'

'Of course,' said Marian.

'Not you,' said Davie, 'I meant Al or Charlie here.' The men who had run after the airman grunted, nodding. 'Dr. Hanson's gone to the manse for a news with the minister. We don't need you.'

He met her eye, briefly, and a wave of regret swept over her, though she could not have said why.

Lexie Conyngham

Chapter Eight

The golden blast of the morning chorus was not as soothing the next morning as it had been that first day. She pressed her forehead against the cool glass of the window and gazed out blearily at the glittering garden. She had not slept: she was used to that, but she was less used to the tossing and turning that had accompanied her long wakefulness. She replayed the events of the previous evening from every angle, but still felt uniformly dreadful.

Forbes had been a bit drunk, she realised that now. They probably had full cellars at the castle, so there would have been no difficulty in finding whisky to drink: he might have been sharing it around amongst the men at the party, too. After the incident at the bridge, he had walked her home in silence, and kissed her on the cheek at her gate. When she had turned back at her door, five or six paces away, he had gone: perhaps he had not trusted himself to behave in his condition, and had chosen to leave abruptly instead. Perhaps he was simply still annoyed. Had she been part of annoying him? She could see why he might have been angry at the general situation, maybe even at Sandy: having a gun pointed at you was never much fun, she imagined, particularly by a man shaking and nervous in the dark, not quite sure who you were. Forbes must have been unnerved, and that along with the discovery that Sandy had not, in fact, stopped the man he should have stopped, the German airman, would not have pleased anyone.

Of course Davie Fraser would not have understood. He was not a fighting man: he did not have to consider fleeing airmen and guns in the dark. It had been kind of him to protect Sandy, she thought, but really, she had been tending to Sandy. There was no reason for Davie to interfere. Sandy had been her patient, and Davie had taken him away to Dr. Hanson, as if he had no faith in her ability to tend to him. It was as if he did not trust her to do her work. Really, he was as bad as that silly old man who had refused to let her treat him, just because she was a woman. She was used to that: it was not uncommon, but it was still irritating. She would have thought Davie would have been more sensible, but there, he was an archaeologist: he was probably old-fashioned.

But, said a more rational part of her brain, as she watched a blackbird putting the garden in order, Davie knew that Dr. Hanson would have light and warmth at the manse, and hot water and probably a medicine cupboard, none of which she had with her at the bridge. The manse was handy, and Dr. Hanson was there and knew Sandy. Why shouldn't Davie take Sandy there? And had he ever given any indication that he had no faith in women doctors?

But that look he had given her as he had left: that had hurt.

It was a lovely morning, and she wondered if she should go up to the hill, and dig at the bones, and focus on that, but the thought of perhaps meeting Davie there just yet was not a happy one. Then she remembered that it was Sunday: neither of them would be digging that day. The paper factory would be in operation despite the Sabbath, she remembered from her conversation with Joy, so she would probably be safe enough going to church. No doubt Davie, too, would be at the factory, and with luck Major Forbes would be sleeping off an aching head. She did not want to see either of them. The way she felt at the moment, however, if she did not go to church this morning she might never want to face the villagers again. Fleetingly a thought reminded her that she was not staying long, anyway, but it somehow faded. However long she was to be here, she did not want her new acquaintances thinking badly of her.

She dragged herself away from the window, thoughts still in a muddle, and went to put the kettle on. Facing church was one thing: facing it without tea was quite another.

She dressed in her second-best dress - her best one still had bits of hedge to be removed from it - and a cardigan, and her serious-doctor hat, and made herself leave the house and walk down to the village. As she passed the junction where the road headed off to the railway bridge, she wondered how Sandy was – and where the escaped German airman had got to. If he had made it past Sandy he had probably left the village altogether. It was surprising he had not left before now. Then she remembered the blood on that sharp bit of wreckage up on the hill: he was wounded, of course. He had been stealing food and lying low, getting his strength back before he made his mistake. Where had he been hiding?

The church was her end of the village, beside the solid block of the manse. The manse was Georgian, but the church was clearly much older, built of granite and sandstone boulders that had been patched together as they were, not worked into square blocks. The tower sat squat at one end, with the door on one side of the building. Spring grass grew fresh around its skirts, not yet trimmed, and around the grey graves in the little kirkyard. She enjoyed the melancholy of kirkyards as a rule, and today it drew her the more strongly as it suited her mood of mild self-pity. Besides, she was early: she must have mistaken the time of the service, for there was no one about at all.

The kirkyard reminded her of Mrs. Geddie's odd remark the previous day at the party, that there were not many names to go round in the village. It was true here: there were Geddies, and Farquhars, and Blaikies, Liddles and Mutches and Anguses, intermarrying and multiplying back through history, and not many other names. Perhaps that explained the oddness of the village. In the corner a rather splendid tall memorial, backing on to the kirkyard wall, marked the family burying ground of the Forbeses: she moved away from that, and concentrated on the ordinary village folk. The graves were a mixture of ages and styles, some with fresh cavities around them where ironwork railings had been removed for the war effort. She wandered between them, trying to fit families together. Soon she was completely muddled, and sat down on an illegible table stone and stared at the place where Dr. Hanson's parents, the murdered man and his devoted wife, were laid side by side. At least that was intelligible, even if it still led her back into the village's myriad stories.

She hardly heard a step behind her but she did notice a sharp little sigh, and turned fast. Davie Fraser was just at the corner of the church, every point of his angular body shouting that he had only just seen her and was intending to creep away. She turned back to the grave, letting him go, feeling the blush burning her face, but instead she heard the tap of his stick and the odd footstep on the gravel of the path, and knew he was braver than she was.

'Good morning, Dr. Cowie,' he said.

'Mr. Fraser,' she acknowledged.

He perched at the other end of the table stone. Neither of them spoke. She could not look at him. With dread she heard him draw breath.

'Sandy's fine, if you're worried.'

'Of course I was worried. But you took him off my hands.'

'I thought you had enough on your hands without caring for Sandy.' He paused, and though she still could not look round at him she saw the tip of his stick, batting the grass around the Hansons' grave. 'Are you proud of him, then?'

'What?' She did turn at that: it was not the question she had been expecting.

'Are you proud of your Major? There's no harm in Sandy, and he worships the Major. He was terrified.'

'He'd let the German airman get past. And he pointed a gun at Major Forbes.' She had never called him Neil, not even in her head, she realised now.

'He was trying his best.'

'His best wasn't good enough, though, was it?' said Marian, her mind on all the excuses she had made for Major Forbes through last night. 'There's a war on: we all have to do our best and more than our best. If Sandy wasn't up to it, what's he doing in the Home Guard anyway? What was he doing guarding such an important position?'

'Because he wants to do his bit, and because there are so few of them that if Sandy hadn't been there on the bridge, no one would have been.'

'I can't see that that would have been any worse,' she said, hating herself even as she said it. She had her eyes back on the Hanson grave now, unable to meet Davie's gaze. 'The airman would still have got away, and Major Forbes wouldn't have had a fright with the rifle.'

'I'm sure he's well used to it,' said Davie drily. She could feel his eyes on her, and burned. She made herself turn back to him, and was shocked at the sorrow on his face. 'You're very hard, you know,' he went on. 'Was it London? Is that what did it? What were you like before, I wonder? Would I have liked you?'

'Davie ...'

But he levered himself up from the table stone and cranked his way off round the church again. She was left with the graves, and the grass, fresh and green and damp, not clarted with weary dust like the London grass, and the daffodils, dancing as if no one had told them there was a war on.

The preaching was good, the one-armed minister taking the text of the mustard seed and explaining to his farming congregation that mustard could be a nuisance of a weed, turning the old story on its head. They nodded appreciatively, taking in the information and storing it for use. The choir was decent enough and to her surprise Lorimer Catto Rennie played the little organ, managing somehow to do so ironically. Davie was not in the church, as far as she could circumspectly see: presumably he had been passing on his way to the paper factory and had wanted a few moments' peace in the kirkyard. Well, she had spoilt that for him, too. Mrs. Forbes sat in the front pew, taking the place of honour, but the Major was not with her: as she had hoped, he must have been sleeping off his whisky.

The church was pretty inside, with rather primitive leafy carvings around the capitals of small columns, and some of the features had the air of not knowing there had been a reformation. The pulpit was pushed to one side and the communion table was central, under a stained glass window showing the Last Supper and, above it, the Crucifixion. As Marian gazed at it she noticed smaller panels in the bottom corners: one showed a praying family, much as the patron's family would be shown on any early religious art, but the other was bright with a large, bearded man on a pyre, arms raised to heaven, and two little white figures watching him. She blinked. St. Angus, then: that's where the story came from. The morning light caught the colours of the flames and the golden white of the two figures, and she surreptitiously wiped her watering eyes. When she focussed again, St. Angus had gone: the picture was that of the burning bush, the figures stones in the foreground, and the usual *Ardens sed Virens* wound around it. Not enough sleep, she thought to herself. And far, far too many stories. She would go back to London this week. At least there if she was not sleeping she was making herself useful.

After the service the minister greeted his flock at the door, making the most of the glorious day. He did not shake hands with them. Marian was one of the last, reluctant to move from the pew as if she could do some kind of penance there. The minister's dark arched eyebrows rose and he smiled as she emerged blinking into the day.

'Ah, I don't believe we've met, though I saw you at the party. You're Mrs. Cowie's granddaughter, I believe?'

'That's right: Marian Cowie,' she said, reaching out a hand automatically. He took it with his left hand, used to the mistake.

'I'm Martin Gauld,' he said. 'I'm sorry I havena been up to visit you but I've been gey busy, and I ken you've been getting about the place well enough. How's your grandmother?'

'Well enough when I last heard,' said Marian. 'She's settled in Aberdeen now, but whether she'll come back to the cottage come the summer or not I don't know.'

'Aye, we miss her, but when you're getting that wee bit older you like to have warmth and home comforts and your family nearby. I hear you've been helping Dr. Hanson?'

'Only a little, while I'm here. I'll be going back to London soon.'

'Oh, aye, oh, aye. That'd be a gey unchancy place at the minute, would it not?'

'I think I can be useful there, though.'

'Of course, of course.'

'Is Sandy all right, then?' she asked quickly, before she lost her nerve. 'I was there last night when – well, just after …'

'Oh, aye, so Davie Fraser said.' She felt herself blush again and hoped he would not notice. 'Look, Miss Cowie – Dr. Cowie, I beg your pardon - will you come back to the manse for a bite of lunch? It's not much but it'll be fine country fare, you ken.'

'Oh, I couldn't, Mr. Gauld …'

'Nonsense. You'd be doing me a favour for then I can take calling on you off my conscience!' He grinned. 'Here's my wife now: she'll say the same. Helen!'

Helen Gauld was slim and neatly dressed in a suit which had been altered a few times, Marian thought. She wore a cap with a little festoon of ribbons bursting from the top. Marian had seen something similar at the seamstress', Mrs. Angus' house, and wondered if it had been made by her.

'You must be Dr. Cowie!' said Mrs. Gauld. Her sweet smile transformed a wide-eyed, innocent face into that of a mischievous girl. 'Mrs. Binnie's my sister: she says you're a great asset if we can keep you!'

'Mrs. Binnie's very kind!' said Marian with a laugh. It seemed that both sisters could make her smile, and suddenly the idea of lunch at the manse was very appealing.

'Can you sing?' asked the minister suddenly. 'We could do with a few more in the choir for Easter.'

'Oh no! I'd be no use for that!' Marian protested. 'I've no voice at all.'

'Then maybe the flowers?' suggested Helen Gauld anxiously. 'Mrs. Angus was down to do next Sunday but she tells me this morning she has to go in to Aberdeen to see her daughter next weekend with the bairn. Would you be able to? It's just the two vases.'

Marian's mother was the kind of woman who ensured her daughters could arrange flowers.

'Of course, if you need someone,' she said. Helen Angus smiled again and took Marian's arm.

'And of course you'll come to lunch just now. It's not chops or anything awkward, you know. Martin often brings people back for lunch on a Sunday, so you're no trouble at all, believe me!'

'Well, in that case ...' Marian thought briefly of the prospect of sandwiches alone in her cottage, still reviewing the previous night in her head. 'I'd love to come, thank you.' The minister and his wife beamed, and led her to the gate to the manse, where a grit path ploughed between banks of budding lavender to the door of the stolid Georgian house. They were already ushering her through the door when she remembered she had meant to go back to London this week, and now she had agreed to do the flowers for next Sunday. Oh, well, if Dr. Hanson would let her help again, perhaps she could make good use of her time.

The hallway was plainly decorated, and furnished with pieces that had probably seen several generations of clergy. Mr. Gauld went to a heavily carved monk's chest and slipped off his shoes, sliding his feet into a pair of homemade slippers. She blinked.

There was a slipper lying in the street, a trail of blood, another slipper, more blood.

'Are you all right, dear?' Helen had felt her sag a little against her arm.

'Yes, yes, thank you. I slept badly last night, then forgot to have breakfast,' she explained with a smile to take away any worry. Helen Gauld frowned into her face for a second, then said cheerfully,

'Martin will take you into his study for a sherry - only tiny, I'm afraid! - while I see what stage the lunch is at.' She pushed Marian gently off in the direction of her husband, who ushered her to an open door off the hallway. 'I promise you, if I hadn't told you there was sherry in the glass you might miss it, so concentrate!'

Marian laughed, and found herself in a stern, dark study dominated by a large oak and glass bookcase filled with grim leather volumes. Mr. Gauld waved her to a comfortable armchair and turned to a silver tray with decanters and glasses.

'Terrifying, isn't it? I feel that bookcase is the collective judgements of my predecessors on any laxity I might grant my parishioners.'

'It's quite intimidating,' Marian agreed. 'Do you use the books?'

'We can't find the key. I don't think that bookcase wants to go anywhere. I suspect they built the manse around it.'

'There since the time of St. Angus,' Marian murmured, accepting her tiny sherry.

'Ah!' said Gauld with an approving smile, 'you've heard of our peculiar patron saint? You'll have been talking to Miss Liddle, then.'

'She was kind enough to tell me the story. I suppose like many of these tales, it's become confused over the years.'

'I daresay,' said Gauld thoughtfully, but she was not sure that he agreed with her. He sipped so delicately at his sherry that there was still a trace left in the glass when he set it down again. 'So, you're settling in well? People being helpful?'

'Oh, yes: everyone telling me stories, of course!' She was used to the villagers recognising this peculiarity in themselves, but the minister raised his dark eyebrows, as though it was news to him. She blinked and went on. 'I've been trying to help Dr.

Hanson, where I can. But I'll be away back to London soon anyway.'

'Oh, yes, you were up at the crash site. I gather you found a body up there?'

'Well, a skeleton, yes. I don't suppose you were here twenty years ago?'

'I was, as a matter of fact. And of course Helen was born here. You'll have to ask her, too, but it's a mystery to me who the bones could be. Some tramp, perhaps?'

'I think it's a woman. A young woman.'

'My! The things they can tell from bones. Perhaps one of the travelling folk, then? Lost from her party?'

'Perhaps. They have specific burial sites, though, don't they? And I think this woman had been properly buried, arms crossed over her chest and so on.'

'Really?' Gauld did not sound as if the news made him happy. The silence lay for a long moment, observed from on high by the bookcase. Marian had a peculiar impression that if one of them did not speak soon, they would be found there, still sipping sherry, a hundred years from now in stony silence, imprisoned by the books. She felt unable to open her mouth, unable to think of any reason to open it. Fortunately, Gauld shook his head a little and spoke.

'And you were there when poor Sandy was hurt last night, too, I gather. Davie Fraser brought him here.'

She found herself blushing, even though she had had every intention of finding out more about Sandy.

'That's right. Apparently the missing German airman made his appearance, and pushed Sandy against the wall on his way past.' She had not meant it to sound as if she distrusted Sandy, or thought him weak, but it came out that way. She blushed again. Davie would be ashamed of her. 'Major Forbes was upset with him because Sandy tried to stop him instead of the airman, and waved a gun in the Major's face. By mistake ...' she added, sheepishly.

'Aye, well, Sandy's always been the one with his hand making straight for the wrong end of any stick, dear love him. Have you met him before?'

'I've seen him about the place. At the party, yesterday, and up the hill when the plane crashed. He's in the Home Guard, I know, but I don't know anything else about him. What does he do?'

'A bit of this and a bit of that. I daresay anywhere else he'd never even have been accepted for the Home Guard. We're that short of people round here, though, and everybody kens Sandy so no one has great expectations of him. Oh, make no mistake, he's a decent lad, never done a bad thing in his life, though sometimes he can frighten people who don't know what he's like. He spent a few months in the asylum once, aye, and he didn't like that much, but we managed to persuade them to let him out again. He's no harm to anyone, as long as nothing much is expected of him, as I say.'

The minister glanced at the drip of sherry left in his glass and raised an eyebrow at it, as though willing it to increase miraculously like the oil in the widow's cruse. His mouth twisted in disappointment, and he went on.

'I met him guarding the railway bridge the other night, on his own then too, would you believe it? I went up to him and he leapt like a deer, and I said, 'Sandy, lad, whatever are you doing out here?' 'Och, Mr. Reverend, sir,' says he, 'I'm guarding the bridge against the Germans coming.' 'And Sandy,' says I, 'what would you do if a German came?' 'I'd say, Friend or Foe,' says he. 'And Sandy', says I, 'what would you do if he said Foe?' That had him puzzled, but then his wee face brightened. 'I'd leave him here and go for the Sergeant, Mr. Reverend,' he says.' The minister laughed, a creaking sound like the saddle of an unoiled bicycle. 'Aye, we're in safe hands while Sandy's on the guard, dear Lord bless him!'

'He can't be as young as he looks, though, if he's in the Home Guard,' said Marian.

'Sandy? Oh, no. He must be – what? Thirty? But he's not like other people, our Sandy, and what would you expect, after what happened?'

For once Marian was genuinely curious. The young lad Forbes had struck, the young lad Davie had protected, was really thirty? Older than she was?

'What was that, then?' she asked.

'Well, once in this village,' started the minister, crossing his legs and settling back, 'there was a pair of fine brothers here, Alec and Dod. They lived up at Essiemuir. They were into everything, always up to mischief, but never up to devilment, if you'll understand the distinction. Alec was a braw, bright, daring lad, strong and fair, and Dod followed him into everything, very nearly as brave as his brother. You'd hear Alec cry out 'Ach, dinna be feart, Doddie! See, I'll go first, and you follow!' and that would be Dod away after his brother. The only way he didna follow was that Dod found himself a girl and married her, and they had a bairn, and Alec was as free as the wind and ofttimes as wild. Then came the Great War, and Alec went to fight without a hesitation, and in the blink of an eye Dod kissed his wife and his bairn and went off after his brother, as he had always done.

'I sometimes think that war is no place for courage,' said the minister. 'Ordinary life requires from us all the courage that God gives us. War needs only a stout body, a steady hand and a solid head. Courage only makes everything so much worse – and I was a chaplain with the Gordons at the retreat from Mons in 1914.' He gestured with his sherry glass at the empty sleeve of his jacket. 'I prayed for courage then, but God knew my needs before me and instead took away my imagination. Around me the most blessed of men mounted up with wings like eagles, ran and were not weary, walked and were not faint – courage was by far a lesser requirement.

'But Alec was a brave man, and he gave everything he could. He was first over the top at every advance. He was the last out in a retreat. He crawled into No Man's Land to pull back the injured, tugging them from the snares of barbed wire, dragging them home through mud and slush. He fought like a tiger, he scouted ahead, he sang as the shells fell and made his comrades laugh and cheer. And through it all his wee brother Dod laughed and cheered with them and was his oppo in all his deeds, for he had always followed Alec.

'Alec was mentioned in dispatches, got the Military Medal, and soon, such was life in those runaway days, he made it to sergeant. It seemed to be that all he had ever lived for, every apple he had scrumped, every ditch he'd tumbled into, every wall he'd climbed, had been training for those glorious days in a muddy field in Flanders. I'd nearly say he loved it, as much as any man could love it. Until one day, when he was leading a platoon through a little wood to the far right of their position. They thought they were well clear of the shelling, but either a stray hit them or they were spotted. They found him by the screaming: they were lucky the Germans didn't find him first. His platoon were all dead, all in pieces. He had never a scratch on him, but when Dod stared in his eyes, he couldn't see Alec there at all.

'He recovered, apparently, though he was demoted again and went back to fighting alongside Dod. But he would wake in the night, in their dugout, and seize Dod by the shoulders and shake him, staring wildly into his eyes, and there were no more songs and there was no more laughter.

'Then one night, Dod awoke to find Alec with his pack on his back, heading for the door. Alec must have sensed Dod's eyes on him, for he glanced back, grinned, and jerked his head, as if to say 'Come on!' But Dod knew where Alec was going, and he thought of his wife and his bairn, and for the first time in his life, he shook his head, and Alec went alone.

'Well, they caught him fast enough, and life was short for deserters. He was put before a court martial, and sentenced to be shot. And Dod's mind was torn apart, for he could have stopped Alec – or could he? - or he could have gone with him and they might, together, have made it away, or he could have gone with him and been caught with him and been sentenced with him, and could have stood facing the firing squad with him, brave and upright and almost his old self again at last. So were the thoughts in Dod's head, the day he was ordered, by some oversight, to join the firing squad and shoot his brother. 'Ach, dinna be feart, Doddie!' Alec cried at the last. 'See, I'll go first, and you follow!'

And so were Dod's thoughts even after the war and for two whole years till one day, the anniversary of his brother's death, he climbed a tree that overhung the lane to the farm, that he'd climbed with Alec, and he tied a rope to a branch, with a knot Alec had invented, and he hanged himself, and followed his brother at last.

'And his wee bairn, Sandy, named for his uncle, eight years old on his dark winter walk from school, he walked into his father's swinging legs, and stared up into his father's black face, and they found him there frozen to the spot, and he's been our own Sandy ever since. The thing is, though,' the minister added, leaning forward to make his point, 'Sandy is terrified to be out in the dark amongst trees. But he had his orders to guard that bridge against some imaginary Germans, and perhaps in his heart there is some of his uncle's courage, and there he is.'

'Lunch is ready!' said Helen Gauld, cheerfully breaking in to the conversation with a flying tap on the door. 'Come along, Dr. Cowie, you must be starving!'

'There, I'm maundering away again like an old man.' Gauld stood with a smile. Marian did not think he looked very old: he had managed to rise from the low armchair without setting down his sherry glass.

'I'm glad to have heard the story, though,' she assured him, following Mrs. Gauld towards the dining room. 'But it's very sad. Did Dod not think he had enough to live for, in his wife and son, without following his brother?'

'It was not that that dwelt in his mind, I think,' said the minister. 'You see, however inadvertently, Dod had committed the sin of Cain, and struck down his own sibling. That was what he could not live with.'

Marian wondered at the word 'sibling'. Why had Gauld not said 'brother'? Cain had killed his brother Abel, and Dod had at least been part of killing his brother Alec. Then the wafting smell of roast fish wound about her, and she thought no more.

Lunch was very entertaining. The Gaulds clearly enjoyed company and knew how to make their unexpected guest welcome, and for a good couple of hours Marian managed to forget about Major Forbes and Davie and Sandy, and even what they encouraged her to say about her work in London did not make her feel guilty about deserting it for a few days. The food was the best she had had for months: clearly, she thought, though it was harder to make the best of clothes rationing in the country, food rationing went much further. She sighed in satisfaction as she waved goodbye and followed the grit path back to the kirkyard, slowing again amongst the graves as she had that morning. The familiar names caught her eye again, spinning her from Angus to Binnie, from Blaikie to Geddie, from Farquhar to Forbes.

A little shiver took her, despite the mild afternoon, but it was not the graves that had chilled her: she could sense someone was watching her, and she spun about to see if Davie Fraser had been waiting to lecture her again. But no one was to be seen. She turned slowly, making certain no one was in sight - surely Davie would not be sneaky and hide if she had sensed he was there – and then hurried past the church, through the gate and back into the square.

Even there she did not feel quite steady enough to climb the lonely road back to her grandmother's cottage. Instead the village drew her, telling her that rather than being nervous she was making the most of the fine day to make another little walk of exploration.

The village was quiet, with the inhabitants either making the most of the Sabbath rest or perhaps working in their kailyards behind the cottages. The road to the south led beyond the village proper, past the village hall where the party had been, to the dressmaker's at the tollhouse, and she knew the main block of the village from the inn at the north, through where it widened into the village square, where St. Angus must have arranged the burning of those Christian girls – wasn't the church said to have been built on the very site of Angus' house? And there was the doctor's house, grandly Victorian with its swelling bays, to the west and the school just up to her left, leaving the village in its shallow valley in between. The east, then, was unexplored, and the turn off, which must run parallel to the road that ran to the railway bridge and on to the station, lay somewhere between the schoolyard and the chemist's. She turned the corner, and found herself on a lane rising easily between two rows of cottages. Much like the ones she had just left, constructed from impenetrable granite blocks, they were nevertheless more uniform in construction, with the air of estate houses about them: even the paint on the doors was the same colour and of about the same vintage. In front of them, contained within walls made from more mortar than granite chunks, little gardens should have been filled with late daffodils and early roses, but instead were raw with vegetable beds. The road surface here was rough and poorly maintained, but her cork soles made it softer on her feet and she meandered on, listening to the birdsong around her, enjoying stretching her legs after an unaccustomedly generous lunch. The cottages, with their angular dormers and little gable over the front door, watched her in cynical surprise as she passed.

As the cottages ran out, the rows ending as though chopped off, the lane passed between two unremarkable gateposts and entered the green chill of woodland. She considered: this was probably the same wood that surrounded the railway bridge, that caused Sandy such distress. Poor lad, she thought: or not lad at all, but poor man. The minister had assured her that he had never done any harm in his state of confusion, but hadn't he said Sandy had frightened someone? Could it be possible that he had harmed someone after all, perhaps killed someone, and had buried them up on the Fairy Hill? If he was in his thirties now, rather than the youth that she had thought him, he might just have been old enough – and he was strong, she knew that. Forbes may have been quite right to be wary of him. And indeed perhaps some of the villagers even knew, and were protecting Sandy. She had heard that such things could happen. In any case … in any case, she needed to be thinking more clearly of what had happened in the village twenty years ago. She needed to consider who had lived here then, and who might have left since. Men off fighting, for example: but the skeleton indicated a slight person. A woman might well be the killer. Where on earth could she start? It was like an Agatha Christie, and she had never found them very satisfactory. How could you confine your suspicions to one small set of people? If it had happened twenty years ago, could she eliminate Davie? Joy? Lorimer Catto Rennie? P.C. Argo? Cammie, anyway?

Perhaps she should think of it more like a diagnosis, she thought, drifting on through the woodland, only half-seeing the path before her feet as she concentrated on the skeleton and its secrets. The signs were what the skeleton itself and its setting could tell her, and the symptoms were the evidence that she received from other people. There was perishing little of it, she thought crossly. Everyone was all too happy to tell her stories, but no one would tell her much about anyone missing twenty years ago. The minister Mr. Gauld had suggested a traveller, but as she had said they had their own places to bury their dead, or took it to a minister – and a minister, as Mr. Gauld should well know, would not bury a corpse up a hill with almost no ceremony about it. It could not have been someone who had just fallen down dead, a tramp dying of the cold, for her hands had been crossed and she had been laid out, as far as Marian had dug, correctly. Had she found any distinguishing features? She did not even know yet if the skeleton could tell her how the girl had died. She gave a little exasperated snort: she had to get back up there tomorrow morning first thing, and do some more digging. Whether Davie was there or not, she added to herself: he could lecture away if he liked. She would be gone soon anyway, and she realised that she did not want to leave the body half dug, or the mystery unsolved. More work, then, Miss, she said to herself sternly, and less lounging around enjoying yourself.

She stopped in the middle of the lane, pulled up short by her own telling off, and instantly felt again that she was being watched.

Could someone have followed her from the church? If so, they must have crossed the village square behind her. Had she glanced around at any point? She could not remember.

Once again, she turned very slowly, feeling like a fool, trying to peer through the trees into the undisciplined undergrowth. The Timber Corps must not have reached here yet, she decided absently. She had almost reached the point she had started at when she let out a loud yelp.

'Caught you!' cried Major Forbes in delight.

'Oh! You made me jump!'

'Clearly!' He was grinning broadly: any annoyance from last night seemed to have vanished. Her heart swooped and she felt a responsive grin on her own face. Sunlight through the leaves caught the colour of his hair just as one would want. 'What on earth are you doing, spinning around in the middle of the drive? Are you coming to see me?'

'To see you?' she repeated stupidly.

'Yes – this is the way to the castle, didn't you know?'

'Of course!' It was obvious now. 'Well, I'm sorry, but I was only here by accident – I mean, I had wandered up here without thinking where I was going.'

'Well, I'm devastated. But at least that means you haven't been swept off your feet by L.C.R. and are coming to seek him out of his hidey hole in the tower. Will you come in for tea?'

She considered, for longer than she thought she would.

'Do you know I'm tired?' she said at last. 'I hope I may say another day? I've had a fine lunch at the manse, and I'm afraid I didn't sleep well last night.'

'Not worried about the German airman, were you? I'm sure they'll catch him soon – as long as Sandy isn't on duty next time. What an idiot.'

He took her arm and began to walk her along the drive, as he had called it, back towards the village.

'Well, he can't help it …' she began.

'Is that what that archaeologist told you? He was very keen to defend him, wasn't he? Taking the poor fool under his wing.'

'But I hear Sandy had a shock when he found his father's body as a boy, and hasn't been right since?'

'That's true enough, but then what's the man doing in the Home Guard? I can tell you, I'd rather face a Nazi with a rifle than Sandy,' he added darkly.

'What do you mean?'

'A Nazi you can predict: he'll act in a sane and sensible fashion. Sandy, well, with him you'd never know.'

'But –'

'Did Fraser tell you they locked Sandy up once before? He was in the asylum down in Aberdeen, and it was probably the best place for him.' He considered a moment, and glanced at her. 'You'll know those places are supposed to be decent enough these days. He'd have been treated kindly. He could have worked on the farm there, felt at home. He probably wouldn't have known the difference.'

'He didn't strike me as that stupid,' said Marian carefully.

'Well, you hardly know him, do you? And nor does Fraser, whatever he thinks. It takes one to lead men before one can really know how they work and how best to treat them, and that's not likely to be something Fraser will ever find out – or would ever find out.'

'Would ever find out?' Marian was glad to see the gates up ahead. This conversation was not going to her liking.

'Maybe it's a good thing he's a cripple,' said Forbes. 'Better a cripple than a conchie.'

Chapter Nine

Her conversation with Forbes had continued all the way to her door. Or rather, Forbes had continued to talk, but she had participated less and less, lost in her own thoughts. Was Sandy a killer? Would Davie have been a conscientious objector, had he had the chance? Had Forbes been following her all the way from the kirkyard, waiting to pounce for his practical joke? She wanted to smile at the thought, but for some reason her lips would not curve and she bade Forbes goodbye without thinking of asking him in for tea until he had long disappeared. She hoped he would have put it down to the tiredness she had mentioned.

She made herself some toast, dressed in her slacks and went to bed early, dozing on and off until dawn, when she rose and bathed in cold water, and changed into day clothes, setting her medical bag back on its shelf. The day was fine again and she breakfasted quickly, then made a little picnic lunch and a flask and headed up the hill, before she could lose her nerve. But Davie was nowhere to be seen, and with mixed feelings she settled down at her little dig site and uncovered the bones.

'Good morning to you, whoever you are,' she whispered. 'I'll just carry on here, if you don't mind. Who are you, anyway?' she went on, as she began to brush earth from the lower ribs she had not yet exposed. 'Are you a local? And if you are, why does no one seem to know you're missing? And why are you here?' She caught herself, feeling stupid, and went on with her work in silence.

When she grew hungry she stopped for lunch, still with no sign of Davie. He must be at the paper factory, she thought, chewing at the spam in her sandwiches as she gazed out over the valley and the village, plotting its stories in the tuck of the hills. As she thought about it, spam was not usually quite that chewy: the bread was growing stale and she had added some elderly pickles from a stone jar in her grandmother's pantry to lubricate the sandwiches. She paused, wondering what precisely she was chewing, then decided it was best not to know. The sharp black tea in her flask did not last long and she shook out the drips before popping the flask back into her grandmother's basket. A few moments more of contemplation, a long view of a rag of cloud snagged on the point of Mither Tap like a scrap of dressing caught in forceps, and she was ready to work again. She settled down on her knees. The job was soothing, in a way, if she did not allow herself to remember what it was she was doing: she began to wonder if this was the charm of gardening, even of weeding, kneeling on the earth, focussing closely on it, feeling it between the fingers and thinking only about the next little move, the next slight adjustment and minor achievement, not about anything outside the work, deliberately not seeing the wood for the trees. The sandwiches sat heavily in her stomach, deterring hunger. The sun inched down the sky but she scarcely noticed, and only when she was finding it hard to see what she was doing did she sit up – and jump.

'Didn't want to disturb you,' said Davie with a crooked smile. 'Sorry – I probably should have.'

'That's all right,' said Marian, awkward. She sat back on her heels. A few days ago she would have told him off for scaring her, but now she did not feel so easy with him. He sat on a rock and contemplated the skeleton.

'How's it going?' he nodded at it.

'Well ...' She had been working on freeing the back of the skull. 'I have just found this.' She lifted the skull gently free of the soil, leaving the vertebrae tailing up to nothing.

'Hm, that doesn't say peaceful death to me.'

'I know.' She fingered the broken dent she had found. A ring of sound bone surrounded three pieces broken from it, but all still aligned correctly – just concave instead of convex. 'She's been hit with something.'

'Perimortem?' he asked intelligently.

'I think so. No healing, so not an old wound, and the bone all in place, implying that it happened and she was laid here with the flesh all still in place.'

'Did she fall on something?'

'Maybe. There's no stone ...' she felt where the skull had lain, '... in the right place for her to have fallen on it here. But even if she died accidentally, there is still the question of who might have buried her decently like this, without telling anyone official.'

'The traditional blunt instrument,' Davie remarked, as she set the skull back tenderly in its place. 'I suppose it's not entirely a surprise.'

'No.' She sighed, and brushed off her hands. 'I don't suppose you were here twenty years ago, were you?'

'You're trying for me as a murderer?' He smiled. 'No, I was blamelessly elsewhere. Well, elsewhere, anyway, which is as much as you can say for a ten year old anywhere, I think.'

She laughed.

'I just wish people would actually tell me where they were and who might be missing, instead of just telling me stories the whole time! Even the minister ...' She tailed off, remembering the minister's story and why he had told her it.

'Oh, yes, you've been to the manse for lunch, haven't you?'

'No secrets in a village,' Marian agreed. 'Except when it comes to this woman, of course. Only stories, stories from every time in history, stories about every family in this village, it seems. Not that they're not all related to each other anyway. And when I say anything about it, everyone just nods kindly and then tells me another, yet another, wretched story! How can I stop them?'

'After all, what's a story?' Davie stood up, staring down at the village. It was the time of the evening when you would have expected lights to start being lit, warming squares of windows and welcoming the workers home for their dinners. The A.R.P. warden was efficient in Burgessie, though. No warm-lit windows till the war was over. 'Some people say a story is a hiding place, somewhere you can disguise the facts, bury them – wind them up in ribbons of camouflage netting. But then you could always say that stories are windows – that all stories are parables, the opposite of a hiding place, the key to understanding something – or maybe everything.'

'I don't care how much philosophical literary criticism you spout at me, you still haven't told me a story yourself,' said Marian sternly. What was the matter with her? She was inviting stories again. Davie manoeuvred himself slowly down on to the grass, still staring down the hill until he lay back, stretching his arms out as if he were easing stiffness from them. He regarded her quizzically for a moment.

'Oh, all right, then,' he said at last. 'But it won't be anything to do with imagined heroics at the paper factory, or even anything to do with archaeology. Evening is on its way, and I'm going to tell you a ghost story.'

'A ghost story?' He had started well: a shiver ran up her spine.

'Well, I could tell you the story of the golden boy that's supposed to be seen around this fairy mound, but you've heard that one already, I gather. And Farquhar had every right to tell you that one, even if it is about my dig site! But this is a story no one else here is going to tell you – no one else at all, I should think. I'm going to tell you a story of my own.'

He rolled himself over into a sitting position, and pulled up his thin leg by the knee, propping himself into comfort against the rock he had been sitting on earlier. He was right: the evening shadows were already creeping around the barrow, and in the dusk his pale angular face and his long beautiful hands seemed to glow a little. He stared through her for a moment, thinking back.

'It was two years after the last war ended, 1920. I was nine. A cousin of mine had come over from Edinburgh to stay that summer, and he came down with what we thought was a fairly general mild fever. We'd stopped being quite so scared of Spanish 'flu by then, so we weren't too concerned. He was ill for a week or so – he complained a great deal of a sore head and he was certainly flushed. My mother had to keep changing his sheets because of his sweating, and he woke me in the night a couple of times – we shared a room – being sick in the chamber pot. He had us pretty worried for a few days, and my mother even sat up with him for a night when the fever was breaking. After that he recovered and all was well, and about a week later his mother wrote to say a pal of his at school had come down with infantile paralysis and was Jimmy all right? I think my mother hadn't contacted her before because Aunt Margaret had enough worries around that time, but now she wrote back quickly to reassure her, for he really was completely well again. All the same, I realised she was watching me at the same time. Ten days passed since Jimmy was ill and she relaxed, but a fortnight to the day from him being ill, I went down with the same thing, headache, fever and vomiting.

'At first we thought – I thought – that like Jimmy I'd be fine in a few days. I couldn't not be – we'd been looking forward to that summer so much that there was no possibility it could go wrong. You see, Jimmy's father had died at Vimy Ridge, but people were starting to pull their lives back together again. My father was home and fit and well, and filled with a sense of our good fortune we were going to take a cottage on the west coast near a Viking burial mound and Jimmy and I were going to dig for treasure. How could some petty childhood illness get in the way?

'But, well, as you know, I didn't get better. I became much worse, far worse than Jimmy, and instead of digging Viking burial mounds I was rushed off to the isolation hospital. My head hurt as if someone was kicking it from the inside, and when the crisis passed – you'll know what it's like, no doubt, no need to dwell on it – I was left in a dim white ward with a dozen or so other boys, all recovering from various nasty infections, all round about my age – the youngest was six, I remember, and the oldest, getting over scarlet fever, must have been twelve or thirteen, and rather above us young ones.

'There was no medication for infant paralysis in those days, and that monstrous-sounding iron lung hadn't been invented. We could, however, benefit from what they were calling physical therapy, that had come out of Europe in the war. It was still a little experimental, I think – each masseuse had her own way of doing things, but I was rubbed and thumped and manipulated three times a day, and my skin sang like the morning chorus. I slept a good deal after each session, and maybe as a consequence I was often quite wakeful at night. If I hadn't been – well, I'm not sure I would have been here now.

'They say that if a limb that was paralysed at the acute stage is still not moving after a month, it probably never will. My arms were both quite mobile, and growing stronger every day – I had worked hard on them, even outside the masseuse sessions, for I couldn't see a future for myself, even then, without writing and lifting books to read - but they would not let me out of bed to try my legs, and neither of them had been much use, so far. The masseuses had a growing sense of urgency about them as they pummelled me each day, and there was talk of applying electricity which I did not fancy at all – it was even more experimental, I think, and I'd seen what lightning could do to trees. I had occasional but vivid nightmares where my legs were blackened sticks, and so, choosing my preferred form of suffering, I lay back and took whatever pummelling they could give me.

'It was a noisy enough ward during the day: even with restricted visiting, a room of twelve boys on the way to recovery could hardly ever be quiet. The nurses were pretty decent, well up to us, as they had to be, and the Day Sister kept us all under control until her back was turned. Night time was different, though: the Night Sister was perfect for her job, a dim light, a warm blanket and a milky drink wrapped up in one serene little clootie dumpling of a body. Nothing, you felt, could go wrong while she was there, and even if I didn't sleep I was rested, calm, soothed by the stillness that seemed to emanate from her. Oh, she was a sweetie!

'But then there was the wee six year old. He wasn't really sick, like the rest of us: he'd had a bit of a fever at school one day, the school nurse had called in a doctor, and he'd been taken to isolation less for the fever and more to give his little bruised body respite from the father's fists and the mother's bottle. He was thin and quiet, and didn't much join in the fun the rest of us had. The Lady Visitors, a fairly frightening assortment of mink stoles and ostrich bonnets let out of my mother's drawing room circle for a week at a time, had brought him a kind of knitted teddy, and he clung to it perpetually, eyes wet and staring.

'One night, when I had been pummelled more desperately than usual, I was lying awake and feeling rather chilled, for a change. The Night Sister was at her desk, knitting comfortably, and must have been in a little world of her own for when one of the nurses came past and nodded to her, she didn't even glance up. The nurse passed up the ward – I was about the middle, with the oldest boy next on my right and an empty bed on my left. As she went she glanced at each bed in turn, though even as she glanced at mine I couldn't see her face clearly, for she wore one of those amazing elaborate head dresses that nurses take such a starchy pride in. I assume they're derived from mediaeval nuns – you certainly couldn't get up to much mischief wearing something like that. She walked slowly, as the night staff all did: they all knew how to walk silently, too, for even though this one had more in the way of skirts than was fashionable even in my distant youth, there was none of the fistling such skirts normally produce.

'She turned at the top of the ward, pausing a moment to glance through the gap in the curtains at the end window. Then she walked slowly down the ward as she had walked up, glancing again at each bed.

'The last bed on the far side was little Arthur, the six year old, fast asleep with his knitted teddy. The nurse turned and went to him, bending over gracefully and touching the boy's forehead. She had her back to me, as she pulled out the plain wooden chair by his bed and settled down in it, taking Arthur's hand. I remember thinking how kindly she seemed, and missed my own mother for a moment's intensity that a nine year old boy would never admit. Then I fell asleep.

'The next morning when we all awoke, there was a screen round Arthur's bed. The nurses were solemn, and would not meet our eyes, and the Night Sister was still there, blowing her little nose roundly into a large, crisp handkerchief. Arthur had dodged his father's fists for good. The doctor on his rounds was heard to murmur to the Day Sister about a missed head injury and the long term effects of malnutrition. After the rounds, they came to take the little body away while the nurses tried to distract us. But Crawford, who was the older boy in the bed next to mine, slid quickly from under his sheets, his eyes on the departing stretcher, and leaned on the side of my bed.

'"She's started again, hasn't she?" he said, low-voiced. He had barely spoken to me before, so I was a bit taken aback.

'"Who? Started what?"

'"Och, come on!" he said, but through his old disdain I was surprised to see something else in his face – fear. At that moment one of the nurses came to hurry Crawford off to some cheering activity, and my first masseuse of the day arrived, and all I could do was wonder what he had meant – or try to, through all the rubbing and thumping.

'Crawford didn't have a chance to finish his conversation till near supper time, by which time I had in my imagination vilified each nurse in turn, Day Sister, Night Sister, the distant Matron, all four cleaners and even Arthur's mother, picturing her climbing through a hospital window, gin bottle in hand, to smother her child. You might think I was very ready to believe Arthur was the victim of a crime, but remember, I was a nine year old boy: I might have been ill but I wasn't out of the ordinary.

'Crawford finished his supper quickly and slid out of bed again as he had earlier, but this time he crouched beside me, hidden from the Sister's desk by my supper tray.

'"Keep eating," he said, "and keep your eyes on your food, and I'll tell you. You were awake last night, weren't you? I saw you."

'"Well, I can't always sleep ..." I started defensively, but he cut across me.

'"So you saw her. The nurse."

'"Which one?"

'"Aw, dinna be so daft! The nurse that sat by wee Arthur's bed!"

'"Well, she must have known – that he was, you know, getting worse."

'"Ach, I dinna ken fit they teach you at they posh schools. Music and Latin and rubbish like that. Have you no heard of ghosts, that you dinna ken ane fan you see it?"

'"A ghost?" Shivers fingered up and down my spine as I thought of the figure pacing up and down the ward, the chill I'd felt, the way I could never see her face ... "Who is she?"

'"A nurse, of course. From lang syne. She comes and walks up and down the ward, up and down, and that's fine. But if she comes to sit by you, you're finished."

'Crawford came from a fishing family up near Peterhead, and I'd always heard that fisherfolk were tremendously superstitious, so while the nine year old in me thrilled at the idea of a ghost in the ward – a killer ghost, at that! – the scholar in me was already protesting. The fact that Crawford was so frightened made me rule out any scheme on his part to make fun of me, but it did occur to me that little Arthur had probably been pretty poorly anyway, and Crawford, who was due to leave us in a couple of days, certainly had nothing to fear.

'That night I fell asleep easily enough, probably because I was trying to stay awake, but some time in the middle of the night I woke with a shiver and there again was the nurse, nodding to the Night Sister who was oblivious over her own notes, pacing up the ward, glancing at each bed with her face obscured by the head dress, a moment at the window at the top, then pacing back down again. I don't think I breathed the whole time, but I did shoot a glance over at Crawford. He was watching her too, his knuckles white on the top of the sheets, eyes staring black. She passed him, passed me, passed the next three beds and paced out of the ward, vanishing into the darkness of the corridor outside just a little too easily to be natural.

'"She'll come a few nights in a row now," said Crawford to me next day after breakfast, "and then there'll be nothing for ages, maybe even a year or so."

'"How do you know?" I asked.

'"My brother's been in here afore, and a couple of his pals knew about her. Word gets aboot." He was trying to sound knowledgeable and calm, but the fear was still in his eyes and his voice. I was pretty sure it was in mine, too.

'"Does someone die every time she appears? Or more than one?" I asked.

'"I dinna ken." He thought for a minute. "If the yin wis eneuch for her, what for did she come back last nicht?"

'"But she didn't kill anyone last night."

'"Naw," he sighed. "She was just hanging around. It's funny," he added, "she looks sorta nice. I mean kindly, like." He drew in a long breath, and let it out. "That just makes it worse, though."

'I nodded, though I wasn't so sure now. How could you tell, if you couldn't see her face? Somehow, the idea of going home was more appealing than ever, and the masseuse that day must have noticed the extra effort I put in to all the physical therapy. If only my damned legs would start working, I might have a chance.

'Again I fell asleep easily that night, exhausted by my efforts. Again, I don't know what time I woke but I was as wide awake as if they had applied that electricity. I should have said that although it was summer, the room was really dark: there were blackout curtains still left from the fear of Zeppelin raids, to encourage us not to lie awake on the bright nights. The only light was at the Night Sister's table, and that was a warm paraffin lamp: between that and the gap in the curtain at the end of the room, a dim light was all that showed any shapes in the ward. I opened my eyes carefully, and surveyed the ward. There was nothing odd in the lower half of the ward: I could see the Night Sister clearly, back at her knitting at the warm-lit desk. Then I rolled my head the other way, and there she was.

'She had just turned back from the window at the top of the ward, and at her usual soft pace, she began the walk down the rows of beds. Left and right she glanced, the elaborate head dress stately as she turned, left and right – and then she turned from her path, and stepped between my bed and Crawford's. I swear I was shaking – I could feel tears trickling down into my hair as I tried not to move. Still I could not see her face, but she turned, pulled out the chair, leaned over Crawford's sleeping form and felt his forehead, in a gesture so tender that it hurt. Then she took his hand in hers, and noiselessly settled down on the chair.

'Then I'm ashamed to say I fell asleep. I don't even remember feeling sleepy. You'll maybe say I dreamed the whole thing, and maybe I did – but in the morning, Crawford was dead.

'This time I was brave enough to ask what had happened, and I asked one of the kindlier nurses.

'"Well," she said, glancing over at the Day Sister, "we don't really know yet, dearie."

'"Are you going to cut him open to find out?" I asked, interested even though the thought of Crawford cut open was fairly appalling.

'She laughed a little awkwardly.

'"Oh, no, dearie!"

'But I was old enough to know a lie when I heard it, and when Crawford's body had been taken away and my masseuse had started her morning's battering session, I was more thoughtful than usual.

'And that night I was most certainly not going to sleep. I refused to drink my milky drink, refused to lie down properly, and instead of insisting, the nurses just exchanged a glance, and nodded. At first I felt I'd persuaded them – but then I wondered. If they knew about the ghost nurse too, if grown-ups knew, didn't that make it even more frightening?

'I lay there in the dark, watching the Night Sister knit, reciting school lessons in my head, pinching my ear or biting my lip when I felt myself drowsing. Now the beds each side of mine were empty, I felt terribly isolated: the other boys could have been miles away, shadows amongst more shadows, their little snores and grunts so distant that they could have been in some other wards, in some other hospital, in some other town. At last, just when I was beginning to think she would never come, there she was, as if the darkness of the corridor took form slowly until her figure was visible, her crisp head dress, her old-fashioned skirts, her pale hands folded in front of her. I felt the chill straight away, and it seemed that at last the Night Sister felt it too, for as the ghost passed her desk and nodded to her, for once she sat up, concern on her usually serene face.

'I felt my fists clench with fear as she began her steady pace up the ward, her head turning left to right, left to right. She passed me, passed Crawford's empty bed, passed the last bed in the row, and paused as always at the window. I wondered if anyone could see her from the outside, and if they did, whether they could tell she was a ghost. What was her face like? Could they see it?

'She turned from the curtain and set out again on her steady progress down the ward. Why was she here? What had happened to her? Did she kill the boys, or did she just know that they were going to die and come to keep them company? A kindly ghost, then, as Crawford had said; a comfort for the dying. I thought of the way she had touched their foreheads, the way she had taken their hands so gently. Yes, there was nothing to fear here.

'She passed the end of my bed again and it seemed to me that she paused very slightly. My heart leapt, but no: on she went, calm and silent. I didn't even bother watching her disappear. Instead I peered up the ward, reassuring myself that the boys up there, as far as I could tell, were all still snoring and grunting and alive. Yes, they all appeared to be fine. I turned to look down the ward – and nearly died.

'There she was, sitting on the chair by my bed.

'Her head was lowered, as if she were praying. Then she raised her eyes, and reached for my hand.

'In that instant, I knew there was nothing kind, no comfort there at all. I let out a cry, and leaped from the bed.

'Of course, I crashed straight to the floor. The boys woke up, the Night Sister jumped from her knitting and scuttled to see what had happened. She called a nurse to help her help me back into bed, but not before I had established two important things – the ghost had gone, without taking me with her to whatever level of hell she inhabited, and one of my legs – just one, but oh! how wonderful! – one of my legs had worked!

'So you see, I'm not entirely sure that fear is such a bad thing. If I hadn't been pushed into quite such a state of blind terror, I firmly believe I would have lapsed resentfully into a wheelchair and never walked again.'

Marian breathed out slowly, finally tearing herself away from Davie's expressive face.

'That was quite a story!'

'Well, it's true,' he said, feeling for his stick. 'Satisfied?' But she could see he was smiling.

'Thank goodness it didn't feature a Binnie, a Geddie or a Farquhar, anyway.' Ah, infant paralysis, she thought, annoyed with herself for not working it out sooner.

'Well,' he said again, levering himself up against the rock, 'I'm going to take a last hoke through my trench before the end of the light goes. There was something in it on Saturday, I thought, a small black circle, so I can't wait till tomorrow to have another poke at it.'

'I'd better go before I can't find my way home,' said Marian. She grinned at him. 'Good luck with your small black circle.' It was strange, but she already felt easier with him again. She tried not to let her mind go back to Sandy and the bridge. Pulling her bits of whin back over the bones, she silently said goodnight to the skeletal girl, and called goodnight out loud to Davie, who was already crouched by his trench, worritting with a trowel. She took her path down the hill very cautiously: it would be an ideal place to break an ankle, and then how long would she be stuck in this bizarre village?

She reached the lane eventually and strode out more confidently, though it was darker here where the dykes cast a shadow over the path. She shivered, thinking of Davie's ghost story. He had told it well: she was already imagining a silent, long-robed nurse stalking behind her, watching her from the folds of a stiff linen headdress. She had known a few scary nurses in her medical career, but Davie's certainly won the prize. Which hospital had it been, she wondered? Did she have any contacts there? Could she find out more about the story – or about Davie?

Then she did hear a step behind her, and froze.

The step had come from behind the dyke, behind the scrubby

hedge. A cow? No: she remembered that was a ploughed field, not a pasture. And in the hedge the birds had stopped singing.

The whole lane flinched when there was an almighty yell from the field she had just left. Forgetting the hedge and its mysteries, she hurtled back up the hill, stumbling and staggering on the rough grass. In the distance she could see the narrow silhouette of Davie, dancing up and down as best he could on one leg and a stick. Relieved he was not reeling in agony on the ground, she ran on.

'What's the matter? Have you hurt yourself? Are you all right?'

'All right? All right?' cried Davie, and she could see his crooked teeth glinting as she neared him, his grin splitting his face like a wireless grille. 'Look what I've found!'

He shone the pathetic strip of his blackout torch down at something at his feet. A strange, angular black shape lay there, and she had to crouch to see it more clearly, reaching tentative fingers to touch something that at first put her in mind of the tip of a wooden leg. But there were three of them, sticking up ungainly towards the dimming sky.

'What …? Oh!' She gently inverted the object. It was a milking stool, or something very like one, low and black with age. 'You dug this up?'

'That's right! The black circle was the tip of one of the legs.'

'But surely it need not be very old …' He was still dancing with excitement, and she hesitated as she spoke.

'Context! It's the context! The layer of soil it's in! It's under things that must have been there hundreds of years ago! But wait: the stool's not the only thing. Look,' he said, breathless, 'at this.' He moved a piece of sacking behind the stool, with the air of a magician revealing the climax of the trick. Under the sacking was a crumpled, blackened object, but its edges gleamed. 'All right,' he said, glancing at her face, 'it's hard to see here. But it's a metal bucket - and I'm fairly sure it's silver.'

'Silver?' Despite herself a thrill ran up her spine. 'You've really found treasure?'

'They're both treasures,' he admonished her, but she could hear the smile in his voice.

'Of course.' She touched the shining edge of the bucket, trying to persuade herself that was what it was, but the shape was contorted. Then her eyes adjusted. 'Oh! There's some kind of pattern on it?' Her voice faded as she wondered if she had mis-seen something, some accidentally crumpled surface, but Davie reached past her and brushed a little more soil off it, revealing a section of pressed whorls and twists, and even, as the blackout torch dribbled light over it, the head of a deer, delicately hammered into the soft metal.

'Oh, my,' breathed Davie. 'I think I'm sleeping up here tonight.'

'You can't do that!'

'I've spent the night in worse digs,' he said. 'I can't leave it. What if something happened to it? And I can't just lift them out and take them home: I'll need to draw them where they are and the light's gone. No, I'll wrap myself in my coat and tuck down against this rock.'

'Sleeping on a fairy hill?' asked Marian, trying to dissuade him with distraction. 'Isn't that a bad idea?'

'I thought you were a scientist! Anyway, I doubt the fairies are busy. There's a war on, you know!'

'Are you determined to stay?' she asked seriously.

'I can't leave it, honestly,' he said again. 'If I stay here I can draw the trench as soon as there's enough light in the morning, then I'll cover it over and go to work at the factory. At least then if anything happens to it, there'll be a record.'

'You're quite mad,' she pronounced, 'but I sort of understand you.'

'That's affa kind,' he said.

'But I'll bring you a blanket, at least. My grandmother's cottage has more blankets than a regiment.'

'Well, I'll not say I wouldn't be grateful,' said Davie, 'but you needn't worry …'

'I'll be back soon,' she said firmly, and marched back down the hill.

In half an hour she was back, with her basket refilled with hot tea and more sandwiches, and as many blankets as she could carry. She had changed into her slacks.

'That's an awful load of blankets,' Davie remarked, taking the basket with good grace. 'It's not November.'

'It's about enough for two,' she announced. 'I can't leave you up here on your own. So if you don't mind, the lassie in my trench and I will keep company with you and your trench, Davie Fraser. I never sleep, anyway.'

She secured one of the sandwiches, took a slug of the tea, and settled back wrapped in her grandmother's blankets against a rock at talking distance from Davie's, while he watched her in silence.

'I know what it is,' he said at last, reaching for a sandwich. 'You're so frightened by the idea of killer ghost nurses you can't bear to spend the night alone in your cottage!'

'Something like that,' she agreed, choosing not to remember that footstep behind the hedge. 'Now, have you any more good stories to tell me? At least they would help to pass the night!'

Chapter Ten

'I thought you said you never slept?' was Davie's cheery greeting when she emerged from her chrysalis of blankets the following morning. 'Out for the count, you were. I'd take it as a reflection on my narrative style if I were a more sensitive soul.' He was already propped against his rock, on his feet, with his sketchbook and pencil curled in his hands.

'Good gracious,' she managed. 'I haven't slept like that since the Blitz began …' She thought about that for a long moment, watching as the slate roofs of the village materialised from the morning mist below. How long had she been living like this, so on edge? And what had she missed while she slept? But there were other things to think about just now. She stretched and reached for the thermos flask, splitting the last half cup between their two enamel mugs. She stood beside Davie, holding his mug ready when he wanted it and sipping her own, while she stared down into the trench. In the grey daylight the upturned milking stool had the look of a dead animal, legs rigid in the air, while the metal pail seemed even less promising, something crumpled up and flung into the metal recycling. But she had faith in Davie: if he said it was a milking stool and a silver pail, she was happy to accept that. Davie took the mug from her hand and drained it, added a few finishing touches to the drawing, and folded the sketchbook shut.

'Can I ask you a favour?' he said, crooked face tilted.

'Mmhmm? I have to help Dr. Hanson today, and before that I have to pick up my coat from Mrs. Angus, but if I can do it around that …'

'I was wondering if you would just take these things back to your cottage for now? I don't want to leave them out here, and I have to go to work. And I don't think I want to tie them on to my bicycle and leave them at the factory during my shift, either.'

'No, fair enough. How heavy are they?' Between them they gently lifted the stool and then the pail from the trench. 'The pail would fit in the basket, now the sandwiches are gone,' she said, then blinked. 'The sandwiches are gone?'

'I was awake long before you, and I was hungry!'

'Well, right, I suppose. Look, if I just turn it like that, it should be safe enough. Now, the stool – that's heavier, isn't it?'

'The wood's wet, I think, from being buried. Here's a piece of sacking. You could come back later for the blankets, couldn't you? Or I could, but it might rain before I'd get back from the factory.'

'Oh, all right.' She pulled up her sleeve to check her wristwatch: it was still only just the back of six. She should have plenty of time: just as well, for Davie was quite persuasive. Between them they wrapped the stool up in such a way that it was both protected and supported, and a loop of the sacking made a useful handle. Davie carried it down to the gate where his bicycle stood, then handed it over, winding himself on to the saddle with his stick tucked in. He seemed to have taken no ill effects from his night on the hillside, though Marian was still suffering from an odd sense of unreality. She had not camped out since she was a child, with her brothers. Waking as the world came into focus around her was unfamiliar, but somehow refreshing – and she had really slept. She did not know whether to be pleased or annoyed.

Balancing herself between the basket and the bundle she teetered down to her cottage. Catching some of Davie's caution, she secured the two artefacts in the only lockable cupboard and for once locked the cottage, too, before she returned to collect the blankets from the dig site. Only then did she allow herself to stop for breakfast, as if that could be a return for daring to sleep.

Nine o'clock saw her walking down through the village once more, south from the square, and off to the old tollhouse where Mrs. Angus the seamstress lived. The two standing stones watched her as she approached, she thought now: it would not be hard to believe they were the last earthly remains of the horrid witch sisters Mrs. Binnie had told her about, outwitted by Canny Annie. Serve them right if they were, she thought with a grin, as she knocked on Mrs. Angus' door.

This time the baby was still asleep, and Mrs. Angus answered the door with knitting in her hand, half a row done. The Royal Marines Band played unusually *sotto voce* from the wireless.

Marian held out the seamstress' own coat that she had lent Marian, brushed and ready to go back.

'Oh, aye, come in, come in,' said Mrs. Angus, sharply efficient. 'A fly cup? I've to finish this decrease while I still ken where I am, or it'll come out a gey funny shape.' She waved the knitting like a little flag: it was an almost-finished balaclava. 'Help yourself: the pot's on the stove and there's a clean cup on the dresser.'

She retreated to prod the baby's cradle into rocking with a practised toe, and counted furiously under her breath. Marian found all she needed and poured herself a weak cup of tea.

'Thirty-one, thirty-two!' said Mrs. Angus, growing louder as she reached the end of the round. 'There, I'll ken if I leave it there. They're just saying on the news there,' she went on, with a sour nod at the wireless, 'that starch isna patriotic any more: I'll have to use gum Arabic. What next? Now, it was your coat, was it no?'

Marian had laid down Mrs. Angus' coat on a chair and the seamstress whisked it up and away, and disappeared into a back room. In a moment she was back with Marian's own coat, showing her the mend. In the warm pile of the woven wool, it was barely visible.

'Oh, that's lovely!' Marian exclaimed. 'Hardly a scar!'

'Aye, aye.' Mrs. Angus examined it herself, lips sewn together till she approved it. 'Sit and have your tea, though: you'll be glad enough of it, no doubt, when you're up a lanie somewhere trying to find Dr. Hanson's next patient.'

'I'm glad enough of it now,' said Marian truthfully, sinking into a Windsor chair where there was some little respite from fabric and wool. On the end of the arm hung a little grey soft felt hat, tufted with scraps of black fabric. 'How sweet! Did you make it? I think I saw the minister's wife wearing something similar.'

'Oh, aye, she has one. Look, see you can change the colours.' She snatched up the hat and reached into a box on the windowsill, flicked off the black fabric scraps and in a moment had fastened on different scraps in a flare of flame colours.

'Oh, that's clever! As many hats as you like in one!'

'Aye, nifty enough.' Mrs. Angus spun the hat on her outstretched fingers, admiring the effect. 'If you've an old beret you fancy doing up, I'll easy put the poppers on for you and make up some scraps. I've done one for my daughter and now all her friends want them, too.'

'I'll see what I can find, thank you!' It would make a change from her awful patient-visiting hat. 'And is all well with your family? I think you said your daughter was in Aberdeen.'

'Aye, that's right. Making camouflage nets. She says I've trained her well: her fingers go on long after the other quines. But not many stories to be found in that, I doubt.'

Marian set her cup down warily on her lap. Was there a story coming?

'They're not so great at story-telling in Aberdeen,' she said quickly. What was she becoming? A museum, a gallery of stories? A book of fairy tales, lavishly illustrated? She could see the pen and ink drawings of loch monsters, witches, ghosts and murderers – and faces, endless faces, inhabiting the village in a long crooked line down the years.

'I think I tellt you before I'd a story to tell you,' said Mrs. Angus, picking up on Marian's anxiety. She had also picked up a jacket from a neat heap of clothes, and found her way to a place where a seam had given way. She nipped a thread with her teeth and slid it into a needle, setting to her work. 'Well, have you the time to listen now?'

Marian glanced at the clock on the mantelpiece, thinking that if it was coming she might as well get it over with. After all, no one seemed to think they had the right to tell her two stories.

'I could listen to part of it now,' she suggested, 'and hear the rest next time.' That would be all right, she thought: she could come back and listen again, if she had time before she left.

'No, no,' said Bathia Angus, more urgently than she had expected. 'A story broken off is like an unravelling seam – if you don't pick it up straight away, who knows where it might end?'

Marian looked again at the clock, calculating, and then realised she was in no hurry at all. Her timetable had not yet been fully arranged with Dr. Hanson. He had not even told her a specific time to arrive. It felt like a small release of tension she had not known she had.

'Well, then, I'll stay,' she said, and the tone of her voice was not as patronising as even she had expected it to be. Bathia Angus carefully rearranged the jacket in her hands to make a new angle, and finished off the first length of thread which she had used with remarkable speed. She replaced it with another in such silence that Marian wondered if she had forgotten she was to tell a story at all.

'A long time ago, before the last war – aye, I think it was maybe during the war before that – a woman ran the Post Office here. She took it over from her father. Her brother was to have done it, but her brother had other ideas and when the father died he leapt off to India before the woman could blink and left her to it. Not that she minded, for she loved her brother dearly, and if she had had to give more for his freedom she would have, and never counted the cost, even though she missed him every day. And it was a quiet wee Post Office, not much different from the way it is today, a few stamps or a telegram, parcels for the farmers or the doctor or the dominie, enough business to keep it going and not too much to wear her out. The pay made her nicely independent, for no man had ever taken too much interest in the idea of marrying her, and if she was not maybe as generous to her neighbours as others of her step in society it was less from a lack of good intent and more from an over-active imagination – she was anxious not to cause offence, or embarrass anyone, for she didn't want to seem above her station in any way. Instead she gave generously when anyone asked, or to the church collection. And she wasna rich, mind, and lived modestly enough, on her own in the Post Office. She had a wee bit put by for when the Post Office no longer needed her. Ach, she was a good wee body altogether. You'd have liked her, or so my own mother said.

'Anyway, two or three of the lads from the village had gone off to the war with the Gordons, and all of them had died on the one day, at Spion Kop, I think they cried it. One of them was my own uncle. The village was hit hard: times here was gey dark, and all was misery.

'Then one day the postmistress had a letter from her brother – now, if you'd brothers yourself you'd know that's not always a common thing! No doubt he minded her fondly when he minded her at all, and on this occasion he said he'd had her in mind on her birthday, raised a toast to her, and had bought her a lovely shawl, which he would send her under separate cover.

'Well, the postmistress was that excited, it was bubbling up inside her. For she had no one that bought her bonny things, or made much of her, for her own wee circle of friends was as careful as she was herself and would have been puzzled how to give anyone a treat, even themselves. To begin with, though, she told no one, for she wasna sure what to say or how not to sound overproud, and besides, she was the kind that, after the first moment's excitement, would remind herself that nothing ever turned out as good as she'd hoped, that the shawl might never arrive, that it might be spoiled by the journey or she herself might take ill and die before it ever came. For her brother was not wholly reliable, you'll understand.

'Then one day, two-three days after the letter came, she was sitting ceilidhing with her friends one evening when the others fell to reflecting that there was never any good news these days, that the world was surely gone to rack and ruin and what was the point in living any longer at all?

'"Well," she said, wanting to cheer the party up and dispel these unholy thoughts, "I had a wee bit of good news the other day."

'"And what might that be?" they asked.

'"Well, I had word from Johnny in Benares," she said, "and all's well with him."

'"That's what I mean,' said old Chrissie Ogston. "It's come to a poor time if the best we can say is that someone's all right."

'"Well," said the postmistress, trying harder, "he's to send me a shawl."

Her friends took the words and examined them for a minute in silence, looking for the pros and the cons, picking at the loose threads to see if they would come away.

'"A shawl?" said Chrissie slowly. "That sounds fine."

'"Aye," agreed the others, and whole mood of the wee room just lifted. "That sounds awful fine."

'"Did he say what like of a shawl?" asked Hendry Farquhar's widow, the one that was – well, ye'll ken that story.

'"Not exactly," said the postmistress, and she allowed herself a wee, quiet smile. "But he cried it bonny, right enough."

'"A shawl fae India," Chrissie breathed, as if it was just starting to sink in. "It'll be bound to be better than what they get in Aberdeen."

'"Maybe even better than Glasgow," said Hendry Farquhar's

widow, for Glasgow was where the Indiamen came in, and Glasgow's warehouses had the finest of all shawls, striped or paisley or self-coloured, the most delicate wool or silk, and fringes that would hang heavy and trig, just perfection.

'"Well, now," said the postmistress, "bear in mind that it's a loon that's choosing it!"

'"Aye, indeed!" And they all laughed, and a few of them had well-kent stories of the times their menfolk had chosen things for them, and they took it in turn to tell them till the teapot was empty the fourth time, and the scones were long gone. The women rose to go, with winces and grunts as their knees and backs told their own stories, but as they went they all patted the postmistress on the arm and agreed that it would no doubt be the finest shawl they had ever set eyes on, and indeed a light had come into all their eyes for the sake of a wee thing of pleasure to look forward to. And more than one of them that night wished their own brothers far off in Benares to send them back a shawl that would be the envy of the village. And the postmistress prayed as she always did for her brother, and slept, and dreamed of a shawl the size of a carpet, of such staggering magnificence that when she woke she laughed heartily at herself and made it, in her head, back into the size of a pocket handkerchief in an unflattering shade of green, just to teach herself not to expect too much.

'Well, the winter weeks went by and the days lengthened, though they were never as long as they seemed to be to the old women of the village. Not a day went by when one or more of them wouldn't be in the post office asking if the parcel had arrived, and soon Easter communions were looming and no shawl had appeared. The postmistress tried her best to forget all about it, and was sorry she had mentioned it to her friends, though their excitement was as contagious as scarlet fever.

'Three weeks before Easter, a big bale arrived for the tiny draper's in the village, the one my own grandmother ran. She was a bitty young to be in the same circle as the postmistress, ye ken. The bale contained the spring shawls from Glasgow, and very fine they were – there was one in kingfisher blue that all the old women felt was very much their colour, and each considered investing some of their savings in it. But they all agreed, every one, that even the kingfisher blue shawl in all its iridescent glory would be nothing beside the one from Benares, and in truth the shawl trade didn't do so well that Spring, for they were all waiting to be outdone by the postmistress's giftie.

'Then, with just two weeks to go to the Easter communions, on a Friday, a cotton-wrapped package arrived for the postmistress. She smiled: not the size of a carpet, then, she thought, at the same time pleased that it had come in a load of other parcels of seeds and the like and no one had noticed it. She blinked at the cost of the stamps, then slid it under the counter with a wee squeeze, determined to wait till dinner time before she would open it.

'The morning went with all the speed of treacle pouring from a tap. Every minute dragged, until she finally turned the sign to 'Closed' and latched the door. Then she made herself go and put the kettle on, deliberately, before she fetched the parcel and a pair of sharp scissors and sat at the kitchen table, carefully cutting the stitches.

'The cotton was double-layered, and it took a little while, going cannily, to cut it away, for she was not the kind of woman to cut the cotton through if she didn't have to. At last, it was undone, and she turned back the last bit, lifted the shawl and spread it out.

'Whatever she had told herself about not being disappointed was forgotten.

'The shawl was squint, though that could be remedied to an extent with a careful pressing. The fringe was uneven, which was less easily fixed. But worse than either, and unfixable, was the smudged pattern, the run colours, the staining, the garish blend of the whole thing. It lay there on the kitchen table like a misbegotten rag.

'She was torn in her heart, wanting to blame Johnny, ashamed of him before her friends, wanting to defend him to them, to protect him in his ignorance, to protect them, too, from the terrible disappointment she knew they would feel. And as she turned it all over in her mind, her heart emptied and she felt as if it had been pressed flat in her despair.

'All afternoon she worked away in the post office without mentioning it to anyone. She supposed she seemed quite normal: she felt herself smile at the customers, nod and respond to questions and comments, and if she didn't speak as much as usual, she thought, at least she could listen more, though in that she may have been deceiving herself.

'In the evening, she closed the post office and made herself her tea. When she had finished, she pushed her chair back and took down the old tin off the mantelpiece, and laid out its contents on the table. There was a little more in it than she had thought, which was good: she could afford something fine.

'The next morning, the Saturday, she did not open the post office, for she was away in the spring dawn to catch the train to Aberdeen. Paying no heed to the city, she crossed quickly from one station to the other and boarded another train, this time to Glasgow. She was not back in the village till after dark. Nevertheless, when she had put the kettle on she set to with the contents of one of her brown paper parcels, and for more than three hours the light still burned in her kitchen. And all the next Sabbath day she said nothing.

'On the Monday morning after that, she slipped a new parcel in amongst the deliveries at the post office, and made sure that she was seen discovering it. The scent of the East was still strong on the neatly stitched cotton, every thread carefully passing through an original stitch hole so that not even her own quick eyes could see evidence that it had been restitched. The Indian sealing wax which she had melted was artfully smeared over the knots. The ash from the kitchen stove brushed over any oddities, and as her friends paid their usual visits to the post office that morning, they could have seen nothing in the parcel to attract suspicion and everything to stimulate the greatest of excitement. To their questions as to her movements the Saturday before, she explained that she had gone to Aberdeen to buy some material for a new summer dress, and showed them the pretty and economical printed cotton which she would take to the dressmaker later in the day. And she invited her friends to come for a drop of tea and a piece that evening, for the grand opening of the parcel and the unveiling of the shawl.

'Not one of them was a minute late as they foregathered that evening. The postmistress had the kettle boiled and a fancy piece or two on a plate in honour of the occasion. Then, when they were all settled, she snipped the knots, unravelled the stitching, folded back the cotton, and with a little intake of breath which she had practised all afternoon, she lifted the shawl from its wrappings to show them.

'It slid through her hands and hung in the lamplight with the perfection of a peacock's tail. The silk shone in blue-green iridescence, the perfectly-knotted fringe hung and swayed and seduced the whole room, so that for a moment not one of them could find a word to say. And Chrissie Ogston finally managed to drag her gaze from this miracle and look at the postmistress, and the postmistress' eyes were wet with tears – "of joy2, maintained Chrissie, "looking round at the lot of us to see could we all see it, too."

'And the tears were part of joy, indeed, for the postmistress could see the delight she had given her dear friends. She watched them touch the shawl almost as if it might flow away at their fingers' ends like a dream, and saw the words forming in their minds to tell of this moment when they went to their homes, when they met again tomorrow, for years to come. She breathed again, and the lovely, lovely shawl, which only last week had hung in the most expensive and grand of the Glasgow warehouses, lay unbelievable in her own parlour.

'Well, she wore the shawl, over her new economical summer dress, to the Easter Communions, and then she laid it in a drawer and never wore it again, for what would she be doing with such a grand thing? And the sad rag that her poor Johnnie had sent her, and for which she had sent such a loving letter back, lay under her pillow, and it was a long time until its queer, Eastern scent had faded away.'

In the silence that followed, the baby in its cradle could be heard snuffling lightly, like a mouse in the skirting board. Marian found she had tears in her eyes.

'That's – that's so sad,' she said at last, 'and yet why? I don't even know why it's sad.'

'Because hope disappointed is terrible, whatever form it takes,' said Mrs. Angus softly. 'Hope of a long life, hope of finding love, hope of someone just remembering you exist and how they should value you. Faith, hope and charity, isn't that what the Bible says? Faith can be lost, and charity refused, but hope disappointed would make the angels weep, or even St. Angus himself.'

'So many different stories,' said Marian, half to herself. 'I suppose every village has its stories, but I've never heard them all before.'

'Och,' said Mrs. Angus, finishing off the seam in the jacket, 'you haven't heard the half of them yet. Have you asked Mrs. Forbes for her story? She has grand stories, as you can imagine.'

'I did ask her at the party, but she told me to try again another time. She didn't say she wouldn't tell me one,' she added, slightly defensively, in case Mrs. Angus thought she had not asked politely enough.

'Aye, well, no time like the present. Dr. Hanson's not expecting you till later in the morning when he's done with his morning surgery.'

'Are you sure?' Marian was taken aback.

'Oh aye. You've time to get along the now to the Castle, if you go along the main road here and in up the front drive. You canna miss it.'

'I'm sure.' She set down her cup and saucer in resignation. 'How much do I owe you for the coat? It's a lovely job.'

She paid and Mrs. Angus helped her on with her own coat again. It was only as she was passing the rounded windows to go down to the main road that she noticed in one of Mrs. Angus's neat stacks of fabric, slithering out of the side by the window, a beautiful peacock silk, flowing like water against the inside of the window pane.

Chapter Eleven

The main road, which had been a toll road, was not much of a main road now – at least, on this spring morning it was entirely devoid of traffic. A tollkeeper in the old tollhouse would not have been busy. One side of the road was dyked with a fairly kept estate wall in smartly-worked granite, like the estate cottages, while the other side had a ditch and hedge, and a view beyond them that spread liberally down over the broad valley and up to the lopsided peak of Mither Tap beyond. Gorse had been draped over some lower slopes, slipping down like a careless shawl, and sheep grazed unhurried in the rough pastures next to it. A train puffed secretly up the line from Aberdeen to Inverness, saying nothing of its going.

The gateway in the walls, which she came upon after ten minutes or so, was clearly superior to the one in the woods by the cottages. The walls curved dutifully to it to rise in high pillars, and there was a lodge, but it was empty and windowless, and the tall and graceful gates lay open, flung wide and abandoned. The drive, however, was better kept, and seemed to have been recently swept of its winter detritus, carving a damp black line through the fresh green parkland.

It must have been another ten minutes before the drive shook itself, like something in Alice, and led her to the large front door of the Castle. The white-harled towers, shabby though they were with wartime neglect, shone against the heaps of mature rhododendrons that were bundled around them, making up for the lack of garden otherwise to the front. It was like many another castle in this part of the world: defensible until the Victorians added their modifications, modest, and happed up well against anything the weather could throw at it. She tugged at a bell pull before she could lose her nerve, and waited.

Would there be servants? she wondered. Perhaps an elderly retainer, or a young maid. What girl would want to work here, though, when there was more exciting work to be done elsewhere? Would Forbes open the door himself? She gave a little shiver.

At last she heard footsteps sharp on flags, and the door was indeed opened by someone in uniform. It took her half a second to see it was Home Guard uniform, and another second or so to realise that the man wearing it was Lorimer Catto Rennie, the archivist L.C.R.

'Good afternoon, Miss Cowie,' he said, giving her a sardonic little bow. 'Do come in, Is Madam expected?'

'No, no I'm not,' she was forced to say, though she was sure he knew.

'I regret to say that Major Forbes is not at home, that is to say he is away,' went on L.C.R., in what he seemed to think a hilarious parody of the best of butlers.

'Oh, is he?' Marian managed, she thought, to be unconcerned. 'But it was actually Mrs. Forbes I was hoping to catch.'

'Oh, she's away too,' said L.C.R., relaxing. 'But come in anyway. They're both away out to visit the seething emporia of Aberdeen, though heaven knows what they'll find to buy there these days. Would you care for a cup of tea? I'm not sure there's milk, and I'm damned positive there's no sugar, but if the resulting infusion comes anywhere near what you would normally dignify by the name of tea, then you're very welcome to it. I was about to venture to have one myself.'

'Well, then,' said Marian, not quite agreeing. The hall was low and dark, with certain lowering portraits that made her feel unwelcome, whatever L.C.R. might say. The chill did not help.

'Are you admiring our poor old family portraits?' he asked. 'It's hardly the National Gallery, is it? This one is the Major's grandmother, a woman so ugly they have to hide her portrait down here to deter intruders. Of course she was tremendously rich. This one is the family's black sheep, a clergyman who turned Anglican and became a bishop in the English church, horrors! Here we have the two Jacobite victims, mother and son. The Forbes of the time was a devoted Government man, but Jeannie Ross his wife, and their eldest son Peter here were hanged for harbouring Jacobites, foolish children.'

Marian stared at the two portraits, hanging either side of a black oak mantelpiece. These, then, were the people Mrs. Geddie had told her about, who had protected Jeannie's brother, the big handsome Jacobite who betrayed them. Mrs. Geddie had never mentioned that the castle in question was this one. Jeannie was an ordinary wifie, to judge by the painting, and her son long-haired and pop-eyed, in the fashion of the day. Neither looked as if they might be related to anyone big and handsome, but then Major Forbes must be a descendant, mustn't he?

'And if you are interested in grim memorabilia,' L.C.R. was continuing, 'this was poor Jeannie's workbox, though why it should be in the hallway is anybody's guess. Too dark and draughty for any work down here. Come along upstairs: I'll show you the portraits in the drawing room. They're equally awful.'

He led the way up a broad stone stair which curled up gently to the first floor.

'The castle began as the usual Z plan tower house,' he continued, without any need of a show of interest from Marian, 'probably designed by George Bell in the 16th. century. The man came to the North East and spent his time churning out Z plan tower houses: you were simply nobody in 16th. century Aberdeenshire without one. Then of course the Victorians got hold of the place and played around with the idea of being mediaeval but could never resist sticking in drawing rooms and bay windows and nursery wings and a splendid new staircase you could hoist a grand piano up. Hard enough to sweep down a little spiral staircase in a crinoline, I suppose, but on the other hand the Forbeses were not rolling in money, even then, so the extensions were for the most part modest. A mercy for the original architecture, and anyway, it could be the salvation of the place. It's no use for large military base or a hospital, and it's much too near the village for a secret installation, I imagine … Here we are.'

'Oh, well, one can see why they might have added this,' said Marian at last. The drawing room was certainly a grand entertaining space, high-ceilinged, with a large empty fireplace centrally placed on one long wall, and three tall bay windows on the opposite side with a view over what must be the gardens, the ones she could not see at the front of the castle. The walls were hung in green silk, lightly gleaming, and the furniture was of the same material, but scattered with embroidered cushions, making the room distinctly more human. Gilt-based lamps competed with steel-framed photographs on corner tables, and the air, though cold, was fragrant with pot-pourri and fresh flowers arranged in a chinoiserie vase.

'They've kept some of the less awful portraits for this room,' said L.C.R., 'on the grounds that they are less unsettling just after dinner. That's Major Forbes' father, the laird.'

'The one who's in India?'

'That's the fellow.'

The portrait was unremarkable to Marian, except that there was a look of Neil, the Major, about the older man's jaw and nose. The eyes, though, were different.

'What does he do in India?' Marian asked.

'Tea, I believe,' said L.C.R. economically. 'If pressed, Mrs. Forbes will tell you he likes the climate, and she does not.'

'Didn't their daughter go with him?' She tried to think who had told her that: Farquhar, the chemist, she thought.

'Yes. This is the girl.'

'What a strange portrait!'

She had never seen one quite like it before. The girl was dressed in a red gown, almost, thought Marian, a robe, in a deep, rich red, disappearing into a shadowy background. Her hair was honey-coloured, long and loose, the colour of her brother's hair when she had met him in the woodland yesterday. Cradled in her hands, in front of her, as if she were handing it out like a treasure to the viewer, the girl held a lamp, the flame steady and true within a glass globe. It lit her face, tilted towards the light, but catching her eyes as she stared straight at the viewer.

'Remarkable, isn't it?' L.C.R. stared up at it, his eyes wide over the pince-nez. 'I could expatiate on the well-handled chiaroscuro, or the depth of the colour of that robe, but that's not what strikes me every time I see it. I've never met the girl, but if she's anything like this … And I never heard of her being married.'

'Tsk,' said Marian, hardly knowing what she was saying in the face of that portrait. 'What would Joy say?'

'Oh, Joy! Joy's delicious. All that well nourished hair, all those long, healthy bones and upholstered curves – everything one could want for a comfortable little fling! Or for intellectual conversation the best bet locally is that little schoolmistress, but she has about as much life as one of those standing stones by the tollhouse. But someone like that girl … you could spend years with her, and still never understand her fully …' He drifted away again, and Marian, embarrassed at his sudden confidence, turned back to the drawing room door.

'I'll come back later, then, I think,' she said over her shoulder. 'Have you any idea what time Mrs. Forbes might be back?'

L.C.R. shook himself like a wet cat.

'Oh, not for hours yet. Do come and have a cup of tea. I have the fire lit in the tower room: it will only take a minute or so, and there's a spare cup.'

She felt powerless to resist as he led her once again up a spiralling staircase, this one much narrower, to the next floor. Here a round room opened out to one side, hung with tapestries faded to almost uniform blue-grey and cosy with firelight. A little desk sat next to the window, and boxes were heaped about, some open, filled with well-ordered and folded documents bound with pink tape. This, presumably, was the slice of the nation's history allotted to him and his guardianship for the duration, his little bit of Edinburgh in Burgessie.

'Here we are: and do take the armchair. Tilt a trifle to your left – yes, that's the way. I fear some of the springs have gone on the right.' He poked his little kettle over the fire, and wiped the dust off the spare cup and saucer. It came to Marian suddenly that he was lonely here in his distant rooms in the tower, despite Joy's physical comforts. The war sends us all over the place away from our friends, she thought. Some of us just cope better than others, I suppose.

'I hear you're digging up on the hill with Davie Fraser,' L.C.R. remarked suddenly. 'But you've found a body.'

'That's right.'

'And not one of the proper archaeological period, either?' he prodded.

'No, nor a new one. About twenty years old, I think.'

'So the police – such as they are around here – will be seeking someone who disappeared around twenty years ago.'

'That's the idea,' she said, trying not to sound as cynical as

L.C.R. 'It's a woman, quite young. How news travels around here!'

'I like any kind of news,' said L.C.R., the charm of his wistfulness quashed by the little acquisitive smile on his thin lips. 'I miss the buzz of Edinburgh. Sometimes Burgessie feels like being condemned to a perpetual Sabbath.' He settled on a stool by the fire, and made the tea. He passed her the cup and saucer, and then with a wink opened a pink tin with flowers on it. 'Do have one.'

It was tablet, a sweet, fudge-like concoction, cut into squares. The smell alone made Marian feel dizzy. She reached into the tin and took one, hating herself at the same time as he smiled another knowing smile. Black market sugar, presumably, she thought, and tried not to scowl. The little corner of tablet was unbelievably sweet to one no longer used to such things: she could feel the sugar dancing already around her veins and arteries.

L.C.R. sat back in his stool and took his own cup and saucer.

'I can only think of the one disappearance I've heard about locally.' He managed to give 'locally' a particular emphasis, as if disappearances in the village might not be quite so socially or historically significant as those in, say, Edinburgh. 'Of course, I'm not a local antiquarian, so perhaps you could try someone else. The parish minister is usually the closest thing to a scholar in a place like this.'

'Well,' said Marian, knowing the signs by now, 'why don't you tell me about the one you've heard of? I'm sure a more cosmopolitan perspective would be helpful.' However short a time Lorimer Catto Rennie had spent in the village, he was as inclined to storytelling as the rest of them. She wondered if it was something in the water.

'Of course, my principal responsibility is the volumes placed in my care by the Keeper of Records. Nevertheless, I feel that if I've been posted out here I should keep an eye on the kind of records that have been generated by places like the Corporation of the City of Aberdeen. No doubt you have the impression, as they do, that the Corporation of the City of Aberdeen, and its county equivalents, have been in place since the time of Methuselah?'

Marian decided that a modest ignorance would be most helpful, and gave a self-deprecating smile.

'Ah,' L.C.R. was satisfied. 'Not at all, not at all. They are mere youths in the history of Scottish administration. Before them were all sorts of bodies, Turnpike Trustees, Commissioners of Supply, Justices of the Peace, which very occasionally took a decision or made a move of almost national importance. Now, of course their records are on paper, and paper is a popular thing at the moment, the War Effort, you know, and all that. I had a nasty suspicion that the Corporation of the City of Aberdeen and the council of the County of Aberdeen might be taking the opportunity for a little clearout, so I nipped down to the, ah, *metropolis*, to express an official interest. In the course of this little tour I felt it necessary to make an inspection of the records – after all, there is no point in insisting they be preserved from the bonfire if they have already succumbed to chronic borealic mould. The Turnpike Trustees' records were particularly legible, and I settled down with a cup of tea and a pipe to peruse their provincial history. Almost immediately, I came on a story involving this village and indeed this house, which of course deepened my attention.

'Now, the Turnpike Trustees in each county were a committee of the great and good – mostly the great – in the area who oversaw the building and maintenance of the turnpike roads. They auctioned off the tollhouses each year – the highest bidder would be given the right to collect the tolls at that particular turnpike for a year, in the hope of making a profit. In practice they were much the same body of men as the Commissioners of Supply, who were the real forerunners of the Council. You'll know there's an old turnpike cottage or tollhouse down by the main road, where it meets the road to Peterhead. You can usually tell them by that distinctive semicircular bay with a window facing each direction, so the keeper wouldn't miss any traveller passing.'

'You mean the seamstress's house? Mrs. Angus?' The house with the roundy windows, from which she had just come. Was she going to have the witches story again, from a different perspective? L.C.R. had delicately wrinkled his letter-opener nose at the thought.

'I believe there is some form of domestic work going on in the place now, yes. Well, the first mention of this tollhouse in the records I read was in January 1801, where the Turnpike Trustees brought up the problem of the absence of the tollkeeper. Now, some of the Trustees were clearly angry at this man, John Mutch, his name was, who had abandoned his post. Others had heard that there was a story behind it, and ordered the clerk to the trustees to make some investigations before the next meeting.

'I turned quickly to the minutes of the next meeting, and there was the clerk's report, engrossed, as we call it, in the minutes. He had visited the village, and found out, from several sources, he claimed (which probably means that he made his way to the inn and paid for a few drinks out of expenses – Mrs. Binnie may well have been the wench that served him) that the said John Mutch was a cripple – a description which in those days covered a multitude of sins – with a beautiful wife, Mary Barclay. Well, the clerk did not specify that she was beautiful, but I think we can deduce that she had some degree of charm, for the laird's youngest son, Thomas Forbes, stopping to pay his toll one day, spotted her and, as the clerk discreetly put it, desired her much. How the lady felt is at this point unrecorded, but apparently, according to the clerk's informants, young Forbes offered Mutch double his toll if he would allow Forbes to spend a night with the delectable Mary. Mutch refused, and the informants said – though from the clerk's tone I suspect he had his doubts – that Mutch was a decent man, and wouldn't countenance the idea at any price. I like to think that the informants were right, though: the honourable cripple, doing his best to protect his lovely helpmeet, rather than some scrofulous miser simply hoping for a better offer if he held back.

'Now, for a couple of weeks after that the young gentleman was seen hanging around a good deal, and travelling up and down the toll road, and one day, when the tollkeeper had a number of heavy vehicles to see through the turnpike, Forbes galloped up, snatched Mary on to his saddletree – is that the right word? I have no idea about these animal matters – and sped off. The good cripple Mutch was said to be 'gey angry' at this turn of events, as one can imagine – the arrogant young gentleman, probably with a fine horse, one of those arched-neck, small-eared beasts with a good deal of white in its eye that you see in the National Gallery, and the gentleman himself finely tailored, groomed and elegant, young, fit and rich, and there goes the lovely lass, her rough cotton skirts about her, her strawberry blonde curls – I like to imagine her with strawberry blonde curls – streaming behind her, her fair skin flushed with emotion, her shocked screams dying away to hopeless sobs as her gallant but helpless husband watches her go. Mutch, anyway, vowed in a terrible voice to fetch back his wife. Being a dutiful tollkeeper, he fetched his eldest son, a fine and decent lad of ten or so – possibly with his mother's good looks, as well as his father's sense of duty – and left him in charge of the turnpike. He snatched up his stick, according to the informants, though they do not tell the clerk whether this was to be a weapon or whether the cripple used it as a crutch, or perhaps both, and he set off bravely. And then, the clerk finishes ominously, John Mutch was never seen again.

'Well, this led to some discussion amongst the Turnpike Trustees. What should they do about replacing him, part of the way through the year? What responsibilities did they have towards his young family, now parentless, and their removal from the cottage? Should they sue Mutch for dereliction of duty, and if so, at what point should they decide that he had in fact abandoned his post? And finally, how could they sue someone who had so effectively disappeared? All the evidence pointed to his previous good record, and because of the dutiful son, through his childish tears, bravely manning the turnpike, the trustees had lost no money. There was a hint in the minutes that the general feeling in the village was that the laird's son had made away with the valiant Mutch (with the exception of a vocal minority who insisted on the involvement of a Mrs. Geddes, a decrepit woman with a certain dark reputation in the area), but there was no trace of a body, and in any case, the laird himself was one of the trustees, apparently at the meeting, so further discussion of that sort must have been difficult, to say the least.

'I read the minutes through several times, and pondered the case. When I returned here, I made a telephone call to my colleague, Dr. John Baird, who has custody – elsewhere in rural Scotland – of the Justiciary Court records for the period, and asked him to see if there was a case there against Thomas Forbes for murder – or indeed for abduction. There was nothing, as I suspected: a mere provincial case such as this would hardly have troubled the Edinburgh courts. I retreated to the library downstairs and found a copy of Burke's *Landed Gentry*, bearing in mind that in some cases Burke wrote first and did his researches afterwards –

a method which I find is not uncommon amongst some historians. Thomas Forbes was indeed mentioned, but as a younger son who did not inherit, he had not much troubled Burke who recorded neither birth, death nor marriage. I approached the local minister, and asked him for the marriage register, but he explained that it had been sent to Edinburgh, so I made another telephone call. My colleague Dr. Thomas Thomson – again, elsewhere in the provinces (I like to imagine us all, little pools I choose to describe as *urbs in rure*, scattered about the wilder parts of our romantic countryside) - found the record of Thomas Forbes' baptism, in 1777, and the baptisms of several of the children of John Mutch and the lovely Mary Barclay. Then there was an alarming record: the marriage of Thomas Forbes, gentleman, and Mary Barclay, widow, in February 1801. I did not like the smell of it. The witnesses, you see, were the minister's maid and Thomas Forbes' manservant, hardly the proper witnesses for a gentleman's marriage. My colleague could not, at that moment, he said, lay his hands on the burial register, which is hardly surprising, as burial registers are much less formal than baptisms and marriages. No one is going to argue with a death, but inheritance can swing on marriage and legitimacy. I left him to search, and returned to Aberdeen. In the library, I found the *Fasti Ecclesiae Scoticanae* – do you know it?' Marian shook her head. 'It lists all the clergy of the Established Church from earliest times to 1900. A scintillating read on a dark winter's night. I looked up this parish and found that the minister of the time was a Mr. Campbell, who had been appointed to the parish by the laird, John Forbes. He seemed a likely candidate for agreeing to marry the laird's son in an unconventional manner. A minor point, but a loose end tied up. I returned to the County offices, and asked to see the Poor Law records. In them, I found that the Mutch children had been given parish relief towards the end of 1800, but that it was stopped in 1801 when their mother had reappeared to claim them. However, they were back on the parish a few months later, as 'orphans' – though that could simply mean that their father was dead. What had happened to those pretty children? with their noble, dutiful brother? The parish had supported them when both of their parents had disappeared, but when did the parish discover that Mary Barclay was still alive? The parish was never slow to pass on responsibility for any charity cases to anyone even slightly more eligible. And then what had happened to return them to the parish in 1802?

'When I returned here, I found that my colleague in charge of the registers had called me back, and had left a message to the effect that there was no trace of a burial register for this parish. With a heavy sigh, I set out for the church once again. There is a Forbes mausoleum in the churchyard, as you may have noticed, with a carved list of the inhabitants in the doorway. There, clearly listed, was 'Thomas Forbes, youngest son of John Forbes of Burgessie, born June 1777, died April 1801.' Now we had children with a dead stepfather, as well as apparently a dead father. With some distaste I explored further about the churchyard – it simply is not very well kept, and I was forcibly reminded of legislation over the years concerning grazing animals in churchyards. I explored without much hope of success, but after a few minutes I managed to decipher a number of plain stones with the name 'Barclay' on them. Amongst them, rather hidden by the wall, was the one I had half-hoped for. 'Mary Barclay', it said, 'wife of John Mutch, died April 1801'. Well! 'Wife of John Mutch'! and died the same month as her supposed second husband! This encouraged me considerably, and I made a determined examination of the rest of the churchyard. I can categorically tell you that there is no stone surviving to the memory of John Mutch.

'I felt the hard surface of a brick wall before me. Where could I turn next? I had no idea. I walked slowly back to this house which I am constrained for the duration to regard as home, mulling over the whole story, how I had seen it from the angle of the church and the angle of, shall we call it, local government. Then suddenly it struck me – I had not seen it from the angle of the Forbes family. I broke almost into a jogtrot and as soon as I arrived back, I sought out Mrs. Forbes to ask her permission to investigate the family papers. She explained that she knew very little about them, but believed the older Forbes papers were in the west tower, and in the absence of Mr. Forbes she was happy to give me permission to examine them.

'The attic in the West Tower is full of rolled maps and tin boxes, and one or two rather splendid wooden trunks. It was hard to know where to start, but fortunately during the winter, when our manoeuvres at the Local Defence Volunteers were somewhat curtailed by the snow, I was able to take a hot water bottle and a candle and spend some time up there. Fortunately, as an archivist I have considerable experience in distinguishing the age of paper and handwriting, so I was able to dismiss a good number of boxes very quickly as predating the time of young Thomas Forbes. Then I opened a box with the initials 'S.T.' painted on it. I could not offhand think of anyone with those initials, but inside I found a number of shirts with the name 'Stephen Thomson' embroidered on them, and beneath them I found, amongst other personal possessions, an account book. Stephen Thomson, it transpired, had been the butler or steward to old John Forbes in the late 18th and early 19th century. The book began with an inventory of silver, glass, and china handed over to Thomson when he took up his post, but I pushed past such trivia of social history and worked my way through the book.

'Thomson began his career very carefully, noting expenses and income in the servants' quarters and very little else. But gradually, as the 18th century drew to an end, he started to mention his other activities and responsibilities, and his fellow servants. For example, in December 1800 he mentions appointing one of the servants to attend Mary Barclay permanently in the summer house, as the housemaid has been complaining of the mud when she has to go back and forth over the garden works. Mary Barclay in the summer house, forsooth! We cannot but hope that it was not a delicate oriental construction, not in Aberdeenshire in December. Then Thomson records asking the laird if Samuel, one of the manservants, is to have a new coat for Master Thomas' wedding, and that the laird, in refusing, was 'much angered'.

'Thomson's life was not an easy one: the welfare of the servants was his responsibility, and he was much saddened, I would say, when one of the maids fell pregnant to the servant of the garden architect – clearly, from that and the housemaid's comment above, the gardens were being redesigned for the new fashions – Capability Brown and his ilk. Then with a degree of weariness he mentions trying to engage a nursemaid for the children in the summerhouse - when they arrive. This must surely be when Mary Barclay reclaimed her children from the parish. Did the parish not know she was there before, or would they, for the benefit of the children's moral welfare, not release them to a woman living in sin in a summerhouse, even with the laird's son?

'Then matters become more mysterious. Samuel, the manservant who witnessed Thomas and Mary's wedding, complains to Thomson that there is someone about the garden at night, and asks Thomson to ask that the gamekeeper should help him patrol about the summerhouse after dark. Thomson notes that the gamekeeper has kindly agreed to this – Thomson would have had no say in the gamekeeper's activities, so this was in the nature of international negotiations. Nothing more is said for upwards of a fortnight, and then there is a shocking entry. I have committed it to memory:

'*Today such an ungodly scene at the summerhouse – Master Thomas stabbed to the heart, Mary Barclay throttled with great marks from Master Thomas' hands still round her throat, and in her hands clutched a bloodstained woollen bonnet, of a common sort. The laird is sent half-mad with it. What is to be done?*'

Marian gasped.

'So they had killed each other? Or had someone 'of a common sort' come in and killed them both?'

L.C.R. smiled thinly.

'My view of the situation is this. Mary Barclay, my lovely strawberry-blonde-haired lassie, was devoted to her poor crippled husband, and would only have married Thomas Forbes, however rich and handsome, if she were sure her husband had abandoned her. Thomas had somehow persuaded her that this was the case, but Mary, having married him and sent for her children, found the bonnet, John Mutch's bonnet, which she knew well having knitted it with her own fair hands. There were bloodstains on it, and she knew in her heart that her new husband had murdered her darling. She went for him with the knife, and he tried to defend himself with his bare hands, but alas, they were both doomed to die.'

'And John Mutch? Where was the body?'

'Oh, well, that much is obvious,' said L.C.R. 'Garden works? A garden architect there? John Mutch is almost certainly under some of that delightful Capability Brown landscaping you can see through the window there.'

Marian went to the window. Further away from the castle was the fur of woodland that spread up the hill to the church, but below in the garden there were certainly some picturesque arrangements of rocks and trees which could well have dated from such a period. She could even see a small building, stone-built and slate-roofed, with pretty windows, tucked into a corner of the garden wall – Mary Barclay's summerhouse? She was pleased to see there was a chimney, anyway, though it had hardly been much comfort to Mary in the end. But if John Mutch, poor fellow, was buried under the rockwork, he was hardly up at the Fairy Hill. Moreover, he was male and over a century old: it would be straining the facts to match him to Marian's skeleton.

'But do you know the worst thing?' L.C.R. had come up behind her, and was standing just a touch too close. 'The final twist? My colleague under whose guardianship are the old parish registers called me again a few days later. He had managed to locate the rather badly written entry for John Mutch's baptism, which took place in 1778. He was the son of an Ann Mutch, with no father recorded – but John Forbes of Burgessie was his sponsor.' He gave a meaningful grimace.

'You mean,' said Marian, 'that John Forbes was John Mutch's real father?'

'Yes.' Lorimer Catto Rennie nodded with a solemnity touched with glee. 'So Thomas Forbes, therefore, killed his own brother.'

A day in Dr. Hanson's busy surgery left her tired, more by the continuously changing human contact than anything else. She and Dr. Hanson had discussed the cases – he was too kind to make her feel she was simply reporting to him – over soup at dinner time, and it was growing dark as she walked wearily back up the hill on her quiet cork soles to the cottage. Black-out was to be from 8.29, she had noted in the *Press & Journal*, and amused herself for a moment by imagining a large house automated so that all the curtains swished shut at precisely twenty-nine minutes past eight, propelled by Heath Robinson strings and levers and set off by a butler with a stopwatch in one white gloved hand and the master switch in the other. She was smiling as she turned in to the path and stopped, surprised, at the locked door. Then she remembered Davie Fraser's treasures, and grinned again as she found her underused key and let herself in.

The stove had remnants of warmth left from the morning and

she leaned against it as she waited for the kettle to boil. Should she try to find a wireless somewhere? It would be company on a quiet evening like this. Back in London she would be waiting for the news at nine, if she was not out somewhere already. There the wireless blocked out the other background noises, but here there was almost nothing to block: behind the quiet roar of the kettle and the stove together, she could hear nothing at all. Or could she?

Was it the draught, rubbing the blackout curtain against the window frame? Had she made sure the window was closed?

She pulled the kettle off the stove, feeling her ears strain towards the window. She held her breath. Davie, come for the artefacts? Surely he would go to the front door, and not walk further than he had to. Someone else coming for the artefacts?

The bang on the front door nearly killed her. She leapt, spilling hot water from the kettle down her sleeve, and ran it quickly under the cold tap before hurrying to the door, heart thudding. Hand on the handle, she paused.

'Hello? Who is it?'

'Dr. Cowie? It's me, Netta Binnie.'

'Oh, Mrs. Binnie!' She scrabbled at the lock and opened the door. Mrs. Binnie on the doorstep was apologetic, with another woman Marian did not remember having met before. She did not look well.

'Did I scare you?' said Mrs. Binnie. 'I'm sorry!'

'No, not at all. I'd just spilled hot water on my sleeve, silly me! What can I do for you? Is everything all right?'

'This is Mrs. Farquhar – you'll have met her nephew, at the chemist's.'

'Mrs. Farquhar? Do come in, both of you. Now, Mrs. Farquhar, what seems to be the problem? Are you one of Dr. Hanson's patients?'

'It's no me,' said Mrs. Farquhar seedily. 'It's one of my lodgers – you ken a couple of the workers from the paper factory stay in my hoose.'

'I didn't, but I do now.'

'Do you ken Miss Joy? Joy Smith-Allenbigh? She's the one that's no well.' Mrs. Farquhar gazed anxiously at her, as if expecting an instant diagnosis. She was skin and bone, with large, dark eyes and protruding teeth that reminded Marian of a baby rabbit she had once had as a pet - even the woman's smooth grey hair was brushed back softly like a couple of long ears from her high forehead, and she wore no hat.

'I'll come at once. Let me get my bag.'

She slid quickly into her newly-mended coat and grabbed her hat and medical bag. Then as an afterthought she checked the kitchen window and the lock on the cupboard again, and made sure she locked the front door after her. Mrs. Binnie watched her inquisitively.

'There's little need to lock the door round here, lass,' she remarked.

'Well, you know doctor's houses – there's always something around that needs to be locked up,' Marian said briskly, discouraging questions. Mrs. Farquhar nodded knowledgeably.

Mrs. Farquhar lived south of the village square in a tall, thin house that had perhaps held a shop at some point on the ground floor, but was now entirely domestic. It was almost directly opposite Dr. Hanson's house.

'She's up the stair,' said Mrs. Farquhar.

'I'll away back to the inn now,' called Mrs. Binnie from the door. 'I hope the quine's all right.'

Mrs. Farquhar backed away from the bottom of the stairs, uncertainly, as a huge black cat undulated down them, almost knocking her sideways when it rubbed up against her brittle leg.

'Oh, Clement!' she breathed. 'Is it your dinner time, my darling?' The great dark eyes were focussed on the cat.

'I'll find my way, shall I?' Marian asked, and edged past the cat and up the stairs. Mrs. Farquhar did not even glance after her.

The first floor had two doors: when she knocked on the second one, there was a faint request to enter. Joy lay in a narrow bed in a room flounced and flowery, but in the midst of the frills she was far from the healthy, active dancer Marian had met on Saturday.

'Oh, you shouldn't have,' she groaned. 'I didn't want to make a fuss.'

'Nonsense: if you're not well – '

'I know: and I have to get back to work. We have a big push on just now.'

'So what's been happening?'

'I woke up this morning as sick as a dog, and I think I've just tired myself out being sick,' said Joy. 'Quite pathetic.'

Marian reached for her wrist to take her pulse.

'What have you been eating?'

'Oh, just the usual in the staff canteen yesterday. Nothing today, I promise you,' she added with feeling.

'What time did you start work yesterday?'

'At seven, as soon as there was enough light. I had breakfast in the canteen at nine – that was toast and that runny jam we get these days. Lunch at two, I think it was yesterday – we do shifts of a kind, all staggered. I had spam fritters and potatoes.'

'And dinner? Supper?'

'Oh!' Joy wriggled a little in the bed. 'I've just remembered. I was thinking I had dinner at the factory, too, but I was on an early shift yesterday so I came home. There was a note from Mrs. Farquhar saying she'd left a carrot pie to cool on the kitchen windowsill, but there was nothing there, so I had a hunt round through the pantry and found some leftover chicken. Such a treat! She feeds all her meat ration to her cat – I daresay you've seen it?'

'Huge black thing? Yes, I have. That explains it – I haven't seen as large a cat in a long time.'

'I think some of mine goes in there, too,' said Joy, without bitterness. 'Anyway, I was chilly so I put the chicken into a bowl of soup that was there, too, and heated it in a saucepan.'

'You may not have heated it quite enough. Half-heated chicken can be dangerous, you know.'

'Can it?' Joy was vague. 'I never learned all that useful stuff. I'll try to remember that one, if this is what it does to you.'

Marian found the chamberpot under the bed, and examined the last of Joy's vomit, delicately taking a sample just in case.

'I'd say that's almost certainly what it is. If it goes on tomorrow, send for me and we'll take a blood test. Or send for Dr. Hanson.'

'She doesn't like Dr. Hanson,' said Joy with an attempt at a grin. 'I'm afraid that's why she's hauled you all the way down here.'

'Then I'll come back tomorrow morning,' said Marian, 'and see you myself. Unless you've been fed to the cat before that.'

'Contaminated meat? No, never!' This time Joy did manage a laugh, and her face began to come back to life. 'You don't think

I'm preggers, then? I did have a couple of dark moments this afternoon, wondering if I was going to bear a child to poor old L.C.R.'

'It seems the lesser of the two possibilities,' smiled Marian, 'but I'll bear it in mind again tomorrow. Are you quite comfortable here? Mrs. Farquhar looking after you?'

'Oh, yes, when she's in. Everybody's busy these days, aren't they?' She gave a little sigh, but more of satisfaction than discontent. 'I do feel a bit better, anyway. If she's around when you go down, would you mind asking if she would do me a slice of bread and a glass of water?'

'I shall.' Marian gathered up the few contents of her bag that she had needed and packed them away. 'Many more of you staying here?' she asked. 'Any of them ill?'

'I don't think so,' said Joy. 'Davie stays here of course, Davie Fraser.'

'Oh? Does he?'

It had not occurred to her to ask him where he lived: he existed between the paper factory and the Fairy Hill. No wonder he had eaten her sandwiches. 'How on earth does he manage on the stairs?'

'He sleeps in the dining room, or what was the dining room,' Joy explained. 'We all eat in what was the parlour, I suppose.'

'Needs must,' Marian agreed.

Downstairs she found Mrs. Farquhar seated at the kitchen table, chin on one hand, gazing at the cat as he ate his dinner of perfectly cooked sausages. Marian explained that she would return in the morning, and asked Mrs. Farquhar to let her know if anyone else in the house came down with the same thing. Then she went home, but before she entered the cottage she walked all the way round it once, checking for breakages. Then she let herself in very quietly, and inspected every nook before she could make her tea and go to bed, dreaming of stealing sausages from giant cats.

Chapter Twelve

She had locked her own front door again, but Marian found Mrs. Farquhar's front door ajar when she went to see Joy next day. The cat, however, was standing guard in the middle of the hallway, and she was briefly reminded of Rob Geddie blocking the passage in the inn that first evening, slow and muscular. Was the cat going to tell her a story too? She smiled at the thought, but slightly nervously. The cat did not smile back.

'Is that you, Dr. Cowie? Do come up!' came Joy's voice from upstairs, and the cat, with a dismissive glance at the staircase, rolled off into the parlour. Marian could have sworn she felt the floorboards straining under its paws, but once it was clear she made for the stairs. Joy was sitting up and dressed, though her usually bright cheeks were still a little washed out. The room was tantalisingly scented with expensive cosmetics, which were neatly arranged on the ancient dressing table.

'At least I had the energy to do my face this morning!' said Joy, waving at them.

'Feeling better, then?' Marian took her pulse again, and tried the sound of her heart.

'Toast for breakfast! No egg, just yet,' she made a face at the thought, 'so I suspect His Excellency the cat got that, too. A pity – Davie could do with a bit of feeding up.'

'Have you been sick since I saw you yesterday?'

'Nothing left to be sick with, I should think. But no, no particular wish to, either. And Mrs. F. said she didn't know of anyone else with the same problem, so it must have been my own culinary skills. I'll remember that one.' She made another face, this one humorously self-deprecating.

'I take it Mrs. Farquhar is out?'

'Oh, yes, she works at the paper factory too. She said she'd leave the door open for you.'

'Shall I make you a cup of tea, then?'

'Gosh, I can't ask you to go running round after me, Dr. Cowie! I'm sure you have much more interesting things to do with your time!'

'Not at all,' said Marian, 'and it's Marian. You make me feel ancient, calling me Dr. Cowie, and I can't be much older than you. I'll go and see what I can find. Do you want more toast?'

'Just the tea would be lovely, thanks so much. But make a cup for yourself, too, yes? A fly cup, isn't that what they call it?'

Marian noticed she sank back against the pillows when she thought Marian could no longer see her, but apart from the general weariness brought on by a day's unaccustomed illness Marian was confident there was nothing else wrong with Joy now. The cat observed her closely from the kitchen table as she made two cups of tea. She nearly dropped them when the animal let out a tremendous miaow just as she was leaving the kitchen, but she was otherwise unmolested.

'Pull that chair over, darling,' said Joy, wriggling upright again on the bed. 'Thanks so much. Did the cat get you?'

'I think I still have all my limbs, anyway.'

'You did well! I'm sure we've lost a couple of postmen since I came here. Mrs. Farquhar claims they've enlisted,' she added darkly.

They sipped their tea comfortably for a moment.

'So what brought you here from London?' Joy asked at last.

'My grandmother owns the cottage I'm staying in, but she's moved into Aberdeen. My boss wanted me to take a break, and this seemed an obvious place to come.'

'No parents?'

'Yes, but they're tremendously busy, too, in Aberdeen. Father's a doctor, and my mother is with the Red Cross. I didn't want to bother them.' She took another sip. 'What about you? What brought you up here?'

'Gosh, I'm not even sure how it happened! I moved here from Edinburgh: Mother found me a job in an office there, but it wasn't really useful, you know? An auctioneer, very respectable, lots of art, but rather glum, too, at the moment. Before that I was in Sunderland in the harbour, but Mother didn't approve. Not of the place, nor of the job, I have to say! But it was such fun. We worked like Trojans and I have arms like a navvy – I went home for the weekend and when I appeared in my dinner gown Mother nearly fainted! Let me think: before Sunderland it was … an airfield, somewhere in Lincolnshire, rather dull job driving a fat old officer from the mess to his office and back, and walking his overweight bulldog in my spare time. Fat old officer was a friend of Mother's, of course, so I couldn't say anything. Slipped off to Sunderland on a rumour one weekend and never went back: she was furious. I think the fat old officer and his dog were quite relieved, though. Before that again? Oh, I managed a stint as a Land Girl before Mother caught me! That was a lark, though the farmer had a touch of Wandering Hands Disease. We dropped him in the duckpond in the end: that showed him. Before that? A spot of office work in Whitehall, but really, darling, I haven't the brains. But I love working! Mother doesn't understand it. And so, I suppose, I keep heading north to get as far as possible from her sphere of influence. Maybe I'll end up in Skye! Is that north of here?'

Marian smiled: in her experience the English often confused romance and latitude.

'You're thinking of Orkney and Shetland.'

'Oh,' said Joy, not the least concerned. 'I told you I wasn't particularly bright. Not like you.'

'You seem pretty bright to me. After all, I'm sure Mr. Catto Rennie has a high standard for his girlfriends' intellect.'

Joy screwed her face up again: it was wonderfully expressive.

'I don't think he cares that much about my brain,' she said, 'but it's lovely to have someone around who doesn't wince at my voice. I know I sound like a hunting horn, but I can't help it!'

'Nor should you!' said Marian impulsively. 'You sound so cheerful always, you're like a tonic.'

'Really?' Joy eyed her uncertainly.

'Really. The B.B.C. should have you on every day.'

Joy laughed.

'I'm sure I'm more use in the paper factory. I just like to know

I'm doing my bit, don't you know? Just like everybody else.' As if reminded, she reached for a small bag of knitting and began to pull out the work in progress, making Marian feel even less adequate than usual. 'L.C.R. doesn't quite understand, you know. He considers the war a personal affront to him, just there to stop him having fun in Edinburgh with all his cultural events and gallery openings and things. They sound an awful bore! So he tries to undermine the whole thing, playing little blackmarket games even though he has no need to. Do you know he never took sugar in his tea until it was rationed? Silly man! And he makes a point of over-filling his bath and all kinds of little petty things. Of course I would never tell anyone – he knows that …' She dropped her knitting suddenly, eyes wide. 'Only now I have, haven't I? Oh, dear: my poor little brain is in a fluff.'

'It's only your word,' Marian reassured her. She had seen L.C.R.'s sugar store herself, but still was not sure if she would do anything about it. L.C.R. took such evident pleasure in it she was sure he had some cunning ruse to hide the stuff if the police went round, and then he would be even more smug.

'We're all absolutely exhausted, which doesn't help, of course,' Joy excused herself. 'I had no idea one person could feel this tired!' At the same time, there was a hint of delight on her face, and it reminded Marian of the kind of tiredness that comes out of a strenuous country walk on a fine day – it went with windburn on the cheeks, and a healthy appetite, and weary limbs stretched out in a hot bath. 'But at least we're all tired together. Well, of course, we had loads to do at the factory sorting things out after the fire.'

'You had a fire? In a paper factory? That doesn't sound too good.'

'Well, you can imagine. It was an incendiary bomb, of course, or rather two. We think it was a tip and run raid, just something left over from Aberdeen – or at least that's what the experts say. It was during the winter … January, I think.'

'How awful. Was there anyone there at the time?'

'Oh, goodness, yes!' Joan laughed. 'The entire night shift was there, of course. I should know – I was one of them! We had quite a night of it! Has Davie not told you about it?'

'Davie was there too?' Her heart skipped. How had he been

able to get out safely? Had he not had enough to put up with?

'Oh – well, if it hadn't been for Davie ... Of course, he wouldn't tell you. He's not that kind of person.'

'Oh, I find him quite chatty,' Marian said, feeling an unexpected need to defend him even from a charge of silence.

'He is, he is! That's not what I meant at all. What I meant was that he's an absolute shocker for not blowing his own trumpet – well, look, I'll tell you all about it.'

Not you, too, thought Marian. This place must be infectious – everyone who stays here develops stories, like cancers. She found herself shivering, as Joy readjusted herself against her pillows with her knitting, and began her particular story.

'We were all working away as usual, with the gramophone playing *In the Mood* which is one of our absolute favourites, and I suppose it was so loud we didn't even hear the planes. But we certainly heard the bombs! They ripped through the roof as if it was a huge sheet of paper, and they landed with an awful whoomph, one in the stores and one just between the production lines and the office. It was frightful, it really was. I've been bombed out before, down in Sussex, but that wasn't incendiaries. I suppose it wasn't a paper factory either, come to think of it. It was only a moment before the whole place seemed to be on fire. Mr. Douglas, that's one of the foremen, he was running round ringing a handbell, screaming at us to get out, and we certainly did. But of course nothing goes according to plan, and I think my abiding memory will be finding myself in a kind of passage between untouched paper rolls – huge things, ten or twelve feet tall – on one side, and ones on the other side that were just a sheet of flame. And I remember thinking 'My face is burning, it's melting!' and 'I'm going to die!' and 'Aren't the flames simply beautiful?' and I could picture, even as I ran, the most stunning ballgown in flame red, and wondered if one could ever catch that depth of colour – watered silk, perhaps? The most ridiculous thing! I'm so shallow, really.

'It felt like hours but of course it was only seconds and we were all flung out by the flames into the snow and the freezing cold outside. It was like a slap on the face, it really was. And already the firewatchers had the bucket-chain running from the river – the buckets are always standing by – and everyone was helping to put out the flames while the foreman was checking us all off on a list. It was all working like clockwork, absolutely lovely. He came up to me and said 'Miss Mutch? Have you seen Miss Mutch?' Miss Mutch was the accounts clerk in the office, and she worked late hours. 'No,' I said, 'I haven't seen her.' He went on down the line and I could hear, over the slosh of buckets, a series of 'No, I haven't seen her,' and then someone said 'Mrs. Harris will know,' because she was the night office supervisor. She retired years ago and she came back to help out, just a fabulous old dear. She told me once that old people never need that much sleep, so she felt she might as well spend the night working for the war effort than sitting reading a book. And then everyone realised that no one had seen Mrs. Harris either.

'There was a hurried consultation, as it happened between Mr. Douglas and Davie and a couple of the line girls, and they said that the bomb had landed between the line and the office. There was a back door out of the office, but it was always locked at night because the safe was in there, of course. Did Mrs. Harris have keys? No one knew.

'And then before anyone really took it in, though Mr. Douglas says he did say he was going, Davie was off, hobbling back to the front door, faster than I thought he could go. And before anyone could possibly have stopped him, he had disappeared inside. Well, I thought that was the end of him, as much as I could think anything at all. The whole building was on fire, though you could still see it was a building. There was an awful pause, and then the firewatchers started yelling at us all and we realised we'd stopped passing the buckets, and of course we started again straight away, and even faster than before. And some of us were told off to empty some of the buckets round the doorway, and of course that seemed even more important to us for Davie's sake and we went faster still. It's amazing what you can do without even thinking about it!

'But we were all still holding our breath even as we swung the buckets back and forth – I had the most shocking blisters on my hands next day, though I didn't even feel the weight at the time. And it felt like an absolute age until we saw some movement in the flames, and there was a hunched figure, and it was just absolutely amazing – there was Davie, with someone flung over his shoulder. He must have the most staggeringly strong arms. People ran forward to help him, and took the body from him, and it was Miss Mutch. The first aiders flocked and in a moment she was coughing and sitting up, and everyone patted her on the back and turned round to congratulate Davie but he wasn't there.

'And this is the thing – this was the bravest thing I ever saw. Davie had already been through the factory to the office and back again. He had been along that passage of flaming paper three times now, once to get himself out and twice to rescue Miss Mutch. You could put that down to impulse, that mad bravery that makes you rush into the road to snatch a toddler from the traffic. But Davie – Davie knew what it was going to be like, and Davie went back in.

'Apparently we kept going with the buckets. I don't even remember. If fifty people willing something to happen could have any effect, Davie and Mrs. Harris would have shot straight out of that building like a couple of champagne corks. But of course they couldn't possibly, and time absolutely crawled, until at last, at long, long last, he appeared – and he had Mrs. Harris over his shoulders.

'Everyone rushed to help again, and pulled them both clear, which was just as well as I don't think he could have gone much further. I thought – I was sure – she was dead and he was dying. They had to roll out the flames on both of them, and someone burned his hand on Davie's callipers – you could see the line of them through his trousers, sort of embarrassing, really. They were both grey, really frightening, and we wrapped them in all the spare clothes we could find and very soon the ambulance arrived and off they went to the hospital at Insch.

'Astonishingly, they all pulled through! Miss Mutch was back at work the next day, though she still had a bit of a cough. Mrs. Harris has retired, though she's not too bad: she's probably balaclavaed the entire Royal Navy by now. I went to see her the other day and the needles were fairly flying! And Davie – well, you know how he is. He and Mrs. Harris were kept in for a week or so with burns and coughing, and then out they came: Dr. Hanson just whizzes people in and out these days, so you could tell he must have been a bit worried to keep them in so long. And then Davie just came back to work and got on with it. It does make you terribly proud to be British, doesn't it?'

Marian nodded, her throat oddly tight. She gathered up Joy's cup with a clatter.

'Well, I'd better be getting on,' she said. 'I think you'll be fine to go back as soon as you feel strong enough: let me know if you relapse at all, but I think you're through the worst.'

'Thank goodness,' said Joy, pushing herself up to say goodbye. 'I hate being ill.'

'You could have told me the story about the fire at the paper factory,' she said. Davie made a grunting noise in his own trench.

'Have you been talking to Joy, then?' He sounded resigned.

'Everybody tells me stories!'

'I hoped she might tell you the one about the time she had to take the fat old officer's dog out for a walk and it got stuck in a rabbit hole.'

'Not a chance.' She brushed more earth from around the skeleton's slim collar bones, scooping the loose soil away with her bare hands, and waited for Davie to speak.

'So she's been telling you I'm the great hero, then?' She could picture his face, mouth narrow and a little twisted, not too pleased.

'Not at all. We both thought you were rather stupid,' she said lightly.

'Stupid?' There was a shuffle as he sat back suddenly on his heels.

'Bravery and stupidity – two sides of the same coin, don't you think?' She sat up herself so she could see him, and grinned. He scowled at her.

'True enough.' He paused to inspect something small in his hand, subjecting it to a minute examination before tossing it over his shoulder. 'War time is ideal for that kind of bravery, isn't it? Lots of gung-ho fools flinging themselves over the top of trenches, laughing in the face of danger, simply because they haven't quite worked out what it is yet. When they do – then we'll see.'

Marian remembered poor Aleck and his shellshock.

'So you think the opposite side is fear and imagination?' she suggested.

'Well, I think fear and imagination are pretty closely linked, don't you?'

She grinned.

'Are you telling me you have no imagination?'

Davie's eyes widened.

'Oh, no, I can tell you, my imagination was working double time that night I told you about in the hospital.' He thought again for a moment. 'And no, I don't think they're the opposite, anyway. Fear and bravery aren't diametrically opposed. Someone who is afraid, but is brave anyway – well, that's more than the big boy's adventure running across France. That's the wee man with the rifle he's too scared to use, standing in the dark guarding a bridge on his own, surrounded by trees that terrify him, because he thinks he'll find his father hanging from one of them again, and all that to do his bit.'

She swallowed.

'You mean Sandy?'

'You've talked to the minister.'

She met his eye, fixed on her in a closed face, acknowledging that he had no right to expect anything of her. She struggled for the words.

'I'm sorry about Sandy.'

At once his face shone, awkward teeth lined up to grin.

'He's a grand lad, and as brave as they come,' he said. 'And he's much recovered now. He's been round to apologise to your Major.'

Marian's tongue tangled around 'Not my Major!' and 'Apologise?', a picture in her head of poor little Sandy marching up that long drive to the Castle to beg forgiveness. That was not right, not right at all, however wonderful and brave Major Forbes might be. She tried to form some kind of protest and stared blankly down at the skeleton for a moment, arranging her thoughts. But instead she said:

'Davie! Come and look at this! No – I'll bring it over.' But Davie was already angling himself to his feet and in a second was peering over her shoulder and into her trench. 'There,' she pointed with a grubby finger.

'Well,' he said, reaching past her to pluck the tiny object out of the soil, 'that's in better condition than my silver pail – which I hope you're still holding safe, by the way, and thank you very much.'

'It's silver, too, isn't it?'

'I should say so. That was – I snatched it up like a very bad

215

advert for an archaeologist, but I assumed it was from the body. Wasn't it?'

'It must have been. It was lying just here: on top of the inner surface of the right clavicle.'

'But that must mean – it has to have been laid there when or after the person died. But this ... I'm absolutely sure this is much, much older than that skeleton of yours.'

'Victorian?' asked Marian. 'The chain is like one my mother has, that belonged to my grandmother.'

'The chain ...' Davie ran it through his fingers, as if they could do the thinking. 'Yes, the chain is Victorian, I should say. Not really my field, but you're right, it's very like family ones. But this little piece hanging from it is not at all Victorian. It's a deer, wouldn't you say? Running.'

'And what's that stone between the antlers? This is ringing bells – did you tell me about something like this?'

'No,' said Davie, 'but I bet I know who did. You had a story from Farquhar, didn't you? The chemist?'

'The golden boy! Yes, that's right.' She struggled to disentangle it from the other stories woven together in her mind. 'Patrick Farquhar's father and the laird – I suppose that would be Major Forbes' father – found an amulet and a sort of gold shirt, didn't they? A breastplate: armour. I can't remember if he said what had happened to the amulet: the breastplate he said the laird took home.'

'I think maybe we need to ask him what happened to the amulet,' said Davie heavily. 'It's possible that there are two, but that doesn't seem very likely to me. What do you think?'

'Well, you're the archaeologist. But no – and particularly not if it was buried with the body.' She swallowed. 'Do you think Patrick Farquhar knows something about this skeleton, then?' The idea of probing the chemist for further information was one she found unusually frightening. Davie blew out through pursed lips, maybe thinking the same thing, and handed her back the amulet, swinging it delicately on its chain.

'Are you no nearer working out who she is, then?'

'Everyone I ask just tells me stories,' she said, but it sounded feeble. She sat back, fingering the amulet. It was warm and smooth, the warmth presumably from Davie's hand though it was almost as if she could feel it warm from the skeleton's living throat. 'Let me think. Patrick Farquhar said the laird took the breastplate. He said they left the breastplate and the amulet in the castle when they went back – came back – to the Fairy Hill and saw the vision. Not long after that, the laird left for India, and Patrick blamed him for his father's death because of something to do with bloodpoisoning when old Mr. Farquhar went to see the laird off at the tollhouse. He didn't mention Miss Forbes, though.'

'I'm not sure Patrick is particularly interested in Miss Forbes or her whereabouts,' said Davie. 'I don't know that I've ever seen him look at a girl twice.'

'Her whereabouts … She's supposed to be in India with her father. L.C.R. showed me her portrait – with which I'd say he's more than half in love – but he never mentioned hearing news of her, or where she is now.' Marian stared up at Davie, half-frightened, half-excited. 'She would have been the right age.'

Davie chewed his lips, staring down at the village. They could see the topmost turrets of the castle over the trees.

'The Forbeses would know she wasn't in India, of course,' he said carefully.

'Yes …' The Major would have been a boy at the time. Would he have known? She could hardly ask him.

'So either the Major or his mother should know – easy enough to ask,' said Davie.

'Do you think so?'

'You're getting to know the Major. You could easily ask him to tell you about his sister in India, and see what he says – and how he says it.'

'Of course. I suppose so.' She still did not like the idea.

'Or you can tell P.C. Argo what you've found and leave it to him – though he doesn't appear to be that interested.'

'And I can't hang around much longer – I must be getting back to London …' It was automatic: she hardly said it loudly enough to hear it herself. 'P.C. Argo, though …' She, too, gazed down at the village, pinpointing the police house for herself. 'I think I'll go down and see if he's at home. After all, I suppose this is evidence, isn't it?'

'Well, good luck. He's not the most approachable man.'

P.C. Argo was just approaching his own gate when Marian reached the police house ten or fifteen minutes later. His expression when he saw Marian was not particularly friendly, but he took the amulet from her with due care and took her in to the little office to sign a statement to go with it. She was about to go on to tell him about the Golden Boy and the amulet found by Patrick Farquhar's father and the laird, when she turned on a different tack.

'You said you knew a woman who used to be a maid at the castle, didn't you?'

'Aye, in Aberdeen.' Argo was still writing in a large and slow hand on a thick pad of paper.

'What was her name again?'

'Jessie Barclay,' he said.

'But that was her maiden name. What was her married name?'

P.C. Argo met her eye, his expression suddenly guarded.

'What for do you want to know?'

'I was hoping to go to Aberdeen and have a quick chat with her, that's all. Somebody told me a story about the history of the castle, and it got me interested.'

'Oh, aye, stories,' he snorted gently, but went no further.

'So where does she live? And what's her married name?'

He gave her a sour look.

'Now dinna you go getting ideas,' he said sternly.

'It would be hard not to get ideas when you're not telling me anything,' Marian said crossly, and P.C. Argo was taken aback.

'It's just – people get notions about it, and there's no need. She married a man called Friedrich Körner, all right?'

'A German?' Marian realised why he had been sensitive.

'Aye, well, his parents were. But he was born in Aberdeen himself. He wasna even interned, ken.'

'So she's Jessie Körner, then? And where does she live?'

'Kittybrewster,' said the policeman, on a long sigh as if he had been holding in the information with his breath. He gave her the address.

'Thank you,' she said. 'I shall go and visit her there.'

'You do that,' said Argo, pulling himself back to his old defiant self.

Outside the police house, Marian paused to fold the paper with Jessie's address into her handbag, and when she looked up again Mrs. Binnie was almost in front of her.

'In trouble with the pollis again, Dr. Cowie?' she said cheerfully.

'That's a fact,' said Marian, smiling back at her.

'Something to do with your skeleton?' Mrs. Binnie fell into step beside her, heading down towards the inn. 'Have you found out who it is yet?'

'I was asking him about the maid he knew in Aberdeen who had worked at the castle, actually,' Marian explained, not wanting to talk about possible identifications just now. 'Someone was telling me a story about the castle and I wanted to ask if she knew anything more about it.'

'That'd be Mr. Rennie, then,' said Mrs. Binnie knowledgeably, 'or old Mrs. Geddie.'

'Anyway, he gave me her address.'

'But you'll no need that. Did he no tell you? She's here in the village for a visit.'

'She's not! Where's she staying?'

'At the inn, just as a friend, ken. Between you and me, I think the main reason she's here is that one of her sons in the Air Force has got the D.F.C., and she wants to blow about it, but then who wouldn't? Do you want to come down with me and see her?'

'Yes, please!' It would be a trip to Aberdeen saved, and a quicker result than she had any right to expect.

The strawberry-blonde hair that P.C. Argo had remembered her by was strung with grey now, but Jessie Körner was still a very pretty woman, rounded by family life and wearied by wartime though she might have been. She was very ready to show Marian photographs of her two handsome sons in their R.A.F. uniforms, and her equally pretty daughter at a sunny picnic. She had what Marian thought of as a silly voice, and a tendency to adjust her hair and arrange her hands as if she was constantly ready to be photographed herself, but she was undoubtedly chatty.

'Miss Forbes? Oh! I can hardly remember her! That was years ago – when I was young, even younger than you!' She paused, as if she were accustomed to some little compliment when she remarked on her own age.

'Were you her maid?'

'Oh, no, dear: I was a parlourmaid, very smart. But it's true, after the Great War the staff wasn't what it had been. When she was getting ready to go to India, I packed her trunks for her. It was all laid out, of course, all I had to do was pack it in. I didn't mind, really – such pretty things, and anyway, I'd already given in my notice to marry my Friedrich, and Mr. Forbes gave me a very generous wedding present before he left – very generous indeed! Of course, I always thought he had a soft spot for me, not that he ever did anything he shouldn't do, never at all.' There was a little sigh there in her voice: she would not have minded too much, Marian thought, if the laird had taken advantage of her just a little. The silly voice grated, but she was amused by Mrs. Körner's wandering from Aberdeen housewife to refined parlourmaid and back again.

'What did he give you, then?'

'Oh, it was very generous! He gave us the deposit for our flat, so we never had to rent. It was so good of him!'

'Generous indeed,' agreed Marian, rather shocked. Was that a common present for lairds to give their maids, unless the maid was more to him than just a maid?

'My Friedrich, well, he was in service then too, but he had already decided to leave and he took up the position of head waiter at the Palace Hotel and he's been there ever since, a very responsible position as you can imagine. And he knows Mr. Argo very well, that's P.C. Argo's father, ken, for the pair of them take care of the air raid shelter for the stair and they have it really lovely between them, all kinds of little improvements all the time, I declare it's almost a pleasure to spend the night there now! But poor Mrs. Argo, she's not very well these days.'

'Oh, I'm sorry to hear that,' said Marian, realising input was required. Mrs. Binnie was busy making more tea.

'Well, it's the worry, I suppose. It's her sister, see: Mrs. Argo's sister Josie was married on a German, a cousin of my Friedrich for that's how they met, and she lives in Hamburg and there hasn't been one word from her since the war started and poor Mrs. Argo frets that much about her, it's terrible to see!'

'That's very sad. And certainly not good for her health,' she added, in a professional tone.

'It's bad enough she doesn't know if her sister's alive or dead, but then of course some of the shopkeepers ken she has that German connexion and they can be awful nasty sometimes. I mean, it's different for us, Friedrich was born in Aberdeen and they all know that, and the two boys in the Air Force – and you can't argue with a Distinguished Flying Cross, can you? My Albert has the Distinguished Flying Cross.'

'Congratulations,' said Marian dutifully, trying not to wonder how you would argue with a Distinguished Flying Cross.

'We're very proud,' Mrs. Körner said unnecessarily. 'And my Sarah in uniform and all. No one would dare to say anything to me about Germans – well, they haven't for a whiley, anyway ...' She finished uncertainly.

'It's good Mrs. Argo has the support of someone who understands, though, like you.'

'Oh, aye, we're great pals, so we are.' Mrs. Körner's gaze wandered off past Marian for a moment.

'So you saw Mr. Forbes and Miss Forbes off, then? Off to India?'

'Well ...' Mrs. Körner frowned, thinking back. 'Well, they went off, of course. And there would have been people saw them off, the big car heading off to the station, I suppose, and them waving goodbye ...' Her frown deepened. 'I don't know that I was one of them, though, now that I think about it. I'm not rightly sure I remember seeing Miss Forbes after I'd packed her things. Now, did I? I saw the mistress, of course, and the master when he gave me that very generous gift – I never expected such a thing! So generous!'

'But you didn't see Miss Forbes.' Marian felt a cold finger on her spine. It was no proof, but it felt like it. Could she have found her answer? Was the skeleton on Fairy Hill Lilian Forbes?

It was all very well during the day, Marian thought, but as soon as dusk came she made sure her cottage door was firmly locked, and now she checked that the windows were latched, too. She was sure there had been scuffling of some kind outside before Mrs. Binnie and Mrs. Farquhar had knocked on her door. It was chilly, and she contemplated lighting the fire, but it would be wasteful: instead she made a cup of tea and a hot water bottle, changed into her slacks, and went to bed.

She lay there in the dark, gazing up at the slanting ceiling she could not see. What were they doing in London tonight? She thought about her fellow volunteers, picturing them amongst rubble and dust and tumbling water. She should have a word with young Macfarlane about tourniquets: sometimes he made a real mess of them. Richard was very neat with a tourniquet: he could turn an old tie into a scientific instrument with a couple of deft twists almost too quick to see. Macfarlane, on the other hand, would never get a job in Harrods tying up parcels. Her own knitting was neater than his knots.

The thumping on the cottage door made her leap in the bed. She had her medical bag in her hand and her shoes on before the reverberations had stopped. Her coat and beret were to hand, ready in the darkness. Only as she reached for the door handle did it occur to her to call out to see who it was.

'It's P.C. Argo,' came the familiar voice, slightly nasal even in a shout. 'I've a medical emergency for you.' He made it sound as though he was doing her a favour, bringing it specially.

'I'm ready,' she said, and opened the door. P.C. Argo's blackout torch flickered over her.

'You sleep in your claes?' he enquired, more observant than she had expected him to be.

'Where's the emergency?' she demanded.

'Down the way. Come on.' He stalked off into the darkness, leaving her to push on her own torch and trot after.

'Where? Who is it?' she asked, struggling to keep up. 'What's happened?'

'You'll see.'

'You're not giving me much chance to prepare.'

She heard him snort.

'A fellow has hurt himself in the old summerhouse at the castle.'

'At the castle? Is it Major Forbes?'

'Naw.'

'L.C.R.?'

'Who?'

'Mr. Rennie, the archivist.'

Another snort.

'Thon creature? Naw. Dinna waste your strength asking questions.'

They passed the inn, silent in the moonlight. A bomber's moon, but no bombers here tonight. She thought of Joy's story of the factory in the fire, and Davie going back in for the second woman. He should get the George Cross for something like that. Whatever word games he played, he had been a hero. They crossed the square to the side road, past the schoolhouse, and she thought she saw the blackout curtain twitch very slightly. What was Miss Liddle watching for? P.C. Argo led the way round the corner into the road that led to the woods, and behind them she was sure she heard the latch of a door, quietly moving. She shivered suddenly.

'Wouldn't it have been quicker to get Dr. Hanson?' she asked, though it seemed cowardly.

'He's away out already,' said Argo shortly. She shrugged at the ordinariness of the answer, and felt better.

P.C. Argo led the way along the rough road and through the gates on to the woodland track, moving with confidence even as the surface deteriorated. She was glad she was not here alone: she was a town girl at heart, not comfortable in the woods at night. Hurrying in darkened London streets she was unconcerned by footsteps and voices around her in the blackout, the occasional slit-eyed car, the hazards of missing railings or crooked paving. Here there were whispers, covert animal movements, that owl again on hushed, conspiratorial wings. She tripped up and let out a cry, but Argo caught her elbow and righted her: the woodland fell quiet, waiting for her to move on. Just as she had here before, she was sure someone was watching her, waiting to see what she would do. Perhaps the woods were haunted – but there were far too many candidates for the position of ghost round here.

It seemed an age before they came to a high stone wall on their right, running along only a few feet away from the path, casting a dark moonshadow over them. Argo did not slow but made his way to a gate, delicately wrought with a leaf pattern in the iron, and pushed it open. Here at last he did pause, at the edge of the moonlit garden, and took stock of where he was. Marian stopped behind him.

The garden sat unreal in the moon's colourless glow. The beds were marked out with little walls, paths running between them, as she had seen it from the castle while L.C.R. was telling her his story of the abducted tollkeeper's wife and the laird's son. The wife had lived in the summerhouse, had she not? Was that where they were going now, to that summerhouse?

The castle was ominous above them, dark and severe against the night sky. Was Forbes up there somewhere? If he looked out, and saw her, would he come down? Was he already down, tending to whoever was injured in the summerhouse?

Did he know anything about the skeleton and the amulet?

Chapter Thirteen

P.C. Argo was still looking about him, like a bird on a wire waiting to take flight. She wondered if he was trying to pick the best route: the paths were overgrown, the plants flowing out of the beds, crisp with last year's unpruned growth. At last he eased forward, walking softly. He gestured Marian to follow.

The summerhouse, as she had remembered, was tucked into a corner, the door facing away from the castle, towards them. The building was ramshackle but she could see it had been substantial: no airy construction but a stonewalled, glazed hut, much more suitable for the summers of north-east Scotland. A wooden door was tucked under the shelter of an overhanging verandah, hard to see at night. The verandah creaked like a heron as Argo stepped on to it, and he froze. The garden was still. He moved slowly forward, and Marian, baffled at his caution, followed again. A faint waft of tobacco smoke tickled her nose, and when Argo opened the tattered door, the cracks visible even in faint torchlight, the smell grew solid.

'In, come on,' said Argo, waving her into the gloom.

'What on earth is going on here? Why all the creeping around?' Marian asked. She could see nothing in the little room, but the tobacco smoke had been joined by a smell of mould, and food, and human waste, and just under the rest the tinny scent of blood. She swung her feeble torch around, and jumped when she caught a movement against the far wall. She focussed.

A man lay on a crumpled makeshift bed of blankets, smoking listlessly. Even in the torchlight she could see he was a dreadful colour. Beside him on a piece of paper on the floor was half a pie of some kind, still in its dish, a scrap of bread, and a tin cup.

'Right,' she said, setting down her medical bag and taking off her coat. She slung it over the back of a mouldering basket chair.

'What's happened here?'

'He has a cut on his side,' said Argo.

She knelt beside the bed. It did not smell good.

'Who is he? Doesn't he speak?'

Argo said nothing. Marian examined the man's face. It showed all the signs of exhaustion, the eyes hostile in dark bony sockets.

'I'm going to pull back the covers here and take a look, all right?'

The man stared at her, but she might as well not have spoken. She gently folded back the blankets. The man's shirt was stained and ripped on one side, and lay unbuttoned. She slipped it back too, and found a nasty bandage inexpertly applied to his lower ribcage.

'This is probably going to hurt, but I need to see the wound. Have you any hot water?' she asked Argo.

'Naw. Cold, though.'

'Cold will have to do. And some kind of cloth.'

He brought her a bucket, which smelled clean, and a cloth which she suspected was his own handkerchief. She soaked the bandage, almost pleased to see the injured man wince as the water touched him: at least he was capable of some reaction. Gradually she eased off the evil dressings, as the man gritted his teeth, eyes scrunched shut, silently suffering. Under it was a single wound, small and round, at the lower edge of his ribcage. She pressed her lips together, and without touching him wriggled lower so she could see more of his side, trying not to block the light from the torch she had set on top of the tin mug. As she suspected, a few inches away from the first wound was a larger, more ragged scar.

'This is a gunshot wound,' she said flatly.

'Aye,' said Argo.

'What's going on?'

'Someone shot him.'

'Why doesn't he speak?' Argo said nothing. She sat back on her heels. 'This is the missing German airman, isn't it?' In the dim light she sensed, more than saw, Argo's shoulders twitch. 'A policeman aiding the enemy? That'll impress your superiors, don't you think?'

'I thought it was your job as a doctor to treat a patient and no ask questions?'

'That's a rather simple view, particularly in wartime,' she said grimly. 'I'm happy to treat this man – heaven knows between you you haven't done a great job so far – but I can't keep this concealed, whatever you've been doing here.' She leaned forward, starting the job of cleaning out the wound with the cold, soaking cloth. 'I suppose Sandy's shot was luckier than he thought.'

'Sandy's no a bad shot,' said Argo grudgingly. Then he sat down heavily on the wooden floor. 'He's my cousin, yon. My auntie was married on a man fae Hamburg, and this is her son.'

'Oh, for goodness' sake.' The skin around the wound was burning hot, and when she felt his forehead it was clammy. 'Have you been stealing food for him?' She nodded at the pie, remembering why Joy had been tempted to try cooking for herself. Argo made an odd affirmative noise, not quite admitting it despite the evidence.

'He was going to get away the night of the party. He'd had to wait until the cut on his leg had healed after the crash – he was gey weak with the loss of blood. I thought a'body would be busy, but Sandy was already out on his patrol and someone spotted him outside the hall and all. It all went wrong. And he heard you was a doctor, someone shouted it, so he tried to get you himself, so you wouldna ken where he was hiding out, but you'd started locking your door like a tounser, and he couldna get in while you were out. He's bluidy useless at the best of times and in the end he got so bad I said I would get you myself.'

'The wound's infected,' said Marian, thinking back to the times she had heard noises around the cottage. A German airman seeking medical assistance – not a possibility she had thought of. She drew over her medical bag and opened it, finding the things she needed by touch with quick efficiency. She had worked in worse conditions. 'If he had handed himself in this would never have happened. He'd have been cared for properly.'

'Oh, aye, is that what you'd have said to Major Forbes and his pals over in Belgium?' Argo asked, sullen. Marian opened her mouth to reply, but closed it again. He had a point. He nodded at the airman. 'Is he going to be all right?' he asked, his tone softer.

'Impossible to know yet. There's an exit wound so I assume the bullet has passed straight out, anyway. He'll need to drink plenty of fluids if he can. Can you get him more clean water? Or tea? Something hot would be good, and he needs to be kept warm and the wound needs to be kept clean. Can you make sure of that?'

'I'll bring you what you need,' said Argo, standing up.

'You'll bring me ...? No, I can't stay here. I have to get back to London.'

'You're no going anywhere till he's better and I can get him out of here.'

A chill ran down Marian's spine. How could she have imagined it would be otherwise?

'No, you can't keep me here!'

But P.C. Argo had something in his hand: he angled his torch to show her a heavy handgun.

'It's his,' he jerked his head at his cousin. 'I'll be leaving it with him, so you have to stay put. I'll bring you a flask of tea before dawn.' He crouched carefully, watching her for any movement, and pressed the gun into the German's hand. Marian saw the wrist sag weakly under the weight of the weapon, but the German was watching her. She swallowed hard, trying to keep the sound to herself. This could not be happening. She was in someone's story, no doubt, knowing this village. Someone was telling her about this happening to someone else, not to her.

She knelt again on the floor, feeling the icy damp of the boards under the fabric of her slacks. The German still kept his eyes on her, and the gun.

'Right, I'm away up the road,' said Argo. 'Behave yourself, Dr. Cowie, and we'll all get out of this nicely.' He eased himself back across the noisy verandah, and disappeared into the garden. The moon, Marian noticed, was already starting to sink, the moonshadows lengthening. She thought she heard the click of the gate, but she could not be sure.

'Well then,' she said aloud. The German's eyes focussed more sharply on her, forcing himself to concentrate. With the new angle of the moonlight, she could see the sheen of the sweat on his forehead. He was not in a good way. 'Do you speak any English at all?'

He made a muttering sound, nasally, the way P.C. Argo would have.

'Was heissen Sie?' she asked, a little unsure of herself.

'Heisse Hans,' he replied, indistinctly. 'Hans.'

'Ja. Guten Tag, Hans,' she tried. 'Or Gute Nacht, or something. Ich heisse Doctor Cowie.' She pronounced the name carefully. 'Sie sind von Hamburg?' She was unsure of the preposition, and hoped she had not said something stupid.

'Ja,' he whispered. Well, she thought, that's about as much as I can manage, unless we want to discuss the weather. It's a fine day today, Hans. What do you think of Adolf Hitler?

She leaned over with extreme care and some pantomime to avoid the gun, and rearranged the blankets over him to give him more warmth. The handkerchief was still wet and she used it to wipe his forehead. The cigarette he had been smoking was long gone, stubbed out in the corner of the floor, and though she did not much care for the smell of tobacco, it had masked the other smells which now crept to the fore once more. She ignored them, and moving her torch she sniffed at the water in the tin mug. It smelled fresh enough, and she lifted it to Hans' lips, encouraging him to drink. He took a sip or two, then leaned away from it.

'Much pain?' she asked, pointing to his wound. 'Sore?'

He frowned, nodding seriously. She opened her medical bag once more and found a powder, mixed it with the remaining water in the cup and again put it to his lips. He drank eagerly, understanding her. He nodded again when he had finished it.

'Danke,' he said. 'Das ist gut.'

'Gut, gut,' she responded, trying to sound reassuring rather than stupid. He closed his eyes, then snapped them open, staring at her distrustfully. She assumed an expression of innocence, hoping it would save her from being shot. But surely he would not shoot her here, so close to the castle? Someone would hear, and he was in no position to run away before they arrived. Not that that would do her much good, but at least he would not get away. No, she thought, best not to make him think of shooting her in the first place.

She settled back on her heels, her feet beginning to go numb. What would Richard do? Well, he would stay calm, in any case. They had never been in any situation quite like this, she thought, rubbing her ankles absently. What would he do? He would find some way to make the airman relax, first of all. His main aim would be to have as many people as possible come out of the business safe and sound, and the airman was the worst injured at present. Then he would distract the airman in order to let Marian slip away to fetch help. Help from where, though? Richard would expect to find the police on his side, not assisting the enemy. But if the team failed him in some way – she swallowed hard at the thought – if the team failed him, he would find the next team and summon help from them.

How could she possibly, on her own, distract the airman and escape from him at the same time? It was so hopeless she smiled. The airman tightened his hold on the gun, as if he suspected her of trying to wheedle it from him. She shook her head, and sighed, and tried to make herself a little more comfortable. Not sleeping was one thing, but this did not look as if it was going to be a relaxing night.

The hours passed. The painkiller she had given him took some effect: his eyes were less sunken, and the fever eased a little. After a long while she roused herself to check his bandages, and noticed him wince again.

'More powder?' she said clearly, pointing to her medical bag. 'Oh, but you've no water.' She picked up the tin mug and shook it out, to show what she meant.

'Nein, kein wasser,' he agreed. He struggled to sit up a little amongst the blankets. 'Ich habe ...' He shoved his other hand under the blankets. It reappeared with a hip flask. 'Fisky,' he tried. She frowned.

'Not very good with painkillers,' she said, and then a thought struck her. 'Maybe just this once.' She smiled to reassure him, and reached for another powder from her medical bag. Hans poured a little of the whisky into the tin mug, and she mixed the powder in with it, giving it a good swirl around before handing it to him again. He sipped at it, made a face, then downed the rest in one mouthful. She could almost see it burn down his throat. He grinned.

'Sehr gut, ja!' He lifted the mug in a pretend toast, and she laughed.

'Sehr gut! Now, you should try to get a little rest,' she said, miming lying down again. He wriggled compliantly back down into the blankets, and tucked the hipflask back where it came from. She waited. In a few moments, his eyes slid shut, and the gun sagged completely in his hand. It was true she had given him another painkiller, but not the gentle one she had first used: this was more like working with Richard.

She gave him a few minutes to settle completely, then rose, picked up her bag, torch and coat, and tiptoed out of the summerhouse, edging along the verandah to avoid the creaking boards in the middle.

She had just reached the corner of the verandah when she spotted a movement at the garden gate. She froze, gripping the railing. The cicatrices of the old wood, the scalpel-sharp edges of flaking paint, dug into her fingers. She half-turned away, hoping that her face would not show up pale in the dark. The moon had vanished now, and a mean dawn was leaking light on to the eastern sky, but it had not yet reached over the garden walls. She waited, but could see nothing more. A fox?

After a long moment, she slid herself down under the verandah rail and into a deep border flowerbed. It gave only a little cover at this time of year, but at least she was not walking on the grating gravel of the path. The garden was a dim maze, but the castle stood shadowy above it and showed her the way. She paused every few minutes and listened, but there was no sound of dispute. If that had been P.C. Argo returning with his pre-dawn tea flask, what was he doing?

At last she reached the castle and began to circle it, wondering if she would have to walk all the way to the front door to find an entrance. But in a moment she came to a set of French windows, part of the Victorian addition to the building. They were unlocked: she knocked gently, sure no one would be awake, but then slipped inside anyway, trying to find the entrance hall and the probable site of a telephone.

There was no telephone in the entrance hall. Feeling more and more embarrassed, she noticed a baize-lined door at the back of the hall: the way to the servants' quarters, she thought. Surely she would find a telephone there, and perhaps some servants, too. She tried the door: it was locked.

Could there be a study or a library where there would be a telephone? She struggled to remember if she had seen one in L.C.R.'s quarters, or in the drawing room, but she had not been thinking about such things that day. It was chilly in the entrance hall, more than it had been before, and if P.C. Argo was hunting for her, surely the French window was the first thing he would try. She drew a deep breath, and walked up the stairs and into the drawing room. There the long curtains had been swept shut and she used her torch to search the room. No telephone. The stunning portrait of Lilian Forbes loomed at her out of the gloom as her torch flashed on it, and she was taken aback again by its luminosity before turning the beam away, apologetic. The fire must have been lit the previous evening, though: she could feel a residual warmth around the fireplace, smell the woodsmoke, and she was aware of a lingering scent of mould and tobacco smoke on her own clothes. Tiredness swept over her. She sank into the corner of a green silk sofa near the fire, tugged her coat around her shoulders, laid her head on the high arm of the sofa, and slid suddenly into sleep.

The lady was sitting opposite her in a room flooded with morning light. Marian sat up and blinked, and then leapt from her seat.

'I'm so sorry! I beg your pardon – I must have given you a terrible shock.'

'You were so soundly asleep,' said Mrs. Forbes, her hands folded on her lap as calmly as if Marian had been invited to tea.

'I came to find a telephone. I wanted to call the police.'

'Of course,' said Mrs. Forbes. 'But there's no rush, is there? You must have a hot drink first: you must be chilled after a night here.'

'I – ' Marian began, but Mrs. Forbes was indeed pouring her a cup of tea in a pretty blue cup Marian was sure was Sevrès.

'And you wanted to hear a story, did you not?'

The cup rattled in Marian's hand.

'I did hear you told a very good story,' she agreed. Had she woken at all, or was she still dreaming? Mrs. Forbes sipped at her own tea, set her cup and saucer on a side table, and wrapped her hands together once more in her lap, her lavender tweed skirt smooth and controlled across her slim knees. She began without preamble.

'Once in this village there lived a woman who loved her lovely daughter. Everyone loved her lovely daughter. Her smile would light up a room, and even when she was a baby everyone wanted to hold her or cuddle her or just be near her. As she grew, she charmed everyone she met. Heads turned the moment she walked in. Grumpy old farmers whittled wooden toys for her, little boys with no interest in children brought her flowers.

'But the woman also had a son, a son whom no one noticed, to whom no one felt drawn, a boy who rarely smiled, who made few friends, adult or child. For this son, the woman had a love so deep, so great, that sometimes she felt her heart would not hold it all, a love such as some women have for their sons alone, a love a husband will never know – unless he had it from his own mother.

'In the sunny summertime, when children run free, the girl was twenty, and already attracting a new kind of admiration, a new kind of love. The boy was eleven, gangly and thin, his eyes the colour of muddy pools, his hair rough as if never cared for. The children had gone their separate ways that day, the boy to catch insects, the girl on some pursuit of her own about her friends in the village. The woman was at home, as women are, and on this day she was baking, the kitchen doors and windows wide to let out the heat, and with it the sweet, hot smells of fresh bread and pastry. Outside the air was humming with bees but little else stirred: the birds were drowsy with the heat, the fields nearby smelled already of harvest to come, the sky was a heavy blue blanket smothering sound, not letting the least breeze through.

'Suddenly she heard running footsteps. She was so surprised that she set down her rolling pin and stepped over to the door to see who could be racing so urgently into the yard. And there was her daughter, fair hair flying, running straight for her.

'"It's my brother!" she cried, her face filled with horror, and the woman's blood ran cold.

'"What is it? Where is he?" She could not bring herself to ask: "Is he hurt? Is he dead?" but the questions were already thudding in her mind.

'"He's in the hill!" And the girl burst into tears.

'Awkwardly, for she did not often hold her daughter, the woman put an arm around the girl, but she could not understand what she had said. She held her daughter, hushing her, while she herself counted to thirty. Then she let go, and waited for the girl to explain.

'"I met him by the stream in Ardo Field. He'd been catching

mayflies over a pool, and he showed them to me, but he said the heat was making him sleepy and he was going to rest for a while on the Shee Mound, and listen to the grating sedge warblers."

'The woman heard the words as if cold water were being poured into her blood. The Shee Mound? Was that the hill he was inside? The hill was said to have caves inside – could he have gone to explore and lost his way?

'"I said goodbye and left him there, and went on down the path towards the village. I was just round the corner when I realised I had left my sunhat behind, so I turned round to go back for it. As I rounded the corner in the path again I could see him lying against the side of the hill, asleep. And then I saw movement across the field, and I glanced round. There, crossing the field towards the hill, was a line of horsemen. I have never seen anything like them. There were about twenty, and they were tiny, and dressed in green and brown – for a moment I thought they were cavalrymen in training till I realised how tiny they were. They were ragged, too, muddy and torn and their ponies all winded and wrecked. They rode right up to him where he lay, and they stopped. Then just beside him, a kind of archway seemed to open up in the hillside. They rode in past him, and – Mother, I don't know how – when they had passed and the archway had vanished, he had gone!"

'The woman did not hesitate.

'"Stay here," she said firmly, and snatched up her rolling pin, and ran up the path to where the girl had last seen her beloved son.

'She soon came to the hill, but of course there was no sign of an archway. She walked once about the hill, examining it carefully, her steps slow while her heartbeat sped. Thorns grew over the top of the hill, but the rest was smooth and green, rising sharply from the flat, grazed pasture around it. She could see why her son might have liked to prop himself on the soft, emerald grass. When she had walked all the way round, she stopped, considering, and fingering the rolling pin. Then she brushed flour from her apron, cleared her throat, and called out:

'"You there! You in the hill! Open your door to me!"

'Nothing happened. She tried again.

'"You there! You in the hill! Open your door to me!"

'Then the thorn bushes shuddered, and in front of her, as if it had always been there, was a high archway – higher than she remembered the hill ever was. The wooden door within it swung open, and beyond was darkness. She took a deep breath, and stepped inside.

'The door closed smartly behind her, shutting out the heat of the day, and for a moment she thought she was in complete darkness. She flung a hand out, expecting to meet a damp earthen wall, but there was nothing. Then the darkness started to glow, and the glow grew brighter and brighter, and she looked about her at a great dazzling ballroom. She glanced quickly behind her: there was a long corridor which she had no recollection of passing down. It ended dimly, and she turned back to the ballroom, for even in the moment that she had glanced around the room had filled with people, people coming gradually into focus and the sound they made growing with them, as if turning a wireless knob could bring up picture and sound together.

'And the people – what people! Her daughter might have seen ragged horsemen, but here were princes and princesses, creatures of light and stunning beauty, shining with grace. The gossamer silk of the ladies' gowns swept and swooped and swung with their dancing: the gold frogging glittered on the gentlemen's coats, and every face, every hand, every lock of hair, every lady's waist and gentleman's calf was so perfect it made the tears rise in one's eyes. The music to which they danced was as intricate as lace, fiddle music and flute music woven into the air, and she felt as if she had never heard music before.

'There was only one being in the room, aside from herself, who did not share this perfection. At the end of the grand room, which shone in a way that owed nothing to the gleaming chandeliers above, there stood two thrones. On them sat a king and a queen, as lovely as the rest. And at the king's feet sat her son.

'He seemed longer than she had seen him that morning as he sat with his knees bent awkwardly in the knot of his arms, and his hair was more unkempt. There was an expression about his face of one who had seen that which he should not, and it hurt her to the heart to see it.

'So, turning the rolling pin in her hands, she strode forward. She paid no heed to the dancers, or to the silvery music, and the dancers indeed parted to let her pass, some with a laugh, some as if she were a pillar or a table, a thing of no note. The room must have been shorter than it appeared, for it seemed that only a few gliding steps took her to the head of it, before she had caught her breath, before she had thought what to say.

'She stood before the king and queen. They wore clothes of a green so true she could not imagine any other shade being called green. Their hair was the colour of snow and bright as starlight. The air about them was scented like fruit and flowers, and she had to concentrate to find a trace of the smell of her own earthly pastry still lingering about herself. She drew breath slowly: courtesy, she supposed, would do no harm. With a glance at her oblivious son, she made the deepest curtsey she had been taught, the one for royalty.

'Rising from the curtsey, she noted that the king's eyes were on her, so she spoke up clearly.

'"Your majesty, I believe you have something that properly belongs to me." And she gestured with her hand towards her son.

'"This?" The king's gesture was a little more dismissive, and she made herself ignore it. "This boy was sleeping in our doorway. We have a right to a tidy doorway, I think you would agree?"

'"By all means, your majesty," she replied. "But he is young and foolish, and made a mistake."

'"Mistakes should be paid for," said the king lightly, his eyes more on the dancers than on her. "The boy has joined our dancing and eaten our food. How is he to rectify this?"

'"Perhaps he cannot," she said, "and perhaps I can. Is there some service I could perform for you, in return for which you would restore the boy to me?"

'The king gazed nonchalantly at her, as if such a thing had never crossed his mind. She was bold enough to meet his gaze.

'"What kind of service did you have in mind?"

'"That would not be for me to say, your majesty," she replied.

'"Well, then, let us think." He made a show of pondering for a moment, then turned to the queen. "My dearest, is there anything you would have the woman do?"

'The queen's gaze flickered a little, then settled on the woman in surprise. She looked the woman down and up again, taking in her floury hands, her workaday summer dress, her hardy sandals and streeling hair. Then her silver eyes returned to the dancers.

'"The lighting of Benarrie is a concern, of course," she remarked without emphasis.

'The woman knew Benarrie, a hill not far from the village. It was unremarkable for anything but the regularity of its peak, a little cone of smooth rock set clear of the gorse and ignored by hungry sheep. The king had considered the matter.

'"Very well," he said. "You must light the peak of Benarrie, around the dragon's tooth. This is to be done with three and thirty candles and no walls, at the dark of the moon. Three and thirty – that should be sufficient, my dearest, don't you think?"

'The queen did not bother to contemplate her again.

'"Adequate," she said.

'"Do you agree?" the king asked the woman.

'"Three and thirty candles lit on Benarrie –"

'"In a circle, round the dragon's tooth."

'"The peak?"

'"Of course."

'She nodded.

'"Three and thirty candles lit in a circle around the peak of Benarrie, at the dark of the moon."

'The king suddenly appeared to be sliding away from her, and her son, too. She reached out, but the whole room was slipping away now.

'"I'll come back for you!" she cried, and at the same time, from a great distance, she heard the king's voice crying,

'"No walls, mark you! No walls!"

'And she found herself on the side of the fairy hill, her rolling pin in her hands and her head singing.

'She was no country woman: she had come from the town. She had to ask a neighbour when the dark of the moon was likely to be, and when she heard that it was to be in four nights' time, she gathered together three and thirty candles and a large box of matches, and waited. Every moment she waited she thought of her son: every moment she slept she dreamed of him. Her daughter was anxious, too, but a sister's care could never match a mother's.

'On the fourth night, she went out at dusk, a late, summer dusk that hardly promised darkness at all. In a basket she carried the candles and the matches and a shawl for when the night turned chill. Once she reached the strange little peak, she began to arrange the candles around it in a ring: she had plenty of time, so she took care to arrange them evenly, set the same distance apart, taking a pride in the neatness of the pattern.

'The sun dropped below the horizon almost before she thought of it, and a shiver ran through her. Up here it was darker than she had expected, and it took her a moment to find the basket with the matches. She fumbled the box open, selected a candle, and began to light them.

'She moved round the peak slowly and deliberately, leaving a little trail of shimmering flames behind her. The candles were fresh and new, and she had kept them in the cool of the pantry so that they would burn longer and more cleanly. They stood quite steady in the mossy earth, and if she flicked the stiff new wicks with a lit match, they soon flared into life. Concentrating on them, in her slow circumambulation, she did not keep track of her progress until suddenly, as she bent to light the next candle, she found it had a burnt wick. She felt it – it was still warm. It must have blown out, so she lit it again, and moved on to find that the next candle had also blown out, and the next. She began to go round the hill again, counting this time, but every candle she came to had blown out, while every one that she could see behind her flamed upright and still. She was not going to be able to light them all at once. What was she to do?

'Leaving the dead candles where they were, she seized her basket and hurried down the hill, stumbling down the path as best she could in the poor starlight. Bottles, she thought, but would the king count the glass sides of the bottles as walls? She was sure he would – then, as she thought of the shiny glass bottles, she had another idea.

'She hurried into the house and started to collect up every small, portable mirror she could find. Her powder compact went into the basket, and a shaving mirror from the bathroom; she quickly unscrewed a plain sheet of mirror from the wall of the downstairs cloakroom, and quietly, so as not to disturb her sleeping daughter, she slipped two hinged sections off her daughter's dressing table. Not enough: what else? The inside of her gold cigarette case – that would work: the shining shovel from the companion set in the drawing room, unused since the winter; a hip flask from the cabinet; a couple of silver salvers, but not the big heavy one. A fish slice from the cutlery cupboard, and finally the worn back of her own silver hairbrush, to match the hand mirror already in. Quickly she counted again – it should be enough.

'She seized a lantern, lit it, and set out once again with her laden basket, letting the lantern lead the way. She had checked the clock and knew she had time, if she was careful and systematic.

'Back on the hill she used the positions of the candles already there to set up a circle of reflection, adjusting the mirrors, setting them against rocks and bundles of moss two for each candle, or sometimes just one if she was clever. Then she returned to her first candle, held her breath, struck a match, and lit it.

'At once, candle flames sprang up all around the hill. She blew out the lantern, just to make sure, and the reflection of the candle at her feet, setting off via the powder compact at her left, definitely came to the fish slice on her right. Benarrie was lit by candle flames at the dark of the moon, all the way round the dragon's tooth. She had done it!

'Without hesitating, she seized her shawl and the lantern, relit, and set off for the fairy hill. Demanding entry as she had done before, it seemed to her that there was a defeated air about the doorway as it opened, and she permitted herself half a smile. The passage was as long and as short as before, and in seconds she was through the sparkling dancers and at the feet of the king. Her son sprawled where he had before, just as if it was only moments before, except that it appeared that his skin was smoother and his hair glossier than before. Again he had no idea she was there. What would happen if she left him here any longer? She tore her gaze from him.

'"Your majesty!" she said confidently. "I have completed the task you required!"

'"Have you, indeed?" said the king, apparently unconcerned. "I suppose we should take a look. No walls?"

'"None at all," she said firmly.

'The king gestured to an attendant, who brought from nowhere a large bowl. It was made of some glittering green stone, as if granite and jade had been stirred together. The king glanced into it, then passed a hand casually over the top. Sparks of golden light turned the bowl into a hollow globe, and in a moment within it was the summit of Benarrie, still encircled with the necklace of mirrored candles flickering.

'"Ha! Quite clever," said the king, passing his hand over the bowl so that the hillside within revolved gently. She found herself gasping as though the movement might blow out that first precious candle, but of course it did not. "See this, my dear," the king nudged the queen. She glanced down.

'"Oh! yes. But then, she has not done what you told her, has she?" asked the queen languidly.

'"She has lit Bennachie with candles at the dark of the moon," said the king reasonably, as the woman held her breath. "And no walls."

'"Three and thirty candles, you said," said the queen. "I do not see three and thirty candles. I see one candle, and an infinity of reflections."

'For a moment it seemed to the woman that the music stopped, and every dancer paused even in mid-step. Now she could not breathe.

'The king shrugged.

'"Then another task must be accomplished," he said. His hand drifted idly over the bowl so that the contents swirled, then one long white finger pointed and the scene steadied. The woman, feeling as though her heart had still not started to beat again, leaned forward to see. In the dawn light, for it must have been dawn outside, was a field of brown cattle.

'"I could fancy," said the king dreamily, "a bowl of warm milk fresh from the cow. And my queen is a great drinker of fresh milk, are you not, my dear?"

'"Wonderful," the queen agreed. The woman wondered if she bathed in it, for the queen's skin was so clear and milk-white.

'"You'll need a milk pail," said the king, "and a stool." The same attendant who had brought the bowl, a creature whose appearance was so vague that the woman found she could not remember it from one second to the next, stepped forward to hand her a silver milk pail and a little three-legged stool of some black wood, dense and heavy. She glanced at her son, but only just in time, for the room was flying away like the view at the end of a swiftly twisted telescope. She heard the king's voice over the music.

'"The pail must be full, you know!"

'The next moment, she was out on the hillside, holding a silver pail and a milking stool, as well as the lantern she had brought. They made an awkward burden, so she tied her shawl through the handles of the pail and the lantern and made a strap of it, slung them over her shoulder and tucked the stool under her other arm, and, dejected in the dull dawn light, she headed for home.

'She was not a countrywoman, as I have said. She was lucky to have recognised the field the king had pointed to as being that of a local farmer. The cattle were neither one thing nor the other to her, but she had lived in the country long enough to know that cows were milked morning and evening, and that no farmer would take kindly to someone found stealing the milk from his cows. It was to be another night-time task, then, she thought: she would go out before dawn tomorrow and take what milk would fill the pail before the farmer rose to milk his herd. She had no idea how many cows it would take to fill a pail, or if she would manage a pail's worth just from one. Needless to say, she had never milked a cow, but she had fed her own two children and surely it could not be too difficult? She had watched milk-heavy cows on the road, udders swaying with their steps, nearly ready to burst. It was probably more a question of popping a bucket under the cow and simply waiting for the gushing milk.

'She hid the pail and the stool in the pantry, and though she was tired enough to drop she made herself go back up to Benarrie and collect the cold candles and dewy mirrors, and pack them all back into her basket. She took them home, and washed and dried them, and put them all away, and only then stopped to have breakfast.

'After lunch and all her daily tasks, she slept for an hour, then rose and went out in the late afternoon to take a closer look at the cattle. It was the right field: the cattle were there, deep reddish brown, most of them, with a couple of clotted creamy white ones. To her alarm some of them had short, stubby horns, less dramatic than long ones, but somehow more efficient. She imagined the quick turn of the heavy head, the rip of the horn through her flesh, and shuddered. But everyone loved her daughter, and her son was loved by herself alone. She made a note to herself to wear a thick coat, and went home.

'She rose two hours before dawn, dressed quickly, found her

thickest winter coat and took the stool and the pail from the pantry. The walk was short, though she stumbled – she could have brought the lantern but again it would have been an awkward burden, and she did not want to draw attention to what she was doing. The faintest light had begun to tint the sky by the time she reached the field, like nothing more, she thought, than the promise of a shine under much-tarnished silver. She unlooped the rope holding the gate shut, opened it and closed it behind her, pulling to check that it was fastened. Then she stepped out cautiously, sensing more than seeing the nearest beast, reaching out for it in the dark as if placating it.

'They must be eager to be milked, she thought, for as soon as they realised she was there they began to gather around her, alarmingly curious. The brush of a horn against her outstretched hand made her shiver, and she had to stop herself backing towards the gate. Well, she thought, they are friendly enough, and she wasn't going to milk anything by standing there. She called up in her mind a picture of her son, lounging at the feet of the fairy king, and drawing courage from it she set the milking stool down gently. She sank on to it, making what she hoped were encouraging little clucking noises, as she would to her own hens. She ran a hand down the flank of the nearest beast, which brought its massive head down to nuzzle her, nearly knocking her off the stool. She steadied herself and the pail and felt cautiously where the udder would be, trying to see with her fingers that great swollen bag of pink flesh. All she met was hair.

'Puzzled, she kept feeling. The hair came to a kind of point and suddenly, blushing hot, she realised what it was. These kindly lady cows were not cows at all – nor ladies, either.

'Horrified, she contemplated the alternatives. A field full of bulls? But bulls did not all stay together, did they? She thought she had heard somewhere that they would fight. The light was growing stronger and she peered hard at the undercarriage of all the cattle around her. There was not an udder amongst them.

'Bullocks. The word finally came to her. She rose up, suddenly mindful of the fairy king's magic bowl, and shook her fist at the sky.

'"A trick!" she cried, and before the last sound of the word had died away, she was once more at the feet of the king. This time there was no mistaking it. Her son's face was taking on a kind of glow, a light that had never been there before.

'The king was watching her, too, for once, with an irritating little smile on his beautiful face.

'"Was it a trick? Yes, my dear woman, I suppose it was."

'"It was quite amusing, you must admit," the queen added, almost managing not to be bored.

'The woman clenched her fists, struggling not to say anything.

'"So, what next?" asked the king. "I suppose we should consider another task."

'"No!" The word burst from the woman's mouth before she could stop it. She drew breath and tried to steady herself. "There is little point in my striving to complete tasks that you have no intention of my being able to fulfil. Your – superior intelligence, your majesty, renders the exercise unedifying for all parties. But, your majesty, tell me, in all your grace and graciousness, is there any way that you will return the boy to me?"

'"But of course!" cried the king expansively. "We will be happy to give you the boy – and to allow you safe passage back to your home – for one small gift on your part."

'"Name it," said the woman, though part of her feared the reply. The king seemed suddenly to grow darker, more intense, as if he had been boiled down.

'"You're sure?" he asked.

'"Name it, and I shall give you my answer."

'The king nodded.

'"Then give us your daughter."

There was a long silence. Marian waited, watching the woman's face. Her gaze was far away. At last she drew breath.

'What more can I say?' she went on. 'For her daughter was loved by everyone, but her son was loved by her alone. He needed her. Her daughter needed no one. And her beauty would be preserved for ever in this strange kingdom, far from mortal decay, from sickness and worry and old age.

'She never knew what the other villagers thought – no doubt they talked, but not to her. Her son, too, was different, more handsome, more charming, as if something had rubbed off on him in his time in the hill, or perhaps it was just that he shone more brightly, once his sister had gone.'

Marian's head whirled. What was true and what was not? The Shee Mount, the Fairy Hill, was it the same one? Was the skeleton truly Lilian Forbes, and if so, what was Mrs. Forbes really telling her?

She heard her own voice tremble.

'Did the girl wear an amulet, a running deer with a red stone between its antlers?'

Mrs. Forbes stared up at the wondrous portrait of her daughter, glowing above them.

'She did. My husband found it at the Fairy Hill. He gave it to her.'

Then they both jumped as a voice came from the doorway.

'Mother, what are you doing?'

Chapter Fourteen

Major Forbes came quickly into the room, and knelt by his mother, taking her hands in his. She raised her head, but Marian had the impression that her eyes were not quite meeting his.

'She tells such wonderful stories,' Major Forbes threw over his shoulder to Marian. 'Sometimes I think she tells them so well because she half believes them herself. Don't you, Mother?' He stroked her face with one gentle finger.

'But Neil, dear ...' Her voice was thin and fine as gossamer. Marian strained to hear it. 'Neil, it really happened.'

Fairy hills and abducted children – she must be suffering from delusions, Marian thought. Perhaps she had had a heat stroke in India or Africa with her husband long ago, and the effects continued. She should be better cared for, not left here virtually on her own.

'Nothing happened, Mother.' His voice was warm and soothing, a hot drink and a pair of slippers by the fire. 'Let me fetch you some more tea,' he added, almost as if he had heard her. He rose to his feet.

'But she's up there in the Fairy Hill, dear, you know that.' Mrs. Forbes' words were firmer than they had been. 'She was buried there, and this young lady has found her, isn't that right, Miss Cowie?'

'Mother ...' Major Forbes met Marian's eye, widening for sympathy.

'Lilian's there, your sister. You know that, don't you?'

Whatever he saw in Marian's expression, Major Forbes stopped, held his breath, and then suddenly let out a great sigh, somewhere between exasperation and relief. He sagged down beside Marian on the sofa. She was half-conscious of the scent of his old sweater, a little smokey, a little earthy, like an old garden shed. She suddenly felt terribly sorry for him. She should not be here, witnessing this family shame, even if she was a doctor.

Major Forbes leaned over and took his mother's hand again, squeezing it gently.

'Well, you'll have guessed by now,' he said to Marian. 'Yes, the bones you found are my sister Lilian.'

'How do you know?' She wanted him not to be sure, to be able to be proved wrong, even if it meant she had to start again herself.

'I was only a boy at the time, but I still knew. Hard enough to hide it, wasn't it, Mother?' His voice to her was tender still, calming, though there was no fight in her that Marian could see. 'Mother was always a little – imaginative. She thought I resented Lilian: she was so beautiful, you know, and kind and sweet and everyone loved her. Father couldn't bear to think of what Mother had done. He helped to hide the whole business, but he left the country. He's never been back. I suppose he knew I would be safe with her, and eventually would be able to keep an eye on her myself. She's been fine for years, really: she's never been a danger to anyone else. But now, if she's becoming more confused ... I don't know. Would you be able to advise us? Where would be the best place for her?'

'I'd need to ask around – discreetly, of course,' said Marian slowly. Mrs. Forbes watched them both, but said nothing, as if she were watching some conversation that had nothing to do with her.

'Obviously we don't want her simply housed with ordinary lunatics,' Major Forbes was saying. Marian was watching Mrs. Forbes still, and saw her eyes widen very slightly. Had she understood that? Or wait a moment – had she heard something? Something outside the room?

She struggled to think. Mrs. Forbes had killed her daughter because she thought her son resented his sister. Brothers and sisters ... so many of the stories the villagers had told her had had brothers and sisters in them, brothers fighting beside each other, brothers sending shawls from India, sister witches in conflict, even brother monsters in the loch. Had they really been trying to tell her something all along? But that would mean ...

Major Forbes certainly had a temper, Sandy could vouch for that. If you kill someone in a fit of temper, are you almost a victim yourself? But then she focussed again on Mrs. Forbes: killing your sister in a rage was one thing – and not a good thing – but trying to blame your own mother for it was quite another.

What was that sound? She was sure there was something outside the closed drawing room door. Had Major Forbes heard it, too?

'Marian,' he said suddenly.

'Sorry, what?' He must have been talking on about burying his mother in some lunatic asylum. She stood abruptly.

'Marian, you do believe me, don't you?' His voice was like honey, his smile that of an endearing schoolboy who knew he had just a chance to get away with it. She tried to smile back. What would he do to her if he thought she had realised the truth?

'Of course I do. Of course. Did you hear something outside the door?' She began to walk calmly across the room, but a sound behind her made her break into a run. Her hand was on the doorhandle, she felt it turn in her fingers, and then the room went bright green. She had a fraction of a second to find that fascinating, before darkness descended.

The first sounds she heard as she came round were confusing. She kept her eyes tight closed, knowing it would hurt to open them, and listened intently, though the pain in her head increased. There were no voices, but she had the impression of more than just Forbes and his mother in the room. What was happening? Had Forbes summoned the servants to help dispose of her? She could hear the rustling of skirts, smell tobacco, but she knew Forbes did not smoke. What was going on? She felt an arm slip around her, a hand brush her hair back off her face, felt herself being gently pulled into a sitting position, and knew she must be showing some signs of resurfacing. Her cheek brushed a rough tweedy material, not the smooth felted wool of Forbes' officer's tunic. The tweed smelled of earth and grass. It must have soothed her, for she slowly opened her eyes.

The drawing room was full of people. There was Mrs. Forbes, still shrunken into her chair. There was Joy Smith-Allanbigh, perched on the arm of Mrs. Forbes' chair and stroking her hand, and Lorimer Catto Rennie, the archivist, standing beside Joy with a proprietorial arm around her as if Mrs. Forbes was serious competition. Dr. Hanson was at Mrs. Forbes' other side, but had a concerned eye on Marian: Miss Liddle was beside him on a stool, knitting calmly, and as if balancing her, Mrs. Angus the seamstress was knitting on the sofa, the leg of a sailor's sock hedgehogged with needles on her lap. Marian blinked slowly, and moved her head very slightly. Patrick Farquhar the chemist was there, carrying a smart ebony baton, and Mrs. Binnie, the innkeeper, was passing a cup of tea to her sister, the minister's wife. The minister himself was alert by the mantelpiece, his one hand on the shoulder of poor Sandy. Cammie and Agnes sat on the hearth, Cammie as usual with his notebook and pencil out, peering round the room and scribbling. And at the window, like some tableau vivant, stood Neil Forbes, handcuffed by P.C. Argo, and held under the watchful eye of Sergeant Leslie and Geddie, the farmhand, not in their Home Guard uniforms but by their stature soldiers. Geddie in particular held himself erect as if someone had rashly accused him of being a coward. No one spoke: nearly everyone was gazing at Marian. She wondered for a moment if she was hallucinating, or dead. But the arm around her was warm, and when she moved her head and met Davie's brown eyes, she was quite sure she was alive. Alive, but completely confused.

The denouement is the wrong way round, she thought. I'm like the detective who has gathered all the suspects in the library to tell them what happened, but instead they all know and I don't.

'How are you feeling, my dear?' asked Dr. Hanson, and the spell broke. Argo and Sergeant Leslie escorted Neil Forbes from the room, his face stoical as if he had been taken by the enemy. He was not a coward, anyway.

'I'm – I'll be fine, I think. What are you all doing here?'

'Ah, well,' said Dr. Hanson, bending down to her and gazing critically into her eyes. 'That'd be young Cammie's doing.'

'Aye aye,' said Cammie in a deep voice. 'Just doing my job, ken.'

'I don't understand.'

'Cammie saw P.C. Argo taking you down the road to the castle woods,' said Davie, wriggling a little to see her more clearly as he spoke to her. 'He followed you.'

'Naughty boy,' murmured Miss Liddle, but her mouth was amused.

'I seen you in thon shed,' said Cammie, with a nod to Miss Liddle. 'And I seen the Hun fella and all.'

'He needs to be in hospital,' said Marian, suddenly remembering. 'He's not well at all.'

'He's on his way to Aberdeen,' said Dr. Hanson, with a satisfied nod at Marian. Clearly he too believed she was not too bad.

'But why is Argo still here? P.C. Argo?'

A curious blank expression passed like a wave over the other people in the room. She decided not to pursue it just now.

'Ahem,' said Cammie, reclaiming the audience with a flick of his notebook. The twine was particularly grubby. 'Then I seen you get away and into the castle. Did you drug yon airman, by the way?'

'I might have overdone his painkiller a little. He was in a great deal of pain,' said Marian stiffly. She caught smiles on the faces of Mrs. Binnie and Mrs. Gauld, who were not descendants of Canny Annie for nothing.

'So I went back to get the Home Guard out,' said Cammie. 'For the airman, a course.' He met Marian's eye. Even Cammie seemed to have known that the castle was not a safe place.

'I'd called at your cottage on the way up the hill,' said Davie, 'to see if you wanted me to take the pail and the stool, but you weren't there and the blackout was still down, so I came down into the village to see if anyone knew where you were, and met Cammie.'

'Then Cammie fetched me,' said Miss Liddle, 'knowing I'd be worried about him.' This time she smiled properly at him, and he basked in it.

'And we were at the chemist's when Cammie came for Mr. Farquhar,' said Mrs. Gauld, waving at her husband the minister.

'And I was taking Mrs. Binnie back her hat when Mrs. Gauld came to tell her what was happening,' said Mrs. Angus.

'And I rang Dr. Hanson, just in case,' put in Mrs. Binnie.

'I've been worried about Mrs. Forbes for a wee while,' admitted Dr. Hanson. 'And since you came here, Miss Cowie – well, probably since you started digging up on the hill, she's been even more frail.'

'She didn't kill Lilian, I'm sure,' said Marian, making things clear, and everyone nodded.

'Aye, it was the Major,' said the minister. 'We've had our notions for years, Miss Cowie, but poor Mrs. Forbes maintained her daughter was in India with the laird. And how could we deny that, with no body found?'

'P.C. Argo never said anything. When I first found the bones, I mean.'

'Well, he wouldn't, dear, would he?' said Mrs. Gauld. 'P.C. Argo's much more interested in what he knows than in what he doesn't know. And he came here years after poor Lilian disappeared.'

As if pulled by a string, they all turned to stare at the remarkable portrait of Lilian Forbes, glowing on the drawing room wall.

'She was beautiful,' said Lorimer Catto Rennie softly.

'She was a lovely girl,' agreed Dr. Hanson.

'Just the kind the fairies would take,' said Mrs. Binnie, but her face was solemn.

Marian drew breath.

'And all your stories – were you trying to warn me?'

The villagers eyed each other, exchanging puzzlement.

'I think,' said Dr. Hanson, 'we were hoping you might tell us one of your own.'

'Oh, everyone has a bomb story in London!' said Marian. 'But we don't usually tell them.'

'I think it's time you started,' said Davie beside her. She turned. His eyes were smiling, but like everyone else in the room he was waiting.

'What should I say?' she asked him.

'You know. Just tell us,' he said. Marian straightened a little, reluctant to leave the safety of his tweedy arm, and thought, thought of her medical training, her childhood, her university years. But she knew she had to face the story at last, and with a sigh she closed her eyes and began.

'When the war started,' she began softly, then cleared her throat and started again. 'When the war started, I was not long qualified as a doctor, and I'd gone down to Guy's Hospital in London to do a special course – do you know, I can hardly even call to mind what it was now? In the phoney war I had a great time, seeing the sights, going to the theatre and dances, all the gay bright things that happened in London before the war really started.

'September last year was when everything changed. It was a Saturday afternoon, lovely weather, and I'd been shopping with a friend in Oxford Street. I bought my new winter coat in Selfridges, I remember. We just got back to the digs we shared when the first wave of planes came over. We thought they were going to split up and bomb airfields out in the counties as usual: we didn't know they had a new idea. I was putting on the kettle and I remember thinking 'They're early – I wonder which airfield's due for a pummelling tonight?' when the ground shook, and the window beside me just fell in, as if someone had moved the glass slightly and dropped it. I abandoned the kettle and ran out into the street, and the first thing I saw was a man's leg lying in the road and a policeman clutching a lamppost, and being sick in the gutter. I drew in a deep breath and nearly choked: the air was full of plaster dust, and then I realised that there were more explosions, throbbing around me. My ears must have been dulled by the first blast. We were in a terraced house in a side street, but the street – it seemed unreal then – the street ended about twenty yards in from where it usually stopped, houses and road just vanished under a heap of rubble. I felt myself reeling, still fighting for breath, but somehow I managed to get my legs to work. I ran back into our digs and grabbed a few medical things I had lying around, then hurried back down into the street. The policeman had finished being sick: he was leaning against the lamppost and I gave him a bullseye to suck, and then we set to, the pair of us, to do what we could do with that heap of rubble. We worked through the night, and all through the next day: it was like a game of chicken. Which would stop first, the planes or us? They sounded the all clear - at first I struggled to think what it was – the following evening. The policeman was sent home by his sergeant, and he took a look at me too and before he had the chance I turned and stumbled back to my digs, through a watergarden of hoses and the piano-plinking of slates sliding from roofs – I didn't even think about one falling on me, leaving the rafters like a fishing net strewn over the tops of the houses, and the heat of the fires and the dark rolls of bodies at the sides of the streets, and when I reached my digs I fell on to my bed and slept till ten the next morning.

'That's what they call Black Saturday. That Monday morning, once I was cleaned up, I went and began the process of finding myself a day job – a medical practice in the East End – and soon I was volunteering with an ambulance unit each night. You'd hope for an hour or so to eat and snatch a nap between work and night, but of course, as the days grew shorter and the nights longer there was more scope for the bombers and less time between work and nightfall, and dawn and work again, so you learned to do with less and less sleep. Look, I know other towns have had it bad, too, even Aberdeen with Hall Russell and Torry, but London has been extraordinary. And the people – well, somewhere between sleepwalking and hysteria, they seem to have some kind of amazing drive to carry on regardless, sleeping under their stairs and turning out clean and tidy next day, even if the house has come down round them. All they need is a cup of tea and they'll plough on.

'You see some odd things, you know. Blast lung is very strange: that's when the blast sucks air from the lungs and just kills you instantly with no sign of injury. It's very uncanny: I've heard of a double decker bus found with the passengers, driver and conductor all dead in their seats, not a mark on them, as if they've just fallen asleep. And blast is just generally – well, if you didn't know better you'd think it was playing games. It can blow down a house and leave everyone inside uninjured round the kitchen table wondering what has happened. It can rip off your clothes but leave you standing. It can fill your mouth with ash and blow you on to your own roof. Everyone has their bomb story. We have to deal with a lot of shrapnel injuries, too: the SC50s explode on impact and fly off in bits. Curtains and upholstery are just left in rags, so you can imagine what it does to people.

'The hospitals are so busy – maybe I should have stayed at Guy's, but we have a job too, to do what we can to help people as soon as possible after they are injured, and take the pressure off the local hospitals where we can. We work alongside the London Fire Brigade and the auxiliaries and the Heavy Rescue, and we all get to know each other because, well, we see a lot of each other, night after night.

'That was how I came to know Richard. I'd probably never have met him any other way. He worked for Heavy Rescue. I know that conjures up pictures of large, muscular men and many of them were, but he wasn't: most of them are council workers who know the buildings well around us and can find their way in and out of them even when they're damaged. Richard was a house-painter – he had a great sense of colour but when I said he should have been an artist he said he couldn't draw for toffee, and changed the subject. He was a little, gentle man, not five feet tall, and very dapper: if you met him away from work he was never without a tie and shoes polished so he could comb his hair in them – I was always teasing him about his hair, which he always wore slicked back to perfection. We had a laugh about it, which I don't know he had with anyone else. He was shy with women, generally, because he said he was too small for any woman to take seriously, and I think he led a lonely enough life for his parents were dead and he lived alone.

'But however careful he might have been about his appearance, he never held back if there was a small space that needed to be crawled into to rescue someone. He was as brave as could be: he said he was very glad to know that even someone as small as he was could make himself useful, but he was much more than that. I can't count how many people and even pets he was able to pull out of the wreckage, and often I've seen him worm his way into a hole not much bigger than a drainpipe, just to hold someone's hand while the diggers tried to get them out from another angle, or just while they were dying, so they wouldn't die alone.

'It amazes me that we must only have known each other a few months. We worked together so often that we barely needed to speak to each other or ask what the other was going to do, we just knew.

'Then one night in March I let him down.

'I'd been out eight nights in a row and working during the day, too – that's no excuse because everyone's like that, but I had a cold and I was feeling sorry for myself, and that night I sent a message to the ambulance unit, and I went to bed. It's a funny feeling, going to bed in London just now and wondering if you'll ever wake up, but I did when the sirens blew and I hid myself in the cupboard under the stairs with the landlady and her smelly little terrier, and wrapped myself in a blanket and went back to sleep.

'The next night I turned up as usual at the unit and we headed out when the sirens blew and worked till dawn. I didn't see Richard all night and wondered why, but I didn't have the chance to ask until we were nearly done for the night. I saw one of his friends from the same crew, and asked if he knew where Richard was. His face screwed up, telling me before his voice could. Richard had been out the night before with another doctor, a fellow called Crompton. Crompton has bad eyesight and a fear of enclosed spaces: Richard had taken a first aid kit from him and crawled into a cellar to tend to a woman bleeding to death down there. The ceiling fell in, and crushed them both.

'I walked back to my digs in a daze, soaked by the cascades of water, tripping over detritus of other people's lives. I hadn't been in love with Richard, or anything like that: but to have lost someone like that ... I think some of the soldiers call it their oppo? It was like losing a limb.

'I did not cry or anything. I knew there was no point, so I just carried on. My supervisor knew we had been close and asked if I needed a night off, but I said no.

'I carried on, as I say, for a couple of weeks. My supervisor kept asking me if I was coping all right, but I was sure I was.

'Then one night we were called out to an incident, a bomb that had hit a children's playground across the road from a row of neat little houses with smart black and white tile paths, where they survived. Air raid wardens were going door to door, knocking to ask if everyone inside was all right. A warden was stopped outside one house, calling and calling.

'"I'm dead sure they're in there," he said as we neared him. "I saw Bert go in with his paper not twenty minutes since - even said good evening to him."

'"Where do they usually shelter?" I asked: it's one of the encyclopaedia of things you can expect a warden to know on their patch.

'"They've an Anderson in the back garden," he said, "but there wasn't much time after the siren for them to get there before this one came down. I think we should take a shuftie, what do you say?"

I nodded, stepping back to take a look at the front of the house. It showed no sign of telltale cracks or broken windows, but no sign of life, either. The warden knocked once more at the door, and with a creaking sigh it simply fell in.

'He jumped back, startled, then called again before stepping on to the door and inside. I followed.

'The family was sitting at the kitchen table, their food in front of them: mince and potatoes, it was. Mother, father – presumably Bert – an older boy in overalls, a younger one in his school tie, and a toddler in a high chair, all slumped and silent. Blast lung, as I've said. And as I surveyed the room, I saw that the toddler had a doll in her hand, a rag doll, and the way it was lying it just looked as if the blast lung had got it, too. And I laughed.

'I laughed until I couldn't stop laughing. The air raid warden turned and stared at me, appalled.

'"What do you think you're doing?" he shouted. "That's my mate Bert, that is! And that's his old woman, and his boys, and the little one!" And he slapped me hard, right across my face, and dragged me out of the room and into the street, and left me there while he found someone competent to deal respectfully with the bodies, as we always do – as I should always do. And he reported me to my supervisor, and, well, she ordered me to come up here and take a rest.'

There was a long silence, and then the minister stepped away from his mantelpiece, and bent to take her hand. He squeezed it slightly, meeting her eye, then moved away. Dr. Hanson did the same. Mrs. Binnie set down her tea cup and sat briefly beside her to give her a hug, murmuring,

'There, now, quine, you'll be the better of that.' Her sister followed, taking both Marian's hands in hers, tears in her eyes. Mrs. Angus and Miss Liddle looked on, approvingly, needles clicking still, and even Lorimer Catto Rennie nodded as Joy threw herself down to envelop Marian.

'You poor darling! I'm in absolute pieces now. Poor, poor lamb!'

One at a time, they acknowledged her, accepting her, letting her know that she was in their eyes all right, no more flawed than the rest of them. Farquhar twitched his head at her, then gently rounded up Sandy and Rab Geddie, leading them to the door, their work done.

Only Davie did not move. He had had his arm around her all

through her story, so she had not seen his face, only felt the arm's steady, warm pressure. She was almost too frightened to see him, but now at last the pressure changed, and he turned to meet her eye.

'Is – this all right?' he asked. His doubt gave her hope.

She said nothing for a moment, wanting to do this right. He held her gaze, uncertain.

'Yes,' she said at last. 'More than all right.'

But as he took her hand in his own free, beautiful hand, she caught a movement by the fireplace. It was Cameron, eyeing them speculatively, and licking his pencil.

'Go on with you, Cammie,' she said, with a sudden, relieved laugh. 'This isn't one of your stories.'

'I thought you'd ken by now, Dr. Cowie,' said Cameron solemnly. He pulled himself and Agnes out of the hearth, and brushed his sister down with an older sibling's authority. 'Everything's a story.'

Glossary

Bings	-	large amounts
Braw	-	strong, fine, handsome
Ca'canny	-	go carefully
Canny	-	clever
Carline	-	hag
Chuckies	-	gravel
Cry	-	call (to call someone something)
Dander	-	walk slowly and aimlessly
Dwam	-	a daze, a dreamy state
Een	-	eyes
Eneuch	-	enough
Fan	-	when (North-East dialect replaces 'wh-' with 'f-'
Feart	-	afraid
Ferm	-	farm
Gey	-	very
Guddle	-	mess, confusion
Guidman	-	husband (archaic)
Harl	-	type of protective covering for wall
Ken	-	know
Loon	-	man, young man
Mannie	-	man (North-East dialect frequently adds '-ie' to any noun)
Michty	-	mighty, large
Minty	-	a minute
Mishachelt	-	misshapen
Onywise	-	anyway
Orra loun	-	oddjob lad about a farm
Peely wally	-	washed out, pale and unhealthy looking
Phillibeg	-	short kilt
Quine	-	young woman
Red	-	tidy
Runk	-	woman of ill repute
Scance	-	look
Shoogly	-	shaky
Skite	-	throw, particularly sharply or sideways
Sojer	-	soldier

Teuchter	-	country person (somewhat insulting)
Thole	-	put up with
Tounser	-	townsperson (pejorative)
Trig	-	neat, well-turned out
Ugsome	-	ugly
Unchancy	-	unlucky, ill-omened
Wean	-	baby, small child
Wheesht	-	hush
Wud	-	mad
Yin	-	one

Lexie Conyngham lives in North-East Scotland and has been writing stories since she knew people did. Follow her professional procrastination at www.murrayofletho.blogspot.com, where you can also join a mailing list to keep up to date with new publications.

The Murray of Letho series, set in Georgian (mostly) Scotland:

Death in a Scarlet Gown
Knowledge of Sins Past
Service of the Heir: an Edinburgh Murder
An Abandoned Woman
Fellowship with Demons
The Tender Herb: A Murder in Mughal India
Death of an Officer's Lady
Out of a Dark Reflection

Stand-alone books:

Windhorse Burning
Thrawn Thoughts and Blithe Bits (short stories)

Printed in Great Britain
by Amazon